This is a work of fiction. Similarities to real people, places, or events are entirely coincidental.

BURMESE CONNECTION

First edition. January 19, 2024.

Copyright © 2024 Ashish Basu.

ISBN: 979-8223785286

Written by Ashish Basu.

About the author:

Ashish was born and raised in India. Over the years, his work in the technology sector has taken him to dozens of countries on five continents. His extensive travels and firsthand work experience in multiple countries have given him the opportunity to see several cultures from a unique vantage point. He enjoys writing fictional stories about the exceptional people and the fascinating places he has seen. Ashish currently resides in Northern California with his family.

1942: Shan treasures

Aung Lung was not happy. At barely twenty, he was still young, but he was already quite frustrated. Aung was deeply troubled by the Japanese occupation of Burma and the tacit approval of that occupation by its leaders. The tribal leaders seemed to welcome the Japanese even though their own people were against it. Aung thought the hill tribes of Northern Burma and his generation of youth deserved better.

Unfortunately, he was in the minority. After he completed his high school and intermediate college in Rangoon, he had hoped that he would go to that exclusive college in India where other Chaofa (Shan ruler) children went. He had even completed the entrance examination that was mandatory for that college. But his life went in a different direction. He was not happy because he was seeing his father and many of the other tribal leaders reading the political situation incorrectly and bowing to the Japanese. Collectively, the leaders of Burma were unable to understand that Japan would not win the war. Apparently, most of them loved Japan because it was an Asian power.

Of course, his father and the other leaders did not see it as "bowing." They saw it as "cooperation" with the Japanese for liberating Burma from British rule. He often felt that his father was forgetting that his grandfather was the Chaofa of his Muang (kingdom). He could not imagine how a descendent of Khun Lung and Khun Lai could be a follower of the Japanese Imperial Army.

Since he had failed to convince his father, Aung tried expressing his views to his brothers, cousins, and extended family. He even tried to remind them of their proud Shan heritage. Most of them were equally adamant. They would not even listen to Aung's reasoning once, so the conversation could not even start.

Neighboring Thailand had chosen the Japanese side, and Aung thought that they could have influenced the Burmese leaders. He was shocked to see so many tribal leaders so inspired by the Japanese Imperial Army and its recent successes in the battles in Southeast Asia. It had a lot to do with that outspoken Japanese officer Suzuki. Aung had heard that Colonel Suzuki often called himself Bo Mogyo and claimed that he was connected with Myingun Min, the Burmese prince in exile.

Most of the elders had started believing in the concocted Minami Kikan stories of Burmese independence. They thought Suzuki's "thirty comrades" would actually create a strong Burmese National Army that could have the capacity to stand up to the British. Aung could not pinpoint where that admiration was coming from. But he reasoned that it could be because of the recent Japanese wins against the British - everyone was surprised by Japan's military prowess. Perhaps the leaders had seen those as Asians finally conquering mighty Europeans!

If the Japanese could defeat the British, so could the Shan or the Karens, just with a little help. Japanese support for the fledgling Indian National Army (INA) assembled with Indian Prisoners of War (POW) in the Malay Peninsula and other parts of South Asia was something the leaders would always use as an example to illustrate their point - as if that one isolated example meant everything in the context of Burma.

He had overheard his father present the case as, "Japan wants countries like India and Burma to be independent from British rule. Aren't the Japanese going to go to Imphal and Kohima with the Indians? We know they are. Aren't the Indians using the Japanese to get rid of the British? We know they are. If the Japanese can do it for India, they can do it for Burma too. After all, Japanese are Asians like us. Just like many of us here, Japanese are Buddhists too; they understand us.

"They would naturally want all Asian countries to be independent, outside European influence. I have to agree with Colonel Suzuki. It just makes a lot of common sense."

The other tribal leaders around his father who were listening nodded their heads in agreement. Just by being Asians and Buddhists, the Japanese were suddenly trustworthy to most of the Burmese leaders! They suddenly understood the Burmese.

Aung was shocked. The Shan leaders were convinced that once independence was achieved, the Shan, Kachin, Lisu, and the other tribes would be well integrated into the Burmese society, and their homeland would see lasting peace, prosperity, and development. Aung knew that several Shan tribal leaders were visiting Rangoon often in their efforts to secure the future of their tribes under Japanese rule. Many of those leaders thought that the Japanese were in Burma to emancipate the Shan, Kachin, Karen, and Lisu people. It seemed that only a minority, like Aung, disagreed with that viewpoint. Aung did not have a problem with being in the minority. He was just mortified by the extent of brainwashing colonel Suzuki and his Minami Kikan team had done.

Aung had been told that Colonel Suzuki was personally involved in the military training of the Burmese National leaders in Japan. To Aung, that meant that Suzuki was serious about pushing the British out. It did not automatically mean that Colonel Suzuki was for Burma and its indigenous people. To Aung, he was not. He was looking after Japan's interests, while telling the Burmese what they wanted to hear.

Aung himself was well read. He studied Japanese Imperialism with great interest because he was initially fascinated by the rising Asian power. His views on the Japanese approach started changing only after he studied the Japanese attacks and atrocities in China and Manchuria. Aung did not believe that the Japanese had any incentive in making Burma independent and training or supporting its armed forces.

In fact, if Burma became an independent country with a strong army of its own, it could become a problem for Japan. He thought the political views of the Shan leaders on the Japanese intent were naive. He knew that the Japanese Army occupied Burma mainly for its strategic location, oil, and minerals. Once they plundered the oil, rubies, sapphires, and jade, they would have no interest in Burma or the well-being of the Burmese. It did not matter to them.

Historically, the Japanese never occupied a country to help and emancipate its people - Aung could not think of one example. Aung's indignation reached its peak when two weeks ago, he secretly saw his father handing over some of the treasured family heirlooms to that local Japanese major from Suzuki's division. He was the local tribal liaison for Colonel Suzuki's team. Aung had heard that the major's goal was to bring the Shan Chaofas and other tribal leaders together.

Those treasures should not have been given away just because someone talked about Shan unity or showed fake respect to the Shan or even learned a few words of their Shan language. Aung asked his father, "Pho, you did not have to give away our family treasures to the Japanese. Those objects were symbols of our Shan cultural heritage. Money cannot buy those objects. The Japanese do not respect our heritage, but you are a leader - you have to. Grandma loved those two objects very much; she used to tell me so many stories about those objects."

His father got very upset and responded, "I don't have to take lessons on Shan culture from you, Aung. I do not need it. If you understood our Shan culture, you would have learned to talk to your elders with respect. You consider yourself wiser than you actually are. I think that school in Rangoon has made you very arrogant. I will do what I, and I alone, consider good for my tribe and my family.

"I gifted the Jade Buddha and the Jade marriage bowl to the Japanese as tokens of goodwill for a good reason. Colonel Suzuki and Major Morita are trying very hard to unify the tribes of Northern Burma. For a strong and independent Burma, the tribes must unify - they cannot remain fragmented with their limited perspective and narrow agenda. If other tribes know of my action, they will also fall in line, and the whole effort will succeed. Burma and the Shan homeland can benefit a lot from the Japanese. After all, we are both Asian and Buddhist cultures. For our tribe, I have to evaluate all options we have in a pragmatic manner. This is not your decision, Aung. Your agreement or disagreement on this matter is not relevant at all. If you are smart, you should know that."

Aung could not believe that his father would ever be like that. He was almost sixty, and he was educated in that famous college in India - he should know better.

Aung said, "But Pho, I think you are reading the situation completely wrong. The Japanese have no real interest in helping Burma; just read what they did in Manchuria and other places they occupied. They are here only for Japan's selfish interest; they do not care about Burma or the Burmese, Pho. The Japanese have a track record of destroying other countries and cultures. You should know that, Pho." His father got even angrier and barked, "I have had enough of you. Get out of my sight and get out of this home; I do not want to see your face in this house again." Aung felt deeply hurt and departed.

When Aung was very young, he had heard stories about that Jade statue of Buddha and that Jade marriage bowl from his grandmother while sitting next to her on a sofa. She always said that those objects brought good luck and blessings to the Chaofa family. The Jade was mined by the Kachins from the Jade mines near Hpakant, and the best carvers of the day carved those. To her, those were almost spiritual and clearly objects of Shan pride; the Jade bowl was used in their family for many generations of marriages. No amount of money could replace those.

The value of those objects could not be measured in monetary terms. Those objects were part of a century of Chaofa family history. His grandmother had passed away, and his father did not seem to care about the Shan heritage. Aung could not tolerate it anymore - he knew he had to do something. After getting banished and leaving his father's Muang, Aung wandered in the jungles for several weeks. He eventually decided that the best way to get rid of the Japanese would be to join the Kachins and their armed resistance against the Japanese occupation.

With that burning desire to expel the Japanese from his homeland, Aung joined the Kachin scouts and started assisting the Allied forces. The Kachins were already helping the British and American forces. Unlike the Shan, they were against the Japanese because of the atrocities committed by the Japanese Army against ordinary Kachin villagers. The Kachin tribal leaders never forgot that violence and never forgave the Japanese Army. As scouts and rangers, they would observe and share information on Japanese troop strength and schedules of trains with supplies and ammunition storage, as well as pinpoint targets for accurate air raids. They also helped in rescue operations behind enemy lines.

Aung decided that he would reorganize that effort and help the Allied forces in a more predictable way by getting informers employed in a Japanese base and by appointing locals as lookout and spotters. He knew his language skills would come in very handy during the war. He was fluent in Shan, Kachin, Karen, and most importantly, English. Over a period of time, he would add a band of dedicated Shan and Kachin fighters; some of those were already experienced in the guerrilla tactics.

These fighters would participate in small arms skirmishes to harass the Japanese Army in the hills - Japanese patrols were targeted often. Initially, his was a very mobile group of scouts and fighters. They never stayed in any one place for long, but their efforts were concentrated around Myitkyina in Northern Burma. Aung and his Kachin scouts chose Myitkyina because it was strategically located; it had the biggest Japanese base and the most important regional airport. The airport was used as a hub for Northern Burma by the Japanese. The British also used the Myitkyina Airport in that manner before they left Burma.

Aung knew that the biggest battle of World War II (WWII) in his homeland would be fought in Myitkyina sometime in the very near future. He wanted to influence the outcome of that battle for his people. When Aung was not in a battle or in a crossfire while scouting, he would incessantly talk about the preservation of Shan tribal heritage and culture if he found a receptive audience. He would also talk about how the Japanese were plundering rubies, sapphires, and jade that belonged to the local tribes. The Shan, Kachin, and Lisu people of the hills were being deprived in every way; the Japanese did not care about the tribes. They knew they had the Burmese tribal leaders on their side.

The Shan cause had become an obsession with Aung. He was also realizing that as a minority ethnic group, the Shan and the other tribes could not remain isolated. Their best option was to engage in the politics in Burma's national and regional levels - the tribes needed a seat at the table. Most of Aung's 1942 went in scouting for the British, but the British efforts were disorganized - mostly unsuccessful because the Japanese were well settled in their defensive fortifications. The Japanese forces could not be threatened because of their control over the Irrawaddy River and the railway track. The river and the railway gave a tactical advantage to the Japanese; those were the best transportation options.

By the end of that year, it was seeming unlikely that the British would ever cross the Irrawaddy River or launch a viable attack on the city of Myitkyina. Aung's hopes were dwindling fast because an ever-increasing number of local leaders were moving over to the Japanese side. To Aung, an Allied victory in Burma seemed like an insurmountable challenge for the British. They were not able to cope; Aung was getting very concerned about the future Burma under Japanese occupation.

Around that time, through his contacts among the locals who worked with the Japanese forces, he was hearing rumors that Colonel Suzuki was being recalled to Japan with a few of his aides. Apparently, the Japanese war office thought Colonel Suzuki and his Minami Kikan were getting a bit too cozy with the Burmese national leaders. Aung was afraid that the Japanese might take the Shan treasures with them to Japan. Aung felt helpless - all he could do was to vent his frustration to his war hardened Kachin comrades in their mountain camp. They were among the few in the whole world that understood his agony.

One day, Aung heard a rumor that the British forces were almost ready to launch an extended campaign in Burma out of Assam and Nagaland in India. His source was a general contractor in the Japanese base, so the information had to be of high quality. He hoped that the British and other Allied forces had learned from their past mistakes. From his side, he decided that he would do everything to get his Kachin scouts ready. He rounded up more scouts, imparted weapons training to them, and surveyed the Kachin Hills for hidden caves, new trails, and streams.

All those measures would come in handy during the Allied campaign. Some Kachins were formidable guerrilla fighters by then; they became very effective in training other Kachins. As a result of those initiatives, the size of the scouts' force grew to several hundred rapidly. Next year, 1943, was very different for Aung. That year brought new promises. The first of those promises were in the form of specially trained British forces for jungle warfare. These were special forces trained as long-range penetration units that were supported by supplies dropped from the sky by parachutes. By design, they did not have any support infrastructure on the ground. These British columns would penetrate the jungle on foot, mainly relying on surprise to target enemy lines of communication, road infrastructure, and supply depots.

Their mobility in the hills was their biggest asset; they were not large in numbers but were seasoned fighters. It was neither easy nor effective for the Japanese heavy armor to run after these forces on the Kachin Hills. Some of the trails were so narrow and steep that soldiers could only manage to march in single file. Even if the Japanese patrols knew of their presence, the topography made it hard for them to take action quickly. The British forces and the scouts became very good at using the terrain to their advantage - they managed to adapt really well.

Kachins were born trackers, they used those skills really well. The special forces carried everything they had and needed for jungle warfare on their backs. That technique worked well in the steep and scrubby hillside of Northern Burma. When the supplies were parachuted to these forces, local Kachins would assist them with load carrying mules or other animals that could negotiate steep inclines. Aung thought this was payback because the Japanese had previously used the same strategy to devastating effect against the British forces there. In the early stages of the war, the British were a bit unprepared; as a result, the Japanese Army advanced and captured Rangoon quickly.

Aung's scout team with its intimate knowledge of the hills and the trails was very effective with these special forces teams. For the first time, Aung thought his scouts were making a difference. By the end of 1943, the British were disrupting Japanese communication lines on a regular basis. These attacks were not lethal blows to the Japanese yet, but these were causes of constant irritation. The attacks were draining valuable resources; some resources took a long time to replenish in wartime. By this time, Allied air forces and navies were threatening Japanese supply lines on air and water all over Asia Pacific. Life was getting harder for the Japanese; it was not easy to sustain supply lines.

If the British destroyed a bridge, the Japanese could repair it in a week or two. But for those two weeks, local logistics were badly stretched. In time, that became the norm, and the Japanese were worried. In some cases, the guerrilla warfare would cause continuous strain in the Japanese supplies and pin them down. The Japanese were faced with a dilemma. If they stayed in the safety of their base; their infrastructure was attacked. If they came out of the base, the casualties went up dramatically. These were very difficult choices for an army that was used to easy victories against the relatively unprepared armies of South Asia in the early days of the war. They had to adapt to the new ground realities.

The Kachin scouts earned a good reputation as fearless fighters and for their assistance to the British special forces. After the British, the American special forces detachments started working with the Kachin scouts, and they reported good experience too. Aung had heard one story in which Kachin scouts found a parachute drop with hundreds of thousands of Indian Rupees in sacks. They had returned the entire lot to the Allied forces. The British and the Americans talked about their honesty, integrity, and commitment. That was how the world came to know about the highly effective Kachin scouts in the Burma campaign. No story of the WWII Burma campaign can be considered complete without mentioning the contribution of these honest, simple, hardworking, fierce fighters from the high hills of Northern Burma.

Kachins were very simple, straightforward people - they were also fiercely loyal. One British commander had written in his field diary that what he liked most about the Kachins was their simplicity.

They were not manipulative like the Burmar and Mon people of the river valleys. The Kachin tribal leaders had to prove a point to the Japanese Imperial Army. They were determined to teach a hard lesson to the Japanese. When the Japanese Army attacked innocent Kachin villagers and burned their homes, they did not anticipate any retaliation. They had grossly underestimated the ability and the resolve of the proud Kachins.

One morning in early 1944, Aung was asleep in his base camp in the Kachin Hills. It was February, so mornings were chilly in the hills. He had also returned pretty late the previous night after scouting work on the Japanese base. He suddenly woke up with a jolt in his hammock because of a noise. It was like a couple of people shouting in the local Shan and Kachin dialect. Aung's scouts knew making noise could expose them to the wandering Japanese patrols - that is why they were trained to operate quietly. Noise in the hills can be very dangerous.

That was what had surprised Aung. His scouts were forgetting their basic training and shouting; their actions could endanger the whole scout camp! Aung was on his feet in a flash with his gun to investigate what was happening. When he got closer through the dense bushes, Aung found a Japanese person in an American type of uniform being held captive by two of his scouts at gunpoint. The captive was being interrogated by two of Aung's new scouts, and they were not understanding a single word of his rapid-fire responses. Aung's scouts were getting frustrated and threatening him by raising their voices in Shan and Kachin. They thought their raised voices would do the trick.

The two scouts were trying to scare the captive by telling him that he would be hung from a tree branch, and then certain parts of his body would be fed to the animals slowly. That graphic description did not have the desired effect on the captive because he did not understand Shan or Kachin. The two scouts were getting agitated.

Aung listened to the exchange for a few minutes and realized that the captive was responding in fluent Japanese; he looked like a person of Japanese origin too. But because of his American style uniform, Aung looked at him and asked him in English very slowly, "Who are you?"

What followed was something completely unexpected! The man answered, "I am a Japanese American member of the American special forces who just entered Burma from India. After we entered Burmese territory, we were told by the British special forces that you were camping on these hills. I came looking for you when your people captured me."

Just to make sure that he was not dreaming, Aung pinched himself and asked, "Why were you constantly responding to my people in Japanese? They are local Kachins with no Japanese language skills. They do not look like Japanese soldiers, do they?"

The American responded, "No, they certainly do not. I thought I might have run into locals working with the Japanese Army, so it felt safer to respond in Japanese. At least initially till I knew who they were. In the worst-case scenario, I could pretend to be a Japanese soldier who got separated from another unit. There are many divisions of the Japanese Army fighting in Burma, so they might not know one another. I was hoping they would not."

Aung asked, "What about your uniform? Japanese soldiers do not wear that uniform."

The captive answered, "I could say that on my way to the hills, I found a dead American soldier and stole his full uniform, so that I can blend in."

Aung told him, "Good story, but you could not have sold that story to the Japanese. They are smart. If they found you, they would have killed you after interrogation. You are Japanese, so as a favor, they might not have used their own blades on you - they would have ordered you to do hara-kiri instead. You don't know how the

Japanese treat their prisoners; I have seen it myself." The man shook. Aung's next question was, "Why are you alone? Where is the team?"

He responded, "I am the advance lookout. I am ethnic Japanese - that was why I was selected."

He informed Aung that the other members of the team were hiding near the nearby stream. Aung said, "First tip, never hide near a stream; that is the first place the animals and the Japanese would check. Anyway, take me to them immediately and walk ahead of me. Please be as quiet as you can; you should not be noisy in the hills; trackers can hear your footfall and plan an ambush from a long distance. Noise draws the wrong kind of attention from the Japanese in these hills."

While walking down to the stream with the American soldier, Aung learned that this special forces unit under General Merrill was new. It was called the Galahad. This unit also had a Chinese detachment with it a mile down the stream. The Chinese and the Americans planned to take on the Japanese together. Aung thought that might work well tactically. The combined forces planned to attack the Japanese lines very hard in parallel, at multiple strategic points.

Once they reached the stream, Aung found nine other Americans in similar jungle uniform waiting. After the introductions, they went further downstream and met with the Chinese. There, only the commander, a twenty-year-old like Aung, spoke or understood English. That day, Aung spent the whole day briefing the Americans and the Chinese commanders in detail. He briefed them on enemy formations, transportation infrastructure, supply lines, and positions of heavy artillery. Aung returned to his mountain camp late in the evening.

The role for his scouts was clearly defined by the Galahad high command; Aung thought it would make them more effective. It seemed the Galahad had taken the scouts into account after talking to the British and then made its own tactical plan. Aung explained to the Americans how the Kachin scouts carefully planned an ambush, using their hand-made pungyi sticks. Pungyi was a smoke-hardened bamboo stake that the Kachins used in combat. The Kachins were sons of that soil - they could use the foliage to camouflage themselves very well. Being natural trackers, they could spot a Japanese patrol many miles ahead of the place of ambush. Those types of actions were not as easy for outsiders, more so for the Japanese soldiers. They could not do it.

In preparing an ambush, the Kachins would select a good site and camouflage the site to appear as natural as possible to casual observers. They would then position their automatic weapons, ready to rake the trail with bullets. After that, they would plant the pungyis in the foliage alongside the path. Once the Japanese entered the area, the fire of the automatic weapons would scatter the Japanese into the undergrowth, where they impaled themselves on the pungyis. The indigenous pungyi stick became a feared and deadly weapon in Burma. Having inflicted heavy damage, the lightly armed Kachins usually disappeared from the area, within minutes, avoiding prolonged engagements. Regular soldiers often displayed too much enthusiasm to stand and fight. Kachin scouts never did that - they knew how to survive. By the time Japanese reinforcements arrived, the Kachins would be long gone.

The Japanese could not follow the scouts all the way to their jungle hideouts. The Galahad forces quickly learned some of the tactics used by the Kachin scouts. General Merrill's Galahad forces had entered Burma from India to build on the successes the British special forces had. These soldiers were well equipped and well-trained US Army special forces adapted for long-range jungle warfare. Some of the Galahad commanders had seen actions in other theaters, so they brought a lot of real-life combat experience with them to the Burma front.

They provided extensive weapons training to the scouts. Participation of the Chinese soldiers was a force multiplier even though they were inexperienced at the beginning of the campaign. Aung liked several of the Chinese commanders and became very good friends with them. This time, the combined American and Chinese forces were able to take the battle to the heart of the Japanese occupation. Many of the Chinese soldiers were in their early teens, really young, but they never gave up and kept fighting. In terms of sheer headcount, the Chinese X Force soldiers were much larger in numbers.

A few members of the Galahad became good friends too. One of the Galahad captains used to say, "When you fight alongside someone in the Kachin Hills, you have to know him really well because in these hills, death lurks in every trail and every stream."

The Americans had a great deal of difficulty in adapting to the altitude, rain, humidity, heat, leeches, and diseases. The terrain was really unforgiving. In the initial stages of the campaign, they were losing more men to diseases, exhaustion, and accidents than firefights. The hills of Northern Burma were essentially the southernmost tip of the Himalayan mountain ranges, among the tallest in the whole world. Some the peaks were really tall, and most of the ravines on the way were thousands of feet.

No amount of training in the plains could prepare the American and the Chinese for what they were faced with in real life. The Kachin scouts taught them a range of survival techniques. They also had difficulties with food supplies and rations because parachute drops were difficult and irregular. The Americans and the Chinese understood the challenges and adapted. Navigating tall mountains in torrential monsoon downpour with heavy loads on their backs was not easy. Initially, it was very hard for the Americans and the Chinese; gradually, they adjusted. Some of the trails were so steep and so slippery with rivers of mud that the load carrying mules would slip and fall in ravines thousands of feet in depth. There was nothing the soldiers could do other than self-preservation. Some sections of the terrain were so high in the mountains that when they woke up in the mornings, they could see clouds floating below their camp, obscuring the view.

On some occasions, parachute drops went haywire because of the cloud cover below their positions. Sometimes, they fell in the wrong hands, and the Japanese enjoyed the food and rations. It took them a while to adapt to the harsh ground realities in the Kachin Hills. Aung and his scouts were battle hardened and ready to assist the Americans and the Chinese. During the first half of 1944, the Americans and the Chinese hit the Japanese hard where it hurt. The Japanese took heavy casualties everywhere and lost a lot of their communication infrastructure.

In about six months of combat, the combined forces advanced hundreds of miles through the harshest jungle terrain in the world, fighting hunger, malaria, blood dysentery, and the Japanese at the same time. Living out in the open in heavy rain and heat took its toll on the human body. Often, the soldiers developed chronic health issues that never went away. None of the battles were easy because Burma's natural topography always favored the defenders. The defenders could easily use the high ground and the river to their tactical advantage.

In the early days of the engagement, several Chinese X Force formations had deadly friendly fire incidents because of poor communication. Aung regretted those unintended tragedies the most - many lives were lost. If there was one thing that held tight till the very end, that was the spirit: the rag tag multinational force knew that they had to win - they had no other choice. Aung remembered several major engagements in places like Walawbum, Shaduzuo, and near his home base in Myitkyina during that period. There were many other battles that he heard about. The American and the

Chinese forces with the help of Kachin scouts engaged in combat with the Japanese Army on thirty-plus occasions. Most of the outcomes were against the Japanese.

Most military observers were surprised by the success of this hurriedly put together coalition of fighters against the more organized Japanese. The momentum of the war had shifted. Perhaps the only difference was that these Allied forces knew that they had to win, and by then, the Japanese resolve was slowly weakening. The Japanese confidence was shaken to the core - they were, in fact, afraid of the Allies by that time. Aung saw the tide turning against the invincible Japanese Army in front of his eyes. Battling Japanese soldiers, hunger, and disease did not come cheap; casualties were high among the Americans and the Chinese forces. During those fading days of the war, Aung was often reminded of his grandfather. Granpho used to talk about Burma's geography protecting its flanks from enemies from the West.

Food and supplies were scarce. In the battle at Myitkyina, the Americans suffered over two hundred soldiers killed. In addition, about a thousand were wounded, and another thousand evacuated for disease. By the time the town of Myitkyina was taken, only a couple of hundred members of the original Galahad forces remained standing. Finally, by early August 1944, the entire town of Myitkyina was taken from the Japanese. The losses and injuries were much worse for the Japanese Army. The Japanese lost more than four thousand soldiers in the battle of Myitkyina. They had realized that the war was lost, and hurriedly organized groups of soldiers were retreating to Thailand.

At an overall level, the war was unravelling for the Japanese government in multiple fronts. By October of 1944, not long after Myitkyina fell in Northern Burma, the tables had turned. The United States 6th Army led by General MacArthur landed on Leyte and eventually liberated the islands of the Philippines. In addition to Allied air forces owning the air over Eastern India and Western Burma, the Allied navy submarines had started dominating the seas completely by this time.

Those were undermining Japan's supply lines in a major way. By the end of 1944, US Marines were threatening the Ogasawara Islands, inevitably getting closer to the Japanese mainland and islands of Okinawa. As bits and pieces of these news items started reaching him in Myitkyina, Aung was thrilled. He tried his best to locate Colonel Suzuki and his men in Rangoon. He wanted to call them out on their false promises, but they had all disappeared.

By the end of August 1944, Aung knew that the war was coming to an end in Burma very soon, and the post war alliances would start settling down. Tribal leaders were already making plans.

Suddenly, alignment with the Allies was in great demand. The Japanese Imperial Army, their vision of Minami Kikan, and praises for their Asian culture were all but forgotten. Aung had become wiser by then, and he told himself, *"Such is the irony of life."*

For the first time since 1941, Aung Lung was optimistic about his and Burma's future!

1945: Myitkyina

It was many summers ago, but Aung still remembered the conversation vividly. Aung was close to his grandparents. One night, Aung's grandfather was retiring for the evening at their ancestral home, when Aung and one of his younger siblings went to him. Both were requesting Granpho to complete "one last" story before they went to bed - Granpho was the best storyteller. He finally did. That story was about the Ahom rulers of Assam who were descendants of a Shan prince.

During the story, Aung asked, "Granpho, other armies do not attack Burma like they attack India. Why? My history books have stories of India getting attacked from the North by different armies."

Before he answered, Granpho smiled and said, "Aung, I am happy to realize that you are actually reading your history books in Rangoon. At least all of your time is not getting invested in football." Then, he patted Aung's back and started answering, "There are three reasons, my son: the harsh terrain, long and intense rains for half of the year, and diseases. The Shans, Kachins, and the Lisu are adapted to this land by the forces of nature; they know how to live on and off this harsh landscape - the invaders do not. A few have attempted over the centuries, but those three reasons always got in the way. Eventually, the risks did not match the rewards. If the outsiders did not come by water or air, they were less likely to establish a foothold in Burma. One of my teachers in India used to call it 'Burma's natural protection' from invaders."

In later years, as the war raged between the Allies and the Japanese Army in different parts of Burma, Aung thought his Granpho's words were prophetic. Granpho was not there to see how it played out in WWII. Burma was naturally protected from the rest of the world with tall mountain ranges on the western flank, northern, and eastern borders. Before the war, it was a British colony with a degree of autonomy that was not very common within the British colonial empire. During the war, three countries - Britain, the United States, and China - fought the Japanese in Aung's homeland in Northern Burma.

Each one of those countries fought with a different set of goals, though. The British Army was in the lead mainly because of the Allied command structure and Burma's proximity to India. When the Japanese Army invaded and annexed large swaths of Southeast Asia, British and Indian troops under British command were sent to defend Burma. The majority of the fighting men in those British Army divisions were of Indian origin. The British goal was to create a buffer around India's far Eastern flank. India was the jewel of the British empire and a major source of wartime revenue for the British crown. Under no circumstances could the British allow the Japanese to invade from the East and occupy India. That was the worst nightmare for the British.

The United States also tried to help Burma as a direct result of pressure from the Japanese Army, but the real American interest was different from those of the British. The United States looked to maintain Burma outside of Japanese control so that supply lines into China could remain open. The supplies traveled into China on land using the motorable road, the road that connected Kunming in China with Lashio in Burma. Supply lines to China were critical at that point because Generalissimo Chiang Kai-shek's forces were already struggling in multiple fronts, and Washington was worried about Mao's successes.

At this point in time during WWII, United States had its Northern Combat Area Command, or NCAC, as a subcommand of the Southeast Asia Command, or SEAC. It controlled Allied operations in Aung's homeland in North Burma, a bit unusual, but that was the command structure. For most of its existence, the NCAC was commanded by General Joseph Stilwell. From 1945,

Lieutenant General Daniel Sultan assumed command of the NCAC after General Stilwell left. For the NCAC, Burma was a priority, and General Stilwell said so in every briefing.

Chinese National Army soldiers formed a major part of the combat units within the NCAC. That was part of the reason why Aung had seen a large number of Chinese soldiers with the Galahad forces in Northern Burma. They had the spirit but needed training to face the war hardened Japanese Army. Albeit different, those British and American worries about Burma were not unfounded - its strategic location was of great interest to the Japanese. By 1944, those fears about Japan's annexation aspirations were coming out in the open for all parties to see. Japan had annexed a large swath of territory very quickly.

The Japanese war ministry was worried about America's industrial production capacity: they knew Japan could never match it. To counter that deficiency, they had decided to go on the offensive and win as much territory as they could. That was war ministry's doctrine of quick decisive victories. They also thought inflicting substantial damage to the Allied forces would discourage America from participating in the war fully. Both were dangerous miscalculations: Japan and the Japanese people paid dearly for those miscalculations and suffered a lot.

On the Japanese side, the Imperial Army wanted to incorporate Burma into its extended borders for its strategic location, oil, and other natural resources. Burma had been exporting crude oil since 1853. During WWII, Burma used to supply much of the crude oil that was consumed all across British India. The importance of that valuable resource during the war was known to the Japanese planners in Tokyo. The Japanese mainland was far away, and the availability of inexpensive crude meant greater mobility for Japanese heavy armor on land. In addition to cutting off supply lines to China, a Japanese controlled Burma could provide security to the expanded Japanese empire. With those goals in mind, Japanese command in Burma was hurriedly reorganized under General Masakazu Kawabe in 1943. Burma was seen like a launch pad.

Right after that reorganization, the Japanese war ministry decided to consider various options for invading India from Burma. As part of that vision of the war ministry, General Renya Mutaguchi was brought in to command the Japanese 15th Army. The war was already going badly for Japan by 1944. Despite that, the leaders in the Japanese war ministry supported Mutaguchi's ambitious idea of starting up a new invasion of India from the Burma command. The India invasion from Burma was considered to be pretty easy by the war ministry in Tokyo.

General Mutaguchi was a respected warrior, but he did not know much about the realities on the ground in Burma. Even his own staff officers were doubtful about his battle plans. He believed that British and Indian troops were inferior to the Japanese troops. Because of that mindset, the India invasion was not planned properly. General Mutaguchi assumed that the superiority of the Japanese troops on the ground would compensate for other deficiencies like the lack of air support by Japanese bombers. They paid very little attention to building and sustaining supply lines. In addition, Japanese planners had inadequate knowledge of the harsh geography; the planning reflected those gaps.

The fact that they lacked support from the bombers of the Japanese air force was widely known. By this time, the air over Burma and India's Far Eastern flank was owned by the Allied bombers; there were regular flights over the "hump." After the debacle in the Malay Peninsula, the Allied command structure was completely revamped, and the Allied troops were fighting with a new sense of urgency. At this stage, they knew losing was not an option. Aung had learned later that the optimism of the Japanese planners about the India invasion was mostly due to the influence of the Indian National Army (INA) on General Hideki Tojo.

Ultimately, from March until July 1944, the Japanese Army fought hard but got bogged down and failed in its goal of getting a foothold on Indian soil. Not just that - most of the Japanese divisions were driven back to Burma with heavy losses of men and equipment. The losses were staggering. The Japanese Army also suffered a significant loss of morale among its ranks. For the Japanese Army, the incorrect assumptions added to the already huge cost in lives and resources. The Japanese had assumed that the "inferior" Indian troops under British command would switch sides overnight and join the INA en masse.

They had widely publicized that the INA was fighting a legitimate battle for India's independence from the British. They invited all patriotic Indian soldiers to join the INA at the earliest opportunity. They expected an uprising against the British as soon as the word was out. The regular radio broadcasts from the Azad Hind (Free India) force and the Japanese Army became folklore in India's eastern city of Calcutta. Much to the dismay of the British, people in the streets and bazaars of Calcutta started imagining the arrival of Japanese ships in their port on the river Hooghly. The imminent British defeat in the hands of the mighty Japanese was the subject of evening chatter in the streets of Calcutta.

Ironically, that widely advertised switching of sides by the Indian troops to the INA never happened. The widely anticipated uprising against the British never got started. On the contrary, the Indian troops under British command fought valiantly and won some of the bloodiest engagements of WWII. The Indians that Mutaguchi used to disparage defeated some of the best fighting formations of the Japanese Army hands down. They proved that they were not "inferior" at all, and ultimately, soldiers of the INA surrendered to the British Indian troops. Weeks later, when small bits of news of the failed Japanese invasion of India would reach Aung and his scouts, they would be overjoyed.

The disastrous India invasion was the turning point of the Japanese Burma campaign in WWII. Japan never recovered. The Japanese defeat at Kohima and Imphal were the largest up until that time, and those defeats effectively doomed the Japanese Burma command. So comprehensive and humiliating were the defeats in Imphal and Kohima that the Japanese Army had to relieve both General Kawabe and General Mutaguchi of their respective commands. The Japanese Burma command and the fledgling INA disintegrated through surrenders quickly thereafter. Some of the senior officers of the INA faced trial in Delhi, India. The British Army regained momentum after its win in India and charged ahead.

Aung Lung was thrilled when Myitkyina fell to the forces of American General Stilwell in August of 1944. That was the beginning of the end of the Japanese occupation. He was overjoyed when the infamous 33rd Imperial Japanese Army under General Honda was defeated in a comprehensive manner and remaining parts of the Japanese Army surrendered. While the formal surrender of the Japanese forces happened in far-away Rangoon, bits and pieces of surrender-related news would trickle down to Northern Burma on a pretty regular basis.

Most of the news came through the visitors who used the Myitkyina Airport. Aung knew that Japan was struggling for its survival by then. Many of the Japanese divisions in Burma were busy planning a hasty retreat into friendlier Thailand. But the retreat was not easy: most were getting caught along the way and captured as POWs. The good news was the Allies treated POWs very differently.

Myitkyina was an important town for both sides not only because of its rail and river links to the rest of Burma, but also because it was on the Ledo Road. That was a huge advantage. General Stilwell and Generalissimo Chiang Kai-shek were planning to rebuild that road. After all, without any formal military training, Aung himself had made that same decision about Myitkyina's importance sometime back.

Aung knew that the fall of Myitkyina set the war for his homeland in an irreversible direction, but it was not over. As if to emphasize that point brutally, soldiers from the 3rd Battalion of the 215th Regiment of the Japanese Army entered the village of Kalagong in Mon State on July 7th, 1945 and rounded up all villagers regardless of age. General Yamamoto's soldiers then shot six hundred plus Burmese villagers. There was no reason for the massacre. The villagers were not soldiers - they did not participate in the war. The villagers did not have to die.

Aung was in his early twenties at this point; he had not seen life for very long. He had vaguely heard about the plight of the Jews in Europe but did not appreciate the scale and scope of that horror. Kalagong laid it bare for him. This kind of mass killing as a result of intense hatred from people of one culture or country for another was unfathomable to him till then. Aung had noticed that attitude earlier in 1942; many of the Japanese soldiers and officers considered themselves to be superior to the Burmese. It was as if the Japanese had the right to decide whether a Burmese person should live or die, and nobody called them out on that.

What bothered Aung more was the deafening Burmese silence. Burmese reaction was muted - he did not hear very many leaders exploding in anger and resentment. As a matter of fact, he did not see much of a reaction at all! Aung's distaste for Japanese imperialism grew even more. Once he heard the news; he could not eat or sleep properly for many days. He suffered from acute depression for quite a while after that event in Kalagong. He hoped that the Japanese soldiers would be prosecuted as war criminals some day in the near future.

During the war and the Japanese occupation, much of Aung's direct and extended family got scattered. Many members of Aung's family perished without any trace; others left the village. Much of Aung's 1945 was spent in search of his parents, siblings, and extended family. The Japanese Army was in a chaotic state toward the end of the war, and that meant tribal militias ruled. It was a total anarchy. A lot of displaced people from Shan States moved to Thailand around this time. Aung would often leave his home base in Myitkyina for several days with a handful of armed Kachin scouts and look for family members in the hills and places inside the Shan State up to the borders between Burma and Thailand. He had not given up hope - he continued trying.

The Shan that went into Thailand were not easy to find. The borders were quite porous, so there was a good chance that his folks crossed over. Thailand had a lot of Japanese sympathizers; Aung always made sure he remained inside Burma and never crossed into Thai territory. Aung knew that Thailand had signed a military alliance with Japan in 1942 and that the Shan States were to be under Thailand's control. Even though Aung did not like Thailand's proximity to the Japanese Army, he knew that there were enough Shan people there to hide his relatives if they were to seek refuge. He sought to locate his family through his contacts in the British and Chinese forces, but none of those efforts succeeded. It seemed that they had vanished without a trace.

Despite all his efforts, till the end of 1945, he could not connect up with any member of his direct family. His ancestral home was flattened by Allied bombers; the village itself had suffered major damage. When he spoke with the few remaining villagers, they said most families had fled toward Thailand. That sort of a vague guidance did not help Aung at all. In addition to the search he was conducting for his family, Aung was also tracking the changing political landscape in Burma.

Several major political events took place in quick succession. Those events changed Aung's homeland forever. In March 1945, the Burmese National Army rose up in a countrywide rebellion against the Japanese. Burmese national leaders like Aung San and others began negotiations with Lord Mountbatten and officially joined the British side as the Patriotic Burmese Forces. It was a good move that helped the Burmese nationalists. By switching sides, albeit toward the end of the war, the Burmese leaders gave themselves the much-needed legitimacy.

At the first meeting, they represented themselves as the provisional government of Burma with Thakin Soe as Chairman. Aung San was the member of the ruling committee of the provisional government. Since the Japanese were completely routed from most of Burma by mid-1945, Patriotic Burmese Forces started formal negotiations with the British in due earnest. Despite the good performance of the British Army in the Burma campaign, it had setbacks that could have been avoided. Much of the British reputation for invincibility had been lost as a result of its many defeats at the hands of the Japanese Army.

Demands for India's independence had also assumed thunderous proportions around that time. In Burma, the nationalists, headed by Aung San and the Burmese National Army, gave valuable support to the British Army in the final stages of the Japanese defeat. As a result of all those factors, the British returned to Rangoon as victors but could not to stay for very long - they knew it when they returned.

Around this time, the British public opinion was also shifting. The appetite for managing colonies far away from the British Isles was not what it used to be. Most British voters did not want colonies in distant places, and they resented participating in war for those colonies. The idea of the colony was going out of favor; the British had to accept that shift in domestic public opinion. Burmese nationalism was like a tsunami by then. The entire Burmese population craved independence. Having seized the administrative reins in the wake of the British advance, Aung San and his men were ready to take over the government right after the war.

Although the British government attempted to put up a brave front, it had to face reality. Its colonial hegemony in Southeast Asia was ending soon. Aung San traveled to the UK in 1947 to negotiate terms for independence. It was widely believed that the world would see an independent Burma under the leadership of Aung San in short order. But that was not to be. Discussions were proceeding in the right direction. When everything looked all set for stability, suddenly, Aung San was assassinated along with his cabinet. That whole event was a shock to all. Eventually, when Burma gained independence, the Federated Shan States became the Shan State and Kavah State with the right to secede from the Union of Burma after a certain period.

None of these developments changed Aung's day-to-day life in Myitkyina materially. The war had ended, but there were local skirmishes among various warring militias every day and all around. Being aligned with the victors, Aung and his scouts were treated with respect by the local militias; sometimes, they were called for advice. They still lived in Myitkyina and worked as a security team for hire.

One morning, he and two of his scouts were returning from a security assignment when they saw a couple of soldiers lying by the roadside ditch. They looked Chinese and looked hurt. One Christian missionary was trying to help them. Aung and his two scouts stopped to help.

Aung asked in Kachin, "Father, could we help you?"

The missionary looked up from the ankle-deep mud on the roadside ditch and said, "You sure can, my son. I think it is the divine that sent you here. I have been struggling to move them. These young men are badly hurt. Both of them need immediate medical attention.

Looks like they have lost a lot of blood already. They are very weak; they are in no position to even stand properly - forget about walking.

"If you and your men can help me to transport them to my church, I will treat them with the medicines we have at the church and look after them till they get better."

Aung understood and sent one of his scouts to commandeer a hand drawn cart from the nearby village immediately. After that, the three of them brought the wounded soldiers to the back of the church for treatment. Aung and his scouts helped the Father set up makeshift beds in one corner, removed the soiled uniforms from the soldiers, and dressed their wounds.

They erected a small partition and made a workspace for the Father. Both soldiers were in their late teens, like Aung had seen earlier during the war. The Father said they would heal quickly and recover from the injuries. The church had its own small supply of medicines - the Father used those on the soldiers. He then asked the two scouts to help him make lentil soup for the wounded soldiers.

"They were probably starving for many days before they landed on that roadside ditch. When they wake up in a few hours, they will be hungry. Hot soup will give them the nutrition their bodies need, and that will help them recover quickly." The Father smiled and commented while looking at the semi-conscious, emaciated faces of the two young soldiers. Aung Lung had not seen such acts of kindness toward fellow human beings in a very long time in Northern Burma.

He had seen so much death, destruction, and suffering around him lately that he had forgotten that such things even existed. *People all around were just struggling so much to survive that there has been no time for higher order values like kindness*, Aung thought to himself. War changed everything.

When they were about to leave, the Father came to Aung and said, "Who are you?"

Aung told the Father about his Shan Chaofa family and then introduced his Kachin scouts, briefly mentioning that they assisted the Allied forces in the war effort. He also told the Father that the wounded were probably part of the Chinese forces that came to fight the Japanese along with the Galahad to provide some context.

The Father said, "Who they were does not matter. Now, they are in God's house; we try to save people here. We have to look after them - we have food and some medicine here. We will talk to them at length when they can, after they recover completely." The Father looked at Aung and said, "Christianity came to the Kachin Hills much before your war, my son. We baptized and converted the first Kachins way back in 1882, and the Kachin church was founded during that year. Kachin literature was accepted by the British government way back in 1895. The Kachin Baptist Churches organization to which this church belonged was founded in 1890. We are familiar with these hills of Northern Burma, my son. We do God's work and try to alleviate suffering. We do know what the war is doing to the people of these hills. It does not help, but people still go to war. Violence cannot solve any problem; it aggravates agony for the aggressors and the innocent."

The Father spoke both Shan and Kachin: he spoke with Aung in Shan and his scouts in Kachin. One of his scouts told the Father his uncle and aunt became Christians just before the war. After a while, the Father said to Aung, "You and your friends have God in your hearts. You are most welcome to stay in the shed in the rear of the church if you like. You do not have to pay rent to the church, but the place might need a bit of fixing all around. You can easily get that done with your boys." Aung was quite surprised by the generosity of the Father.

He accepted the offer and also told the Father to let him know if they could help the church in any other way. In two weeks, he and his two scouts converted that shed meant for farm tools into a functional home for themselves. They started liking it a lot. Gradually, Aung got to know the Father well. On some evenings, after his day's work was done, the Father would talk to Aung about the Kachin Baptist Convention and its work. From him, Aung came to know how American Reverend George J. Geis, a Baptist minister and anthropologist, came to North-eastern Burma in the 1890s and started promoting Christianity amongst the local Kachins and Shans. Most of the Kachins and Lisu were animists at that time. He established missions throughout Kachin and Shan States. He traveled extensively to preach and also wrote about his experience. Since then, more and more Kachins came to the church and showed greater interest in the universal message of the gospel.

The Reverend tried his best to understand the hill tribes. Hundreds from the distant north came down to Myitkyina on bamboo rafts for the first time to hear the story of Jesus. The Reverend Geis frequently reported on his travels in the hills. He talked about his growing friendship with the local people, the opening of the first location in the mountains, and the substantial site that the government had granted. Kachins responded to the overtures by the Reverend with a lot of respect. Aung was amazed by the scale of the effort. He had no idea that the church had done so much for the tribes in such a short time. Most members of his scouts team sheltered around the Myitkyina Airport road; that place was getting crowded for the large team of scouts.

Aung knew that the support they had from the British and Americans would dry up soon after the war was over. Aung was hoping that the tribes would have a chance to influence independent Burma, but he was not sure. The Burmar and Mon folks who were Japanese leaning were already switching sides to the Allies. They were better positioned to control Burma's national agenda, and they knew it. Aung and his scouts had no steady job or source of income, so he started planning some vocational training for his scouts. They were also helping the church in running a school for the Kachins and a field hospital on Sundays. Food and supplies were scarce, and abject poverty was everywhere, but the optimism for the future of their homeland kept them happy and motivated. Everyone was thinking that the difficult times would pass, and all ethnic minorities would have a better future in independent Burma. They had high hopes because in independent Burma, the Burmese would make decisions about their peace and well-being.

Reality turned out to be quite different. Aung was ecstatic when Burma became independent. But his euphoria did not last long. During the first few years after independence, insurgencies continued unabated - sometimes led by the Red Flag Communists or the White Flag or led by army rebels calling themselves the Revolutionary Burma Army. Remote areas of Northern Burma were controlled by Kuomingtang (KMT) forces after Mao's victory in mainland China. Burma accepted foreign assistance in rebuilding the country in these early years; continued American support for the Chinese Nationalist military presence in Burma continued to be a problem.

Burma refused to participate in the SEATO, or Southeast Asia Treaty Organization, and did not support the Bandung Conference of 1955. Burma generally tried its best to be neutral in world affairs. It was one of the first countries in the world to recognize Israel and Mao's People's Republic of China. By 1958, the country was beginning to recover. Aung and his scouts started getting odd jobs in local security - protection of government facilities. Economic activities were picking up slowly. However, politically, Burma was breaking apart in its seams. The political situation became very unstable, when U Nu survived a no-confidence vote in parliament only with the support of the National United Front. The National United Front had communists among them, so they were not liked by everyone - many saw them as Chinese plants. Army hardliners saw this as an opportunity, and then Army Chief of Staff General Ne Win was "invited," or he "invited himself," to take over the country. It was a matter of semantics.

By this time, Aung joined the Shan Federal Movement because he thought that was best way to help the Shan cause. He visited Rangoon dozens of times, met with the leaders, and thought he could agree with their vision of autonomy, peace, and prosperity for the Shan people. It was becoming clearer to Aung that the Shan needed to be part of the national platform in Rangoon. The Shan were not the ethnic majority in independent Burma, so isolation in the hills of Northern Burma was not a practical option. Having seen armed struggle from close quarters, Aung knew its limitations. He was doing his very best to convince his leadership to focus on education, health care, and development of the Shan.

He told them, "If those issues are addressed, many other things will automatically fall in place. People should see the difference."

During one of his trips to Rangoon, Aung met Suu Myint, the sister of one of his Shan comrades. Her elder brother introduced the two of them. Suu Myint had finished high school and was wanting to go to culinary school. Her parents did not like the idea of culinary school at all, so they sent her to Rangoon to be with her brother and decide. Together, they were supposed to figure out if she could study hotel management or join the upcoming tourism industry in some way. Aung and Myint fell in love quickly, and the frequency of Aung's Rangoon trips started increasing. Myint's brother had known Aung.

He knew Aung from his days at the intermediate college they attended, and he loved Aung for his honesty and his passion for the Shan cause. He had said so to his sister when she had asked him about his impression of Aung. Myint and Aung had a number of interactions in the presence of others and one-on-one. Aung was reticent, and Myint was the polar opposite. She talked all the time. Rangoon was still recovering from its wartime devastation and carnage, so Aung and Myint's romantic outings were limited to the immediate vicinity of Rangoon University.

Her brother studied there and lived nearby, so she was familiar with the neighborhood. During his fifth trip, Aung asked her out and somehow mustered the courage to ask her if she would marry him. Aung was a shy person, and during his four years at school in Rangoon, he knew only one girl. That girl was a distant cousin who was studying to become a nurse someday. So, what occurred in the case of Suu Myint was not normal for Aung. Something happened to him that day, and he felt he could not wait. After Suu Myint agreed, they spoke with her family and her parents. Myint's brother introduced Aung to a few of their relatives around Rangoon. The war had dispersed their family.

Aung still remembered his last question to her that day: "You know me now, directly as well as through your brother. If there is one thing you want me to change what would that be? If I know it, I promise that I will try very hard to change it for you." Aung knew he was not like a regular husband. He neither had a regular job nor a steady income. Marrying him was not an easy decision - it could mean much uncertainty. He thought it was fair that he asked that question to Myint that day because she was making a very difficult choice for life.

She did not wait for long, and she said, "I respect and support your commitment to the Shan cause, but when we have a family, our children would have to come first. I hope that would be acceptable to you."

Aung was not prepared for that particular statement, so he had to think for a bit, and then he said thoughtfully, "That would be acceptable to me, and I would remember that commitment."

Later that year, they decided to get married in a simple ceremony in front of his Shan comrades. She came from a Shan family, so the marriage was out and out a Shan affair. Aung stayed in Rangoon for a few days after their marriage and then returned to Myitkyina with Myint. His scouts had set up a one-bedroom apartment. The apartment was on top of a store - it was more comfortable than the hammocks and tree branches.

The caretaker government led by the army and Ne Win provided immediate stability. It paved the way for new general elections in 1960. The new elections returned U Nu's Union Party in government with a majority, but not much of governing happened. Each stakeholder was pursuing its own narrow agenda. Increasingly, Tatmadaw and its staff officers had greater influence on everything. Nothing moved in Burma without their explicit or implicit approval. Despite the good start Ne Win had, the situation did not remain stable for long in Burma.

There was political bickering from all quarters. As soon as the Shan Federal Movement started talking about the prior promise of a "loose" federation, the others in power started calling it out as a separatist movement that would definitely hurt Burma. They said that the Shan Federal Movement was undermining Burmese national unity. The Burmar and the Mon leaders often said that the Shan insistence on the government's agreement to the right to secession was happening at the wrong time. Some folks often called it treason or revolt from within.

Aung could not understand this dramatic shift in attitude in the same people that had expressed support for the idea. The only good news of 1960 was the birth of Aung's son. He and Myint named him Win Lung. Win was born in a local hospital in Myitkyina. On the day he was born, the Father from the church in Myitkyina came and blessed the mother and son. As ethnic Shans, Aung and Myint were both born Theravada Buddhists via their families, but because of the life they had led both had developed a very inclusive view of religion.

They were both schooled by life during war. Rituals and bigotry often associated with organized religion meant nothing to them.

They had both seen how so-called nonviolent Buddhists perpetrated extreme violence against fellow Buddhists in the Mon state, and they had seen the same treatment against the Muslim Rohingyas in the Arakan state. An outward allegiance to an organized religion without any real commitment toward tolerance had no appeal for Aung and Myint. They felt quite comfortable without any outward or visible attachment to any organized religion. If anyone asked, they said they were not sure as yet.

Both Aung and Myint had developed a liking for Kachin Baptists. Kachin Baptists in particular had a message on inclusion that resonated with both of them. Aung, in particular, loved their humanity. Their developmental programs were helping the hill tribes a lot; that also mattered. It was not just Aung's wartime experience with the church in Myitkyina - some of his scouts and their families liked the KBC's inclusive approach. He did not go to the church to pray every Sunday, but he continued to assist the church with its educational and social programs for the Shan and Kachins. Aung had developed a personal bond with the Father at the church in Myitkyina. In time, the vocational training program they started became widely popular.

Win resembled Aung closely like a carbon copy. In the Western tradition, he would have been named Aung Lung Jr. Aung, Myint, and baby Win did not have much material comfort in Northern Burma in 1960, but they were happy in their austere home in Myitkyina. Burma remained a very poor country post-independence, so one area of focus for Aung was to find a steady job and a source of income. He now had a family to feed, so he knew he had to do something about it sooner than later. Aung had seen the ravages of economic hardship among the tribes, and he did not want those to touch Myint or baby Win ever.

For the first thirty odd years of his life, the Shan cause was all that Aung was about. After Win's birth, he realized that he was responsible for the well-being of baby Win and Myint. If it was not him, someone like him could pick up the Shan cause, but Win and Myint had no one else - they had no backup. Aung had to deliver a decent quality of life to his wife and son. Unlike others, he had no extended family on either side to lean on, so, Aung took the responsibility of looking after Win and Myint very seriously. He had always remembered the question Myint had asked when he requested her to marry him in Rangoon, so he had to act.

General Ne Win had already succeeded in stripping the Chaofas of their feudal powers in exchange for comfortable pensions for life. He staged a coup in 1962, arrested U Nu and several other leaders, and declared a socialist state run by a council of senior military officers nominated by him. They were all his own people. He effectively got rid of the last traces of the civilian government. Essentially, his band of brothers from the army ran the country according to their personal priorities. Self-interest was above all else for the corrupt generals.

After the 1962 Burmese coup, the status of the Shan States and the Chaofas' hereditary rights were completely removed by the military government. At that stage, Burma was what Ne Win and his band of generals decided for her. She had no views of her own - nobody even asked. Some people in Rangoon called Ne Win's style of governing a necessary form of "benevolent dictatorship" for Burma's quick advancement. Aung could see the dictatorship part clearly but could not sense the benevolence part. At least there was none toward the Shan or the other hill tribes: they had learned to suffer in silence.

Independence usually brings progress and development in its wake, but Burma was an exception. There was very little progress and virtually no development immediately after independence. The fact that independent Burma was a multiethnic society that had different priorities did not seem to be a consideration for Ne Win. Most of the Burmese people had no independent voice; there were no real national elections in sight, so no one really knew what they wanted. As Aung had feared, the hill tribes had no influence in the national conversation.

The minority tribes were excluded from the agenda. Aung was surprised to see the process of national reconciliation implode; his Burma had become a fiefdom run by a few lords who made decisions for the many. Those few lords cared about their ostentatious lifestyles and their inflated egos, not much else. The downward slide toward fiefdom happened rapidly, and all opposition was stifled systematically.

After General Ne Win's declaration, a part of Aung felt that he had wasted his life thus far. In twenty years' time, he had come one full circle with almost nothing to show for it. Shans had no peace, no prosperity, and no say in the Burmese national government in Rangoon. The only difference was now the oppressors were the Tatmadaw full of Burmar and Mon people rather than the Japanese or the British. In some ways, the outside occupation was better because the locals were united; among the locals, there was empathy and understanding of one another. In Aung's opinion, Burmese fighting against Burmese was worse because the biggest loser was Burma.

That was hardly any consolation for Aung. To him, his youth, the bloody battles he fought, the sacrifices he and his comrades made as part of the resistance, and the sleepless nights he spent in hammocks and tree branches in the Kachin Hills were all a colossal waste! He could not imagine baby Win living his life under the army. Aung was desperate to give Win a chance. Gradually and very painfully, Aung was realizing that he would not be able to achieve that goal in Burma.

Aung felt dejected and broken. He wanted to hide his agony but didn't know how. He also did not know how things fell apart so quickly.

2020: San Diego trip

Kip Kimura's early morning start was going great! Kip knew he had to plan a trip soon to meet up with Dr. Kang, the researcher in the High-Performance Wireless team, at the SCRIPPS Institute in San Diego. That team at SCRIPPS was consulting with Kip's company for a wireless infrastructure project in Thailand. A couple of times, he had almost booked his tickets, but something important always came up, and he ended up postponing the trip. He always told himself that it was a day trip to San Diego, after all, and he could plan it any time he wanted with a week's notice to Dr. Kang. Dr. Kang always made himself available.

This time, however, several things fell in place. Kip himself was not over committed; United Airlines had his favorite seat in business class at the right price; Dr. Kang was available, and because of the lockdown, Kip had agreed to drive down to Dr. Kang's home office in Chula Vista. So, with all the stars aligned the right way, Kip confidently decided to make the trip. The project was not on a tight schedule, and they knew that the wireless technology specifications could change again.

Kip Kimura had obtained a license and started "ConSec" in San Rafael, California, almost immediately after he took early retirement from the US Army. The idea of ConSec, or Consulting in Security, came from Kip's army buddy Tim Kramer, who eventually became co-owner of the company. ConSec specialized in physical and cybersecurity, breach prevention, mitigation, and conflict resolution internationally. Tim and Kip had a unique set of skills in ConSec's area of specialization because they were involved in similar work for the Armed Forces and US Department of Defense (DoD). They still maintained their connections with the DoD and the US Army.

The conflict resolution part of their work required Kip and Tim to have a very wide network of international connections. Some of those were through the government agencies, and some of those were outside the formal government structures. That practice was Kip's area of focus. As the world became more connected, one side effect was social media. With social media taking over the world, tribalism increased considerably. Whether it was election interference in a foreign land or fighting a pandemic, or other kinds of nefarious media influencing, tribalism was out and about everywhere you went.

Much of ConSec's recent work focused on resolving those types of conflicts, identifying the sources, and preventing those from reoccurring. As a team, they were never short of work; people knew about them in ConSec's niche market. They were not rich yet, but with a steady caseload from law enforcement teams all over the country and their contacts in the Department of Defense, they were busy. That was part of the reason for the delay in planning the trip to San Diego, California.

Kip's Lyft driver dropped him at the San Francisco International Airport with plenty of time to spare. Kip managed to check his email and even finished the coffee he purchased at the terminal. He was quite elated when he saw that the flight was departing on time. With COVID-19 lockdowns everywhere, one could never be sure when the flights actually departed. With so many new restrictions, a lot could go wrong; most of the airlines were not yet allowed to sell all the seats. *Some flight routes might not be commercially viable*, Kip thought.

He hoped that the US Congress would be able to approve a financial relief package for the airlines. After the flight took off into the bright blue California morning, Kip settled down in his seat and opened his tablet to watch the Netflix movie he had not finished last time. The WWII true story was about three brothers saving several hundred Jews in Northern Europe by hiding them in a dense forest. For over two years, the brothers ran a small makeshift village of Jews in the middle of the forest. It had its school, communal kitchen, and ragtag security force. Kip loved the first hour of the movie - the acting and the direction were great. Adversity really brought people together.

Several minutes after the flight reached cruising altitude, just about when the flight attendants were getting ready with their service carts, a passenger started feeling unwell. She was three rows behind Kip's, so he could not see much, but he could feel the anxiety in the voices of the flight attendants.

After a few minutes of tense discussion and snippets of conversations from a couple of passengers near her, Kip heard the senior flight attendant say, "I would go and talk to the captain. He might consider landing in Burbank so that she can get immediate medical attention. We are not far from our destination of San Diego, but Burbank is even closer - could make a difference of fifteen minutes."

With those words, the flight attendant went away for several minutes. When she got back, she said, "I tried to explain, but the captain is reluctant to consider landing in Burbank because it would change the connecting flight options from San Diego and save twenty minutes. He did not think it would make a material difference, also Air Traffic Control might not be able to clear us for landing immediately."

On hearing that statement from the flight attendant, the passengers who were nearby started reacting. A male voice that sounded elderly said, "Twenty minutes can make a lot of difference when someone is unwell. You go and say that to your captain, young lady."

The flight attendant seemed to make an attempt to say something, "Sir, I understand, but -"

Before she finished her sentence, another lady's voice picked up the thread, a bit more aggressively, "What is wrong with your airline people? Why are you worrying about flight connections when someone is unwell? Someone's life is more important than your flight schedules. You know, planes will fly tomorrow, the day after, and the day after that. Jesus, Christ, I cannot believe this!"

That last bit of lecturing opened the floodgate! More passengers spoke up; several of them had graphic tales to tell - stories of suffering uncles, cousins, and aunts started coming out of many seats. One lady spoke of a very sick aunt who got stuck on a plane in New York last month for three hours just because the captain parked the plane away from the gate, and the passengers were bused to the terminal. Her sick aunt had to wait for her wheelchair, which took a lifetime to arrive.

They asked the flight attendant to go and talk to the captain one more time and persuade him. The experienced flight attendant realized the direction in which the conversation was going and how quickly things could go south. She left before things went out of control. This time, the flight attendant came back quickly and said that the captain had agreed, and the flight would land at the Bob Hope Airport in Burbank in about twenty-two minutes. *Pretty quick*, thought Kip.

Kip watched the whole thing unfold and wondered if he should inform Dr. Kang that he would be delayed for his 11:00 a.m. meeting in Chula Vista, but his AT&T iPhone had no bars, so he decided to wait for the plane to land. On landing in Burbank, he would have signal and could call then. He was still hoping that he would make it to Chula Vista, San Diego, for the meeting. He started watching their plane descending into the Bob Hope Airport through his window.

Upon landing in Burbank, the sick lady was stretchered off the plane, and the other passengers were asked to wait in a quarantine room adjacent to the terminal building. Kip noticed a stern looking lady in the corner of the bare room they were in.

As he and a few other passengers approached, she lifted her gaze and said, "Please fill out this yellow application form, and then form a line on the left side of my desk. And please stay six feet apart; we observe social distancing at the Bob Hope Airport, no exceptions. We have a very high standard of passenger hygiene at this airport, and we want to keep it that way." Nobody disputed her claims, so she shifted her focus on her tabletop.

The form had questions about their general health, travel plans, if they had a fever, if they had visited Wuhan in China recently, etc. It stated that the nurse would take body temperatures with a thermometer. It also said that depending on their answers on the form, passengers could be quarantined at the state-of-the-art quarantine facility located at the Burbank Airport. Apparently, the quarantine facility was so comfortable that some passengers wanted to stay there longer!

After his experience so far, that was the last thing Kip wanted, even if the facility was state-of-the-art, so he followed the instructions. While they were departing, the nurse handed each passenger a set of disposable latex gloves and two surgical masks. She also advised each of them to wear a mask at all times in the Burbank Airport. Kip was happy to note that mask wearing in public places was gradually becoming a norm, at least in California. The whole process was long and inefficient to say the least, but he liked the fact that people were following the process. As Tim would say, "It is the process of compliance that protects people," not the intent. The nurse took a lot of time, but eventually, she let all passengers go back to the main terminal building. All first half flights were already gone - short hop flights were a lot fewer, anyway.

Kip got back to the airline counter at the terminal and found the only options were late evening flights. Then, he went to the rental car counter and found that cars were readily available, and he could potentially pick up the car from AVIS in Burbank and drop it off at

AVIS in the San Diego Airport. The distance was not much, but if he opted to drive in a rental car, he could be stuck in LA traffic for hours. Traffic jams on I5 South were legendary. Interstate 5 (I5 for locals) and other routes to San Diego through the city of Irvine were all likely to be clogged with traffic at that time of the day. The last time he had tried going that way, he was stuck near the UC Irvine campus for three long hours!

Ultimately, Kip decided against going to San Diego. Instead, he called Dr. Kang, explained the situation, and re-scheduled his meeting for a later date. After he ended the call with Dr. Kang, he got back to the terminal building to check the options for return flights to San Francisco and even Oakland. He checked with United, Delta, and Southwest Airlines. The earliest outgoing flight was around 8:00 p.m., which meant he would be home around 11:00 p.m. at the earliest.

As he was checking the flight schedules, one thought occurred to him. He could simply go to his friend John's house in Glendale and borrow his old car for a drive back to San Rafael. John and Kip were in high school together in Boulder, Colorado, and they had always stayed in touch. Lately, they had not met each other in a few months after the COVID-19 lockdowns. The last time John was visiting a studio in Emeryville, he did not have time to drive down to San Rafael because he had to fly out of Oakland Airport, so they missed each other. Then came the lockdowns. Everybody had to drastically cut down essential and non-essential travel by air. As it was, John did not travel much for work. Kip was the one who did, so he might as well make up for the missed opportunity in the Bay Area. This was a good time for Kip to meet John and his son Joe. He knew John's wife was at her parents' place in Santa Barbara looking after them. The extended lockdown had complicated life for the elderly more than others could even imagine.

With a little luck, that option could get him home probably by 4:00 or 5:00 p.m. Kip's next call was to his friend John. As expected, John Abreo was at home because of the lockdown; his post-production company had switched to "working from home" mode. John readily agreed to lend the old Acura Integra to Kip. He said that the old car was only occasionally used by his son, so Kip could borrow and keep it for a few days. John's son was college bound, but the admission he was longing for was not in hand yet, so Joe did not have a use for the car during the lockdown, and it stayed parked roadside. John said the car had not been serviced in a couple of years, so Kip should keep that in mind.

Kip knew he would have to visit Southern California (SoCal) in a week, he could always drop off John's Acura during his next trip. In a few minutes, Kip picked up his backpack, came out of the terminal building, called a Lyft ride, and left for John's house in Glendale. Like many folks do in Los Angeles, Kip's Lyft driver used some shortcuts and made it to Glendale quickly. As he was alighting from the Toyota Camry curb side, Kip could see John doing some yard work. His yard needed attention after the recent rains - leaves were scattered all over.

On seeing him, John called out, "Hey, Joey, come and say hello to Uncle Kip - he is here."

By the time Kip climbed the two steps onto the porch, Joe was out greeting him. Much as he would have liked to, Kip could not hang out with John and Joe for long because John had work. John had to do a series of conference calls with his creative director. John's company was outsourcing parts of the shooting to a company in Austria where the COVID-19 lockdown was less intense and movie production was going on uninterrupted. Like Norway, Austria managed the lockdown well. They closed the country early and opened early, and movie production was continuing there as per US CDC and local guidelines.

Joe told him that he was hoping to get admission in University of Arizona, that he had a good GPA, but his SAT scores were low. Joe thought he did not make it in the first list of admitted students because of his SAT scores. Kip encouraged Joe to stay positive and said that his admission would probably come through because of the low volume of international students this year. Kip had read that news item on the internet and also watched the president of the University of California system say so to a reporter on live TV. Joe said he was hopeful because some of his classmates had just started receiving their scholarship and admission offers. After a while, Kip picked up the car keys, joined John and his son Joe for a quick falafel sandwich lunch, and departed for San Rafael.

He topped off the gas talk in a Shell gas station on Los Feliz Boulevard and picked up a few bottles of water and a bag of snacks for the six-hour drive back. He knew once he reached the Interstate 5, he would have a pretty smooth drive at this time of the day. Because of the recent wildfires in Southern California, there was a rerouting of traffic on I5, based on what he had heard on the car radio - Kip hoped that would not impact him too much. He should be able to manage.

As he headed toward I5 Northbound, Kip told himself that he had made a good decision; there was really no point in pushing himself to go to San Diego today. It made no sense to him. It was not a great idea to just wait in Burbank Airport till 8:00 p.m. for the next flight and then learn that there had been a schedule change. Travel had really become a nightmare in 2020 because of the lockdowns. In terms of traffic and driving, it was not just San Diego - he had to take into account the driving distance to Chula Vista as well. Within minutes, Kip drove out of Glendale and hit the freeway, and the car handled itself well. That was one thing he liked about the cars made by Honda. Like his friend John, he liked cars made by Honda for their reliability. The traffic on I5 was light, and he was making a steady seventy-five miles an hour.

After all, ninety-six thousand miles is not that big a deal for an Acura made in the early 2000s, Kip told himself. The temperature outside was seventy degrees and sunny; it was indeed beautiful California weather for driving. Given the beautiful weather and the broadcast from the local PBS station, Kip did not need to stop soon. He crossed the suburbs of Los Angeles, Bakersfield, and decided to do a gas refill and coffee break. He stopped over at a gas station and an adjacent Denny's at Buttonwillow. After he filled the gas tank, as he was departing the gas station, he heard a noise coming from the undercarriage of the Acura.

He ignored it for several minutes as he went around the overpass and merged onto Northbound I5. He thought the noise was caused by the vibration of a part that had become loose. Kip thought that it may be a loose body part, and at steady freeway speed, the vibration and sound would subside. It did not quite work that way as the sound increased steadily - it did not change with speed. As he was crossing Kettleman City and going toward Coalinga, the sound increased considerably, and he had to stop on the shoulder right after the junction of I5 and State Highway 33. For a few minutes, Kip sat inside the car and thought about the options he had. None of the options seemed very appealing.

Finally, he thought maybe switching off and cooling the engine might help. Kip switched the engine off, let the car cool down for fifteen minutes, and attempted a restart, but this time, the engine would not even start. When the car didn't start after several attempts, Kip realized that it would be dark in a few hours, and he did not want to be stuck on the shoulder of I5 after dark. With cars traveling on I5 at eighty-five miles an hour, that would be a very bad idea in the middle of nowhere in the truest sense of the term. Also, towing might not be available by the American Automobile

Association (AAA) after dark, so he decided to call the California AAA toll-free number from his iPhone.

The emergency roadside service of the AAA said that the estimated arrival of a tow truck from Los Banos was an hour later. So, Kip went inside the car, switched on his blinkers, and waited. He wanted the speeding cars to see his car parked on the shoulder because of the blinkers. An hour later, a very impressive looking AAA towing truck came and parked about fifty feet ahead of Kip on the shoulder. The car had all kinds of lights on its sides and also on top of the driver's cabin. The driver came down from the truck, took Kip's membership card and driver's license, and filled out some paperwork. After that, he tilted the cargo section of the tow truck and winched John's Acura on the tow truck - the Acura fit into the flat cargo bed pretty well. The bed could accommodate sedans and trucks.

As soon as Kip settled on the front passenger seat, the driver started his drive back to Los Banos. The first AAA approved auto shop they ran into was full, so the tow truck driver had to take Kip to Dick's Auto Repair a bit further down the road toward Merced. Kip got down and explained the problem to Dick, the owner. Dick nodded his head and said he understood the issue; he said he had repaired this type of problems in the past. He said it was quite common with old fasteners.

He explained that some of the fasteners used in the undercarriage had become loose. And those had to be replaced with original Honda or Acura parts as soon as possible; otherwise, the larger parts would sustain damage, which would cost more. He was hoping that the problem would not be complicated because that Acura was his only transport back to San Rafael, and he was delayed. Dick had the Acura lifted in his repair bay and inspected the undercarriage with a powerful flashlight designed for inspection.

After doing a visual inspection, he hammered a few places and declared, "I can repair it - it is not going to be expensive, about three hundred dollars or so, but it will take time because I have to get a spare part from another store in Morgan Hill. I can get it done in eight hours tops." When he heard the time estimate from Dick, Kip's heart sank; he realized that he was looking at the possibility of spending the night at sleepy Los Banos, for which he was not prepared. Not the ideal situation to be in, but Kip had seen much worse days in the US Army.

Dick went inside, made a couple of calls, and came to Kip with a smile. "Good news and bad news: the good news is the part is available and it is coming; the bad news is it will take two extra hours. I'll have my night shift guy get it all done, and you can pick up the car in the morning."

Kip could drive long distances for ten to twelve hours in the daylight, but he was not a good night-time driver because he had a tendency to doze off. Kip reluctantly decided to spend the night in Las Banos to avoid night driving. Dick's shop was on Highway 152, and on his way in, Kip had seen a Walmart. One block from there, across from the Walmart, there was a La Quinta Inn. Kip was in no mood to go and look for another hotel.

Kip decided to visit the Walmart first because he felt there was a high likelihood that he would get a room. *Los Banos cannot be crowded with visitors at this time of the year*, Kip thought. Kip had to do a bit of shopping at Walmart for toothpaste, razors, and bottled water. After Walmart, Kip went to the La Quinta Inn to check if rooms were available. Luckily, rooms were available, and the front office staff were very helpful - they even ordered pizza for him. There were few guests, and Kip took a room on the third floor to avoid the white noise from I5.

Kip was in no mood to step out again for dinner, so he had accepted the hotel manager's offer for the pizza. Los Banos was almost in the middle of California and on I5, so the hotel was not heavily booked during the week. As soon as he was inside his room, Kip called Tim in San Rafael and filled him in about his stay in Los Banos.

Tim joked and commented, "Some people prefer the scenic route to get back to San Rafael from Glendale - what can I say? Please enjoy your vacation. I will see you day after tomorrow, then." After that, Tim ended the call.

The day had been long and tiring, so Kip had a shower, finished his delicious hotel ordered pizza, watched the news on CNN for a half an hour, and went to sleep. In many cities in the US, there were Black Lives Matter protests. In several cities, the protests had turned violent toward the late evening hours. The next day, before breakfast, Kip called Dick for a status on the repair. Dick said that they had more delays, but the car would be ready for pickup by 10:00 a.m. It didn't matter to Kip that much because it would still be mid-afternoon when he would reach Highway 101 near Gilroy. He would switch to Highway 280 eventually, but he was a lot more worried about the traffic on Highway 101. Once he was past the bottleneck, in San Jose, Highway 280 was manageable. He had no way to get a better sense of the traffic on the way. *I will cross that bridge when I get to it*, thought Kip.

His next traffic nightmare could be the Sausalito bound traffic on the Golden Gate bridge, but he thought he could deal with it. Kip had a leisurely breakfast of eggs, bacon, and a lot of black coffee. After that, he walked around the block and completed his three-mile daily quota of brisk walking. Los Banos was a pretty quiet place; Kip liked the simple working-class town. Visitors were probably there only because of I5 or the University of California, Merced to the East. It was also a route to the Yosemite Park, not a popular one but a good one, and there was a lot less traffic.

He used the hotel Wi-Fi, cleared all his emails, sent the two documents Dr. Kang had wanted, and then left for Dick's auto shop. On arrival at Dick's repair shop, Kip noticed that the brown Acura Integra was ready and parked outside - Dick had even washed the car thoroughly. Dick profusely apologized for the delay and said that while the repair work was going on, someone had called about the car and his mechanic talked to the caller. Kip asked him what the call was for, but Dick did not know; he went inside to check with his mechanic, but the mechanic had already stepped out for early lunch. Dick said their lunch break was usually one hour, but he was not sure if the mechanic would return in an hour. He had left early for a doctor visit that had to be today.

Kip was in two minds, but in the end, he decided not to wait any longer and risk traffic delays on Highway 101 North and then on the Golden Gate Bridge. He did not want to get caught in traffic on 101 or even 280. Kip paid Dick's invoice with his American Express and headed for Highway 152 Westbound; he would now be on 152 West all the way till Gilroy, California. For a regular Tuesday morning, traffic on the road was light, and Kip made good time. The car was driving like a charm. Clearly, Dick knew what he was doing - the noise was all gone. The ride quality was very good for a 2002 Acura. *Gasoline cars of that vintage were made really well*, Kip thought. He had to admire the build quality of the Japanese cars - so reliable after so many years on the road.

After a couple of hours, Kip arrived in Gilroy and merged into 101 Northbound. There was a small roadside brush fire near San Martin, so for about three miles, Hwy 101 had only two of the four lanes operating. Contrary to his expectations, Northbound 280 was completely clogged with traffic near Palo Alto, and that slow down added at least twenty-five minutes to his travel. Most of the crowd was for the Venture Capital firms and Hewlett Packard campus - some for Stanford University. There was a demonstration going on at the Golden Gate Bridge toll plaza. He saw that the protesters were carrying signage that said, "Make America Great Again" and "Four More Years." He knew who those protesters were. Finally, around 6:30 p.m. after crossing the Golden Gate Bridge, Kip could see his lane. Roads were wet - it had rained a lot over here!

What started out as a short-day trip to San Diego finally came to an end a day and half later! He was really tired from the long drive. Kip parked the Acura next to his Jaguar on the driveway, opened his garage, and went inside. Once inside, Kip made some coffee and sat down with his laptop to clear his email. His flat screen TV was on mute. Kip saw on CNN that the Black Lives Matter protests were now happening in multiple cities in the US simultaneously. Some of the CNN analysts were saying that professional sports teams from the NBA and NFL would soon join the protests. Kip thought it was about time. He was tired of seeing examples of racial discrimination on TV weekly; it was like having two legal systems in the same country. What bothered him even more was that the government and the folks in power were still mostly in denial.

If Kip had time, he would have liked to go to San Francisco and join one of the protest marches. He made a mental note to check the schedule and check if he could go. If he drove down to San Francisco, he would have to commit himself for a full workday. That was the only reason he had not been able to go. He did not have that kind of time right now, but he would in a month or so, and at that time, he would most definitely make a plan with Tim and drive down to San Francisco. Because of the lockdowns, parking in the city had become much easier.

Next morning, Kip woke up at 5:00 a.m. so that he could start the day early after his run on the trail near Marin Headlands - he got back after his five-mile route. He came back from his run, showered, and was about to sit down for breakfast when his landline phone at home rang.

The display had John's phone number from Glendale, and as he picked up the phone, he could hear Joe's excited voice at the other end, "Uncle Kip, I made it into the university; they have even offered me the Electrical Engineering honors program I was waiting for. I might get good financial aid as well."

"Wow, wow, Joey, slow down," Kip said, "we were talking about this only yesterday at your house in Glendale. I am so happy and thrilled for you. I am sure you would become a great electrical engineer someday. Anyway, very big congratulations!"

He really felt great for the kid. After a couple of minutes, John came on the line. John said, "Kip, I never thought I would bother you like this, but could you please drop off the car this week? Joe will need it on the campus because there is no other form of transportation."

Kip replied, "No worries at all, John. I had to visit Southern California next week anyway for a project in San Diego. Could I bring it over on Thursday, say midday?"

"That will be awesome. Thursday any time would be all right, Kip. You decide, I don't want to impose," John said.

He realized that John was feeling a bit awkward, but in reality, it was not an inconvenience for Kip's schedule at all. He thought he would let John know next time they met face-to-face in Glendale. Kip disconnected and started planning. *If I'm going back to SoCal, it might make sense to connect up with Dr. Kang in San Diego*, he thought. After a few minutes of thinking, Kip discarded that thought. It was probably better to keep the schedule flexible for now, at least.

Finally, Kip decided that he would start early on Thursday, drive to Glendale, and return the car. Only after that was done would he plan the rest of the activities. After his last trip got disrupted the way it did, Kip thought that too much detailed planning was not very wise. If he could plan to drive in off-peak hours, he should be fine because the distances in SoCal were not far. After dropping off John's car, if things went as planned, he could easily rent a car from Glendale or Burbank Airport.

He could drive down to San Diego; he would use United Airlines on the way back. He had lots of unused miles for 2020, and in their mileage program, some miles could expire. Kip wanted to bounce off a few ideas with Dr. Kang about the Thai wireless job. No big deal. Kip spent most of Wednesday in meetings with his partner Tim. He briefed Tim on the ongoing cases and made sure that Tim had all the case files, copies of agreements, email addresses, and contacts for the priority items. After his last trip got extended, he had become wiser.

1963: Bangkok

After many months of deep contemplation and weighing all options available to him, in 1963, Aung decided to leave Burma for good and move to Thailand. He and his wife talked about the agonizing decision of leaving their homeland and living in a foreign country for hours on end. After two full years of roaming around in temporary shelters in the border regions around Chiang Mai, Aung, his wife, and young son managed to sign up as residents in a more organized refugee camp.

Those two years of hopping from shelter to shelter were particularly hard on three-year-old Win. In addition to the lack of physical comfort, his friends, toys, and surroundings changed too frequently for his liking. Win felt unsettled, and Aung felt sorry for Win and Myint. The organized refugee camps provided more stability and security to the residents. The advantage was organizations like the International Red Cross, Doctors without Borders, UNHCR, and local Non-Government Organizations or NGOs had access. Stories from these camps got out.

There were regular schedules for school going kids for food distribution, basic health care, and vocational training. There was even a class for learning Thai and English, taught by a Thai schoolteacher from Bangkok, that met twice a month. The Thai government did not want the Shan to migrate into Thailand. For the Thai government, the Shan were illegals who were an unnecessary drain on Thai public resources. Most of the programs in the camps were run by non-Thai social welfare organizations. The Thai government wanted to keep the Shan contained in a small area - most of the Shan never, ever went outside their camps. For the Thai government, the Shan were simply unwanted.

The government did not recognize them, so they could not access any public service. The refugees mostly survived through the handouts. They also received donations from the United Nations, international charities, other governments or NGOs. As unwanted illegals, if the Shan folks ever got lucky and managed to get employment, they were almost always underpaid and exploited. There were brokers who arranged work for the refugees for a fee. Many of those were part of the organized racket that did the exploitation.

In the newspaper reports and informal channels, there were numerous stories of local Thais taking advantage of Shan refugees. If those cases of exploitation were reported to the authorities, they mostly looked the other way, so the practice largely continued with impunity. The refugee camps of Chiang Mai were a living hell as it was, and the attitude of the Thai government made it worse for the helpless refugees. Aung was not sure if it was by design or simply accidental.

Compared to most of the other Shan, Aung was more educated and more aware; therefore, he was more worried about their long-term prospects in Thailand. He knew that for him, his wife Suu Myint and his son Win, the camps of Chiang Mai could not be a viable option for very long. By the end of 1965, Aung rose to a leadership position among the Shan within the refugee camp. His role included coordinating food distribution, arranging vocational training, and coordinating basic health care. Because of the outside donations, the camp had some resources of its own. From time to time, his role would involve him talking to the International Red Cross, Non-Government Organizations, charities, and Thai government officials for resources for the camp.

In 1965, during one of those NGO reviews, Aung was asked by the refugees in the camp to appeal to the NGO. The management of the NGO was doing a review, and the refugees were asking for more food and medical supplies. As one of the leaders, Aung prepared a meticulously detailed case and made a passionate plea for help with resources during his presentation with a lot of data and anecdotal evidence. Aung knew he had made a good pitch with all the data and projections; now, he and the officials had to wait for the NGO decision.

As he was finishing his speech, Aung thought he recognized one of the NGO administrators. His name was different, but his speech and the way he conducted himself were eerily familiar to Aung. Aung felt that he had met that man before, somewhere. He mentioned his feeling to Myint, and she advised him to stay quiet because if the man was not who Aung thought he was, he could get offended.

Her words of caution were, "Avoid any unnecessary exposure with the Thai people here. We cannot go back to Burma with baby Win. Burma is far too violent."

As he went to bed that night, Aung remembered who that man was and why was he looking so familiar despite his Thai name. The man was his friend from Chinese X Forces. Chiang Liu was part of the Chinese forces that were fighting alongside the Galahad. In the beginning, the Chinese forces were inexperienced: they had no idea about the schedules and patterns of the wandering Japanese patrols. As a result of this naiveté, the Japanese could target them often. The limited training the Chinese forces received in India meant that they were not quite ready for the Japanese onslaught. That said, these Chinese forces with the Galahad were still better than many others.

Their contemporaries fighting inside China were much worse; inside China military operations were impacted by the corrupt KMT. There were reports of financial mismanagement by KMT leadership all over. Greater access to equipment and ammunition and less influence from the Chinese leadership eventually turned the four Chinese divisions within the NCAC into formidable fighting forces. In the end, they could be trusted a great deal more in combat than others.

Among those who were fighting in the Kachin Hills, there was a concern for their inadequate training. In the early days, once, Aung was next to a Japanese patrol well hidden in the bushes, and he heard Japanese soldiers boasting that they could use the Chinese for target practice at will. The entire Japanese Imperial Army would come to regret that attitude later in the campaign. The NCAC Chinese divisions fought hard because they knew they had to win - losing was not an option.

Chiang and his boys were caught in one of those crossfires with the Japanese in a steep hillside. The Chinese were not expecting a Japanese patrol, but the Japanese lookouts had heard Chiang's noisy team pass by on a trail and were ready to unleash its firepower on them. By the time Aung's scouts reached them, Japanese guns had inflicted heavy damage to Chiang's team, and their mules and Chiang had fallen in a ravine after getting shot. Without the scouts, Chiang would have died. On his own, there was no way for him to escape from that ravine.

Aung saw the scar on his left fist during the NGO meeting. That scar was caused in that unexpected battle with the Japanese troops in the Kachin Hills. Chiang should remember Aung's help in 1944; in that skirmish, he had almost lost his life. He was lucky to be alive. Aung's scouts had rescued Chiang from the ravine with ropes and makeshift pulleys and had given him medical treatment in hiding for two weeks. Chiang was really young and fit; that was part of the reason why he recovered from the trauma. Initially, it was touch and go for many days.

After Chiang recovered from his injury a month later, Aung had personally taken him across the Kachin Hills to the command post of the Chinese forces so that he could be reunited with his division. Aung was lucky: Chiang's NGO and its staff were not closely supervised by the Thai authorities in the camp and outside because it had some connection with a member of the Thai royal family. Once he recognized his friend, during Chiang's third trip to the refugee camp, Aung mustered enough courage to go and talk to him in person. Aung had to be careful - Chiang had a new Thai sounding name. Thailand had a fair number of ethnic Chinese people, so he blended well among them.

Aung had no doubts in his mind - also, the scar was a definite giveaway. When he was alone, Aung asked, "Can I ask you a personal question?"

"Sure," said the man, smiling.

Without any preamble, Aung said, "Were you known as 'Chiang Liu' in the Kachin Hills during the Japanese occupation of Burma? I hope my direct question does not offend you in any way. If you are not Chiang, I am sorry - I hope I have not offended you in any way. You look just like him in every way. You have that scar just like he had on the same hand in the same place."

Aung knew it was Chiang, but he was not sure how Chiang would react to Aung confronting him. After a full ten seconds, Chiang spoke, "And you are my friend Aung Lung of the Kachin scouts? We fought against the Japanese side by side in the Kachin Hills near Myitkyina in Northern Burma. I almost died on those ravines; how can I ever forget that? I have been waiting for you to open up for two of my trips here."

Aung was in a state of shock. He said, "Why were you waiting for me to open up first? Why didn't you ask me directly during your past trips?"

Chiang clarified, "Most of the Shan that migrate to Thailand do not want to be found. I assumed that about you too. You are a friend. I will never be the one to identify you. If you did not want to be identified, I could understand the possible reason behind that decision. If you do not want to be found, that is how it would be as far as I am concerned. I know that the Thai government is not very friendly to the Shan folks that migrate from Burma."

Though quite unusual, Aung understood the logic Chiang had just presented to him. After that, the two of them did a lot of catching up. They talked at length about Aung and his family's options. Chiang was now married to a Thai lady with connections. He had settled in Bangkok, and he knew several high officials in the Thai government. He had a business of his own to supply food and produce to restaurants. On the side, he assisted this NGO to retain his connections with the royal family and to look good. This NGO was for his image, Chiang said. He said this NGO opened a lot of doors for him that would otherwise be closed. Aung did not completely understand the context, but he decided not to push.

During their hourlong interaction, Chiang told Aung that Aung's best option was to get new identities for him and his family and move to Bangkok. Initially, Aung resisted the idea with all his might because he did not want to compromise and give up his Shan identity. The eternal Shan rebel in him protested violently, but Aung had to be pragmatic for baby Win and Myint. It was not just him anymore - he could not gamble with Myint's and Win's lives and well-being. He had given that commitment to Myint. After three visits to the camp in Chiang Mai, Chiang convinced him that with a Thai identity, his family, particularly Win, would have a better shot at life. Win would have many options that he could not imagine if he remained a refugee in Chiang Mai.

Aung's day-to-day life was pretty bleak in the refugee camp. Aung knew that he had to do better for Myint and Win. In his head, he reasoned that if he was able to get out of this hell hole of a camp, he might be able to help the Shan cause a lot better. After four months of agonizing tug-of-war between staying in the camp and going to Bangkok, Aung relented. During his next trip to the camp, Chiang collected a lot of information from Aung and Myint to build up the case for their Thai residency paperwork. He filled in a few forms and had Aung and Myint both sign those forms. With a portable camera, Chiang took several pictures of the three of them for the application.

After that, Chiang made arrangements with a law firm in Bangkok for filing the Thai residency paperwork for Aung, Myint, and Win. He said to Aung that he expected all three of them to get legalized as permanent residents of Thailand in a few months. It was not an easy process, but with so many refugees from neighboring countries, things were still a bit chaotic in Thailand, so Aung and his family's residency applications were approved without much scrutiny. The right connections Chiang's NGO and his in-laws had with the royals helped.

Aung, Myint, and Win had their Thai paperwork for permanent residency in hand by 1966. Aung did not expect it to happen that fast; his family's experience did not match the experience others had. Thai residency allowed Aung to live anywhere he wished and work in any profession he deemed appropriate and was qualified for. He and his family could travel inside Thailand, own property in Thailand, and access public health care and other services; in return, he was required to pay taxes. That was a decent bargain, Chiang had said to Aung. At one level, Aung was happy to leave the camp, but at another level, given how his residency paperwork was obtained, he was worried. His worry was more for his family and less for him. He did not show his worries to Myint and Win - he hoped that they would have more stability now.

One thing Aung knew: this was the better of the two bad options he had. The refugee camp was not a long-term option for him and most importantly Win. Thailand was not just a foreign country for the Shan - it was also hostile. The Lungs were leading a communal life in the refugee camp; they had very little that they could call their own. When the paperwork came in, there was not a whole lot to prepare or plan for. They could leave immediately, and they did.

Chiang had cautioned Aung that after the paperwork came in, the Lungs should not hang out in the refugee camp in Chiang Mai for too long. It would draw unnecessary attention. Aung completed the unfinished work he had at the camp, and through an agent, he had their second-class train tickets booked for Bangkok. That was the least expensive way to travel to Bangkok from Chiang Mai. Thai trains were not bad before the war, but the train journey the Lungs had was long, hot, and uncomfortable with lots of delays. It took them nearly a full day to travel from Chiang Mai to Bangkok's main transportation hub Hualamphong Station.

Luckily, Myint was able to pack some fruits from the meagre food supply at the refugee camp for the journey. The track had seen bombing in multiple sections, and the train had to stop. Stopping and slowing down happened in many places where repairs were taking place. Before the war, the Japanese and Thai governments were rebuilding the tracks - they had taken on some expansion as well. When Aung stood on the station platform in Bangkok for the first time as a Thai resident, he did not feel elated at all. Deep inside, he felt like an imposter who cheated his way out of a horrible life using questionable means. Aung felt awful for abandoning his beloved Shan people.

Once Aung, Myint, and Win landed in Bangkok, Aung had to find work and a place to stay. For the first week, they stayed at a youth hostel near the station so that Aung could go and meet with Chiang easily and often. Chiang's NGO offices were located near the main station. Since Aung had no local transportation, the family ended up staying in the youth hostel longer than they had originally anticipated. Chiang had a lot of connections in the food and restaurant industry. Most of the waterfront restaurants procured their produce from Chiang, so he talked to many of the owners about various operational issues. Word of mouth was a good way to reach potential employers, Chiang said.

After two weeks, Chiang told Aung about the owner of a Chinese restaurant near the Bangkok waterfront. Chiang supplied produce to that restaurant. That Chinese owner, Mr. Lin, was looking for a manager who was educated and could also double up in other roles. The restaurant was doing quite well but could not hire too many employees on its small payroll as of yet. During one of his visits from the youth hostel, Chiang told Aung that Mr. Lin would like to meet Aung.

If it was all right, he could ask Mr. Lin to come to the offices of the NGO, and Aung and Mr. Lin could meet up there - the back office had a closed space where the meeting could take place. Aung readily agreed; he needed to support his family, and he needed a job as soon as possible. Aung met Mr. Lin face-to-face in Chiang's office on the appointed day.

Mr. Lin asked Aung, "Are you good with numbers? What about dealing with people of different nationalities and cultures? We get a lot of Americans and Europeans in Bangkok."

Aung responded, "I have always been very good with math and numbers. Math was my strongest subject in high school and intermediate college. If the war had not broken out, I would have studied math in college. More than anything else, I love dealing with people of different cultural backgrounds. I think I connect well with people, and I have worked with Americans and Europeans before and made many friends.

"Also, I can communicate in English reasonably well - I studied in English schools." Aung also told him frankly that he had a family to feed, so he needed the job. Mr. Lin liked Aung and his answers, and he said that Aung was straightforward and willing. Aung was not sure if it was his answers or Chiang's reference that actually made a bigger difference.

In any case, after the meeting, Aung was offered the job of part-time manager; part-time cashier, and whatever else the restaurant needed. Mr. Lin told Aung to be flexible about his new role. Aung happily accepted the job offer and immediately moved Myint and Win to a one-bedroom apartment in a low-cost neighborhood in Bangkok. Thus, they started a new phase. It was necessary to move out of the youth hostel so that he could get started with his new life. The work was demanding, and the hours long, but Aung did not mind. Initially, he had to take a small loan from Chiang to make ends meet, which he paid back after his own salary was regularized by Mr. Lin. Gradually, Mr. Lin started delegating more and more of the managing to Aung.

In a short time, Aung was doing the day-to-day management of the restaurant. Aung was doing the very best he could - he was working extremely hard, and he was flexible. In 1968, just a couple of years after Aung joined, one evening, Aung was tallying the receipts at the cash register, and Mr. Lin came up to him. Every evening, Aung had to match the sale with the receipts as a good bookkeeping practice.

He said, "Aung, I need to talk to you about something."

Aung said, "What is it, Mr. Lin? Oh, I know, I am sorry about the chef's complaint about our pork supplier. I promise I'll talk to supplier again and get him to supply our pork. Some new people in his team had caused the confusion - I assure you it is sorted out and will not happen again."

Mr. Lin pulled up a chair and sat down next to the cash register, raised his hand slightly, and said, "I am not talking about meat supply issues at all, Aung. I know you are doing your best to take care of the supplier logistics; sometimes, things go wrong despite your best efforts. I am old enough to understand that fact of life. I need to talk to you about a different matter altogether - that matter is not connected to this restaurant. I have to talk to about a different opportunity." He paused for a bit and said, "I have been thinking of expanding my restaurant business. Now, I think I have found the right opportunity in Pattaya City. I have just bought a struggling Thai restaurant there. It has huge growth potential immediately - I want to go there and run it myself."

That was a lot to take in, but Aung managed to say, "That is great news, Mr. Lin. Thanks a lot for letting me know."

Mr. Lin looked up and added, "Not just that. When I am away in Pattaya, I would like you to part own this restaurant and run it as the manager - as if you were me." On hearing that, Aung had a range of emotions go through him; he felt elated, but he also sensed a bit of uncertainty. He was not sure if this restaurant would remain a stable business, and if it did, for how long. On the whole, he was pleased because Mr. Lin was giving him more responsibility and recognizing the contribution he had made so far.

Aung knew that Mr. Lin was a fair-minded person. In the end, he said, "I am very grateful to you for your trust in me, Mr. Lin."

Mr. Lin concluded the conversation by saying, "I will let you know the exact dates and other logistics in a week or two. I know you will do a good job and make this restaurant successful. Initially, I would spend a few weeks at a time, but in about a year, if things go well, I might have to move to Pattaya City permanently." Mr. Lin explained that Pattaya City was experiencing huge growth, and with the US investments, that growth was expected to continue for many decades to come. Since there were fewer places for good Chinese food in Pattaya City, Mr. Lin thought his timing was just right. Mr. Lin had hoped that there would be other opportunities in Pattaya's hospitality sector where he could invest.

Pattaya was a fishing village until the 1960s. Tourism started before but began growing during America's engagement in Vietnam. As American servicemen and contractors began arriving on rest and relaxation trips in the waterfront, the need for different cuisine and other tourist services grew. Americans and Europeans loved the place - they started coming by the hordes.

Large groups would often arrive in Pattaya from other countries and stay there for days, enjoying the welcoming waterfront and the beautiful weather almost all year. Pattaya City's popularity among westerners grew a lot, and the word of Thai hospitality spread far and wide. The south end of the beach gradually became known as the "Strip." Mr. Lin was a cautious businessman; Aung knew he would have thought through this whole decision for a long time. In a short period of time, Mr. Lin's new restaurant project was quite successful.

In 1970, he decided to move to Pattaya to run the new place and invest in a small tourist resort nearby. Before departing for Pattaya, Mr. Lin offered part ownership of the Bangkok restaurant to Aung, and he also gave him time to arrange funds. Mr. Lin thought that was the best way to recognize Aung's contribution in the Bangkok restaurant and also keep him engaged there. When Chiang came to know of it, he was pleased for Aung. Aung knew that he did not have access to that much funding at short notice, but he said he would give it a good try. It took Aung some time and a fair bit of running around, but it worked out. Aung managed to raise money from his friends and with a small bank loan became part owner of the Bangkok restaurant in 1971. His life had changed.

Once again, Chiang was a big help in arranging references for the bank loan and convincing others that if they gave a loan to Aung, he would pay it back. Aung felt eternally grateful to Chiang; he did not know how to repay him for his help in this lifetime. Chiang told him that was what all friends do - that he was not doing anything special for Aung for which Aung had to thank him. By then, eleven-year-old Win was going to a local school, and the family had moved to a two-bedroom apartment on top of the restaurant that Mr. Lin used to use.

That arrangement worked out very well and became a necessity because Myint was helping in the restaurant full time; living upstairs saved money and valuable time. Aung did not know that Myint had worked in a restaurant in Rangoon. Now, he saw why she wanted to go to culinary school - restaurant business was her calling, she excelled at it, and she did not even have to try. Myint was a natural in the restaurant business. She was a talented chef, and she enjoyed working at the restaurant. Win was already a good student and a voracious reader. Win read everything that he could get, and he always asked for more.

Whenever he found time, Aung would educate him on Shan heritage and Shan culture, and the two of them would discuss the political dynamics of post-war Asia. Very quickly, Win learned to speak in the Shan dialect, and the Lungs started to speak only in Shan among themselves. For his age, Win knew a lot, and he understood Aung's concerns with respect to Burma and Asia. Sometimes, he asked incisive questions that Aung could not answer. Win had a very analytical mind. Aung thought Win had the potential to become a very good attorney or doctor someday if he had the opportunity. To the surprise of his teachers, Win was doing really well in school. He loved learning and it showed. Aung could see a bit of himself in Win; he also loved learning.

Win once asked him about the rationale for Shan Chaofas in accepting the pension option from the Burmese government, and Aung had to admit that even he did not know what motivated that decision. What were the Chaofas thinking? Win had a lot of questions on the Thai government and the role it played in neighboring Burma.

Aung could not answer most of those questions. Win wondered aloud why the Thai government decided to be on the side of the Japanese at the start of WWII. For many such questions, Aung would encourage him to talk to his teachers, even though some of Win's questions were politically incorrect in Thailand. At Win's age, knowledge was more important than political correctness, Aung thought. Political correctness could wait for a few years. As they settled down in the relative safety of Bangkok, Aung was still haunted by the plight of his beloved Shan people and his homeland. He could do nothing sitting in Bangkok.

Despite his best efforts, he was not able to do much for the Shan. During days and evenings at the restaurant, Aung had no time for anything else, but early mornings were his alone time. He would often get up early and take a long walk around the waterfront, thinking about how he could get more involved in the Shan cause. There were no easy ways. On weekends, if Win was not planning to go to the central library for reading, he would join him. Aung would talk non-stop about the opportunity lost for a peaceful and prosperous Burma.

An overwhelming sadness gripped Aung because he could see that the tribes were losing critical time. With the passage of time, people would tend to forget the key issues and what was committed to the tribes. By this time, Aung was convinced that the Burmar and the Mon people of the valleys were controlling the national conversation on government priorities. The Shan, Kachin, and Lisu were living like foreigners in their own land, devoid of any real sense of belonging or any real say on anything. The tribes did not participate in the political process in the early days, and later, they were not invited. They had no seat on the table for discussing Burma's national agenda. Dissatisfaction and unrest were brewing among the tribes like Karen as well - they had their own militia, which was involved in major violence.

Whenever he could, Aung would visit Chiang and get updates from him on what the NGO was seeing in Chiang Mai and its assessment of the situation across the border in Burma. Since Chiang was so well connected, Aung had also asked him to be on the lookout for his direct and extended family. Aung knew that Chiang was doing his best, but the search was very difficult. Because of the open hostility of the Thai government, Shan refugees that crossed into

Thailand did not want to be found, and that made the search process a lot harder. If they were found, the chances of exploitation increased significantly - even the law enforcement harassed them at will. By then, Aung was giving up hope.

Chiang was doing really well. Aung thought he had a flair for relationship building and spotting business opportunity. During one of his visits, Chiang told him that he was planning to get into fishing by investing in a couple of large fishing boats and buying ownership of a seafood warehouse on the waterfront. Aung wished him luck in his new venture. Given Chiang's flair, Aung knew both businesses would do well in a relatively short period, and they actually did. During their "walk-n-chat," Aung would explain to Win how the Chaofas, including his own father, had made a series of wrong decisions, including aligning with the Japanese in 1941. Once Aung described to Win how his father gave away symbols of Shan culture to a Japanese major called Yoshikuni Morita just as a "token of goodwill." That major was trying to unify the tribes. Japan wanted Burma to be one country ruled from Rangoon - not multiple principalities in different parts of the country.

He told Win about the argument they had and how he had left his home for good. That memory still haunted Aung in Bangkok. More than anything else, he felt terrible about parting ways from his father in that manner. If he had known he would never see him again, he probably would not have done it that way. His father was a good man. He had been too much of a pragmatist, had read many signals from the Japanese wrong, but he did all that for the good of his beloved Shan, not for himself. He was a Lung; personal gain was not a priority for him. He was pursuing the wrong path, but he sincerely believed in it.

On Win's request, Aung took out a napkin and drew a pencil sketch of the two objects he was talking about. Win would listen to his father's stories and assessment of the Shan situation with rapt attention. In due course, Aung and Myint were able to connect up with a couple of other Shan families in Bangkok. One of those Shan families was originally from Thailand, and one family originally came from a different part of Shan homeland in Burma, but not from Aung's clan.

They started meeting on social occasions and during Shan festivals - everything they did had a Shan connection. For Win, the Shan emphasis in everything they did or thought about was a bit overwhelming at times. Sometimes, he would get tired of that single-minded obsession. Even though he was only eleven, Win could sense that other Shan families were not as passionate as his father toward the Shan cause. He noticed the difference and liked that his father was different; Win's exposure to the Shan cause and its nuances was nearly complete. Win knew more about the Shan and the other tribes of Burma than most by then.

On his own initiative, he learned even more from his books. Win picked up Aung's passion for reading at an early age, and in Bangkok, he had the tools and resources to pursue that passion. Aung and Win would go to the main library in Bangkok on some weekends and read for many hours. Spending many hours reading books on Asian cultures became a hobby for Win. Sometimes, Aung came to the library with Win and read to update himself on the current politics. By this time, Aung was tormented by the misfortune of the Shan State Army, or the SSA, in Burma. At that time, the highest organ of Shan State Army was the Shan State War Council, which was chaired by the Mahadevi (Queen) of Yawnghwe. As combatants, local Shan villagers were recruited by the SSA and sent to the leadership school they had set up.

It taught the fundamentals of military organization and operations, intelligence gathering, and an introduction of international politics, pretty basic stuff for soldiers. In 1971, its political wing, the Shan State Progress Party, was formed to tackle various problems faced by the Shan State Army. Yet another organization called the Shan Unity Preparatory Committee was also formed to unite other Shan rebel groups. The formation of this group was a good sign in one way - it proved that the necessity of unity was understood. On the whole, Aung was dismayed.

The Shan had too many organizations, no unity, and every aspect of their effort was fragmented and disorganized. Burma's government did not work for all its people; it worked for the privileged few. In that kind of environment, there was very little hope for the hill tribes; they were set up for failure. Aung knew that this lack of unity will make it easier for the Tatmadaw and others to take advantage of the Shan. Aung was also concerned by the rising tide of opium trade in the Shan State. He knew that the Shan State had a vast share of global opium production; it probably produced a third or a bit more of all the illegal opium in the world. The opium trade was growing in the black market, and addiction was increasing among villagers. Most operators used China as the conduit to go to the market - the global consumption was up. As the global consumption was growing, so was the harvest. No one was doing anything about the opium trade that changed the situation on the ground.

The government did not seem to care; they simply looked the other way. Reports of addiction-related and overdose-related deaths were all over. Sometimes, multiple cases were reported within the same village or same family. Burmese print media was stoic about it, as if none of those reports mattered. Even the resident Shan seemed quite indifferent. The government and its main instrument of terror, the Tatmadaw, provided a tacit approval for growing opium so that they could then sell it on the black market, using China as a conduit.

Much of that money was pocketed by the corrupt generals and Chinese merchants. That money also funded the acquisition of illicit arms trade in Northern Burma. Food was scarce, but the local militias that worked for the drug lords were never short of arms and ammunition. The resident Shan community in Burma was not making any organized effort toward lasting peace, education, and development. To Aung, it seemed like they were expecting outsiders to solve their problems. They seemed disengaged and isolated. When Aung was not busy with his restaurant, he would constantly talk about the Shan. Win participated in the conversation like an equal. He liked the fact that his father valued his opinion. Aung said so frequently in front of others.

In this manner, without realizing it, Win became a defender of the Shan cause as well. His view was his father's viewpoint; his voice was his father's voice. Win trusted his father's judgment so completely that he was picking up a bit of Aung's cynicism as well. Win liked the idea of being different from his Thai classmates; he used that as a motivation to do better in his studies. Many of his Thai classmates called him an outsider and treated him differently most of the time. Around this time, a conflicting set of emotions were coming into Win's young mind.

A small part of Win was beginning to dislike his father's obsession with the Shan. A part of him wanted Aung to be like other fathers, live day-to-day, focus on the here and now, and play with him just like other fathers. As a family, everything they did or planned had to have a connection to the Shan culture or tribe. Socially, they mixed only with Shan families in Bangkok; they celebrated only Shan festivals. Politically, they discussed only the Shan homeland and its future as if the rest of the world did not exist and their current life in Thailand was all rosy and had no problems. Win could not resolve these conflicts.

Every now and then, Win thought his mother was not wrong when she got upset and said only a part of Aung was with them. "His soul is still in the hills of Burma with the Kachins; he never left his scouts. In his mind, he is still fighting for the Shan," was the way his mother would put it when she got upset. Once or twice, some Thai kids in his school had called him "refugee." They used the word in a derogatory way, but Win was not offended. He felt secure in the thought that he had an indelible Shan identity within him that could not be taken away from him. Both Aung and Myint did not have any extended family on either side after the war. Win never saw any relatives or cousins growing up - for a long time, he did not even know that was not normal.

The only time he saw any conflict between his parents was when Aung would go over the top talking about the Shan cause, and Myint would say she was tired of hearing that all the time. She would say that Aung was not the only Shan person in the world, that there were others who could and should think about the well-being of the Shan tribe. Myint felt that Aung had done enough for the Shan in his lifetime. As a Shan herself, Myint was also sensitive to the Shan cause, but for her, Win and Aung came first. At times, she used to find Aung's obsession with the Shan cause completely suffocating. To her credit, she never tried to influence Win directly. Win had to decode Myint's feelings himself.

Myint was a very talkative person, but influencing others was not her business. She left that task in Aung's capable hands. Aung could engage others in a conversation and then make them see what he wanted them to see. Both Aung and Myint were fair-minded; they did not take sides in an irrational manner. Their Thai employees liked that a lot about the Lungs - the Thai staff had become like an extended family.

Back to Glendale

On Thursday, the iPhone alarm woke up Kip sharp at 4:30 a.m. It was still dark outside. He showered, had a quick bite, got ready quickly, and hit the road by 5:15 a.m. This time, he packed his carry-on bag with clothes and a few other essentials. The drive through the Golden Gate bridge was foggy, but it gradually cleared as he drove into the valley near Menlo Park. After Palo Alto, it was flat, and Highway 280 was almost empty.

Traffic was very light at that hour of the morning, and he made it to I5 near Los Banos in less than three hours. It was yet another beautiful California day for long-distance driving, Kip thought and immediate scolded himself. He remembered how a similar beautiful day had turned out to be not so beautiful just two days before. Traffic on I5 picked up as he got past Coalinga - but nothing unusual other than a truck with tomatoes dumping some of its cargo on the shoulder of I5 because of a brake problem. CHP officers were redirecting traffic there. Luckily, it was the trailer unit, so it should get cleared out quickly.

He was able to make good speed all the way to the outskirts of Bakersfield. Kip stopped over briefly, got himself a tall latte and snacks, and also filled the gas tank. This time, the car drove really well, and Kip kept thanking Dick for the good repair job. Traffic on the outskirts of LA was really heavy; it was past the peak hours but not completely. When he was almost at the outskirts of Los Angeles after the hills, his cell phone rang. The Acura Integra did not have automatic hands-free phone hook-up, so he had to get the phone out of his pocket, and by the time he did, the call disconnected. He wished he had a cell phone hook-up in John's Acura Integra or at least that he could use the tools like Apple CarPlay. On seeing John's home number as the calling number of the missed call, Kip relaxed.

He thought John called to check when he was arriving, and since he would see John soon, Kip did not bother to call back.

For a second, Kip thought it could it be something else, and then he discarded that idea, thinking that John would have called a second time. Kip and John spoke multiple times in a week anyway, so there was no reason for John not to call if a really important issue had come up. He decided to wait and talk to John face-to-face in a bit in Glendale. He was almost there. At last, after six hours of driving, he managed to reach John's Glendale neighborhood. When Kip came closer to John's house, he saw a sheriff's car parked next to John's Tesla, so Kip parked on the road. He picked up his bag from the trunk, locked the Acura, and rang the doorbell. John's yard was looking clean and well maintained.

When John opened the door, Kip could see a sheriff's deputy sitting on the couch where he and Joe had sat two days before and discussed mundane stuff like Joe's college admission, GPA, and SAT scores. Kip kept his backpack in the foyer and entered the living area. John was calm and collected, so Kip thought this could be a routine matter for which the law enforcement needed John's expertise on video. Kip wanted to congratulate Joe, but he was not around anywhere nearby.

He knew that John assisted the local law enforcement with digital video archives and video forensics whenever he had time, so he was not entirely surprised. When he was inside, John said, "Kip, let me introduce you to Deputy Scott; he is here actually to see you. I tried calling you before you arrived, but your cell phone kept ringing. You might have been on the road when I called." Kip knew he had missed John's call. He said that he was on the outskirts of LA. He had thought John was inquiring about his arrival time, but now it seemed it was something else altogether.

Kip was still taken aback. He could not fathom why a sheriff's deputy would come to John's house to see him. John did not seem tense, so Kip relaxed a bit and prepared himself to listen.

Deputy Scott smiled and said, "Not the kind of welcome you expected. Am I right, Mr. Kimura? I am sorry I had to surprise you like this." Like John, Kip was used to dealing with law enforcement frequently during the course of his firm's work, but this was indeed a complete surprise to Kip.

Kip was wondering if something was wrong with Tim, but then his wife would have called. Finally, he did the only thing that he could do. He extended his hand toward Deputy Scott and asked, "How can I help you, Deputy Scott?"

"Nice meeting you, Mr. Kimura," Deputy Scott said warmly. "Just Scott will do - we are among friends here. Thanks also for your help to our brothers in the US Department of Defense in those cases. I was in the army too. Rangers. It was before your time."

Kip realized that Scott was checking on him already, and clearly, he was well prepared for what was in store. John had gone inside. He emerged with a tray that had a few cans of soda, iced coffee, and empty glasses and ice cubes in a separate jar.

"Gentlemen, please help yourselves," John said, pointing to the soda and coffee and sat down next to Kip. Kip picked up a soda and wiped out the condensation. John seemed to be ready for a long chat. Kip sensed some anticipation.

Scott took a soda, cleared his throat, and said, "Mr. Kimura, we have a complicated situation at hand. You were seen driving a reddish brown 2002 Acura Integra on 15 on Tuesday that had a number plate that we were looking for. Correlating data from our traffic cameras, we tracked the car to a repair shop in Los Banos on Interstate 5. Dick's, I believe. We called the repair shop and got the VIN number of the repaired car, and interestingly, the VIN number and the number plate did not match the California Department of Motor Vehicles (DMV) records. DMV records show John as the owner of the car, and the Vehicle Identification Number (VIN) number matches, but the number plate does not match the DMV number allocated for the car by the California DMV.

"It seems that somebody switched the number plates. Since I happen to know John, I called him yesterday and shared this information with him. John told us that you were bringing the car back today and I could check it out. That is why I am here today. When you are ready, let us step out and take a closer look at the car. I think you parked on the street, so let us walk over after we finish our drinks. It seems to me I might have to get our forensics team involved in taking a closer look at the car. I am not expecting to find anything, but we still have to take a close look. That is required in California, and as per our department policy, this one seems like a professional job."

Kip was not expecting this - he was totally surprised. He suddenly remembered the call Dick had mentioned at his auto repair shop. Maybe he should have waited for Dick's mechanic to get back to the shop from his long afternoon siesta. That must have been Scott's team, he concluded in his mind.

Kip took several seconds to process the information and then asked, "May I ask you why you were looking for that particular number plate on this make and model, Deputy Scott?"

Deputy Scott seemed a bit uncomfortable, but said, "I can't share all the details with you right now but let us just say in connection with a break-in investigation. It is a complicated investigation. We do not have many leads other than the fact that a reddish Acura Integra was seen in the neighborhood. The timeline of the break-in broadly matches the sighting of that Acura in the vicinity. We attempted to trace the owner of that number plate, but so far, not much luck - we couldn't locate her."

Kip was speechless. He did not know how to react to that news. In a few minutes, Kip led John and Deputy Scott to the parked Acura outside, and three of them looked at the number plate. It was indeed different from the DMV record John was holding. The letters and digits didn't match. It was clearly switched recently. They also noticed that the number plate was mounted with different types of screws. Those are not the types recommended and used by the California DMV.

Deputy Scott took a few pictures with his phone and spoke first after they went back into the house, "It is quite clear that the plates were switched by someone who was in a tearing hurry. Where is that car usually parked, John?"

"On the roadside pretty much where Kip has parked it now. That has been its place for months since February of 2020," John confirmed.

"We have a single car garage. After I bought my Tesla in February; we ran out of space because my wife uses the garage for her SUV. In fact, I use the driveway for my new Tesla."

Kip heard Deputy Scott say, "So if somebody wanted to do the switching after dark, it would not have been very hard."

Kip could not help but say, "But why? What is the connection between the break-in and John's old car? John rarely takes this car on the road; this car could not have been involved in anything?" Kip had another question for Deputy Scott. "Who was the owner of the number plate that was planted on John's car?"

"One Ms. Tracie Wilson of Culver City; last time we checked; she does not exist. She seemed to have vanished without a trace," responded Scott quickly. Kip realized that they were caught in a mess! This was a well-planned set up to buy someone more time.

Deputy Scott was a bit more forthcoming this time, and he said, "Street cameras captured a red Acura Integra in the vicinity where the break-in happened in West Hollywood."

John was aghast and commented, "Someone switched the plates. That someone is trying to frame me by switching the number plates deliberately, but frame me for what?"

Deputy Scott responded, "It seems that way, John, but I assure you we will find out why. This is not a coincidence at all, John." He then turned to Kip and said, "Mr. Kimura, can I ask you a question? Are you in town tomorrow morning?

"Assuming you are, could I request you to come over to our office and meet up with the detective in charge of this case? Considering some of your recent successes, you might be in a unique position to help us with this particular investigation."

Kip had no idea where that was coming from, but he agreed to meet Detective Bloder the next day at the police headquarters. Deputy Scott told John to apply for a new license plate from the DMV and gave him a copy of the police report so that Joe did not have a problem if he drove the car. Joe was disappointed when they met him, and John told him everything. John understood Joe's point and said the forensics team would take only a day.

Deputy Scott advised that Joe's plan to take the car to his campus over the weekend could still work because the forensics team from the police department would need access to the car for a day for DNA and other evidence. John and Kip had a long drink and conversation after Deputy Scott left for his headquarters. John told him that the break-in had happened several weeks ago. It was one of those many incidents in LA.

He knew about it because it was in the newspaper, but he had no reason to connect that event with his old car - he was still in a state of disbelief. The victim was a movie producer and director of Asian origin who was well-known in John's circle of movie folks. John also said that he knew Deputy Scott and Detective Jeffrey Bloder very well from his past video work. The video archival work he did with the police department involved both of them, so when Deputy Scott found out it was John's name from the DMV records, he called immediately. Deputy Scott had also asked John about how he knew Kip and a bit more about Kip's background and work as part of ConSec. Deputy Scott also asked about Kip's business partner Tim and his background in the US Army.

Kip knew the rest of the story. Kip requested John to accompany him to meet up with Jeffrey Bloder the next morning, and John agreed because it was his car, after all. He felt violated and he needed to clear his name. Kip decided to accept John's offer to sleep in John's guestroom for the night, so he had some time on hand to call Tim in San Rafael and fill him in.

Tim listened carefully and said, "Seems like we're on to something here, Kip. Our firm has never worked with the police department in Southern California in the past. Since the opportunity has presented itself, I think we should take it. Look at it as a business development effort in Southern California, Kip. Who knows? We might benefit from movie connections! All the best to you, Bro. Needless to say, there should be a formal engagement, and they should agree with our terms and fees."

Kip felt the same way. John and Kip drove down to Deputy Scott's office first thing in the morning on Friday after breakfast. Deputy Scott ushered them in and took them to a conference room. The conference room had a ceiling mounted projector, bottled water, coffee, and doughnuts; he had clearly planned for a conversation that would take a few hours. In a few minutes, a very smart looking tall and lean man in his early forties joined them.

John got up and said, "Howdy, Jeff! Long time, you have stopped coming to Glendale area."

"Great! And you, John? I was beginning to think that you have forgotten us" said Jeffrey Bloder smiling. Kip could sense traces of a private joke between John and Jeff.

Kip was introduced to Detective Bloder by Scott formally. The first thing he said to Kip after a short nod was, "Can I call you Kip and can you call me Jeff?" Kip was amused, but he liked the way Jeff introduced himself. Jeff was carrying several papers in a folder.

He readily agreed - he was a big believer of informality. John had said a lot of good things about Jeff, so he knew he would enjoy working with him. Once all of them settled down with their coffee, Jeff switched on a projector and started the briefing. The first slide on the screen was an exquisite looking bowl, and the second one was a Buddha statue. Both seemed to be made of decorative stone, and both were expertly carved clearly by the best artists and carvers. The third slide presented the front and bird's-eye view of a West Hollywood mansion. It was a very nice and sprawling Spanish hacienda architecture, very well designed and probably even better maintained.

Jeff cleared his throat and started talking, "Kip, the first two slides had what were stolen in the break-in, and the third slide presented the place. That was the owner's mansion in West Hollywood from where those two objects were stolen.

"Several weeks ago, a wealthy family in West Hollywood reported a break-in in their mansion; two highly valued ancient objects were stolen in that break-in. The mansion had a security guard and cameras everywhere, but nothing unusual was picked up by the cameras or the guard. The most interesting thing was that the thieves did not touch any cash or valuables even though some of both were strewn all around. The owner is a well-known movie maker with several hit movies.

"Nothing else in the house was disturbed either, so much so that the family did not even realize that something was missing! Sometime back, the insurance company that insured the objects inquired about their insurance premium because it was coming up for renewal. That call from the insurance company made the owner open the family safe and realize that the safe was forced open by a professional, and two of the extremely valuable ancient Burmese jade artifacts were missing.

These artifacts were given to the grandfather of the current owner during World War II in Burma - both were hundreds of years old. We are confident about that estimate because the family that gifted those used the objects for various religious and festive rituals for three to four generations. The artifacts were with this particular family for eighty odd years in Japan and the United States. Naturally, the owner was distraught, and he reported the incident immediately. Initially, local police investigators did not have a whole lot to go on; they were even finding it hard to establish the fact that a break-in happened at all. We almost went back to the owner frustrated and told him that other than his words, we had no supporting evidence. There were no leads at all.

"But after a few days of careful backtracking of residential and traffic cameras in the neighborhood, the police department found a hooded figure and a reddish Acura Integra in the immediate vicinity. After a few days, that car was spotted on Hollywood Boulevard, and our high-resolution street camera was able to digitally enhance the numbers and letters in the number plate. When we put a trace on that number plate through the DMV, we found that it belonged to one non-existent Tracie Wilson in Culver City. We think she passed away recently. There was no record of any relative, friend, or next of kin.

"The last time traffic cameras saw the car correlated well with the owner's recollection of the timeline for the break-in. After we were able to decipher the number plate of the car, we intentionally leaked the news to some of our beat reporters. That was when the police department issued an alert for that number plate across the state."

Jeff paused for a bit, had a sip of his coffee, and then said that he made some inquiries with antique dealers and auction houses after he spoke with the insurance company. He spoke with the big auction houses like Christie's, Sotheby's, as well as a couple of boutique places that specialize in Asian artifacts. Luckily, there were plenty of them nearby.

In Kip's tablet, he noted that, all the auction houses had consistently told Jeff that based on the description and provenance alone, the artifacts should be worth hundreds of thousands of dollars each, most likely in the millions. Four separate insurance companies had also told Jeff that the fair market value of these type of objects might have doubled or tripled in the last year because of the place of their origin. The part of Burma where these objects came from is effectively a warzone, almost inaccessible, so replacement could be very expensive. Insurance premiums would have to take that fact into account, and as a result, premiums could increase.

The owner, however, saw the objects as cultural treasures of the tribe that had gifted those objects to his grandfather during WW II. In his view, the tribe faced war, oppression, and all forms of human rights violations for generations since the British left Burma. That, in his view, was all the more reason why their cultural heritage should be preserved. He would like to honor his grandfather's wishes by returning these objects to its rightful owners if he could locate them. The tribe thought these objects had some spiritual connection to its ancestors, and the owner did not want the objects to fall in the hands of petty thieves.

As a matter of fact, the current owner's father did make multiple attempts to return those objects to the tribe, but he could not.

All his efforts through the Burmese Embassy in Washington, DC, were in vain. The Burmese Embassy was not at all interested in helping them. The owner had no intention to sell the objects and had said that he would spend any amount of money to get those back. At this time, he was much more worried about seeing these two ancient artifacts tossed and turned around in the hands of petty thieves in skid row. He was quite wealthy, so he would not hesitate to finance a full private investigation. He said he could not forgive himself if some dubious black marketer acquired them.

After Jeff finished, no one spoke for a few seconds, and then Kip asked, "But why me, Jeff? You gentlemen could have conducted this investigation easily. You have the expertise and the jurisdiction. You could have probably recovered the objects with your own resources."

Jeff responded, "Oh, that was Scott's idea after he learned about your work from John and did some reference checks. He can explain that part well. Scott thought this case might have a different historical context than our typical investigation - we focus on catching thieves."

Deputy Scott winked at Kip and said, "That incredible investigation you and your partner Tim did in Hong Kong a few months ago reminded me of this case. We need your kind of expertise, Kip." Kip absorbed the information and then talked about the paperwork they would need to get started. Clearly, these folks had thought it through, and it appeared that they knew what they were doing. It was time to get moving.

Kip observed that, Both Scott and Jeff explained that finding the original Shan owners in Burma was a priority for this investigation. After the current break-in, the owner did not feel comfortable keeping these valuable objects in his home, or any home, for that matter. Since he has no children, there is no one in his family to look after those objects after him. Keeping those objects in a private home is also getting expensive because of the increase in insurance premiums. No one can deny that the fair market value has quadrupled, and it is likely to increase even further in the future simply because of the scarcity and obscurity of that part of Burma. For all those reasons, the owner would like to return those objects to the Shan tribal family who originally owned those. He thinks these treasures should go back to the owners so that they can decide how to share these with the next generation of their tribe.

It was their decision to make, not his. Kip understood the context and where Jeff and Scott were coming from. He walked them through the typical terms and conditions pertaining to ConSec engagements. Jeff said that most of those were pretty standard in their third-party consulting engagements and that it was no problem. His department was used to this type of arrangement. After that was out of the way, Jeff called the owner and set up a face-to-face meeting at West Hollywood for the very next day. It seemed Jeff had already given a heads-up to the owner.

The owner told Jeff that a detailed briefing would take several hours, so all three of them should keep their schedules flexible and plan to have a working lunch with him. Jeff said that would be acceptable if that was not difficult for the household to manage. Jeff emphasized that the detailed briefing to Kip by the owner was mission critical, and that they would do whatever it took to get that process done. Kip had to agree with that point completely - he needed as much information as he could get.

It was decided that both Jeff and Scott would pick up Kip from John's house at Glendale in the morning and go to West Hollywood together. Jeff said he would brief Kip about a few specific things on the way. Kip was very impressed with the socially distanced COVID-ready functioning of the entire police department. It seemed like most people were working normally with masks and social distancing - they had adapted well. Kip was hoping for a vaccine, and he was hoping for a better 2021.

Bangkok to Round Rock

Thailand found itself in a hotspot post World War II, not by design but by chance. In its neighborhood, there were fights going on in almost every direction, in Vietnam, Burma, Indochina, and even in China as Mao's forces were stamping out resistance. In 1954, when the Southeast Asia Treaty Organization, or SEATO, was formed, Thailand became a US partner in a tearing hurry, as if it could not wait. While the war was being fought between the Vietnamese and the French in Indochina, Thailand attempted to stay neutral, but that came at a price.

Then, the conflict became a war between the US and the Vietnamese communists, and at that point, Thailand had no choice but to join the US side. It did so quickly without wasting time. With the advent of the Cold War, the West began to look to Thailand as a potential buffer against the rise of communism in China and Southeast Asia. In a large swath of communist dominated states, it was an island.

Thailand sent troops to join the United Nations forces during the Korean War and participated in other international efforts to make people forget about its wartime association with the Japanese. The establishment of Mao's communist regime in China increased Thai fear about the spread of communism within Thailand. That fear drove Thailand toward the US at a greater speed. By the time Aung and his family moved to the Thai capital Bangkok, the US influence in Thailand was strong and growing. The Thais loved the Americans and the Americans reciprocated; gradually, the Thai culture started showing that influence.

Around this time, the United States poured huge amounts of economic and military aid into Thailand to fortify Thai infrastructure and boost its military and police forces. This massive financial support laid the foundation for an economic boom in

Thailand for many generations. That growth spurt continued almost steadily for many years. Almost every sector was seeing a healthy demand. Several sectors of the Thai economy, including the hospitality and tourism industry, benefited from that cash infusion. Aung's Chinese restaurant business was benefiting from this economic boom big time. His revenues were growing, and he and Myint found it hard to keep up even with three hired Thai hands. Even though it was not fancy or large, the food was good in Aung's restaurant, and they served a fusion cuisine - not just Chinese food.

Myint was very creative with the cuisine, and she was always inventing new recipes. She could not go to culinary school in Rangoon, but in Bangkok, she was able to practice that fine art in her own restaurant to her heart's content. In the first few months, she had completely redesigned the menu and made it a lot better. Mr. Lin visited once, and he himself could not believe it. He said, "My old restaurant has been transformed by Myint; I am so happy to see this."

The three Thai employees Aung had hired were very good in building relationships; customers liked being served by them. Gradually, the good word spread, and once or twice a week, Aung's restaurant started seeing large groups of foreigners coming by. Every now and then, Aung was also getting catering orders for NGO fundraising efforts through Chiang's contacts - those were big engagements.

On many occasions, Aung's restaurant hosted groups of American soldiers that were in Thailand on a short visit. There were arrival parties or farewells all the time. One such occasion would always remain etched in Aung's memory. This particular group of mostly young men was fairly large and loud: they were probably on a short break from a field posting in Vietnam. There was only one man who was not very young - he was also the only one in civilian clothes. They came in early, started with some Thai beer, and continued for dinner till midnight. That was not unusual at all - many groups did that to extend the socializing. More Americans were coming to Bangkok because of Vietnam. Many of those newcomers knew of the good food and service at Aung's restaurant through references and common friends.

Aung had asked one of his hired staff to look after that group. A few times that Aung had to go their table when they had questions, the group was very appreciative of the food. When Aung came to that table for the third time to deliver some specially done pot-stickers, the man in civilian attire called him aside. He was about the same age as Aung, maybe just a little bit older, but much taller.

Others in his group were still talking loudly, so he came close to Aung and said, "Have we met before in Bangkok or elsewhere? I think have seen you somewhere. I cannot remember exactly, but I am pretty sure we knew each other."

Aung looked at his face and even he felt a tinge of familiarity but could not quite remember, so he replied, "You look familiar, but I am not sure where we met in the past." With both of them unsure of where they might have met each other in the past, the man went back to his group and started nibbling at the food. Aung noticed that he kept looking at him several times; he seemed very familiar to Aung as well.

About a minute and half later, that man got up from the group table suddenly, toppling a couple of empty beer bottles. Members of his group from his table looked up; they did not know what had happened. Aung heard the noise and looked up from the kitchen window.

The tall man in civilian clothes came toward him and embraced him in the tightest of bear hugs possible and exclaimed, "I remembered. You are Aung Lung of the Kachin Hills? We met in 1944." The other soldiers at the table had stopped talking - they were looking at the two of them.

Aung looked at the man once again and said, "I just remembered too. You are Jim, the Galahad captain!" The tall American nodded.

As the two of them hugged each other again, there were cheers all around, particularly at the table where the Americans were eating and drinking. After a while, when the Americans were ready to leave, Jim came back to Aung and said he would come back the next day to do a bit of catching up. It had been a long time; both of them had grown older and wiser. Aung told him that he would look forward to that and reminded him to come a bit early before the restaurant got crowded.

At night when they were in bed, Myint asked, "Who was that tall man? What was the hugging all about with that tall man?" Aung had to tell her how it all started in early 1944 - the whole fascinating story of his association with Jim and the Galahad and their improbable victory against the vastly superior Japanese Army in the hills of North Burma.

After the British Indian Army's efforts failed to threaten the Japanese in Northern Burma, they decided to rely on special forces. In 1943, those specially trained jungle warfare soldiers called the Chindits entered Burma from India. They did not turn the tide but made a dent in the Japanese supply lines and, more importantly hurt, Japanese pride and the belief in their invincibility. Right behind the British special forces were General Merrill's Galahad forces. They were sent to Burma in 1944 along with the Chinese X Force; Aung had made many friends among the Chinese and the Galahad. Jim was with the first team of Galahad forces that came in contact with Aung's Kachin scouts in early 1944. Aung still remembered how two of his new scouts captured Jim's Japanese American intelligence officer and interrogated him in Shan and Kachin. Jim's man was funnier - he was responding in Japanese!

Even though Jim and his team were very well trained in jungle warfare in India, it was not easy for them to adapt to the hills of

Northern Burma. They had to deal with malaria, amoebic dysentery, and typhus, and then if they survived, the Japanese. Many did not survive for long. The Galahad forces were always low on ammunition and other supplies. They also had insufficient food rations as the norm, but they still marched ahead. In Jim's case, he came down with a bout of blood dysentery in his first week. His condition worsened quickly.

He was drinking water from the streams directly, and the water was contaminated with bacteria and parasites. Aung's scouts took care of him and a couple of other members of the Galahad in their camp. Once he recovered, Aung taught Jim to boil water with basic resources in the jungle, to drink boiled water, and a range of survival techniques used by the local population. They had to deal with leeches, dysentery, cerebral malaria, scrub typhus, and other diseases. Jim was a quick learner; he learned the techniques himself and had all his men learn the skills. The Kachin scouts were good trainers - they passed on what they knew as the sons of that soil.

Jim lost nearly twenty pounds in two weeks, he and the Galahad soldiers had to rough it up while being in a firefight with the Japanese. They were a spirited bunch, and in the end, they managed it well. After the long grind, when Myitkyina fell to the British, Jim and his surviving team were there to celebrate the hard-fought win. General Stilwell personally came down to Myitkyina to award medals to the surviving Galahad soldiers. Aung still remembered how the exhausted and injured were airlifted to India and how he and Jim said goodbye to each other on the runway of Myitkyina Airport during a torrential monsoon downpour. Jim was weak - he was still recovering from his injuries.

Aung had read that after the war, the American and British press called the Galahad "Merrill's Marauders" named after General Merrill. Apparently, the name became quite popular in the Western press. Aung did not mind that characterization; marauders they indeed were - ask the Japanese! Jim trained Aung on weapons; his finely tuned shooting skill was entirely because of Jim. All those long-lost memories that seemed like a lifetime away were flooding back, as he was recounting the story with Myint. Aung was reliving his time in the Kachin Hills a quarter of a century later, in Bangkok of 1972 - Myint could sense it.

Jim came back the next day at 4:00 p.m. sharp because the restaurant opened at 6:00 p.m. Over several cups of tea and two rounds of beer, Aung and Jim did a lot of catching up. Jim told him that he was a colonel in the US Army at that time, and he was in Thailand as a consultant. Toward the end of the conversation, Jim asked why Aung was not seeking asylum in the United states. After all, he had helped the US Army, and he was a friend of the United States. Aung said he had not thought about it, and he had no idea about how the process for seeking asylum worked.

Jim promised he would find out more from his friend at the American Embassy in Bangkok, and he would be happy to sponsor them for their US Asylum application. Jim said that moving to the US would be better for them. As a parting remark, Jim said he knew Aung was passionate about the Shan cause, and Aung would have a better chance of working on that cause in the US than in Thailand. The truth in that parting comment hit home with Aung. Given the situation in Thailand, Aung had to agree with Jim. Several weeks went by after Aung and Jim spoke, and nothing happened, so Aung almost forgot all about it and immersed himself in restaurant work all the way. About five weeks later, Jim showed up at the restaurant again at 4:00 p.m.

This time, Jim was not alone. He came with another younger man in tow - that man was in a suit and tie and spoke formally. Jim introduced that man as Mr. Cooper from the US Embassy in Bangkok. Mr. Cooper told Aung that Jim had discussed the topic. Political asylum for Aung and his family was mentioned to the US government officials as well. In his opinion, Aung and his family had a good chance of getting approved quickly. The current situation should help Aung's case, he said. Because of Aung's help to the US Army at great personal peril and US Army officers corroborating that, he had a strong case for asylum if he decided to seek it. Most asylum seekers did not have as strong a case as the Lungs did. Mr. Cooper said that to Aung over and over again.

Mr. Cooper thought it was a great option for the Lungs, for Win in particular. They should rebuild their lives in the US in a state they liked and in a manner they loved. They would have all the freedoms. Mr. Cooper asked Aung to fill in several forms and talked to him at length. Much of the conversation was recorded in a small tape recorder, and Mr. Cooper made copious notes in a thick yellow notebook. After that, he talked to Myint as well, and Mr. Cooper spent a lot of time with Win. He kept saying his own son in Maryland was the same age as Win. He said Win was bright and he would do well in the US school system.

Mr. Cooper spent a lot of time explaining the healthcare system in the United States. Aung did not understand most of it. The concept of health insurance was quite complicated to Aung to wrap his mind around. He thought he would ask Jim later and understand it better if the asylum application came through. Aung felt he had plenty of time on hand - there was no need to rush everything. Unlike in Thailand, refugees were treated well in the United States. They had rights, according to international laws. Around that time, the US government was planning to draft a plan for the Hmong from Asia, so the wheels were already spinning. Cooper also told Aung that the paperwork for his Thai residency was dubious - he would have to handle that part carefully.

Jim indicated that for the purposes of US records, Aung's Thai residency would not be recognized. His case would be treated as though he applied for asylum straight from the camp in Chiang Mai.

That distinction was not material for Aung; he felt like an imposter in Thailand anyway. Many asylum seekers ended up crossing borders illegally, so that was not unusual. Jim hung out a bit longer after Cooper left and asked Aung if he had a preference for any US state to live in.

Aung said, "I have no idea. Until you talked to me, I had not thought about this."

Jim seemed to have expected that and responded, "Anticipating that, I have told Cooper to consider Texas for you guys. I am in Dallas, Texas, and if you guys are in Texas, I could reach out and help you settle down. Cooper will not know the city or state until the process moves forward, and he hears back from the State Department, but it is good to be prepared." Aung could see the logic in Jim's thinking, so he agreed. Myint had several questions for Jim on US schools. Jim answered her questions, and he advised her to practice English. That was not very hard to do with the customers at the restaurant.

Win was already studying English, and Jim asked him to accelerate the pace and practice speaking English with his friends. Aung sat down with Jim and calculated the expenses that he would have to pay. After the calculation and currency conversion, he thought financially he would be all right. A few days after Jim's visit with Mr. Cooper, Jim came by for an hour and informed Aung that his asylum application had been submitted to the US government. Jim also said that the war in Vietnam was not going well for the United States and that he would have to travel back to the US for two weeks to brief his bosses in the US Army on the political situation unfolding in Vietnam. Aung was also reading about the Vietnam War and how it was going in the local newspapers.

Jim promised that he would touch base after he got back to Thailand; he felt his US stay could get extended. Jim's trip to the US got extended, and instead of two weeks, he came back after two months. By then, he had become a regular at Aung's place. He would typically show up during early evening and leave late. Win loved talking to Jim in English; he loved Jim's war stories from various battlefields even more - Jim had an endless collection of stories for Win. Jim never got tired of telling stories to his "favorite kiddo," he would say. Aung called Win "Kiddo," so Jim switched to "Kiddo" or "My favorite Kiddo" pretty quickly - both Jim and Win loved it. Gradually, that became the norm.

By the end of 1975, Aung received a letter from the US government that said that his case for political asylum had been approved, and the papers would arrive in Bangkok in a couple of weeks. He was also told that the US Embassy in Bangkok would guide him through the next steps. Within a week of that, Jim came by again with Mr. Cooper, and they explained the process to Aung, Myint, and Win. The process was well laid out. The goal was to make it easy for the asylum seekers to get to the US, adapt to the local rules, and settle down in the new country. Aung thought they were being treated like customers.

Jim also advised Aung to start the process of selling his restaurant and wrapping up their stay in Thailand. The war in Vietnam had ended, and Jim was planning to relocate to the United States permanently. Win had to seek a transfer from his school as well. With the fall of Saigon in April 1975 and Laos and Cambodia firmly under the communists, Jim's engagement with the US Army was ending as well. Suddenly, Thailand was surrounded by communists all around. Jim told Aung that he would join his father's engineering service business for oil industry in Dallas in a few months. Aung, Myint, and Win were thrilled to learn that Jim would be physically in the US as they tried to settle down in their adopted country - perhaps even close by.

Jim had become a member of the family. Jim's counsel was very important for Aung. The very next day, Aung visited his friend

Chiang at the Bangkok offices of the NGO. Aung told him that he wanted to sell the restaurant and leave Thailand. Chiang did not ask too many questions because he knew that Aung felt like a foreigner in Thailand. He advised Aung to reach out to the previous owner, Mr. Lin. Aung liked the idea because he was grateful to Mr. Lin, and he felt if there was a deal to be made, Mr. Lin should have the first right of refusal. After all, it was Mr. Lin who had started that restaurant and hired Aung a few years before. Aung and Chiang promised to stay in touch with each other always. Aung told Chiang that he would always be grateful.

Mr. Lin had a nephew who wanted to relocate from Lampang to Bangkok, and Aung's restaurant could be a good deal for him. If the transaction was kept within the known circle of friends, then the possibility of exposure with respect to Aung's Thai residency would be less as well. Aung could see the point, and he readily agreed - Aung knew he had to meet Mr. Lin. The next week, Aung went to Pattaya City and met with Mr. Lin; he was mighty pleased to see Aung after a long time.

He said that he would ask his nephew Sujin Lin to travel from Lampang to Bangkok and meet with Aung and Myint immediately to consummate the deal. Mr. Lin's nephew Sujin Lin was so keen to follow up with the proposition that he arrived a full day early. Sujin agreed to the terms and accepted Aung's offer. Myint thought Aung should have been able to get a better deal for the restaurant, but Aung knew they did not have the luxury of time to explore other options. Also, Aung had a debt of gratitude toward Mr. Lin - selling the restaurant to his nephew as Mr. Lin desired was the least Aung could do. As per Aung's terms, the new owner agreed to keep their Thai staff employed.

Those Thai employees were working with Aung and Myint from the very beginning; among other things, they would provide continuity for the customers. Myint was really sad to part ways.

While Aung was concluding the business transaction and property transfer paperwork with the Thai government, Myint focused on getting the transfer certificate from Win's school and also saying goodbye to the local Shan community. They decided to host a parting get together at their restaurant during their last week in Bangkok. For the local Shan, Aung had become like a leader, so many of the families said they would miss the Lungs in Bangkok. Just before they were about to depart, the US Embassy in Bangkok confirmed that they would eventually live in the state of Texas, as Jim had originally requested in the application form.

They were thrilled to learn that they would now be in the same state as Jim. Win went to the library and started reading about the state of Texas and told Aung that its capital was in a city called Austin. It was a big state that bordered Mexico on the South; it had a long coastline along the Gulf of Mexico. Jim's town of Dallas was one of the biggest cities in Texas and was toward the Northeast. It was about three hours' drive from Austin by car. In Texas, most people used cars for everyday travel.

Finally, after concluding all their affairs in Bangkok in mid-1976, Aung and his family boarded their flight bound for Los Angeles, California. The airline was called Pan Am. Contrary to what Aung had thought, leaving Bangkok was a pretty emotional affair. Aung realized the attachment and fondness they had developed to their life in Bangkok only when he was leaving it for good. He and Myint promised the staff that they would visit again, and the new owners would take care of them. Shujin was there, and he promised to take care of the staff.

Their Pan Am flight was very long because it had stopovers at Hong Kong, Tokyo, and Honolulu, Hawaii. Win slept through the flight. Because of his age, his body adapted quickly. Aung and Myint could only take small naps because their body clocks did not adjust that quickly. Each time the plane had a stopover, Aung, Myint, and

Win would get off, walk around each terminal, and see different types of stores, people, and cultures. Hawaii was most interesting - it seemed like a melting pot. They saw a wide diversity of people at the airport. Even though they were exhausted, they enjoyed that part of the journey.

When the Pan Am plane was approaching Los Angeles, Aung looked out through the window. Los Angeles seemed to be a huge city, much larger than Rangoon or Bangkok. The city seemed to have the sea on one side and hills as well. By the time they landed in Los Angeles International Airport, there were US government people waiting for them; they had to fill out a series of forms. They were also issued temporary identity documents on arrival. Aung was told that they would live in a city called Round Rock in Texas. It was apparently very close to a city called Austin, which is about three hours by car from Dallas where Jim was. Aung felt it was good news to be so close to Jim.

Win thought the name of the city was funny. "How can a rock be round?" he wondered.

After they got out of the terminal building with their meager possessions, they walked into a waiting bus. There were two other Asian families like them that had migrated from Asia. They spoke a different language, so all of Myint's multiple efforts to have a conversation were in vain.

Those Asian families did not speak a word of Thai, English, or Shan. Aung realized that they had obtained asylum from a different part of Asia. Looking at that family, Aung realized that they would see diversity at a whole new level in the United States.

Even the people who migrated from Asia could look and speak very differently. Jim had mentioned it to him in Bangkok, but he did not register it. Aung was looking at his newly acquired homeland through the bus window and thinking that he was in his fifties, almost retirement age for some people. But for Aung, it was the beginning of a new phase of life, literally a world apart. Aung found the refugee resettlement process in the US to be efficient and sensitive. Myint was very happy too; she thought Win would do better in the US, and because of that, she was willing to accept any challenge or hardship that came her way.

After just a few days in Los Angeles and Austin, Texas, they were sent to their temporary accommodation in Round Rock. It was a nice and clean two-bedroom fully furnished apartment will all utilities. Round Rock was a small city - literally on a freeway called Interstate 35 or I35. For important things, most people drove down I35 to Austin. Aung was shocked to see so many cars; people drove in their cars even for the smallest of errands. In Texas, the cars were much bigger than the cars in Bangkok, and gasoline prices were cheaper than what Aung had seen in Bangkok. Cars were the main mode of transportation in Texas.

The resettlement agencies at federal and State levels took care of everything during the first few months, including spoken English lessons for Myint.

Aung noticed that things moved fast in the US. Within a couple of weeks of arriving in Round Rock, he had opened his first bank account in the US, gotten social security numbers for the three of them, and started the process of getting driver's licenses for him and Myint. A driver's license was needed for many things. Win's admission to the local school in Round Rock was done as well; they simply needed to check the residence address. With his identity papers, he was admitted on the same day. Aung and Myint were pleasantly surprised.

Win was already liking the school because of its small size and the freedom it provided. Win loved his school library and the fact that he could borrow any number of books he wanted. Win enjoyed the speech and debate club in school; he was so enthusiastic that he joined a total of three clubs. Win's experience in school was very different in the US. Unlike in Thailand, he found that difference of opinion was not discouraged. People were free to express themselves and articulate their views on any topic as they pleased and in a medium, they liked.

There was a local city run library nearby; in one visit, all three of them were issued membership cards that they could use to borrow books on any subject. Aung and Myint had to take driving lessons and then take driving tests with the Texas Department of Public Safety or DPS, Aung passed the driving test in his first attempt, but Myint had to retake the test because she was not used to parallel parking. She needed two attempts to pass that requirement. Jim visited them during their second week in Round Rock; he advised Aung that he should start thinking about the restaurant business he talked about.

Aung preferred to buy a functioning restaurant so that he could leverage the existing location and the customer base. He had outlined his preferences to Jim.

Funds from the sale of Aung's Bangkok restaurant were converted from Thai baht to US dollars already, and the bank had informed Aung that he could use the funds from Thailand. In addition to that, Jim said Aung would be eligible for bank loans with the help of the resettlement agency. Aung liked that option, and he completed the paperwork and got the funds arranged for purchasing a restaurant at a short notice. In the US, things happened fast. Jim said he would talk to the local restaurant association and request their help through a contact. Aung's idea of buying a restaurant was looking like a possibility soon.

In February of 1976, Jim got word that a Mexican restaurant was looking for a suitable buyer because the owner wanted to move to California to be with his extended family. They had just relocated. The restaurant was in very good condition, and it had all its clearances from the government. All it needed was an external facelift and signage.

The owner's desire to go to California was the main reason driving the decision to sell. It worked quite well for Aung; the restaurant had all the necessary ingredients that Aung and Myint were looking for. Their experience in Bangkok had taught them a lot. Aung made an offer and purchased the Mexican restaurant in less than a month. Like he had done in Bangkok, in time, Aung converted the restaurant to an Asian fusion cuisine restaurant with the type of menu Myint had created for their restaurant in Bangkok. There was only one thing Aung insisted on doing differently this time. That was the name - he wanted a distinct name that people would notice for miles on I35.

He decided to call it "The Shan" with a prominent signage visible from I35! It was mounted on a tall pole, so the signage was visible for many miles in either direction. Not many people in Round Rock knew about the Shan at that time, so Aung and Myint had to educate almost every diner and every family that came in for a meal. Aung enjoyed that opportunity, but Myint did not enjoy it as much.

"Let the cuisine speak for itself - don't overwhelm people," she would say to Aung.

The restaurant was between Austin and Round Rock, actually pretty close to Austin with easy access to I35. It was also a variation from the typical Tex-Mex combination food that most other places offered at that time in Round Rock. Texas was a fairly large state, but the variety of available cuisine in its cities was not that much because the immigrants were mostly Hispanic. People from Austin could easily drive down and come for an elaborate dinner with family and friends.

The immigrant Hispanic population preferred Mexican cuisine, so other than steakhouses, that was all Round Rock had to offer. Aung and Myint knew the restaurant business, and in due course, their new restaurant became quite popular because of the quality of the food and its service. Aung and Myint started hiring locals quickly like they had done in their Bangkok restaurant. In Round Rock, they hired a bunch of hard-working Spanish speaking staff. Aung and Myint liked their work ethic and no-nonsense attitudes; many of their new hires were really young. Most of the local staff they hired came originally from Mexico, then crossed the border near El Paso for a better quality of life. Many still had families back in Mexico waiting for their visas. For Aung and Myint, those folks became part of their new extended family in the US in a short time.

During some days of the week, they started to have a long wait list, so Aung started accepting telephone bookings. He quickly hired dedicated staff for the busy evening hours. In the US, people ate out more frequently - that is why restaurants were always busy. Special local events like a big movie shooting in Round Rock brought a lot of people to the restaurant. The crew liked the food at The Shan and spread the word among their friends and families. That was a lucky break.

They also had local chapters of Rotary and other organizations use the restaurant for their special meetings, and the proximity to I5 was a big help. In less than five years, Aung's restaurant had carved out a name for itself because of the great food and quality of service. Because of the success of The Shan, Aung was able to pay off his loans and even invest in a small single-family home in Round Rock, which was closer to Austin on I35. House prices were low in Round Rock because that charming city was still a bit unknown. It was a gem that was not discovered.

Myint decorated their new home with a lot of Shan and Kachin artifacts shipped from Burma. The three-bedroom house was not very big but had a large backyard where Myint could grow her exotic Burmese herbs for her special cuisine; she had Shujin Lin ship some seeds to her from Bangkok. She was very protective of her secret ingredients like specially grown Burmese red peppers. She also did experiments with long grain brown rice for her Burmese Shan dishes.

Win finished high school in 1979; he was among the top students in his class. Some of his teachers were really surprised to see how quickly he adjusted to the American system. Aung was not. He knew Win was a very bright kid and if anything, the American system would be easier for him compared to the very restrictive system he was used to in Thailand. In America, the system offered a lot of flexibility, and Win excelled with ease. More than anything else, Win enjoyed the freedom of expression he had in America. By mid-1979, Win came to know that he was accepted in many Ivy League schools for admission in the East Coast - he was offered admission wherever he applied.

Aung and Myint wanted him to go to any university he wanted to, but in the end, the decision was Win's. After looking at all his options and associated costs, Win decided to opt for the University of Texas at Austin with a full scholarship. He decided to major in Economics and International Relations in undergrad with the eventual goal to study International Law. Win wanted to be a specialist; that meant exposure in a wide range of areas and also a stint with the US government down the line. Win was clearly up to it; he took it seriously. When Jim asked Win why he was not accepting one of the admissions he had secured on the East Coast, Win simply said that UT was good enough for him - he had thought it through. Jim said he agreed with Win's approach.

He had done a lot of research, the school was good, the faculty was great, and it offered him a full scholarship. He said, "Uncle Jim, the rest is up to me, isn't it? If I cannot make it work here, what is the use of going to Boston or New York?" Aung saw a new resolve and confidence in Win as he was growing up: he was smart, analytical, and opinionated. Aung loved what he saw; Win was a lot like he was in his youth in Rangoon. America had brought out the best in Win, Aung thought.

Aung and Myint were very proud. On the day of Win's high school graduation, Jim drove down from Dallas and spent the whole day with the Lungs. High school graduation in America was very different - it was a big celebration inside and outside the school. In most Asian countries like Burma or Thailand, high school graduations were barely noticed. It was like a steppingstone - it was never a big event.

Jim was thrilled; he hugged Win and told him, "Kiddo, I am proud of you. Now I know where I should go if I need help with International Law ever."

Win smiled and said, "Sure, Uncle Jim, no fees for you anytime, anywhere. You just have to call me, and I will be there. For the next few years, I will prepare myself so that I can actually help if you ever have a real need. We will have to see when the time comes."

Jim told Win to let him know if Win needed internship experience. Jim could easily arrange that within one of his group companies; they took a lot of interns from the UT system each year. He told Win that some of his UT batchmates would be headed their way for work anyway. Win said he would love that option and he would reach out to Jim in due course.

The Lungs from the Shan homeland were living their American dream.

West Hollywood

As agreed during the visit to the police department on Friday, Jeff and Scott arrived at John's house in Glendale at 8:30 a.m. on Saturday morning. Kip was ready, and both Jeff and Scott declined John's offer for a quick coffee, so they were able to leave for West Hollywood immediately.

John wished them luck and said, "If you need me for any more information on the car, call my cell number."

It was a short drive to West Hollywood from Glendale, but Jeff and Scott had decided to avoid freeways and use Los Feliz and Santa Monica Boulevard instead. That meant more signals and a bit more travel time, but they were moving at a steady speed instead of staying parked on the freeway.

After a few minutes, Jeff said, "We are going to West Hollywood, not far from the Los Angeles Holocaust Museum - twenty-five minutes' drive."

Those minutes went by discussing the Los Angeles Lakers and how the National Basketball Association would adjust its schedule to make it COVID safe. They arrived at the Morita mansion a bit later than expected, well after 9:00 a.m. because of a roadblock and construction diversion. Like other cities in California, Los Angeles was getting a head start in road repairs and other construction projects during the lockdown. The elegant mansion was a bit offset from the road, so Scott drove through the security gate into the semi-circular driveway and parked underneath the extended second floor balcony. The mansion was surrounded by walls with carefully planted overlapping vines on top. The vines obscured the brickwork entirely and gave the impression of a naturally occurring green hedge all around the property.

Since they were late, Jeff got out as soon as Scott parked, climbed up the steps, and rang the doorbell. The large wood paneled doors opened almost immediately with a musical sound. Clearly, they were expected. A lady in her fifties opened the door and said so in as many words in slightly accented English and added that Mr. Morita was waiting in the study. She said her name was Emma. From her accent, Kip though she could be from Colombia or Argentina - her accent indicated that she had been in the US for a while. Kip was training his ears to detect Spanish accents from different countries. He practiced that skill diligently with all five languages he spoke; it helped him understand people better.

Once they went upstairs, she opened the study door with one hand and asked if they would like coffee or tea. Scott and Jeff both asked for black coffee, and Kip opted for green tea if that was available. She said it was available and she would go and get their drinks. Kip noticed the interior of the house was decorated with paintings of different styles, but mostly oil on canvas. He saw a beautiful stone sculpture as well - it looked like one of the Indian classics from Ramkinkar Baij influence.

As they entered the study, Kip saw a man in a green polo shirt, tweed jacket and khakis look up from his MacBook, get up from the desk, and greet them. His desk was in a corner at the very end of the book-lined study not directly visible from the door. For a man of Japanese origin, he was tall, slim, and had mixed features - he seemed to be in his early-sixties.

Nick Morita walked around the desk, came closer, and extended his hand toward Kip and said warmly, "Kimura San, Koniichiwa. O Genki desu ka?" That took Kip by complete surprise.

Kip was not used to "Kimura San" and Japanese greeting. Most people called him Kip and started with a "Hi," but he understood the formality and reciprocated. He said, "Nice meeting you, hope you are doing well too, Morita San."

Then, Nick turned toward Scott and Jeff and told them, "Jeff, Scott, thank you gentlemen for making time on Saturday - I really appreciate it. I know you are busier due to the COVID-19 lockdown. I was just reading in the *LA Times* that violent crime has increased substantially during the lockdown; even automotive, property thefts, and burglaries are up. Really bad times." Nick led them toward a round coffee table with six chairs at the other end of his study.

"That we are - both our departments are indeed very busy during the lockdown, Nick. Our call center is buzzing with calls for burglaries and thefts," Jeff responded, and Scott nodded. They both seemed to know Nick well. As Nick was finishing, Kip saw Emma bring a tray with their drinks and put it on the table next to Nick's desk. She also brought a pot of tea for Nick along with some delicious Japanese rice cookies.

Nick went back to his desk, closed his MacBook, and came back and joined them at the coffee table. Nick carried a folder with him with some photographs inside. After they settled down, Jeff was the first to speak.

"Nick, we would appreciate if you could give Kip a detailed description of the break-in that took place - please do not leave out any detail, even if it appears outwardly insignificant. As I said to you over the phone, Kip's firm has some unique expertise in this area - we could leverage that. If you agree, we would like to engage Kip's firm to work on this case."

Nick seemed ready. "I agree," he said. "I did some reference checking on Kimura San's work in Asia after you called, and I agree with your assessment. I do think he is the man for this."

"Excellent, let us start the briefing right from the very beginning," said Jeff with a smile on his face. Scott did not say anything, but he had an "I told you" expression on his face. Kip felt a bit uncomfortable.

Nick cleared his throat and looked at Kip. "Kimura San, before we start, let us get to know each other a bit. I do not mean to be intrusive, but since you are also from Japan originally, I'm tempted to ask, where is the family from? Your parents' ancestral home in Japan, for example?"

"No intrusion at all, Nick, that is normal. Both my parents and their parents were from Sendai area in Miyagi Prefecture. Our ancestral home is not far from where the Sendai Shinkansen station is today on the Tohoku Shinkansen line. My father went to college at Tohoku University and then worked at the Seiko Epson plant in Nagano for a while before settling down in Boulder, Colorado. He had to have mountains and ski slopes around him all his life. I was born and raised in Boulder until I joined the US Army out of the University of Colorado. I have been all over the world while I was in the US Army - much of my time was spent in Southeast Asia. My business partner Tim and I started our company right after we both took early retirement out of the US Army.

"I used to read and write Japanese, but I have not practiced those skills in many years. Thanks to my mom, I can speak and understand it if I need to. To be completely honest, I am not quite used to 'Kimura San' and the Japanese greetings. Please feel free to call me just Kip."

He paused for a bit, hoping that was enough. Since both Jeff and Nick had been checking on him and his work separately, he was not sure if there was anything more he could add. Kip absorbed people and places like a sponge; he did not worry about where they came from or what they did. He accepted most people as just people, and that worked pretty well for him. He did not have to wait for long.

Nick took a final sip of his tea, cleared his throat, and started talking with an emphatic "Arigato, Kimura San. My family is from the Kansai area. My father's side and my mother's side came from Samurai families from the Nara area in the Kansai region. You may or may not know Nara - it is a small ancient city not far from Kyoto. It connects with Kyoto by means of a local train line. Nara was the well-known capital of Japan in the eighth century - it is a UN heritage city. The city of Nara is well-known now for its world-famous Tōdai-ji Temple.

"My parents came to the US in 1955. I was born and raised in Seattle. I moved to Los Angeles many years ago because of the college I went to, and then I stayed because of my work in films - my company produces movies. But let me start this story from the time of my late grandfather. That should provide you with the context and the timeline. The historical significance of the two objects should be clear to you. Most of what I am going to say to you is what I heard from my grandfather directly during our many visits to his home near Kyoto. I was very close to him when I was a little boy. I learned many foreign languages from him; after those lessons, I always bugged him for wartime stories. That was how I learned the details of this great story."

Nick continued, "My grandfather was a very talented student of linguistics in Kyoto University before World War II. Just before the war broke out, like many other young men in Japan at that time, he joined the army. He eventually went to the Imperial Military Academy and the school for intelligence officers in Nakano near Tokyo. In due course, my grandfather got promoted and as a young major got assigned to the Imperial Army's intelligence operations. He was posted in various places in the Malay Peninsula, in Singapore, but eventually, he was sent to Burma. He adapted to the multiethnic culture of Burma and developed a working knowledge of a couple of local languages very quickly. At that time, the hills of Northern Burma had mostly Shan, Kachin, Karen, Lisu, and other tribal people. Burmar and Mon people were concentrated in the river valleys and big cities; they pretty much dominated Burmese national politics centered around Rangoon.

"Some tribes, like the Shan, already had some autonomy. Some of their princely states or small kingdoms were recognized by the

British but nominally ruled by local rulers called Chaofas. You can imagine - it was not easy for the occupying Japanese forces to navigate this multiethnic demography and further its cause of an independent Burma. At least on paper, that was what they were committed to do. My grandfather's efforts and his flair for relationship building was noticed by Colonel Suzuki, the leader of the Japanese intelligence in Burma.

"At some point in 1942, my grandfather was acting as the principal Japanese liaison for the Shan and Karen tribes in Northern Burma. Many of those tribes were seeking independence from the British. Some of them had their own armies and militias that were loyal only to its tribal chiefs. My grandfather's task of making them see a collective victory in Burma's independence was not easy. Each tribe had its own agenda; they were unwilling to leave their comfort zones.

"Grandpa often got frustrated by the petty politics of each tribe. In the end, most tribal chiefs agreed that his efforts helped, and many of them thought he was a genuine friend of Burma. At that stage of the war, my grandfather actually thought Japan would help the hill tribes.

"He eventually got disillusioned and frustrated by the Japanese war ministry, but that was a bit later after he was recalled from Burma. While he was in Burma, he did everything he could. In 1942, he received two very special gifts from one of the Shan tribal chiefs; these objects were given to him as a token of appreciation for his efforts. The Shan Chaofa said so in a handwritten note and put his personal seal on that note. It would have been impolite and politically incorrect not to accept those gifts, so Grandpa accepted the gifts with humility and said so.

"The first object was a jade marriage bowl used in traditional Chinese and Asian marriages. The fourteen-inch bowl was made of green Burmese jade with exquisite finish and carving on the outside with Chinese Kanji inscriptions. There are some etched drawings on the inside as well. The second object was a fifteen-inch Buddha statue made of white jade. Both objects were decorated with Burmese rubies; both were also exquisitely carved by the best jade carvers of the day.

"The quality of the Jade mined in Hpakant, Northern Burma, and craftsmanship by local tribal Shan and Kachin carvers was just awe inspiring. While this liaison and tribal unification effort was going on, some in the Japanese Imperial Army become concerned about Colonel Suzuki's pro-independence stance and authority over the Burmese Independence Army. That concern gained momentum inside the Japanese war ministry in 1942, and as a result, the intelligence team and my grandfather were recalled to Japan. Grandpa returned in late 1942.

"For the rest of the war, Grandpa worked in the Japanese war ministry by overseeing logistics - he basically became a back-office person. While Grandpa worked in Tokyo, these two objects along with others he had collected in Burma remained in our ancestral home in Western Japan. Grandpa had a room built for his wartime collection of precious artifacts. Once, our house in Japan caught fire and that room was destroyed, but he had it reconstructed. The fire took place before I was born; I only heard the stories of that fire from Grandpa and Mom.

"Grandpa knew the historic and cultural significance of those two objects; he thought they were safer in the Kyoto area because the Allies would never bomb Kyoto and its vicinity. He was right in his assessment; Kyoto was never bombed even though much of Japan was. In my childhood when we visited my grandparents, sometimes, these ancient objects came up in dinner time conversations. Grandpa would always recount the story and say he would have no problems in returning these objects to the rightful Shan owners if he could find them and authenticate the ownership. When Grandpa passed away, my dad got that task of locating the Chaofa family that owned those objects and arrange for their return. Dad discovered it was not easy.

"As I said, the importance of these objects to the Shan tribe was not lost on my grandfather. My father made many efforts to locate the original Shan Chaofa family in the late 1970s through the Burmese Embassy in Washington, DC, but none of those efforts were successful, so we became the keepers. That part of Burma is not easily accessible, so we did not have very many other options. Since my father's passing, I have been looking after the two objects - I have no idea what would happen to these objects after me. Every year, I would register these, purchase insurance, take those out once for professional cleaning, and put those back in the safe. After this house was constructed and the rear wing expansion was completed in 2001, the objects were kept in the safe in my mother's room in the rear. I felt that was the best place. I purchased a special Israeli made safe and had the safe wall mounted during the construction of the rear wing; the whole thing is well concealed. That Israeli safe was a state-of-the-art technology when I purchased it. Nowadays, that particular brand is out of production.

"My mother's health is fragile; she spends most of her time in that room or in the adjacent patio. My mother believes those objects are spiritual and brought good blessings to our family; she says she can feel the presence of those objects in her mind and in her bones. I do not know how to explain such feelings to you gentlemen rationally because it makes no sense. Since we do not open the safe more than once or twice in a year, I thought my mother's room is the best place for the safe and its contents - it is well hidden. Until very recently, till I discovered this break-in, I never regretted that decision. It made sense, and it worked out pretty well for us. After the break-in, I am not sure."

Nick paused for a bit and opened the folder he was carrying. "I had taken a few high-resolution pictures of those two objects last year; here are those pictures for you, Kimura San."

Kip had seen the slides in Jeff's office, but these pictures were a lot better. Nick was a movie guy, so he probably took those with his professional camera and used his expertise well. He saw the picture of the marriage bowl at first and then the Buddha statue in full color and ultra-high resolution.

He agreed with Jeff; the word *exquisite* did not do justice to these objects. They were both one of a kind - clearly designed by the best artists, made with the best jadeite mined in Burma, and probably carved by the best jade carvers of the time! Kip's first impression, based on his limited knowledge of valuing jade, was that together, the objects would exceed millions of dollars in fair market value. It might be much more at auction, particularly if the history and provenance were taken into account - those objects could not be replaced easily. Probably, the thieves who planned this particular break-in knew a lot about those objects and their ancient history. It was premeditated and well-planned.

After Kip put the pictures back in the folder, Nick continued, "Several weeks ago, I got a call from the insurance company that I work with. The caller said that my policy for those two objects is coming up for renewal and the fair market value has increased. He said that I would see a significant increase in the insurance premium, that they have no choice but to raise the premium. I told the insurance agent that I am not selling or auctioning these ancient Burmese artifacts to anyone.

"Both objects are in my private collection and those are going to remain there. Therefore, I did not think I should pay an increased premium because of fair market value. The agent went on explaining that the fair market value had doubled, and we went back and forth arguing on the phone for a full ten minutes. We had multiple phone calls, fax, and email exchanges with variations of the premium quotes as well. I was basically asking him to make various adjustments to lower the premium. He did make a few adjustments on the coverage, but the premiums did not change materially. Thereafter, the agent couriered a whole folder of paperwork that they had collected to assess the value. Clearly, the company had spent time and money to justify the increase in premium. I asked my secretary to file all the paperwork away.

"A few more weeks went by; I had started talking to other insurance companies for quotes. Some of those were quoting even higher premiums, so the matter could not be settled easily. As I made those calls to insurance companies and the haggling continued over phone, fax, and email, I realized we had not done the annual cleaning of those objects. So, a few weeks ago, I went to my mother's room to get the two objects for cleaning - that was the first time this year. We do not open the safe in Mom's room unless we have a genuine need.

That was when I discovered that the safe was forced open and the objects were missing! I called Jeff immediately, and the very next day, I went to his office and met up with him and Scott. I lodged a formal complaint about the break-in. You know the rest of the story from them, Kimura San. My main goal is to get the objects back and return those to their rightful Shan owners. I would like to see the perpetrators brought to justice, but that is not my primary goal - I am worried about the objects. That is where we thought you would be able to help us."

"If I have to establish a timeline, when would you say you actually saw the two objects for the last time?" Kip asked after Nick finished.

"That would be about three months back. I do not remember the exact date, but three months would be a good estimate," Nick responded after thinking for an additional minute. Kip had several other questions on the events before and after; Nick answered all those questions patiently. Kip made several digital notes on his hand-held digital tablet.

The summary of Nick's answers would read somewhat like this. He did not appoint any new staff or household help in the last three months; Nick's mother did not remember hearing any noise or seeing anyone suspicious near the safe or her room. The house was never completely empty. Nick had one travel to New York in three months for a motion pictures trade show; he was away for only two consecutive nights. For both of those nights, Nick's sister-in law came from Irvine and stayed in the house with his wife and mother. Then came the COVID lockdown. After the lockdown was announced, all air travel and other non-local visits were canceled. So, no change in the routine.

The only visitor Nick could remember was his cousin Ichiro Morita visiting from Osaka for one night. There were no unusual events. The only minor incident that was somewhat different was a bunch of people working on the electrical supply lines on their access road. Nick knew about it because the electric utility company had informed him, and they got a formal permission via email. Not just from Nick - they got permission from all house owners. One of the crew members from the local utility Southern California Edison Company had come by to shut off electricity from outside on the day Nick left for New York. Nick's wife Emily talked to him just as Nick boarded the limousine for the Los Angeles Airport. They got the repair done promptly.

Emily talked to him outside the door about the shutoff and when the electricity would come back on. After Nick he returned from New York, his wife told him that the same man in a hard hat and Southern California Edison Company uniform came back after a couple of hours and switched the electricity on from the outside. They didn't even feel that the electricity was not there for three hours. They thought the utility company did very well by keeping them informed and also completing the electricity line repairs on schedule. SoCal Edison had also informed Nick that the repair work was done, and they did not plan any more interruptions. Nick received the email in his personal account

Kip had many more questions, and Nick answered all of those in great detail, so the process took a long time. Kip pulled out an Android tablet and made some notes for himself. In the meantime, Emma came with another tray and left more fresh coffee and green tea along with some delicious rice cakes.

After Nick finished answering all of Kip's questions, Jeff said, "Nick, we have to update you on a few related developments that have taken place here and in Glendale recently."

That was when Scott described in detail that one of the neighborhood cameras picked up an Acura Integra roaming the streets. He also showed a couple of very grainy pictures of a hooded man driving the car; the man was careful. None of the cameras were able to capture a full-frontal view. It seemed the person knew where the cameras were and prepared accordingly. On seeing the pictures of the car and the hooded figure, Nick said he could not recognize either. Jeff asked if Nick would like his wife to see the pictures, so at Jeff's request, Nick's wife Emily Morita came in and saw the pictures. Jeff asked her if any of the household helpers or handymen or contractors she might have used in the past had a similar 2002 vintage Acura Integra.

She looked at the picture carefully once again and said she did not think so. She could not recognize the hooded driver either. After Emily left, Scott described the incident with John's Acura and its number plate.

Nick heard the whole update and then commented, "So, the plot thickens now?"

Jeff responded, "It certainly looks like that, Nick. This was no ordinary break-in; there was a plan, and it looks like we ourselves or someone else has somehow disturbed the original plan. I think the switching of the number plates is a reaction. One of the perpetrators, or an accomplice, was shaken a bit by the news leaking in the press and wanted to hide. He found a suitable car roadside and went for it.

"Whoever did it, he or she planned it very well and executed it even better. We have to explore multiple avenues; we need to know the who, and we also need to know the how. From your description of how the objects came to your family's possession, it seems to me that we might have to travel a bit to unravel the why part completely. I am speculating a bit here because I do not know for sure yet. Are you broadly in agreement with those high-level thoughts? We'll need your approval."

Nick thought for a bit, processed what Jeff had said, and said thoughtfully, "I think I agree with you, Jeff. We need to unravel this mystery, and this could go in any direction. These treasures belonged to an ancient tribe in the hills of Burma; I do not want to see these treasures fall in the hands of petty thieves in the Los Angeles underworld. Money is not a problem for me. I would spare no expenditure to fulfill my grandfather's wishes of returning these to the rightful owners. If you gentlemen think Kimura San can assist us getting there, I am happy to pay his fees. I'll sign the paperwork, and I will have my accountant set up an expense account for Kimura San's use effective immediately. Let me know if you need anything else."

Finally, Kip had one last request. He asked Nick if they could see where the safe was. Nick gave them a tour of the seven-bedroom, two-storied mansion and then took them downstairs toward the rear. The rear suite opened into a very nice Japanese garden and a koi pond. It had a nice hillside view from the covered patio. Nick knocked and entered his mother's room; he spoke with her for a few seconds and invited the others.

Kip heard Mrs. Morita say to Nick, "Daijobu desu."

Nick's mother Keiko Morita was wearing a beautiful Japanese kimono with intricate needlework; she was elderly, easily in her nineties, but looked healthy and sharp. She did not get up from her reclining chair, but she waved everybody inside with her hand. Kip looked at the wall-mounted safe carefully; it was a well-made safe that had an electronic locking mechanism. On the outside, it was hidden behind an enlarged poster that was framed and hung with recessed hinges on one side. The poster was from Akira Kurosawa's *Rashomon.*

The picture frame opened like a real door on hinges, and that was how the safe was accessed. If one did not know, one could look at the wall, appreciate the framed poster of the famous psychological thriller, and go away. The safe was very cleverly hidden in plain sight. There was no major external damage to the safe, but when Kip opened it with his ballpoint pen, he could see a that the locking clasp was bent, and a couple of wires were dangling inside. Several holes were expertly drilled into the safe from the outside.

Scott said, "I have some pictures of the inside; I'll email those to you."

Kip said, "Thanks" and turned to Nick. "Did you call the manufacturer of the safe and discuss the damage?"

Nick said, "That was the first thing I did. This particular model is ten plus years old; they do not make it in the US anymore. They got one of their senior technicians to talk to me. He said somebody with good knowledge of the locking mechanism must have done it because it is not easy to force open these types of safes. He also emphasized that the process takes many hours; if the holes are drilled incorrectly, the plate inside breaks and fuses, and the safe can never be opened by anyone. The technician commented that our thief was an expert locksmith; otherwise, he could not have placed the drill holes so precisely. He apparently had a very good hand for precision drilling too. He must have had complete access to the safe for many hours. He knew he had time; he was not in a rush. You cannot do that kind of precision drilling in a rush. We design our safes with the assumption that thieves do not have uninterrupted access. If that assumption is invalidated, then we cannot prevent an expert from gaining access."

Kip made a note in his tablet and then walked out into the wrap-around patio. Mrs. Morita had another recliner at the patio at the other end. Kip stood there for a couple of seconds and noticed that if someone sat in the recliner in that position, that person could not see the safe. The angle was not good because the wall blocked the view. Kip thought he had seen everything he needed to see for now, so they said goodbye to Nick's mother.

She nodded and said, "Hai, Sayonara, Arigato." Jeff and Kip both looked thoughtful; wheels were spinning in their heads. When they got back to Nick's study, Kip asked for a list of temporary staff and residents at the mansion and their working hours.

Nick had it already; he said he would email it to all three of them with the contact details and reference information. Nick said that he had informed his mother and wife about the break-in; no one else in the household knew as of yet. Kip and Jeff did not want to publicize the news. Nick mentioned that they had a full-time housekeeper, Emma, their cook Selma, and their security guard Jim. Carlos, the gardener, worked twice a week. Nick's secretary Martha worked on Tuesdays and Thursdays, and his mother had a physiotherapist who visited her for a massage twice a week - typically on Tuesdays and Thursdays, but not always on the same set of days. His visit days could change based on other patients he looked after; Nick was under the impression that Jack was a pretty sought-after physiotherapist. Kip asked him how he formed that impression, and Nick said it was based on Mrs. Morita's inputs.

Selma, Emma, and Jim, the security guard, had been with the family for over five years. Carlos, the gardener, was supplied by the landscaping company that was known to Nick's neighbor. Carlos had worked on the neighbor's property for many years. Nick had hired Martha about a year ago; she had worked for a Hollywood post-production company before this assignment with him. Nick had worked with that post-production company for two of his movie projects, but he did not know Martha Wilson at a personal level before hiring her. He got to know her as a person only after she started working here. The physiotherapist, Jack, was recommended by Mrs. Morita's doctor from UCLA Medical School a few months before. Nick himself had called UCLA. She had started complaining about joint pain sometime back.

Her doctor, Dr. Marshall of UCLA Med School and Hospital, diagnosed it to be an early onset of age-related arthritis and said regular physiotherapy was the best form of intervention at that point in time. After Jack started the regular massage sessions, Mrs. Morita had been feeling a lot better. Mrs. Morita thought Jack's massages were really helpful. Nick's wife Emily restored old paintings; her art supplies and her client deliveries were handled by Jim, at the gate most of the time.

Those transactions and FedEx or UPS deliveries were received by Jim and brought into the house later unless Jim was informed that an urgent delivery was expected. Emily's client interactions happened from her email and her personal cell phone. Since those transactions were fewer in number, she managed her communication from the MacBook in her studio. Emily's work required her to go to art galleries and auctions sometimes; those were infrequent and as a result, quite easy to plan.

After the conversation ended, they took a break in Nick's study and had some sandwiches with him. As Nick had said, it was a working lunch, not elaborate, just tasty and simple. The lunch break allowed them to compare notes and action items.

As they started eating, Scott said, "Nick, do you suspect any of your staff, or can you think of any one of them doing this to you?"

Nick thought hard for a minute and said he could not name any suspects. He did say, however, that some weeks before, he had a premonition that something wrong was going to happen - it was just a strange feeling. After that, he had asked Jim to stay at his post at the gate throughout the day. He had no rational basis for suggesting that to Jim, but he could think of nothing else to do.

Also, Jim was very receptive to the idea; he thought being alert always helped. So, they went ahead. He told Jim that Emma would serve packed lunch and coffee to him at his post. Jim was quite willing to change his routine; so was Emma - it generated little extra work for her. Since that directive, Jim was coming inside the mansion only when he was using restrooms. Nick had no idea if his action helped in any way, but his strange feeling went away after a couple of days. In his own mind, Nick rationalized it by thinking he had done something right.

Kip thought he had enough information for now. On his cue, Jeff spoke, "Nick, thanks a lot for such a comprehensive briefing covering every aspect. We have everything we need from you for now. We should get going now, but we might reach out to you via phone or email if we need any clarification on any of the topics we covered. If you think we missed anything or we should check something, please let me know. Kip will need to talk to your house staff one-on-one at some point, but soon. Given the way this break-in happened, someone from inside had to have a major role. We need to know who, why, and how. The how part is critical because your household is very organized with well-defined roles for each occupant. This break-in was a clear violation of the trust you placed in one of your staff members; we do not know who that is as of yet. But we would know in a few days' time for sure.

"When you described your conversation with the safe technician to Kip today, I could not help but thinking. The list of people who could have had access to the safe for an extended period of more than one hour during the last couple of months could not be that long. Just that input alone would shrink the list of suspects significantly to just a couple of people, I would think. That input was something very useful.

"I think our challenge is to establish the 'how' now. I think the 'who' part has become a lot narrower now. But even if we know the who, until we can establish the 'how' that can withstand scrutiny, there is no case. The 'who' will simply deny all wrongdoing, and we would not even have a case to prosecute. Personally, I do not think we would get a break easily, so we have to shake up a few trees. In this case, I do not believe we will get lucky and have people coming to us with their confessions ready in hand. We are probably dealing with people who have executed this kind of operation before.

"The detailed planning was quite impressive. We should also remember that the switching of the number plate in John Abreo's parked car in Glendale was a deliberate act by someone who felt threatened by our investigation. Clearly, the strategic leak we had planted with the newspaper reporter helped, but even that could have complete deniability. The planner of this break-in made sure he or she had razor tight alibi for the participants in this ambitious scheme.

"But the person who did the switching of number plates realized that he had just lost his anonymity and he could be vulnerable. As soon as that realization dawned on him, he decided to get rid of that number plate in a tearing hurry. He probably chose a location not far from his home or place of work, found a very similar looking car, and switched the number plates. It is time we start some old-fashioned real detective work and find out who had the motive and the opportunity. Luckily, our list of names has shrunk. We will make sure that one of us calls you early next week to give you a status update. Kip wanted to check out several things before we talk to your staff. We would try to finish those in the next couple of days before we question the staff."

Nick said, "I cannot thank you gentlemen enough." He got up and said, "Bye for now."

Lungs in America

Win finished high school in 1979 and enrolled at the University of Texas (UT) at Austin. For his undergraduate degree, he majored in Economics and International Relations. Win worked harder than everyone in his class and finished his degree requirement for both majors in four years flat in 1983. He remembered their lives in Bangkok and even a little bit of Chiang Mai. He felt he was privileged to be able to go to UT, Austin. He wanted to utilize every minute of it. Some of his professors and faculty advisors were surprised, but Aung was not.

He could see that Win was able to adjust to the American system rather easily. After his undergraduate degree was completed, there were multiple avenues and many different conversations on options. Myint felt that Win could join their own restaurant business and grow it - she loved her restaurants. But Win's mind was made up: he wanted to pursue a career in International Law. He wanted to specialize in international trade negotiations, the United Nations, UNHCR, conflict resolution, human rights, and international climate change initiatives.

Jim visited the Lungs from Dallas whenever he could. He had joined his family business after the war; it was not very difficult for him to pull himself out if the Lungs had a need. Jim came by on a weekend from Dallas and spent the day with the Lungs. Win's plan to go to law school after he completed his bachelor's degree was discussed at length; it was a commitment for several years, and then there would be bar examinations. If there were doubts, those had to be brought up before the multi-year commitment was made. Win had no doubts. His mind was clearly made up, and he started preparing for admissions.

Jim agreed with Win's decision, not just that he reminded Aung and Myint that Win talked about doing law many years ago in Jim's presence. Even though Win was an adult by then, Jim still called him "my favorite kiddo."

As was Jim's habit, he concluded by saying, "My favorite kiddo is always right - in this case about studying International Law." That settled the conversation on that subject; everyone was actually happy. Win liked the fun way Uncle Jim settled the issue for all.

Aung already knew that Win was vigorously preparing for law school, so a few weeks later when Win came home one evening and announced his admission, Aung was not surprised. "Pho, Mom, looks like I made it to The University of Texas School of Law or Texas Law at the University of Texas at Austin."

When Myint called Jim in Dallas and let him know that Win had made it into Texas Law, Jim screamed in delight, "I am so proud of you, Kiddo; I know how selective that school is. Ask Dad when is the party? I'm coming for a big and noisy party!"

While Win was studying law at UT, Austin, another important development took place. A Thai restaurant in Austin was getting auctioned by its lender, a local bank. The issue was non-payment of bank loans. The location was very good; it was bang on Highway 183, not far from the Arboretum. That neighborhood was the happening place in Austin, so the restaurant would see a lot of customers on all days of the week, even on weekends. Aung felt the location was great. Aung did some due diligence through his restaurant association in Round Rock and found that there was no major issue in the paperwork; it was mostly the non-payment of bank loans as the bank stated. He then called Jim and requested Jim to use his contacts for another round of reference checking. Jim knew a lot of good people in the government because of his stint with the US Department of Defense.

He did his research and thorough due diligence through his contacts in the government. Jim made some calls and found out that the previous owner had problems with the Immigration and

Naturalization Services (INS) as well. He had employed a couple of people who did not have the appropriate work visas, so the INS was pursuing him for some fines. None of these were causes of concern in Aung's case. With Jim's inputs, Aung decided to bid for the restaurant with most of the savings he and Myint had been able to set aside from The Shan in Round Rock. Because of those savings, funding was not going to be a problem this time; he might not even require a bank loan.

A couple of months went by, but nothing happened. And then in the third month, when Win had just gone back to his university after a short vacation at home, Aung and Myint were drowning in the increasing workload of their restaurant in Round Rock. One evening, the phone rang at the Lung residence in Round Rock.

The caller said, "I am Rex Brown from Nations Bank. Could I have a word with Mr. Lung about his buying bid for the Mung Thai restaurant in Austin?"

Myint said, "Sure" and handed the phone over to Aung.

Mr. Brown started without preamble, "Mr. Lung, we at Nations Bank have decided to accept your offer for the Mung Thai restaurant in Austin. If you are still interested, we would need to set up a face-to-face meeting with our lending team in Austin to go over the process and sign the paperwork." Aung realized that the process was suddenly moving at a faster clip; this time, he had prepared well.

And then without waiting for Aung, he asked, "Would the 11th of next month at 2:00 p.m. in Austin work for Mr. Lung?"

Aung realized he did not have much choice, so he said, "I would be happy to make myself available on that day along with two of my associates." By that time, Aung had adapted to the fast pace.

Mr. Brown gave him the address in Austin, shared the list of documents Nations Bank would expect, and then concluded the call with a "See you at the offices of our bank in Austin in roughly two weeks. Please make sure you go through our checklist and bring all the required documents. We do not want any last-minute delays; that is why we are giving you much time."

Aung looked at the address and realized it was quite close to the UT campus, so he called Win and asked him to block his calendar. Win had a court hearing he had planned to attend, but he was happy to reschedule that and planned to make himself available on that day. Then, Aung asked Myint to come along. She was not interested in going to Austin, but she insisted on Jim's presence. Jim's opinion and advice mattered a lot to all the Lungs.

Aung had to call Jim and request him to come over to Austin. Jim was available, so he said he would be happy to drive down from Dallas. Aung, Jim, and Win went to the Austin offices of the bank on the appointed date and time.

The paperwork was long but not very hard because a lot of due diligence was already done by the bank, and Aung had brought all the required documents with him from Round Rock. Aung was quite organized, and it was visible that day. Aung wanted to look at all the compliance certificates and regulatory clearances for the building and the restaurant space. Most of the documents were in order because the space was part of a strip mall and a larger building - the building management had taken care of most of the regulatory clearances. There were a couple of violations reported by the utility company for the gas line and electrical switch box. As the new owner, Aung was supposed to contact Austin Energy and other service providers get his new account set up for all the utilities and services.

The bank said that it would address the violations and also get the place professionally cleaned and disinfected. The bank also put Aung in touch with the contractor for interior and exterior decorations and signage for the restaurant. That contractor had worked in that mall for several other businesses, so he was familiar with the building and its statutory clearances from Travis County offices. He was already vetted.

With the official process out of the way, after receiving the cashier's check Aung had brought, the bank handed over one set of keys to Aung. The bank said the second set of keys would be sent to him after the violations and cleaning were taken care of. The repair folks would need access to the space for their repair work in the interim. Aung stepped out of the offices of the bank and let out a sigh of relief. He told Jim and Win that he had discussed the name of the new restaurant with Myint, and she thought it should be called "Shan Austin." That name would lend legitimacy and make people recognize the place, and both Jim and Win liked the idea very much.

The name Shan Austin also had a rhythm to it. Aung was all about Shan, but Myint wanted to recognize the US and its prominent places as well. She was "eternally grateful to America," she would often say. Jim and Win knew that, and they both liked that spirit of giving back in her. The Lungs were Americans now, and Myint wanted to display that in action, example, and spirit.

Jim commented, "Down the line, you guys could call the other one 'Shan Round Rock.'"

Aung said, "That is the idea - we would take up that task of new signage, menus, etc., when we do the renovation of that one next year."

Aung also told them that Myint had suggested real authentic Shan decoration for the Austin restaurant. "Great idea," said Jim. "But it might not be easy to get Shan artifacts in the US or even get those shipped from overseas in a timely manner."

"If you could, that would be unique in Austin and probably all of Texas."

Win promised to do a bit of research and get back to Aung in a week. Aung had an early evening celebratory meal with Jim and Win at Win's favorite restaurant, El Cerrito. It was good, but not as good as The Shan in Round Rock. *In any case, people in Austin will soon have a choice of great Shan cuisine*, Aung thought. Aung was thrilled with the acquisition of Shan Austin. After seeing off Jim on his way to Dallas, he dropped off Win at the UT campus in Austin before driving back to Round Rock. When Aung reached home and briefed Myint on the day's events, she was ecstatic. It was her dream to have another Shan restaurant to spread the word about Shan cuisine. The next few months were very hectic for the Lungs. Based on their past experience, Aung and Myint knew that they would need to invest time to bring up the Austin property to their high standard. They made several checklists and distributed the tasks, but still, there was an awful lot to do.

The first thing they did was to promote Mauricio, the first Hispanic young man they had hired in Round Rock when they started, to manager, and they gave him complete managerial responsibility for the Round Rock property. Then, they hired Mauricio's elder brother Roberto from a local steakhouse. Roberto was already an experienced manager, and they asked him to manage Shan Austin right from the very beginning. Myint designed the menu with a consultant; she got a lot more creative.

The two brothers, Mauricio and Roberto, were also given complete freedom to hire local staff to work under them. With those two key hires in place, Aung shifted his focus on getting the exterior and interior work done. Along with that, they also had to complete various registrations. The City of Austin and the offices of Travis County had different registration requirements. Myint displayed a lot of creativity in developing a menu that was suitable for the local palate. Produce and supplies were no issues because their suppliers in Round Rock could service the Austin location easily. Win helped a lot with promoting Shan Austin among his local contacts in Austin. Because of their past experience, Shan Austin started without any hiccups. They planned to run advertisements in the *Austin American-Statesman* before the inauguration.

The process of getting authentic Shan decoration proved to be much harder than Aung had anticipated. Win made dozens of calls each day. As a by-product of the main activity, he got connected to the Shan refugee organization in Washington, DC. To his great surprise, he even located a few Shan families in Texas and two in the Austin Metro area - one family had come before them. But none of those contacts could help in locating the artifacts Aung and Myint were looking for to decorate Shan Austin. Win even called the Burmese Embassy for help.

Finally, Win called Uncle Jim in Dallas mentioned the difficulty to Jim. Jim quipped, "I knew it; remember I said that to your dad?"

Win remembered the conversation outside the offices of Nations Bank in Austin. Eventually through Jim's old contact in Bangkok, Win was able to connect with a supplier from the camps in Chiang Mai, Thailand. That supplier sold Shan artifacts made by the Shan people in refugee camps of Chiang Mai; he could ship the stuff. But he had to have a lead time.

The supplier said he could supply all the items in Aung and Myint's list, but the lead time would be twelve weeks at the very least. When Win mentioned twelve weeks, Aung was disappointed because that would be well past the inauguration day. The deputy mayor of Austin had accepted the invitation for inauguration along with members of his staff. At that stage, Aung could not let his restaurant association and other supporters down by changing the date. Even if it became a relatively low-key affair, the inauguration had to happen on the agreed upon date. Changing the date was not an option Aung could consider.

Once again, Myint came up with the best idea that salvaged the situation. She suggested that they try the Indian store in Austin - they had a lot of Asian Indian artifacts. They could use the temporary decorations to stage the inauguration and for the first couple of months for the interior and then replace those when the shipment from Chiang Mai arrived in Austin. Jim was thrilled with Myint's idea. Jim said that the typical Indian artifacts were different from the ones made by ethnic Shan. If the Indian store had stuff that was made in the Eastern Indian state of Assam or Nagaland, those would be very close. Naga artifacts would be almost indistinguishable for most folks.

Some Shan people live in those Indian states - they could just get lucky and find what they were looking for. Myint drove down to the Indian store on Mopac Boulevard in Austin, and she was lucky to find an assortment of Naga artifacts. She bought them all.

Some of them were so good that Myint said, "These will remain in Shan Austin even after the shipment arrives from Chiang Mai." Shan Austin had its inauguration by the deputy mayor in 1985 in full regalia. The shipment from Chiang Mai arrived ten weeks later, but the contractors took another week to assemble some of the larger artifacts. Aung was particularly proud of the two model Shan horses at the entrance; those two horses framed the entrance of the restaurant when customers walked in. Almost everyone wanted to know more about those short horses. Aung loved every opportunity to talk about those.

Shan Austin became a popular destination for people who liked to try different types of food, particularly with the large international student population and faculty at UT Austin. Austin was still a university town, and the UT influence was everywhere in the city. Myint liked that about Austin. Aung and Myint started getting a lot of visibility as successful restaurateurs. Since both their restaurants fell under the jurisdiction of Travis County, the county officials started seeking their opinions on other business matters as well. Small business success stories were fewer in the county at that time, so the Lung businesses got a lot of attention from the county's small business team.

The area had the Texas state capital with the state government and UT Austin - those big organizations got all the local media attention. That is why sometimes, county officials would go out of their way to seek out success stories from small businesses. After a few months, the profile of the Lungs and their family's remarkable journey from the Shan homeland in Burma was published in a local newspaper. Aung and Myint became mini celebrities in the small business circles of Austin overnight.

Win was enjoying the celebrity status of his parents more than anyone. He would often joke with Jim, "Uncle Jim, can you please look for a publicist for Dad? Next time, he will need a makeup artist as well." Jim would laugh on the phone and say that he would indeed be on the lookout for a publicist and the best makeup artist for Aung.

His new notoriety as a successful restaurateur was a source of major discomfort for Aung; deep inside, he was a private person. He would often request Myint to represent him on official visits and functions set up by the Travis County office. Myint adapted to her role as an ambassador for the restaurants and for Travis County. She became quite adept in articulating the core values of the businesses and how the county supported them with financial incentives and policies.

The Lungs and their businesses soon became the favorites. Both restaurants were now run day-to-day by Mauricio, Roberto, and their hand-picked staff. While Aung focused on finance, regulatory compliance, marketing, and local outreach, Myint remained completely involved with the food quality, suppliers, and overall customer experience. The Lungs knew that many things went into crafting a high-quality experience in a restaurant; the staff who delivered that experience to customers mattered a lot. If the staff were motivated, things became a lot easier. That is why they treated the staff like family.

From their past experience in Bangkok and Round Rock, Aung and Myint knew that the quality of food and experience were the most important assets for any good restaurant. Those were difficult to create and even harder to sustain. They had a razor-sharp focus on those elements. The Lungs were lucky to have a very dedicated band of local staff; they treated the Lung restaurants as their own family businesses. Aung and Myint were almost like their parents, and the feeling was mutual.

Mauricio and Roberto had come to the US from Mexico when they were very young; one of their uncles sponsored them for their US residency. Aung and Myint treated them like extended family. Having been refugees in their past lives, they knew how it felt. Jim had encouraged both brothers to file paperwork for US residency for their parents and helped them connect with a couple of good immigration attorneys in Dallas. Both brothers were really grateful. Sometime toward the end of 1986, Aung received an unexpected phone call from a Shan person from Washington, DC. The caller said that he was connected with the people of the Shan Independence Movement in exile in the US. They were a group of a few hundred people who always kept the flame burning.

He and his comrades wanted to request Aung to join them and help them promote the Shan cause in the US. Their meetings were typically once a year, but they stayed in touch via phone, fax, and other means. Their main goals were seeking support for the Shan cause from the US Congress; they also did year-round fundraising for the Shan. The funds they raised went to Burmese charities in Thailand and to International Red Cross teams working in Burma. The caller also mentioned that he was able to locate Aung because of the tabloid story on Shan Austin published in a newspaper in 1986. Aung smiled to himself when he heard that bit - *that was why he did not like publicity.*

Aung told the caller that he would be happy to help but, he did not think he would be in a position to do much travel outside of the Austin area. The caller said he understood Aung's reservation. He made a personal request to Aung to consider making at least one trip to Washington, DC, during their next meeting in 1987. The caller was very polite. He called Aung a senior leader of the Shan Independence Movement and spoke with Aung in the Shan dialect. Aung was very happy; he kept telling Myint that he would like to go and participate in the DC meeting. After talking to the caller, Aung thought that the Shan cause was alive and well - it seemed to be in good hands too. But he also knew how complicated the Shan problems were, and those were not easy to address.

In the evening, he called Win and told him about the conversation. Both Win and Myint felt that Aung should definitely go once and reconnect with the people involved with the Shan cause in the US. That was how Aung got introduced to the Shan activists in exile in the US. For several years, Aung had been a bit out of touch. Now, suddenly, he was able to get a lot of updates on local conditions of the Shan inside Burma. It was like drinking from a fire hose. Most of the updates were depressing; some updates were much more depressing than others.

Among other things, Aung painfully learned that Burma in the 1980s still treasured its days under Japanese occupation from 1941. To make that point loudly, Burmese President Ne Win met Emperor Hirohito in Japan in 1981. He awarded Burma's second highest civilian title to members of Colonel Suzuki's Minami Kikan team. These awards were to Colonel Suzuki's team members. Colonel Suzuki, being the great leader, he was, had received that award from Ne Win earlier. Ne Win had high praise for Japan's and Colonel Suzuki's roles in helping Burma achieve its independence. President Ne Win also felt that Burma as a nation needed to do more to recognize that effort by Japan. In his communication to the Japanese, he said so emphatically.

Some of those news items were like a slap on Aung's face. Aung wondered, *could that really be the will of the Burmese people?* Aung had witnessed the way the Japanese Army had killed six hundred plus unarmed Burmese in Kalagong in 1945. Even the suffering of Japan's own citizens in Hiroshima and Nagasaki should have been known to the Burmese by then. Those deeds were all caused by the same misguided Japanese government, its aspiration for annexations, and its corrupt army officer corps. Colonel Suzuki was part of that mix.

Aung was convinced that the world at large was not holding the Japanese government accountable for all its wartime atrocities. But Ne Win giving awards to the Japanese aggressors for their role in 1941 and 1942 in the name of the Burmese people - that was taking the hypocrisy to a whole new level. Aung knew he and those who shed blood with him were on the right side of history; they picked up arms to protect their own homeland and its people. They did not to attack others. But he also realized painfully that just like in 1942, they were again in the minority. And just like in 1942, no one who mattered was willing to listen!

Their views did not matter to those who were in power. Aung also learned about the dramatic increase in the narcotics and opium trade in the Shan State. He was told that many Western aid organizations and NGOs believed that the drug lords in the Shan State had the implicit support of the Tatmadaw. He saw depressing pictures taken by UNHCR and the International Red Cross that showed two generations of Shan villagers consuming the illicit drugs together inside the same hut. Aung read many accounts of the tribes getting tortured by the army.

It seemed they had no influence on today's Burma; their very existence in their own land was threatened. The mainstream Burmese press and the Burmar and the Mon population chose to look the other way. Some Hollywood stars made movies about the atrocities and human rights violations to draw international attention. But those actions did nothing to change the situation on the ground. Several generations of the tribes were suffering or dying silently in the villages.

When Myint heard these news stories, she was quiet for a long time. Then, she broke her silence and told Aung that she had had enough of the Shan cause. Her advice was, "You have done all you could; you cannot do anything more. It is time for the next generation of leadership to take over and manage. The Shan have to learn to help themselves, and if they cannot, then this is the destiny of the Shan."

Aung could not make it to the meeting with the Shan exiles in 1987 because he had a long bout of the flu that kept him in bed for three weeks. The dates in 1988 did not work out either because Win was graduating from law school, and Jim insisted that they should celebrate together with a big party in Dallas. Aung was a bit preoccupied with their new home as well. Toward the end of 1988, Aung and Myint bought a five-bedroom single-family palatial home in Austin and permanently moved to Austin. They sold their Round Rock property to Mauricio and his brother; they had plans to bring their parents over. They needed a bigger house before the parents arrived. Aung's old house near I35 worked out great for Mauricio and his family.

Aung's new home was on Balcones Woods Drive, slightly off Highway 183. It was pretty close to the Arboretum and Shan Austin; both Aung and Myint loved their new place. Among other things, the Lungs invested in a well-appointed home office for Aung and Myint so that they could run their restaurant business without stepping out, and if they stepped out, it was a short drive. There was a suite for Win just in case he decided to operate from there at some point. There was a guest suite specially prepared for Jim with his favorite interior decorations. Jim promised Aung and Myint that he would visit often.

The Shan exiles meeting for 1989 worked out great for Aung, and he attended it. He arrived at the Washington, DC, hotel a full day in advance to familiarize himself. Aung wanted to know the key people and get connected to the cause all over again. They sat around a round table on the day of the conference and endlessly discussed the priorities for each tribe. They formed a number of different committees and distributed various reports, tables, and action items. Most people around the table were in their fifties, much younger. He realized that he did not understand many of the current problems of the Shan; the political dynamics was different now. Much to Aung's dismay, he learned that post-independence, Burma had become a country that was fighting with itself all the time. It did not need an external enemy.

There was no unity - no room for a common cause among the various ethnic groups. As one of the senior delegates, Aung was asked to speak a couple of times. Finally, he went to the podium and picked up the mic; he looked around the audience and then started to speak.

"I am Aung Lung, a Shan from Northern Burma. I am almost seventy now, much older than most of you. I left my home in my twenties, picked up a gun, and started fighting the Japanese Army in the Kachin Hills. In 1944, the Japanese occupation of Burma ended. But my struggle for the Shan has not ended because the Shan are still suffering. The only difference is that the fight is now with the different set of enemies. Having been at it for nearly half a century, I have realized that armed struggle cannot be a solution to the problems faced by the tribes. Their problems have to be solved politically, with participation from all.

"As a collective, we have to win politically; armed struggle inside Burma or financial assistance from the outside would not be enough. The first step toward that goal is participation. The Shan and the other tribes cannot isolate themselves in their corner of the country. They must participate in local and national politics. The desire for change has to come from within. The Shan have to rise up for their rights and lasting peace and prosperity in the Shan homeland. In my youth, I was for armed struggle. Now, I am not because I have seen its limitations.

"Today's Shan have to confront their adversaries with the same courage and conviction as my generation did in 1942. The Japanese Army was among the strongest in the world at the time, and we were mostly unarmed and untrained. That disparity did not deter us; today's Shan should face today's adversaries with the same level of commitment. They should own their problems. External agencies like this group can enable that process - can act as a catalyst - but cannot do it for them. With the current realities in Burma, the top two priorities for this group should be education and health care for the resident Shan population. If education and health care are addressed, many of the other problems like addiction will reduce in scope and complexity.

"Educated people make better choices about their lives and livelihood. Many of you might not believe it, but I said these exact words to the Shan Federation leadership, of which I was part, in Rangoon after the war ended in 1958. The Japanese occupation had ended, and the British had left. I thought leaders of newly independent Burma would understand; I thought the Shan Federation leadership would understand. Ironically, both did not, and here I am preaching the same truth today from the same play book. We lost time; I feel disappointed.

"I repeat those words today, after thirty-one years, with the hope that you will understand the importance. The current Burmese government is very insecure because the whole world knows what they are doing inside Burma. Their abuses are widely seen. They know that someday, they will be held accountable, just like we have seen autocratic rulers being held accountable in other countries in Asia and Africa. From the outside, we must let them know that we are watching; the independent democratic institutions all over the world are watching. The current Burmese government and its blunt instrument, the Tatmadaw, will have fewer issues with education and healthcare programs. Those programs will be seen as apolitical. Those programs will have a greater chance of success if we do the planning well.

"Those programs could eventually be the covert carriers of your influence from the outside. I would also advise the Shan exile group to plan a stronger physical presence in Chiang Mai in Thailand. Last year, I had connected the leadership with my old friend's family in Bangkok. My friend's NGO has good connections with the Thai government and some members of the royals. I would encourage this leadership team to use that Thai connection and build up a channel of communication from there. Because of its proximity, Thailand can be a good base.

"Please consider engaging with the resident Shan population in the Shan State as much as you can, in as many ways as you can. In my life, I have seen the limitations of armed struggle; believe me, engagement is a more effective tool in the long run. From Chiang Mai, Western influence can spread inside the Shan homeland. The Shan must not have an adversarial relationship with the Thai. If the Thai government and NGOs support us, our quest will become easier and will have a greater chance of success. Most Thais can understand our struggle.

"If there is one thing I have learned over the years, it is 'politics matters,' whether it is local between Northern and Eastern Shan or it is national in Rangoon. If a tribe or community ignores politics at local and national levels, it will do so at its peril. We have to galvanize the resident Shan population for greater participation in local and national politics in Burma. You can help create grassroots organizations that will encourage participation and engage the resident Shan. To control their destiny, the Shan have to learn to engage in many ways."

After a couple of rounds of discussion, several of the senior leaders started agreeing with Aung's viewpoint with respect to their priorities. There was almost unanimous agreement. The deep insight on the Shan that Aung brought on the table was unusual. Aung had seen poverty and hunger from close quarters. Most of the current leaders had not lived the life that Aung had. Aung was not giving them a tactical solution to every problem faced by the Shan. He was trying to make them self-reliant; he was preaching that self-help is the best help.

None of the current crop of leaders had left a life of relative luxury and willingly chose to live the life of a commoner. None had taken on one of the most powerful armies of the time, just with the support of some untrained Kachins, fought, and won. In their lifetime, none of them had seen the death, destruction, and despair Aung Lung had seen. The respect for Aung Lung, his sacrifices, and his commitment to the Shan cause was palpable in the entire conference room in Washington, DC.

None of the admiration touched Aung on the inside because he did not consider his efforts a success or himself a role model for others. If anything, he felt more dejected, and a strange sense of hopelessness gripped him. Deep inside, he thought these folks were trying to solve a problem that most of them had only read about in books. They did not feel the problems in their bones. He liked them for staying committed to the cause, but the fact was that most of them had not lived the life of a Shan in Burma.

A couple of times, Aung almost asked himself, *"Who are these people? Why are they even talking about problems of the Shan without any real direct experience?"* A part of Aung felt that he had wasted his own life going after the Shan cause in his youth, but that was his life. Now, he was dragging others into that same struggle. He had no right to drag others into that quagmire. They probably had families to look after - sons and daughters to raise.

If they got involved a lot more, members of their families would suffer a lifetime of disappointments just like his family members had. Aung could not ask others to waste their lives.

Aung felt conflicting emotions, frustrated on one hand for not having confidence in the leadership around him and guilty on the other for expecting them to rise up for the cause. He was sure of only one thing: if any of them considered Aung Lung to be a role model, that person would have a lot of suffering. These days, whenever anyone appreciated his contribution toward emancipating the Shan, Aung felt sad, and he thought he did not deserve any praise at all because ultimately, he did not deliver. He felt like an imposter who was getting high praise in a different setting while his Shan folks were still living like destitute in their own Burma.

That conflict did not sit well with Aung. He often corrected members of the Shan leadership in exile when they attempted to praise him or his efforts. He constantly told them that he tried, but he had not been able to help much, so they should not praise him. Many could see his viewpoint; only a few could see his battle scars and the deep-seated agony for his tribe. Aung did not believe he deserved praise. One good thing he felt was the scale of the fundraising effort by this leadership team. Those funds collected in the US could do a lot of good among the poor Shan in Northern Burma. A small amount collected in the US went a long way in Northern Burma because of the exchange rates and the black markets. He himself contributed generously and made a passionate plea to others for US dollar contribution in due earnest.

In his own assessment, he had given his best, done everything he could, tried everything he knew; but in the end, his efforts did improve the lives of his beloved Shan people. When he got back to his room in the hotel that night, Aung called Win at work from Washington and described his experience like he used to do very often in Bangkok. He told him how he felt, how he reacted to the praise showered on him.

Win was a very smart and keen observer. Win had become his most intelligent sounding board for decades; he was uniquely qualified. It seemed Win was not at all surprised; he sounded like he was expecting it.

When Aung asked him about it, Win said, "Pho, let us talk about it after you get back home. It might be you who is living in a time capsule; you might have overreacted. Today's Burma is not the Burma you left in 1945; it has changed. The people and the issues are different."

Aung asked him, "How so, Kiddo? Please explain yourself."

Win said, "I promise, I will, Pho. It will take time. So, you and I will sit down with some Thai beer and talk about this for several hours after you get back to Texas; I have to brief you on a few topics. Please go to bed now."

Aung responded reluctantly, "Okay, I will go to bed. I have an early morning flight to catch for Austin anyway."

Preparations

After Jeff, Scott, and Kip returned from Nick's house on Saturday, they met for a debrief in Jeff's office. The first thing Kip said was that he needed to plan an extended stay in Los Angeles and needed to be mobile. Jeff called his administrative assistant and had her set up one of the boutique hotels on West Pico Boulevard for Kip. He also got her to rent a brand-new Volvo SUV with comprehensive insurance coverage for Kip that had no limits on the miles logged. Jeff said that the advantage of the boutique hotel was it was less crowded and more secure in terms of internet and wireless communication. This facility would make it easier to access secure servers in Jeff's department if needed.

Jeff also briefed his admin on the expense account Nick had set up so that bills could be sent to Nick directly, and this effort would not get bogged down by the department's approval process.

Once all that was out of the way, he turned to Kip and said, "Where do you want to start, Kip? I think talking to the staff should be pretty high on your priority, right? I want you to take the lead; I will do whatever you ask me to do. It's your show now - Scott and I will support you all the way."

Kip said, "I would like to get back to San Rafael for one night to pack my stuff along with some equipment I'll need. I will be back in LA on Sunday night, so it will be great if we can plan the chat with Nick's staff on Wednesday. Before that, I will do a bit of due diligence. I think we ought to plan one full day to cover everyone and everything. Some of Nick's people do not come every day, so perhaps Nick can let them know informally that he would like them to come on Wednesday without disclosing my planned presence to investigate the break in. On Monday and Tuesday, I will be in Los Angeles working on the case but more toward preparation and set up."

Jeff heard the whole thing and commented, "Sounds like an excellent idea to me. Since you want to get back to Bay Area tonight, I could have you dropped off at the airport."

Kip said, "That would be great."

In a few minutes, Kip booked himself on United from Los Angeles International Airport (LAX) to San Francisco International Airport (SFO) and informed Jeff that he would need to be dropped off in Los Angeles Airport in one hour. Jeff said he would ask someone from his team to drop him off; within minutes, Kip was on his way to LAX. The roads were not crowded, so he arrived quickly.

After he landed at San Francisco International Airport, Kip took a Lyft ride to Tim's home in Sausalito first. There he had a simple dinner with Tim and his wife. Kip had called earlier from Los Angeles Airport, so it was not a big problem for Tim's wife. Once dinner was done, Kip briefed Tim on what he had heard from Nick over a bottle of Napa Valley 2002 merlot.

Tim thought long and hard after Kip finished and said, "I think it is clear; someone from inside the Morita mansion had to be involved big time. So, to begin with, everyone inside that house has to be suspects. My guess is we will be able to rule out Nick, his mom, and probably his wife quickly. That will still leave us with the housekeeper, the cook, the security guard, the secretary, the gardener, and the regularly visiting physiotherapist recommended by the UCLA doctor.

"Any one of those six people could have the opportunity and the motive. Also, some of Nick's assertions about references have to be checked thoroughly - he might be assuming things. As you know, reference checks can be a can of worms; lots of unanswered questions get answered there. Primary, secondary, and tertiary references lead to a lot of issues. You remember that case we had in Cambodia last year!

"For example, he might have appointed the gardener based on a neighbor's recommendation who did not actually use the gardener's services. Basically, primary, secondary, and tertiary references, as you know - sometimes, those are the big holes. Again, in that list of six people, we might be able to rule out another one or two relatively quickly. Some members of the Morita staff have had continuity of service in the Morita household with integrity and no complaints.

"That data point will work in their favor, but longer duration of service could also result in easier access, so that will have to be carefully examined. But for this break in explaining the 'how' part could be the most important because the Morita household seems to be a tightly controlled environment. The roles are well defined, and the cameras are always watching. And people can change too; a good person can behave badly under duress or unexpected financial hardship.

"Pressing charges, conviction, etc. will be downstream activities expertly handled by Jeff and Scott. I do not think we should worry about that part of the operation. As you and I talked, they have the jurisdiction, knowledge, and expertise. Once we have figured it out, we should leave that part in their capable hands and exit; the timelines associated with those steps are long. ConSec cannot help in that area."

Tim paused for a second and started again, "But even after we are able to focus our energies on two or three people, it will be a challenge to establish the 'how.' From your description, this break-in appears to exceptionally well-planned and executed; no one person could have executed a perfect job like this break-in. It would have involved a lot of coordination. The more I think about it, the 'why' seems to be money. Money as the motivation makes sense; a couple of million is a lot. For some reason, the amount of money or the interest in the objects increased recently. We have to retrace steps and see if there was any such event that increased the value and drew attention from the wrong kinds of people. The effort for the break-in remains same, so if the fair market value increases suddenly, the thieves get a much better return. Nothing else makes sense at this point with the information we have."

Kip agreed with Tim's initial assessment almost entirely, except in one very important aspect. After Tim finished, Kip added, "I was thinking of outside help as well, Tim. When you think of two objects and their actual dimensions, those objects were large, and jade is heavy. It is not possible for any of our shortlisted six to simply walk out of the Morita mansion with those in their pockets or small laptop bags. Those large objects would require a fairly large duffle or roller bag.

"So, the perpetrators had to have external support and help on the outside to whisk the objects away after extraction. Not just that, if the break in was for some easy money, the perpetrators had to know the value of the two objects. After having gone through so much trouble to extract those from the safe, it is unlikely that they would be careless with the transportation aspect. They would have planned that part well. My guess is that part was well-planned, and that would mean more people and resources on the outside. I have a feeling that was where a 'look-alike' of John's old Acura Integra got involved, and the fear of exposure led to the swapping of number plates."

Tim looked at Kip and said, "Excellent point. We have got to figure out the 'how' part as soon as possible; a lot of things will be explained when we do that."

Kip told Tim that jade sits between 6 and 7 on the Mohs scale of hardness compared to 10 for diamond, so it is not as hard as diamond. But on the toughness scale, jade is rated higher. Jade is rated "exceptional" whereas diamond is rated "good." These thieves would not have worried about a minor fall - they would have known the material properties of jade. For objects made of jade, such events would not cause any scratches or real damage. That made the job easier for the thieves. They would have had more options for extraction and transportation.

Tim listened carefully and then asked, "Have you considered someone hiding the objects inside the mansion after taking those out of the safe? Maybe those were taken out of the safe but not taken out of the mansion as yet? I think that could be within the realm of possibility." Kip knew Tim was playing Mr. Devil here. That was their common practice; they used that technique to weed out noise from the compelling logic. Kip had thought really hard about that.

Kip was ready with a response, "I did consider that possibility in great detail, Tim. Like our legendary mentor in the army used to tell us, I tried putting myself in the shoes of the thief. If I were planning it, I would break the safe only when I had a sound extraction plan in place. Until then, I would leave the two objects inside the safe. Taking those out of the safe and hiding those in a suitable place inside the mansion is risky, and it delays the process of selling. The thief had payments to make!

"Also, please note that several weeks have gone by in the interim. So, even if hiding the objects inside the mansion was in the realm of possibility when the theft took place, it is probably not so anymore." Kip paused for a second and continued, "That is why on my way back on the flight from Los Angeles, after a great deal of thinking, I have ruled that possibility out for now. We may have to revisit this assumption later, but for now, I would like to assume that those objects were taken out. Depending on how other parts of this investigation unfold, we might have to reconsider that thought. If those are out, those could be brought up for public or private sale any moment.

"We have to do our very best to stop the thieves from selling the objects. They have had a head start, but if we can, we need to slow them down. If we succeed, they will get desperate and make mistakes. The good news is, these objects are not like liquid cash that you cannot trace. It is hard to sell these types of artifacts as it is; now, it should be even harder. I have also alerted Jeff and Scott that we might have to get permission to access the bank accounts of some of the potential suspects. All we need to know is if any of our preferred suspects have had large unexplained deposits." Kip paused. Tim was already nodding his head.

Tim agreed with the logic and said, "You said the Moritas have cameras everywhere and also on the boundary wall, so you should be able to review the footage for many days, right?"

Kip nodded and said, "I think so, and I hope the camera coverage is good with no dead zones." Kip continued," I was thinking of ways of finding out if these valuable objects have come up for sale. There should be ways to let potential buyers know that these are stolen, and the law enforcement folks are in the lookout."

Tim agreed, "If we are able to do that, we will buy ourselves some additional time for search and recovery. I see where your mind is going. Makes sense to me - that is our highest priority."

After that, they divided a few tasks between the two of them to be done on Monday and Tuesday toward preparation. Since Tim had other cases to work on during the day and Kip was likely to be on the road quite a bit in SoCal, they both agreed on a late evening daily call. Kip decided to take the late evening flight from San Francisco to LAX on Sunday. He packed light, but he made sure he had all the electronics and surveillance gear. He thought he would need those in Los Angeles. On arrival at the boutique hotel Jeff had set up for him, he realized that it was a very comfortable place with all the facilities he would need and much more. He left the hotel phone and fax numbers with Tim and also left a voicemail for him reminding him to call the major antique dealers in the East Coast, particularly in the New York metro area.

He went to the restaurant attached to the hotel, had a quick dinner, and went back to his suite. After he set up his laptop, he sent Jeff an email and informed him that he was back. He informed Scott via email as well.

Jeff called almost immediately. "Hey Kip, welcome back to the city of Angels. Your secure internet connection and new cell phone are both up and working already. Hope you like the hotel and the location. With this set up, you will be able to access some of the documents and files on our servers securely. Our IT guy has set up a secure VPN access for you so that you are good to go; I feel you might need that flexibility.

"If you want to check on our suspects or their finances or access public county records, those can be arranged as needed. You had said you will get some of your own electronics with you from Bay Area - hope you were able to do that."

Kip responded, "That is great, Jeff. And yes, I got the electronics I wanted. What about the false identity paperwork, business cards, and documents I had requested from you and Scott as an antique dealer or broker working with a private collector?"

"Scott is still working on that. He is talking to a big player in that space and setting you up as a senior consultant. It will look and feel totally legitimate, and the story will stand. He told me it will all get done by Tuesday."

Kip was happy with that update; it was critical to his plan to work quickly. Kip finally inquired, "What about the staff interviews on Wednesday in West Hollywood?"

Jeff responded, "Nick has arranged that as well. You have to be at his place at 10:00 a.m. You have Nick's email ID; please send him an email with a copy to me and Scott and explain how you would like to conduct the interviews. Nick has confirmation from everybody except the physiotherapist; he has a prior patient appointment. He will come only if he can reschedule that one. As you had asked, Nick has not disclosed your role to anyone as yet, but eventually, he will have to say something about who you are. Please explain that part in the email. Depending on what you recommend, Scott or I or both of us will join you - we are available."

Kip said, "Will certainly do, Jeff" and hung up. Kip looked at the number of people he would have to talk to at the Morita mansion on Wednesday and put them in three categories: red, yellow, and green. From his own perspective, interviewing people in category red was most critical to the investigation. He put Nick and his mom, Keiko Morita, in green. Nick's wife Emily, Emma the housekeeper, and Selma the cook went in category yellow. Finally, he put Martha, Nick's secretary; Jack, the physiotherapist; Jim, the security guard; and Carlos, the gardener in category red. Keeping people in color-coded bins helped structure his own thoughts. This was Kip's standard method.

In his email to Nick, he said that Martha, Jim, Jack, and Carlos would be the highest priority for face-to-face meetings at the mansion on Wednesday. After meeting with them, he would meet with Emily, Selma, and Emma; hopefully, they would not need more time with those ladies. He thought about having Jeff or Scott joining the meetings on Wednesday. After a great deal of contemplation, he decided to request both of them to come in for the interviews, if possible, in full uniform. In his investigative work, Kip had paid a lot of attention to psychology.

Kip's rationale was, if there was a connection to the break-in from inside the Morita mansion, seeing Scott or Jeff in uniform would imply that the good guys are on the lookout. And just that impression could make the perpetrators uncomfortable and slow them down. Kip explained the rationale in an email to Jeff and Scott. His intuition told him that he needed to buy time. He had to buy more time any way he could. Before going to bed, Kip sent out an email to Jeff and Scott and explained the context. He really thought that the optics of two uniforms at the Morita mansion would go a long way. He hoped that Scott and Jeff would agree with his viewpoint; there was indeed a small chance that it may not have any impact. *We will see*, Kip thought.

The next morning, Kip woke up at 7:00 a.m., a bit late by his standards. Since he was not going for a run, he decided to take a sneak peek at his email and saw that both Scott and Jeff had agreed with the suggestion, and they planned to be at the Morita mansion in full uniform at 10:00 a.m. Nick had also responded, stating that he agreed with Kip's idea of introducing himself as the insurance broker working with law enforcement to assist them in the search.

"That should work," he said.

Nick had sent the final confirmation that Jack would be there on Wednesday. With those two action items out of the way, Kip could focus on his preparatory tasks. He had a short list of boutique antique dealers in SoCal who specialized in South Asian artifacts; he would make sure he got in touch with those today. He finished all those calls in less time than he had allocated; these people were not very talkative. They listened to Kip with a lot of attention, particularly when Kip was describing the type of Asian artifacts his private client was looking for.

Nick had already provided the residence addresses of his staff. Kip took those addresses and marked those on a detailed map of the Greater Los Angeles area. Martha's address was in Culver City, Carlos had an address that was in El Segundo, and Jack lived in Inglewood. Jim the security guard lived a bit far off in Long Beach, so he marked that place for late afternoon. In Jack's case, there was a work address listed as well; that was the Ronald Reagan Medical Center of UCLA at the Westwood Plaza. Kip had planned to check out each of those places on Monday, so he got up to get ready. He did his mandatory 100 push-ups and three-minute planking and showered; after that, he went downstairs and had a wholesome breakfast at the restaurant in the hotel. He got started after that with the places to visit recorded in the car navigation screen.

Kip's first stop was to go to Culver City. Martha's place was a two-bedroom single family home facing the street. Kip had run the address in Zillow and established that the property was purchased in the last two years. The kitchen had been remodeled, and a den was added in 2019. Zillow showed that the property had gone down in valuation quite a bit. From Culver City, Kip went to El Segundo. Like the locals in Los Angeles, he avoided freeways, and it worked well. Carlos lived pretty close to the East Imperial Highway, but the multi-unit property faced Lomita Street. From the Spanish advertising all around, it seemed like a predominantly Hispanic neighborhood. From El Segundo, Kip decided to hop over to nearby Inglewood to check out Jack's address. Jack's address was on Magnolia Avenue not far from the Oak Street Elementary school. The building was pretty easy to locate; it seemed like a multi-tenant facility from outside. It was a quiet working-class neighborhood. Kip hung out for a bit to watch - nothing unusual.

It was a neighborhood with few home offices of plumbers, electricians, and landscapers. From the outside, the house seemed like a multipurpose dwelling with a warehouse-like entrance on the first floor. It did not look like a conventional office entrance. The second floor looked clearly residential from the outside, but Zillow listed the location as mixed use, and so did Redfin. Kip concluded that the first floor was probably used by a business, and the second floor might be used by the same business for housing its staff. It was all speculation, but that was all he had for the moment. He made a mental note to revisit that.

Kip's drive to Long Beach from Inglewood was harrowing to say the least; Highway 405 was clogged like a parking lot most of the time. It took him an hour and thirty-five minutes. Since the car was not moving much or moving less than five miles per hour while going and returning, Kip was able to make a few calls using the automatic phone hook-up. By the time he arrived near the destination in Long Beach, it was almost 4:00 p.m., so Kip decided to stop over at a Starbucks to get a sandwich and coffee. It was a blue-collar neighborhood - all busy folks.

After he finished his coffee, he went and checked out the property on Lime Avenue; it was a single-family home with a cast iron fence and an iron gate. Given the low height of the fence, it seemed more for decoration and less for safety. It was a mixed neighborhood that had some small shipping and logistics businesses, clearly connected to the port of Long Beach. With all the addresses validated, Kip made sure he took pictures of each place and tried to locate the nearest street camera that was visible. He'd email the list of street camera locations to Jeff.

"Who knows? That errant reddish 2002 Acura might show up in the vicinity of one of these houses, and the traffic cameras nearby might capture it," Kip murmured to himself. Kip had even more traffic on his way back; by the time he arrived at his hotel, it was seven in the evening. On the way back, two of the antique dealers he had left messages for returned his calls. Both said they had not seen objects like a marriage bowl and the Buddha in the market, but since Kip's wealthy client was so interested, they would be on the lookout and spread the word. Kip was amazed to see how well his hurriedly crafted cover story worked. Clearly, Scott had done a great job of building up the background!

Jeff and Scott were the ones who painstakingly built the case history, credentials, and the concocted stories to support the cover. Kip saw the efficacy of the cover when he made his morning calls. Kip's cover story was he was representing a Hollywood movie mogul who had heard those objects were in the market and he wanted to buy those at any price for his private collection in Palm Springs. He also demanded to keep it quiet because it is a private - not a public - collection.

He had also told the dealers that his client would compensate the dealers at higher than market rates, so their interest was palpable. Because of his unusually long drive back, Kip was able to call Tim and brief him on the specific addresses he checked out in LA and on the feedback from the dealers. Tim was not surprised; he had similar experience with the calls he had been able to make. Nobody seemed to be talking about the two objects they were looking for. Maybe they had not hit the market as yet.

Tim said, "Let us hope your interviews go well and we get a real lead. I called all the big and small antique dealers and asked them to spread the word. In addition, I also called our old US Army buddy who is currently with US Customs at LAX, just in case. I alerted him; he said he would be on the lookout too. He said it is unlikely that US Customs will get to see those objects. He said that smart thieves know many ways to avoid customs."

On Kip's checklist, he had one major action item that was pending for Tuesday. He had made a short list of insurance agents and companies that dealt with Asian artifacts. He went through that list and shared it with Tim via email. They decided to split that list and follow up; Kip's list had six names. Tim took the top three and said he'd call those, so that left three for Kip to call.

Tuesday morning, Kip woke up at his usual 5:00 a.m. and went for a run along the West Pico Boulevard. After he came back, he showered, finished breakfast, got ready, and called the Ronald Reagan Medical Center at UCLA. To his surprise, no one recognized Jack's name in the two separate physiotherapy teams. He then called Geriatrics because Nick had said his mom's doctor had recommended Jack, but even there, no one recognized his name. One of those two had to be Jack's contact!

They also said that doctors often recommended outside service providers who lived near their elderly patients, and that list would be available only with the doctors. Kip knew that he would have to go back to Dr. Marshall's team soon because in this case, they would be the ones who did the referral. Kip called after one hour, introduced himself as Mr. Morita, and requested to be connected to his mother's orthopaedic surgeon. This time, the office connected him to Dr. Marshall's nurse, and from her, he got the names of twelve individual physiotherapists. There were four companies that worked with Dr. Marshall's patients as outsourced contractors. One of the four companies on the list had the same address as Jack in Inglewood who provided physiotherapy services. That was probably the address of the company, Kip thought.

Since the Inglewood company's address matched Jack's address, Kip assumed that Jack could be employed by that company. When Kip visited the place on Monday, Kip had seen that company's name on the warehouse-like entrance. The usage of the upper floor was not clear. *But why would Jack's office address and residence address be the same?* Kip had wondered. *Did the company provide the residence to Jack? Was Jack trying to hide his actual residential address?* Those questions in Kip's mind were not answered at that point. Kip did not like the roundabout way because that meant Dr. Marshall actually referred the company, not the person. The actual person doing physiotherapy could have been easily replaced by the Inglewood company. He called Tim immediately and requested him to check on that company - Inglewood Physio Inc. Tim told him he would get on with it at the earliest and also activate his local resources in Los Angeles. Tim and Kip had a lot of contacts who did their odd jobs; these were very capable people.

Tim also told Kip that he had reached out to the Shan leadership in exile in Washington, DC, through his contacts. This was an example of the value that Kip, and Tim brought to the table in many of their investigations. Through their extensive network of global connections, they could connect the dots very quickly anywhere. In this particular case, a potential private buyer could come from Asia. If that happened, they wanted the Asian buyer ecosystem to know that the objects were stolen. The best way to do that was to inform folks of the same cultural background. Tim had informed that group to let him or Kip know if the two objects came up in any discussion - buying, selling or anything else. The Shan representative said that they would do so. Both Kip and Tim agreed that they had to stop the objects from hitting the buyer's market. If they could not stop the sale, they had to delay the process as much as possible. Unfortunately, time was not on their side.

Given the large number of rich private collectors in Asia these days, if the objects hit the market, they would disappear very quickly. Tracing those after purchase would be a lot harder. Kip was hoping to create a fear and uncertainty factor so that a sale could not be consummated. Tim's Shan contact had told him that it would not be difficult to trace those objects because those were quite unique. He also promised that he would spread the word widely within the exiled Burmese community. He did say to Tim that there might be Shan families from Northern Burma who received political asylum in the US who could know about those specific objects. He promised Tim that he would get him the phone number of a person who might be able to help. Kip knew that type of a list would not be very long. And they would genuinely try to help because of their ethnic background. They would not want those objects to fall in the wrong hands and become untraceable.

On Tuesday, Kip also had a series of calls with Jeff to make sure that he could have access to the tracking devices he had requested for three or four cars. While on the call, Jeff also updated him on the receipt of permission from cell phone companies for location data for a few of the cell phones Kip had alerted them on. Both of those options were backups for Kip; he had decided that he would use those only as a last resort. Scott had already got the process completed for Kip's new identification as a consultant attached to one of the top antique dealers; Kip would use that identity at Morita's. In addition, he had acted on Kip's request to get an IT security guy from his department who could set up a tracking mechanism for messages. One of Kip's requirements was that the tracking should not be detectable easily for a few weeks at the very least. He wanted to know if anybody was reading Nick's emails without Nick knowing about it. He also wanted to make sure that the perpetrator was not alerted before Kip was ready.

Staff interviews

Wednesday started bright and early. It was a clear, crisp summer morning in Los Angeles. As they had agreed on Tuesday, Kip met Jeff and Scott on the street outside the Morita mansion at 9:45 a.m. to go over the plan of action. They had agreed that the staff would be told that the two valuable artifacts had been stolen from the mansion. Nick was on board with the idea. All of them felt that a disclosure like that at the outset would lend legitimacy to the interviews. If there were any guilty parties, they would most probably react to that news, and that reaction was exactly what Kip wanted. Kip was an expert in reading body language.

When they went inside, they found that Nick's study was set up for the interviews. Nick was not planning to join as he had told them earlier. Emma, the housekeeper, greeted them and said that she would be the one who would look after them and fetch whoever they wanted to talk to. Jeff told her to give them half an hour to set up, get them some coffee, and then ask Nick's secretary Martha to join them. Emma nodded and went away. Scott and Kip quickly set up their laptops and a couple of video and audio devices. Kip had a couple of powerful hidden mic and camera combination pods set up that would feed directly into his MacBook Pro. By the time Emma brought them coffee and tea, they were all set up and ready to conduct the interviews.

Jeff said to Emma that she could inform Martha to come over on her way back. Emma nodded and indicated that she would get Martha. The conversation with Martha Wilson was businesslike. She was older than Kip had thought, probably in her early forties. She looked smart and confident. Martha confirmed that she had worked in the back office of various post-production companies before taking the part-time job with Nick Morita. The post-production work for two of Nick's movies were done by her previous company in Burbank; both movies were a great success. At that time, Martha had seen Nick a couple of times.

When Nick was looking for a part-time secretary cum admin about a year ago, the CEO of the company Martha worked for had recommended her to Nick. Martha confirmed the street address in Culver City as her home address; she said she lived with her husband. Her paternal aunt had lived nearby but had passed away. Martha said she had not known Nick personally earlier.

In response to Scott's question about her husband's profession, she replied, "He works in the film production industry." Scott's questions about relatives and siblings were also dealt with - all were short and cryptic answers. With respect to the question on the two objects that were stolen, she said she had no idea what those were, where they came from, or how they looked. Jeff apparently did not like the last part of her answer; his facial expression clearly showed that. Kip thought Jeff was doing it intentionally. It was like telegraphing "I hear you, but I do not believe you, and I want you to know that." Clearly, Martha had made a conscious decision to lie.

When Jeff described the two valuable Asian artifacts that had been stolen from Nick's safe, Martha's reaction was very professional. She said she was shocked to hear that and promised to help in any way she could. Jeff said he or Scott would reach out to her if they had additional questions. Martha agreed and on Jeff's request wrote down her cell phone number on Jeff's notebook. Kip could see that Jeff and Scott were highly skilled in this high art of talking to suspects. Both were controlled; it was really hard to assess what they were actually thinking unless they chose to signal it. Jeff also told her that if she planned to go out of Los Angeles, she should inform him or Scott.

She asked Jeff, "Am I a suspect, Detective Bloder?"

Jeff said, "Ms. Wilson, the investigation is in its early stages; at this time, we are making the same request to everyone, including the Morita family members. By that definition, everyone is a suspect, including some of the Moritas." Martha did not react to that answer, but her facial expression said an awful lot to Kip.

She clearly did not like that line of questioning and that well-rehearsed answer from Jeff Bloder. After Martha left, Jeff went out, located Emma, and requested her to send Jack in fifteen minutes. Once Jeff came back, all of them compared notes for a few minutes. Martha's reaction on hearing about the break-in had registered as "unusual" for all three of them. Jeff said he felt upset by the way Martha denied any knowledge of the two objects. Nick had told them it was she who filed the docket from the insurance company. That docket had a lot of valuable information on the two objects; that was why Jeff felt she was being arrogant, deliberately. Martha knew that they spoke with Nick.

Kip had to agree with Jeff's assessment. Scott felt she was showing an attitude. The way she asked Jeff if she was a "suspect" was also a bit unusual. "She did not seem surprised at all and was prepared" was the way Scott put it. Only Kip seemed to have picked up on two other bits of information; those were her street address in Culver City and her last name. He wanted to share those bits with Jeff and Scott. He was just about to elaborate on his observation when Jack walked in through the door, so Kip had to postpone that conversation for a different time.

Jack Slim looked younger than the age they had on file. He was dressed in smart casuals and seemed confident and engaging. Scott did most of the talking with Jack. He started out with how he got to know the Moritas. Jack stated that his company contracted physiotherapy services for Dr. Marshall at UCLA all over greater Los Angeles, and when Dr. Marshall's nurse made a request to the Inglewood company, he was assigned to this job to care for Mrs. Morita. Jack openly admitted that he had never been to UCLA Ronald Reagan Medical Center or met Dr. Marshall personally. He said he focused on his work and on his patients; his only goal was to make them feel better. If he achieved that goal, he thought he had done his duty. Who gave the assignment was not important to him. Kip detected an unnecessary defiance here.

Nothing to argue there, Kip thought. He made a mental note of that comment; he needed to talk to Nick on that specifically. According to Jack, Mrs. Morita was pleased with his work, so the contract was renewed after the first month, and he had been visiting her since then regularly. Kip had independently confirmed with Nick that Mrs. Morita's lower back pain and stiffness in the ankle joints were indeed a lot better since Jack had taken on the physiotherapy - he had to be good.

Jack also confirmed the place from where he had done his chiropractic and physiotherapy training. Jack said that he was working with this Inglewood company for eighteen months and lived in a studio apartment on the second floor of that same building in Inglewood. As the three of them had decided, Scott explained in great detail that the hidden safe in Mrs. Morita's room was broken into, and he also described how precisely the holes were drilled in the safe.

Jack paid a lot of attention to Scott's words. Scott also emphasized that the manufacturers of the safe had said that the thieves seemed to have worked on the safe for many hours. Jeff described in great detail how they thought the wall mounted safe in Mrs. Morita's room was accessed and the locking mechanism was destroyed. He deliberately pointed out that it was the room and the only room where Jack spent most of his time when he was in the mansion.

Other than a momentary flicker in his eyes, Kip did not seem to see any reaction from Jack. Once Scott finished, Jeff asked Jack, "Does Mr. Morita always receive massages in her room, or do you use the recliner in the patio as well?"

Jack thought for a second and responded, "Lately, she has been complaining about pain in her ankles; sometimes, we use the patio recliner. For her massages, she would be on the recliner, and I would sit on a small stool near her feet and work on her ankles and toes."

Kip and Jack both exchanged glances. "And typically, how long are your physiotherapy sessions, Jack?"

Jack replied, "Depends on how bad her arthritis pain is that day, but typically, one and a half to two hours, including all the exercises she does."

After that, Jeff repeated his request about letting him or Scott know if Jack had any reason to leave Los Angeles. Jack said he would. Jeff also made him write down his cell phone number. After Jack, they had to talk to the landscaper and gardener, Carlos Domingo. Carlos told them that he and two other friends were owners of the landscaping company Nick had engaged for the lawn, gardens, and the koi pond. Carlos came to the US from Tijuana twenty years ago and got his US green card five years ago and lived with his wife and son in El Segundo.

He said that location was very convenient traffic-wise. His wife was from Juarez in Mexico, but she spent her teen years in El Paso, Texas. She worked in the facilities management team in DirecTV in El Segundo. Her workplace was two miles from their home; that was why they decided to move to El Segundo from Pasadena several years ago. It was a great decision; she got to work in four minutes, and his son's school was close by as well. Carlos was clearly shocked to learn that a break-in took place and two very valuable objects were stolen; he said he had no idea.

He said that Mrs. Morita was a very good lady. He always bowed and said, "buenos días" to her in the mornings, and she always responded with a very warm "Ohayo gozaimasu," the Japanese "good morning." She wrote it down for him in English letters on a sticky note - that was how he knew how to say it. He did not work on Mrs.

Morita's garden other than blowing the leaves. Jeff went through his routine of taking the cell phone number and letting Carlos know that he should let him, or Scott know if he went out of Los Angeles. Carlos said he was not planning to travel anywhere this year, but he might go and see his ailing father in Tijuana, Mexico, next year. He would be happy to inform Jeff if he did travel. Carlos came across as a straightforward, hard-working person.

Carlos said he would like to help in any way he could. As he got up to go, Scott asked him what type of car he drove. Carlos gave him the make and model of his GMC truck and the trailer with his gardening gear. He also said that he parked it near the gate outside so that Jim could keep an eye on it while Carlos was inside working on the grounds. Carlos was familiar with the neighborhood because he also worked in the adjacent property of Mr. and Mrs. Baker; it was Mr. Baker who had recommended Carlos to Nick. He had known the Bakers for five years.

As soon as they finished with Carlos, Emma came in with a tray full of all kinds of sliders and coffee and other beverages. Nick followed her closely into the room and said, "The three of you were talking non-stop for three plus hours; I thought I'd request you to take a quick break and join us for a quick bite. Nothing fancy, just some sandwiches." He looked at Emma and pointed her to the coffee table in his study for the food; she duly obliged, put the tray on the table, and disappeared. Kip felt it was really very thoughtful of Nick to have planned it this way.

Jeff and Scott updated Nick on the interviews so far. Kip made sure he mentioned the fact that Jack was actually part of a company that did outsourced physiotherapy work for UCLA. Kip asked Nick if he knew of any financial strain faced by any of his staff, and Nick said he did not. He also said other than Selma or Emma, no one was really that close to the Morita family. Even if they had problems, they might not confide in the Moritas. Emma and Selma might discuss such topics with his wife Emily; they were close. After some contemplation, Nick said that even Jim might talk about such difficulties with him, but he could not be sure. Nick used to know Jim's father well for many years, so there could be a bit of personal connection there. Nick did not think Martha or Jack would.

Then, Kip had a very important question for Nick. He asked, "Nick, we would like to see how your workspace is organized and how your email system is set up. Jeff's IT guy will stop by later to talk to you about the email system and check if there was any intrusion."

Nick said, "Why don't you gentlemen come along with me? I will show you the workspace right now. It would take only a few minutes; it is on the same floor on the other side." They went along and saw that Nick's workspace was essentially two rooms; he sat in the bigger room inside, and Martha used the outer room. Nick's office had another door, but that was blocked with a shelf. There was a small balcony attached.

In order to access Nick's office, they had to walk through Martha's office. She looked up and smiled at them. Nick's office had his desk and racks with movie tapes on all sides on floor-to-ceiling racks. Nick also had several Emmys and other awards on display in a small glass case. Martha's office had a landline phone and printer cum fax; it also had several file cabinets. Nick's many awards were neatly arranged on one side. There was a rack-mounted computer server with routers and cable modems, and there were many wires dangling from the rack on one side.

After looking at everything, Kip asked, "Nick, do you keep your office door locked or is it kept open normally?"

"It is usually open," answered Nick.

"Are all your emails automatically copied to Martha, or do you send the emails to her only if you need her to work on something?"

Nick thought for a while and then replied, "I use two email accounts. From my movie company email account, all emails and attachments are copied to Martha by design. We do it that way because we have to pay our service providers on time, and those bills are emailed. That is the easiest way to run my operation from the home office. I see all her work emails as well because I am always copied by design.

"From my personal account, no email goes to her unless I decide to send it. On a need basis, if I want her to follow up on something, I might send emails to her selectively from my account. For example, after following up with two insurance companies for quotes for my household valuables, I might ask her to follow up on the third company on my behalf. In such a situation, I'd forward that particular mail trail from my personal email account to Martha. That way, she has the context and the contact information for subsequent follow-ups."

The implication of Nick's last statement was not lost on Kip. He had seen what he wanted to see and get a feel for. He said, "Thanks a lot, Nick; that clarifies. My understanding is a lot better now." Jeff and Kip exchanged meaningful glances as they went out. Scott also had his eyebrows raised and a serious look on his face. When they got back to Nick's study, Jim the security guard, was waiting for them. He said Emma had asked him to come, and he had come two minutes before them.

Jim was a very pleasant person, barely past his teens - probably in his early twenties. He looked even younger. He asked them how they were doing and if he could ask Emma for more coffee or tea for them. All of them said "no." Jim told them that he lived in Long Beach with two older brothers and his mother. Both his brothers worked in the Port of Long Beach. His late father used to work in the movie industry; he had known Nick for many years. He had passed away four years ago. Jim said he joined Morita's almost as soon as he joined evening college five years ago. Jim's father's past work with Nick was the connection; for his college timing, this job worked out perfectly.

Jim also said that he was hoping to join the movie industry after he finished college. He wanted to pursue a degree in art.

Jim was in total disbelief when he was told that a theft had taken place from inside Mrs. Morita's suite. He said Nick, Emily, and Nick's mom could be disappointed with him, but he had no clue. Jim said his father always told him that the Moritas are good people and he should not let them down, but that was how he felt about this break-in. He had not seen or heard anything unusual; he could not remember anything that was out of the ordinary. A few weeks ago, Nick had called him to his study and advised him to be extra vigilant and not to leave his post except for restroom breaks. Nick did not explain the background, and Jim had no reason to ask; he simply followed Nick's instructions.

Jim had been following that directive to the letter. He confirmed that lately, he had stopped coming inside the mansion for lunch. Emma got him a sandwich, or he ate whatever Selma cooked on a given day. Selma would also send a flask with hot coffee for him a couple of times a day.

If he needed more, he would call Selma on the intercom, and Emma or Selma would go over to his post and deliver it. The only time he left his post at the gate would be to relieve himself a couple times during the day. Ever since Nick spoke with him, Jim had been hyper alert. Even though Nick did not share the details with him, Jim had assumed that there must have been a reason. Jim was intrigued because this was the first time Nick had done something like that. Like Nick had, Jim did mention the work done by Southern California Edison on the day Mr. Morita was to travel to the East Coast. Jim gave a pretty detailed description of what happened; it matched Nick's description entirely.

He also explained why he remembered the details of the SoCal Edison repair work. "This is a very quiet neighborhood with a few large houses; that is why I remember that repair work. If this were our area in Long Beach, I would not have remembered because it happens all the time." After Jim left, Jeff requested Emma for more coffee. Scott suggested that the three of do a bit of debrief on the interviews so far.

After Emma brought a coffee tray and some cookies, Jeff was the one who spoke first. "Let us hear your take first, Kip. I saw you made copious notes on your tablet. You have been largely quiet as your cover required except for that little bit of conversation with Nick, which ended in a very suggestive note, if I may say so." Kip smiled at Jeff and Scott both; he was not surprised that they had both noticed.

Kip said, "I have to agree with you, Jeff. From what we have seen and heard so far, I am convinced beyond a reasonable doubt that someone from inside the mansion had to be involved. The only questions are who and how?" Kip paused and added, "Here is how I'd paint the picture. Martha would be at the very top of my list of 'persons of interest.' It is quite possible that Martha heard Nick's haggling with the insurance agent in all its gory detail. She had the agent's side of the story, so she knew that the value of those objects had doubled by the estimates of the insurance company. That information was credible; the insurance company did good research.

"Assuming money is the motive here, as my partner Tim believes, she then made a very elaborate plan to extract the objects from the safe for cash. In his hypothesis, we have to assume that Jack had to be her accomplice because he had uninterrupted access to the safe. From our interviews, we now know that Jack was not vetted the way Nick had thought; in fact, he was not vetted. I would start looking at those two suspects in some detail right away. In fact, of all the staff members, Jack is the real wild card. We also learned that he does use the patio for his massages regularly. I have checked the angle. If Mrs. Morita is on the recliner, she cannot see the safe from that position; the wall corner blocks the view. It is theoretically possible that Jack would have taken breaks from his massage and worked on the safe for many days. We have to explore that angle in detail and understand how he made time for it. He was a total professional, so no DNA evidence or fingerprints."

Kip paused for a bit and then continued, "So far so good, but there are a few problems with this hypothesis. The first problem is how did the objects get out of this mansion? The objects are big; if you want to transport both, you need a box or a bag. A large duffle bag or a cardboard box could do. As Jim confirmed, no one was seen carrying anything unusual outside. Martha comes to work with a small purse in hand, and Jack enters this mansion empty handed. If either of them carried a box, Jim would have noticed, and that would have been seen as 'unusual,' and he would have alerted the Moritas immediately.

"That was probably why Nick had asked him to be hyper vigilant. The thief had drilled holes on the steel door of the safe - we saw those holes. The drilling would have made noise and required a powerful hand drill and maybe a crowbar or a large screwdriver. How did those hand tools come onto the property and go out of the property unnoticed by the mounted cameras? All are points to ponder, I am afraid. I noticed that Jack was wearing a long white coat like the doctors do; that coat could provide the cover for bringing in the drilling tools and taking those out. The other challenge with this hypothesis is we have to establish that Martha and Jack were in it together or at least knew each other; a gut feeling won't do. So, we have a few holes."

When Kip finished, Jeff said, "Interesting hypothesis, I have to admit it makes a lot of sense, even though we all know that the theory has some holes in it. But since this is among the better theories we have right now, we can agree on a few next steps. We can keep an eye on Martha. We can do the same for Jack for a few days; we can also request permission from their financial institutions for disclosure of any windfall deposits or transfers. Some of the measures we discussed are less intrusive and therefore requires less formality; I think we should start with those at the earliest. The electronic surveillances you had planned - Kip, those can also start. Monitoring of the few traffic cameras you identified could start as well. I have received the list you sent me.

"For now, I'd like to include Carlos in our shortlist of suspects as well. When our IT person shows up later, I'll have him check on the intrusion of Nick's files and set up the tracking we discussed. He is very good and professional. With a simple setup like what Nick uses, expect him to get it all done in one afternoon, maybe just a couple of hours. He will report back to me as soon as he is done here. I would pass on his feedback to you both. If all goes as planned, expect a call from me later this evening. We need to know what went on here."

When Jeff finished and took the final sip of his coffee, Scott looked up and said, "I had a couple other points, Kip. How would you connect the reddish Acura Integra seen in this neighborhood with your theory? And then, why go all the way to Glendale from here to swap the number plates?

Kip responded, "I do not have a good answer to that question as yet, Scott. What I have for you is a possible answer. That car would have been part of the getaway strategy with the two objects inside. I have not figured out 'how' as of yet. The swapping of number plates in Glendale could be explained by convenience of proximity."

Scott asked, "What do you mean? Please elaborate a bit."

Kip answered, "Someone connected to this break-in probably lives or works near John's Glendale neighborhood and happened to see a similar car parked on the road for an extended period of time. This person probably observed the car for a day or two and figured out that the car is not driven frequently; it remains parked for extended periods of time. The fact that the Acura was not driven frequently was a huge advantage. The perpetrator expected to buy a few weeks' time by picking that particular Acura; that was an extremely smart thing to do.

"My decision to borrow the car from John to get back to Bay Area was a pure coincidence. If I had not borrowed the car from John, you probably would not have known about the swap because no one would have driven that Acura on I35. For another two or three weeks, our perpetrators could have been doing their planning and execution for Plan B or C."

Both Jeff and Scott nodded. Jeff commented, "I agree, that is a possibility. In the absence of a better theory, let us assume that and proceed. In order to make progress on a case like this, we have to pursue multiple avenues, and this is as good as any other avenue."

With that, Jeff got up and said, "I've got to get back to my office, so let us catch hold of Nick, update him on our progress, and brief him on the next steps. We can talk on the phone later in the evening or first thing tomorrow. At this stage, let us not reveal names to Nick because that might cause change in behavior toward his staff. Our IT person will call me tonight after he finishes here, so if we talk later, I will have his inputs as well."

After that, the three of them met up with Nick and updated him at a high level without mentioning Martha and Jack explicitly. Then, they left the Morita mansion. By the time Kip returned to his hotel, it was almost 6:00 p.m. He took a shower, freshened up, and had a long call with Tim. He briefed him on the hypothesis the three of them had.

He also explained the holes in the theory that they had seen themselves. Tim said he would think about it overnight and call the next day. Before Tim hung up, Kip asked him to activate ConSec's local contacts in Los Angeles for Martha and Jack, and he emphasized the urgency. *Putting a couple of private eyes on Martha and Jack would be a great idea*, he thought. Tim had used these contacts in the past for another case in Los Angeles; they proved to be very useful. These were locals that did a non-intrusive 'staying in touch' for a daily fee. Kip liked the euphemism Tim used to describe their work. Tim always considered them a valuable asset in their line of work. They all had other day jobs, so the service was relatively less expensive. Some of them were security guards during the night shift, some were retired from law enforcement, and most of these loosely organized guys would moonlight for a few hours for a fee. The business model was very similar to application-based drivers of Lyft. Tim loved their very low overhead operation.

Sometimes, formal permission for physical or electronic surveillance was long and cumbersome to obtain, so Tim preferred to depend on these types of resources. In many investigations, formal surveillance was not needed, or it was needed at a later stage for collection of evidence. For this investigation, for now, this was a great next step. These guys were smart; they knew how to do the job without breaking any laws and keeping a very low profile and disappearing into the woodwork when they were not needed. Tim had great experience with them in their past cases.

Kip had already run this by Jeff and Scott. Jeff said, "If you decided to do it as a private citizen, I could not stop you, since no laws are being broken; I cannot take your guys into custody."

Kip got the point and decided to invest in at least three or four days of "staying in touch." Tim agreed. For his working hypothesis, it was critical to establish that Martha and Jack were working together - at least, they knew each other to begin with. Kip had a few other requests for Jeff and Scott. He wanted them to do a thorough background check on Tracie Wilson in Culver City. She was the lady who owned the reddish Acura according to the DMV. Kip mentioned the strange coincidence of Martha having the same last name and living in the same city. Kip told them that there was a high chance that Tracie was a close relative of Martha's. If that was the case, they needed to validate that information and find out how the two were related; that could explain a few things.

Scott had not noticed it initially, but Jeff already had, so he had no hesitation in doing the background check. Kip told him, "I know you have told me that she is 'non-existent,' but somebody had to do the DMV paperwork in her name in the past. We need to know who that was, and if that person is connected to Martha. If she is truly non-existent, who drove her car? I have a feeling you might find that Tracie lived in the same street or very near Martha's house in Culver City. It is just a guess, but I am beginning to feel that I could be right."

Jeff gave him an intrigued look but did not say anything immediately, but he finally spoke, "Hope you are realizing one thing, Kip. Even if we can connect Martha to this break-in, we are a long way from formally charging her with anything. In order to do that, we have to show motive, we have to have evidence, and we would also need to show that she benefited from the break-in. We will need witnesses and will probably have to trace the stolen objects to build a case that will stand in a court of law. I am not saying you are wrong; actually, you may be right, but we are still a long way off. If we understand the challenge, then we will be better prepared and do the due diligence patiently. I am simple trying to deflate your enthusiasm a little bit so that you do not run too fast and stumble."

Scott nodded thoughtfully and said, "We are far from pressing charges as of now."

Kip saw the bigger point Jeff was making and understood that Jeff was simply cautioning him from jumping to conclusions. Assuming that the case could be prosecuted right away could endanger the investigation big time. Kip thought for a few seconds and told Jeff that he understood. He also emphasized that pressing charges would be entirely up to Jeff and Scott; that was not his area. Jeff's last comment changed Kip's attitude; instead of taking it negatively, he decided to take it as constructive input. He understood the context and the challenges they would face.

That meant they could potentially do the investigation in two parts; part one would deal with Nick's priority, which was finding the objects and returning those to the original Shan owners; part two would deal with prosecution. Jeff was essentially encouraging Kip to stay focused on part one; part two had many variables that were not under their control, and it mattered less to Nick. Part two would require Jeff and Scott to have extensive discussions with the district attorney's office and other parts of the law enforcement apparatus. Kip neither had the knowledge nor the time for resolving part two. Tim had also stated that categorically during their conversation last time. Tim did not want an extended involvement from their company's perspective.

Myitkyina revisited?

The Shan exiles meeting for 1989 was a disappointment for Aung. After he got back to Austin, Win spent a lot of time with him and explained to Aung why he was not surprised when Aung expressed his disappointment on the phone from Washington, DC. Win told him that in 1942, all the tribes in Burma were fighting for Burma's independence. There were two participants in that conflict, the outsiders (British or Japanese) and the Burmese. The tribal fissures were probably there at that time as well, but under the surface, they were not visible every day. Independence was the cause around which they united; all parties understood that was the highest priority for all. After independence, each tribe started fighting for its agenda, so there were many participants in that internal struggle. The Burmar, Mon, Karen, Kachin, and Shan tribes had overlapping interests in development, health care, security, mining, etc. They all wanted a share of the pie.

Aung and his scouts made a difference in fighting the Japanese, but now the Shan cause was one among many. Even within the Shan cause, Northern, Eastern Shan had slightly different priorities. Win thought Aung should not have expected them to be unified because in the eyes of the current leadership, there was no one cause to unify around. Aung was not sure he understood Win's logic entirely, but he accepted the explanation and decided not to take an active role in the affairs of the DC based Shan in exiles team as Myint had said. He did not have as much energy as he did before. In 1990, Win married his law school classmate Laura Matsumoto and started a private law firm in Austin called Lung, Matsumoto LLC. Win's marriage was a large gathering for the Lungs with their lifelong relationships with Jim, Mauricio, his brother, and extended family, and other connections through the two restaurants. Win and Laura's friends from the university and the law school and Laura's family from Chandler, Arizona joined in as well.

Things were going pretty well for the Lungs. Suddenly, a year after the marriage, Myint fell ill. Her chronic heart condition had been aggravated, and despite the best medical care, she passed away within six months. It was a shock for Aung and Win, and also for Laura; she got to be with her mother-in-law just for a few months. Aung was acutely depressed after Myint's passing. Jim came and spent a few days with Aung in Austin.

Before departing for Dallas, he called Win aside and told him, "Kiddo, since this house is so centrally located with so much space, why don't you and Laura move in with Aung? He will be thrilled. You guys can even have a home office here if you like. Aung is getting old; he does not have a whole lot of time left."

Win said, "Thank you, Uncle Jim. I will certainly talk to Laura and let you know." After Myint's passing, Aung withdrew from the outside world almost entirely and started focusing his energies on the restaurants and their hired staff.

Both businesses were doing really well, so Aung's operational involvement was less than before, but he still managed the bigger issues. The Shan group from Washington, DC, tried to reach out to him a couple of times, but he did not feel like participating because of his past disappointment. After checking with Win, he introduced Win to them and told the office bearers of the Shan exile group to call Win's office number if they wanted to reach him. By 1993, Win and Laura moved in with Aung and made the home look like it used to when Myint was there. Win loved to be surrounded by his mother's memories in her own house as she left it. Laura understood that, and because of that, she agreed with the suggestion to move. As Jim had predicted, Aung was thrilled to have Win and Laura around with him all the time.

He would get a lot of pleasure in getting Shan Austin deliver Laura's favorite food at their home several times a week. A memorable year for the Lungs was 1995. That year, Win and Laura welcomed their twins Andy and Becky. Aung was overjoyed when he saw the twins for the first time at the Seton Hospital where Laura had given birth. No one remembered how the next couple years passed in the Lung household because the babies were at the center of everything. Their grandfather was enjoying every minute of those moments with the babies; that was all he wanted to do. Aung's only regret was Myint did not get to see the grandchildren; she would have loved them. Aung thought he was truly blessed to be able to see his grandchildren.

In 2001, Tropical Storm Allison brought storm force winds and heavy rains to the Texas coast. Some parts of Texas like Houston recorded over thirty-five inches of rain and major flooding in many areas. Allison spawned over twenty tornadoes and caused over forty deaths in the state of Texas. When the storm hit the Texas coast, Jim happened to be in Galveston visiting some of the oil rig projects his company was working on. He and his team of engineers had to visit multiple locations in pouring rain, hurricane force wind gusts, poor road conditions, and poor visibility. Southern Texas got battered by Allison for several hours. Trees fell, cars were swept, and buildings got damaged.

On one of those late evening site visits and night-time drives back to the city, the driver of his SUV could not see a downed tree trunk on time and drove into it at a very high speed. The traffic cops would later discover that the tree had probably fallen minutes before the SUV came by. Later, when Aung heard about it from the traffic cops, he called it "destiny." The ensuing collision caused the SUV to tumble, and Jim and the driver were gravely injured. The news reached Aung and Win a day later, and they both drove down to

Dallas immediately. By then, Jim had been airlifted to the hospital in Dallas, and he was listed in critical condition.

Almost immediately after his arrival in the hospital, his doctors had to perform multiple surgeries. When Aung and Win arrived in the hospital, he was still in ICU and barely conscious. After many hours, when Aung and Win were allowed to see Jim, his speech was still slurred because of the heavy dose of sedatives.

He smiled at them and told Win, "Be well, Kiddo." Seeing Uncle Jim in that condition was particularly hard for Win; Jim was his rock, invincible. Win and Aung both lost all self-control and poise and wept uncontrollably in front of the ICU staff and several members of Jim's extended family. The hospital ICU staff probably understood the extent of their grief; they gave them as much time and space as possible. They were very understanding.

Aung was thinking, *If Myint were here, she would have wept just like us.* It was lucky for her she was not with them. Aung and Win waited in the hospital for Jim to recover, just for another opportunity to talk to him. Aung and Win did not get what they hoped. Despite all the prayers from Aung and Win, they did not get another opportunity to talk to Jim. Those three words, "Be well, Kiddo" were Jim's last words.

Aung kept telling the nurse that Jim was an extraordinary man, a great American hero who had fought in several wars and won. He should be able to recover; the medical staff must do everything. The nurse would listen to Aung's tearful monologue and nod silently. Win told the nurse that he was ready to give blood just in case there was a need. She agreed and tested Win's blood group just to be ready if a transfusion was needed. Father and son tried everything they could, all avenues they knew.

After twenty hours of waiting, the duty doctor came to the distraught father and son duo and spoke, "For his age, he was quite fit, but when you are over eighty, your body cannot cope with blunt force trauma the way it could when you were much younger. I am so sorry for your loss. I think I can see that he meant a lot to you." Aung almost collapsed; Win had to quickly grab him and steady him on his feet. Win himself was not doing all that great either.

The doctor also assured Aung and Win that they did everything they could, including getting Jim airlifted directly to the hospital. Aung was inconsolable. Jim's sudden passing away was extremely hard on Win. He was a grown man now; he understood the uncertainty of life. It was the suddenness that he found hard to accept. Jim had treated him like his own son from the time he was eleven or twelve years old. He was like a father to Win, maybe even more so than Aung's in some ways. Aung's obsession with the Shan cause made him inaccessible at times; Jim was there for Win always. From his teenage years, Win had always taken Uncle Jim for granted; it was so hard to change that habit.

Whenever Win needed a balanced view on anything, he went to Jim. From his Bangkok days, Jim was like a friend, philosopher, and guide for Win. Jim's absence made Win realize how important Jim was to him. Win had to take several days off to mourn and also to travel to Dallas for Jim's funeral. Win went through the next several days like a sleepwalker; he had no idea when the days started and when they ended. He kept thinking of so many unfinished conversations he had planned and needed to have with Uncle Jim. He missed Jim a lot. About a week later, Win drove down to Dallas for Jim's funeral service. After the funeral service in Jim's Episcopal Church in Plano, Win was walking to his car while wiping tears and clearing his blurry vision.

He suddenly felt a hand on his shoulder. Because of the tears, his vision was slightly blurred, but he recognized the man. It was Jim's personal attorney Tom; Win had met him a couple of times in the past. During his law school years, he had interned with Tom's law firm, so he knew Tom quite well. The frequency of their informal communication was less lately, but they knew each other really well. Win realized that Tom had something very important to say.

Tom asked Win to stop for a moment, came closer, and said, "I need a moment with you, Win." They both then walked to Tom's car, his driver opened the door, and after they sat down in the rear, he gave them both two bottles of drinking water.

They both drank some water and then Tom spoke, "This might come to you as a complete surprise, Win, but you ought to know that in his will, Jim has left all his company shares and a substantial number of other holdings in your name. As a result of the ownership of the majority of the company shares, you will automatically get Jim's board seat. You will also get an executive position till you decide to retire or pass it on to someone of your choosing. I will need your signature on this paperwork right away."

Win was speechless; he knew Jim had never married and had no children of his own, but he had half a dozen nephews and nieces. He also had a dozen cousins in the extended family in and around Dallas. He was totally at a loss to utter a single word.

He gave a stunned look to Tom and stammered, "But why me, Tom?"

Tom answered quickly, "Only Jim knew the complete answer to that question, Win. But if it makes you feel any better, I did ask him when he had me draft that will several years ago. His answer to me was, 'My wealth and my company's future will both be better off in Win's hands than in those of the members of my family or my extended family.'

"As his friend for thirty-five years all the way from the university, I had asked him to think about it for a day. He came back to my office the very next day in the morning and said, 'Are you happy now, Tom? Nothing changed; you have only delayed the process by one full day - we just lost time.' His mind was made up, Win."

Tom paused and then continued, "Obviously, you meant a great deal to him, Win." Win did not know what to say. His eyes were tearing up again; he wiped tears from his eyes one more time and signed the paperwork Tom had taken out from a folder. After signing the papers, Win returned the bunch of papers and the folder to Tom. Tom said he would be in touch for the quarterly board meeting dates and a few other formal procedures.

Win's voice was choking up; he could barely speak. He said bye to Tom and ran to his car for the drive back. Win's mind was in turmoil; he had no idea that Uncle Jim would do such a thing. When Win got back to Austin, he told Aung and Laura about Jim's will. They were both in a state of shock after they heard the story that Win had heard from Tom in Plano. Aung and Win sat together and wept all over again for a very long time.

After a long pause, Aung said, "In the Theravada Buddhist tradition practiced by the Shan, we believe in reincarnation. In some past life, somewhere, in a different place and time, Jim would have been my own older sibling from a different mother. I felt that way ever since I met him for the first time on the banks of a stream in Burma."

Aung's grief was palpable; for him, the world had suddenly become very empty. A part of him did not want to be in this world anymore. After Jim's passing, it took a while for life to return to normal. Win and Laura's kids were the main reason why the Lungs had to get back to normal life; both kids were in school by then, and there were a host of other activities around them. Both Andy and Becky were very active kids. That kept Aung occupied most of the time because he loved teaching them, helping them with their homework, and doing their errands. They also did a "celebration of life" event for Jim in Shan Austin that was very well attended. Win invited members of Jim's extended family and all the key executives from Jim's company. He had to start working with them on a regular basis from then on.

Lung, Matsumoto LLC. was doing good work as a law firm, but its international work was not very visible to the world. In 2002, Win and Laura decided to improve their international credentials, and as part of that plan, Win joined the US State Department as an attorney for Asian affairs in 2004. Win's Asian background and fluency in Burmese and Japanese helped. The idea was to work in the State Department for a few years and gain experience with the UN and International Criminal Court. That sort of exposure was necessary for their law firm to differentiate itself from others in the field. He and Laura were consciously trying to develop that capacity and networking in Lung, Matsumoto LLC.

International affairs, human rights issues, and building relationships at the UN and International Trade Commission were their areas of focus. As part of the State Department, Win's work required him to be in Washington, DC, frequently. He negotiated a special deal with his bosses and set up a small office in DC, but it was agreed that he would mostly operate from Austin. He did not want to be away from Aung, Laura, and the kids for too long, but he was ready to travel to DC if needed. Because of the long hours Win was putting in, it became manageable.

Win was spending more time on State Department work by 2006 and 2007. The timing was just right; the president was from Texas, and there were a lot of advisers around him who were from Austin and UT. It was pretty easy for Win to find friends, classmates, and contemporaries in DC that he could depend on. In 2007, Win got involved in several high-profile international negotiations and meetings for the State Department; he contributed positively in all of those. He visited South Korea multiple times and did a lot of due diligence on the discussion with North Korea in early 2007. That effort and the other initiatives by the State Department eventually culminated in North Korea's agreeing to shut down its main nuclear facility. It was a new beginning.

Toward the end of 2007, he also contributed a lot in the United Nations and brokered an independent investigation of Pakistan's Prime Minister's assassination, though ultimately, he did not join the UN investigative team led by a Chilean diplomat. Win worked in several other hot spots at that time; much of the work he did was not visible to the outside world. By 2011, it was becoming clear in the State Department that the US president could visit Burma (called Myanmar by then) sometime soon. It could be the very next year during a major regional conference in Cambodia. Burma's military rulers were desperate to show to the world that they were just like any other democratically elected government. It seemed the US administration was also willing to entertain their overtures just to make a new start.

Given that political dynamic, the State Department decided to send a team of officials to check out the place before the presidential visit in November 2012. Win Lung was selected to be part of that delegation because of his background and his knowledge of Burmese and Shan. When Win mentioned the travel plan to Aung, he was ecstatic. Aung made a long list of people and places for Win to meet and visit. Aung told Win to definitely visit his Shan State and Myitkyina in Kachin State; Aung specifically asked Win to visit the church in Myitkyina.

Win and the US delegation flew to Rangoon (called Yangon now) and spent a day in the city. They decided to pay a visit to the university, where the US president might be requested to address the Burmese people. When the others were inside the auditorium, checking its security, vantage points, exit routes, communication towers, etc., Win asked the driver to take him around a bit in the vicinity. Win saw some of the students and faculty; the students were very curious. He remembered this was the place where Aung had met Myint for the first time in 1958. After that short visit, they drove 200 miles north to the new capital Naypyidaw. The Burmese government was very keen to show off its new state-of-the art capital; Win was not sure of the purpose. After the official discussions were concluded, Win took a few days off on a personal visit. He drove for four hours by car to Heho in Taunggyi District in Shan State to catch his flight to Myitkyina.

He reached Myitkyina after almost four hours of flying; domestic flights within Burma were not crowded. When he landed at the airport, he took a deep breath and tried smelling the air. He tried to visualize his father and Uncle Jim fighting the Japanese through incessant shelling to reach the outer perimeter of the runways. He tried to imagine a young and wounded Uncle Jim receiving his medal from General Stilwell at the airport. This was a homecoming visit for Win.

He could almost visualize the tired and emaciated faces of his father and Uncle Jim in his mind. He also tried to picture how his father and Uncle Jim parted ways when a cargo plane flew Uncle Jim and his wounded comrades to an Indian base hospital from here. Win felt he was rewinding a film and watching it again and again in his mind. Win never got tired of that movie. This visit was like a pilgrimage for Win. He was standing on the same scorched earth that two brave men he admired most fought for and almost died for. His contact in the local government had booked him in a hotel near the Myitkyina University; the hotel was nothing fancy but quite spacious, nice and clean.

The Irrawaddy River wove through the city like a loop and was visible from the hotel. The river views were even better from the rooms in the upper floor. As he was taking numerous pictures of the river and the people, Win realized that he was at his place of birth. This was where he was born when the city rose up from the wartime destruction. He decided to rent a car with a driver for a couple of days and visit a few of the places Aung and Myint used to talk about. For the next two days, Win visited many different places in Myitkyina, particularly those he had heard about from Jim, Aung, and Myint.

He tried to locate the hospital near Geis Memorial Church where he was born; there was a hospital in that neighborhood just a couple of blocks northwest from the church, but he was not sure if that was the same hospital. Win made an attempt but could not locate anyone who knew what happened in that neighborhood in 1960. Based on Aung's description, he tried to locate the place where they lived as a family, but that place seemed to have a Hindu temple of ISKCON now. Win could not be sure if that was the exact place, though. He stopped over at a few other places described by Uncle Jim for great food, but the descriptions did not match the businesses in present day Myitkyina.

His last stop was at the Geis Memorial Church on Munkhrain Road. That particular place was at the top of his own and Aung's list. The church looked just like the way Aung described it; the sheds in the back were still there, bigger and better. The Kachin Baptist Convention now had a big compound next to the church; it was the global headquarters of the convention. Win got out of his car and entered the church. He was wondering if he could have a short meeting with the Father, and just as the thought crossed his mind, an elderly man in local dress walked by.

He stopped after a few paces, turned, and asked in English, "Can I help you, my son?"

Win said, "Yes, Father, you probably can. My father and his Kachin scouts stayed in a shed behind this church around 1947. He asked me to come and visit the church and hoped that the church and its congregation are well. My father speaks highly of this church."

The Father looked at Win, smiled, and said, "That is very generous of your father. He was probably here during the time of one my predecessors; I don't know which one yet, but I can try to find out. Your father will be pleased to know that this church and its congregation are doing really well. As part of the Kachin Baptist Convention (KBC), we have grown quite a lot. From its headquarters here in Myitkyina, KBC now manages 300 Churches and 15 associations with over 400 ordained ministers. In a couple of years, we are planning to have our local chapters in the United States."

Win said, "That is a very impressive accomplishment, Father. My father will be indeed pleased. Do you have anything from that time in the church?"

The Father thought quickly and said, "We do have a few things I can show you; please follow me, my son." The Father started walking toward a small room in the rear that looked like his office.

Once there, he pulled out one dusty box file and started going through the contents; after a few minutes, he showed a few grainy black and white photographs from mid-1940s. Most were taken inside the church compound. In one of those, a Father in a robe was standing next to three men in traditional Burmese dress. Win recognized the taller man in a split second; there were two other men with him. All were in traditional Burmese dress worn by villagers, and they seemed very happy. He pointed to the picture and said, "That's my dad. Wow, I never knew he looked like that in his youth."

The Father looked at the picture one more time carefully, wore his reading glasses, and then added, "Exactly as I had thought. He was here with one of my well-known predecessors. After I came to the church, I was told that your father and those two Kachin men rebuilt the roof of that shed and all the shelves still in use inside the shed. It is used as a large storage space now. Let us walk over there and see their handiwork that has survived a lifetime. We still use what they built; please thank your father on my behalf and that of the church. Also let him know that one of those Kachin men with him in the picture joined the Baptist church later and became one of our ministers. After the war, that Kachin scout studied Theology in a KBC managed college."

Win said he would certainly pass on the message. Before leaving the Father's office, Win took a picture of the grainy black and white photo and its description from the box file. After that, they went to the shed and saw the roof and the shelves all around. The large shelves were now used for storing supplies of the church and religious literature of the Kachin Baptist Convention; those were stacked on those shelves in vertical piles. Aung and his men had probably worked non-stop for many weeks to build those large heavy-duty shelves. The Father said that Aung and his Kachin scouts had helped in other church activities as well.

Win asked him why he thought so. The Father said, "Now that I know exactly which predecessor of mine spent time with your father, I remember reading about several other programs that started for the Kachins and Shan during his tenure in the church."

Win asked, "Like what, Father?"

"The church had launched multiple educational campaigns and vocational schools for the Kachins and the Shan. After your father's Kachin scout became a minister of the KBC, he continued the educational programs and started several new ones. Today, the KBC runs several major schools that teach Theology at the college level to train its own ministers." Before they parted ways, Win gave his contact information to the Father both in Austin and in DC. He also asked the Father to connect him up with the various KBC chapters in the US.

Win also took his email and social media information so that he could stay in touch. The Father gave him a comprehensive list of KBC chapters in the US and requested Win to get in touch after he returned to the US. The Father promised to do more research on the programs that Aung started and to send a detailed email to Win so that he could inform Aung in the US. Win took an early morning flight out of Myitkyina the next day. In his mind, he had a whole new appreciation for his father's passion for the Shan cause. He realized that his father had started living for others pretty early in his youth. The journey his parents had to go through from this nondescript city in Northern Burma to the capital of Texas in the US was just mind blowing.

He realized that a lot of things could have gone sideways for them as a family during that transition. His father guided the whole transition through very turbulent waters like an expert seaman, making the right calls for him and his mother. He was indeed lucky to have had friends like Uncle Chiang and Uncle Jim. But then, they must have seen something special in his father to have helped him so much. Both of them treated Aung like a brother, and so did Aung. Uncle Jim had told him what drew him to Aung. It was his unusual humanity.

Uncle Jim had said that the deeper reason for Aung's passion for the Shan cause was driven by that same humanity. Win took Uncle Jim's observation seriously. As he grew older, he also realized that Aung lived for something larger than himself all his life. The Shan and the hill tribes were deprived of their humanity by the British first, then the Japanese, so Aung fought for it. Later, it was the Tatmadaw and its officers, so Aung kept fighting; he couldn't stop. His appreciation for Reverend Geis and the Kachin Baptists could also be explained the same way. Aung was not a particularly religious person. He was drawn to Kachin Baptists because of their humanity - not because they were Christians; he would have liked them as much if they were Buddhists. Religion had little to do with his liking for Kachin Baptists.

Win had asked Aung about his religious belief once, when he was in UT. Aung had responded with a question of his own, "Why are you asking about religion, Kiddo?" Win had just completed his undergrad at UT Austin at that time, so he already had more formal education than Aung. He wanted to feel secure with a religious identity that others could relate to and understood. He thought they needed that as a family as well; a part of him felt that Aung had not thought about it. America knew diversity; people were used to different of cultures and religion, but they needed to understand clearly where they belonged.

In Win's world of UT, he had already seen a lot of diversity, and he knew people were generally tolerant. But even that diversity and tolerance had its limits. So, Win had responded to Aung, saying it is necessary to align with Theravada Buddhism or Christianity, but probably not both. If it was either, people could relate to them easily. If it was both, people would not understand, and they would not be able to relate to them.

Aung had responded again with a question, "Why is that, Kiddo? Why do you need a stamp on your forehead that states your religion? Why would you feel comfortable if your forehead had 'Christianity' or 'Buddhism' written on it? Will it make you happier? Is it for you or for those others in the society who want to box you?" This time, Win realized that Aung was trying to teach him something profound. So, he did what he used to do from his talk sessions in the Bangkok days. He just remained completely quiet. He knew if he remained quiet, Aung would feel compelled to clarify. That strategy had worked for Win in the past, and it had worked again. Then, Aung talked. He talked and talked nonstop for over two hours, passionately. Aung started with a famous story of the Kachin Baptists. According to the story, the first Baptist missionary arrived in Burma from the West way back. Upon arrival, he asked the then Burmese king for his permission to preach the message of the gospel among the Kachins. The king was dismayed; he told the Baptist missionary that the Kachins were unsophisticated animists. It would be easier for the Baptist missionaries to preach to his dog instead of the Kachins. To Aung, that story was not a joke; it was an example of how devoid of humanity the ruling class was. Not just Burma, that was true in many places.

To him, it was the story of a monarch who felt very entitled to judge, but not compelled to do his duty. After the story, Aung asked Win, "Kiddo, would it have mattered if that king was a Buddhist or a Hindu? To me, it would not. Societies and political classes are a bit like that Burmese king in the story. Both often focus on form over substance. They would like me to, but I do not want to write who I am on my forehead. If I tell them who I am, it is easier for them to deal with me, to stereotype me, to place me in a box - they know. That is not for me. It has nothing to do with me; it is for them. That is why I refuse to conform and box myself for them. I would not like to be stereotyped. I want the world to judge me by my deeds, not by my words or tall claims. I think the main purpose of religion is to provide its followers with a moral compass. If the compass is missing, what is the use of putting a stamp on my forehead? I would have no use for it.

"At their core, every religion in the world teaches you to be a good and compassionate human being. If you can commit to be that, you can be of any religion."

Win was blown away by the way Aung articulated his perspective on life and religion. He saw the role Uncle Jim played in his father's life and his in a whole new light as well. Uncle Jim had a very similar view of the world and life; it was eerily similar to that of his father. Both did not judge people easily. If they ever did judge, it was based on deeds, never talk. They judged the Japanese in WWII in that way by the deeds of the Japanese Imperial Army. Like Aung had said, Jim and he must have been siblings in their past lives.

As the plane took off, he thought he should be eternally grateful for the life he had. After he got back to Washington, DC, he reached out to the Shan organization in exile that Aung had been in touch with. Win told the Shan organization that he would try to help their cause as much as he could. He also encouraged them to reach out if they needed any legal counsel or advice from the State Department. He thought he could educate them on the focus of the US government and the State Department so that they could align themselves better and benefit. Major parts of the US government goals matched those of the Shan leadership in exile; they just had to articulate and map those better.

The Shan leadership appreciated Win's gesture very much and said that they would stay in touch. Win remembered Aung's favorite quote from his childhood days in Bangkok. Aung heard it from his grandfather; in Shan, it was said differently, but the closest English translation would sound like "The flame must not be extinguished." His father had a lifetime commitment to this cause; Win made the same commitment.

No leads, dead end?

Kip, Jeff, and Scott were back at the Morita mansion of Friday. They still had to talk to Nick, his wife Emily, Nick's mother Mrs. Morita, Emma, and Selma. Just like Wednesday, they started early. As they had agreed, they started with Mrs. Morita. There were two reasons for that. One, she was an early riser, and two, they did not want to keep her waiting, upsetting her daily routine. She was in her nineties; that was why Nick had made that specific request. Kip met Jeff and Scott on the street outside of the Morita mansion twenty minutes early to go over the plan of action. They had agreed that the nature of the discussion would be a bit different on Friday. With Nick, Emily, and Mrs. Morita, the focus should be on what they saw or heard or noticed. With Emma and Selma, they would have to focus on their personal background as well.

On Kip's advice, Jeff had called Nick and briefed him on their theory that Jack had unfettered access to the safe for extended periods of time. When they went to Mrs. Morita's room, she was already up and drinking her morning tea, sitting on a tatami. Nick was with them; he explained the purpose of their visit to her in Japanese; she listened to Nick for a few minutes and nodded her head.

After that, she looked up and asked them slowly in English, "How can I help you gentlemen?"

Jeff started by asking her about her daily routine and then shifted the conversation to her physiotherapy sessions with Jack. Mrs. Morita said, "I spend most of my time inside this room. Around 6:00 a.m., I go outside on the patio to do Usui Reiki and then feed the fish in the koi pond and water my Bonsai in the garden. By 7:30 a.m., I am inside. Unless I have a physiotherapy session on the patio, I do not step out till the evening. Sometimes, the patio gets pretty hot in the afternoon because of the sun. Usually, I do a bit of haiku reading on this tatami every day.

"I eat my lunch and dinner in this room. I step out for another hour late in the evening to do yoga."

"What about your physiotherapy days?" asked Jeff.

"On those days around 10:00 or 10:30 a.m., Jack gives me a massage in this room on the recliner. After the massage, he typically asks me to do a few stretch exercises for about twenty minutes. Lately, my ankles are giving me a lot of trouble, so he would often massage my ankles on the patio and then have me do ankle and leg exercises fifteen minutes for each ankle and leg - in total, about thirty minutes."

Jeff had a couple of other questions for Mrs. Morita. "Did you hear any unusual sounds during your massage sessions in the last couple of months? Also, did you ever see Jack carry any machine or drilling equipment?"

She responded, "No, I did not; my hearing is not very good, and Jack always had a background music playing during the massage sessions and the exercises that follow. He says it helps in concentration." After a pause, she added, "I do not think I saw or heard anything unusual except one day several weeks ago. We were in this room that day; suddenly, all lights went out and Jack's music stopped. After that, he continued massaging only for a little bit and left before I did my exercises. That was very unusual for Jack because he never left early; he always comes on time and leaves after about two full hours.

"I told Jack that there was enough natural light so if he wanted, he could continue. Jack seemed a bit unsettled. It was as though the rhythm was gone; he decided to resume in the next session, which he did. Jack has a good hand; my ankles are a lot better after the massage and the exercise sessions I had with him. Afterward, when Selma came with my lunch, I asked her, and she said that the electricity people were making repairs in the road outside, and that is why they had to cut power. If I remember right, the lights were back in a couple of hours."

After she finished, Kip looked around and noticed that her recliner was facing outside; it was a pretty heavy piece of furniture. If Mrs. Morita was reclining and doing her exercises facing outside and concentrating on her feet with music blaring, she would not be able to see what Jack was up to toward the head of the recliner. Each massaging session could give uninterrupted access to the safe toward her head for thirty minutes easily, maybe a bit more. Uninterrupted, quality time with the safe.

As they left Mrs. Morita's room, Nick commented, "I can see the plausibility of your theory, Kimura San. I think Mom helped us nail down the timeline."

Kip and Scott nodded. Jeff spoke, "Nick, right now, it is just a theory; we have to do more work to prove it. There could be some gaps in our understanding." Scott nodded in agreement as well.

Jeff continued, "Kip has uncovered a few other avenues we have to explore; I want to set your expectations right. It is not going to be easy for us to establish a rock-solid case easily."

Nick said, "I understand."

Nick went back to his office, and the three of them met Selma in the breakfast nook at the kitchen. Based on Jeff's phone call on Thursday, Nick had informed Selma and Emma of the break-in. When Scott asked her about it again, she said she said she had no idea that the Moritas had such valuable objects in the house. She also said she was shocked because everyone in this house was so nice. Selma also said that the Moritas treated all of them like extended family, so any member of the staff getting involved in the break-in was unthinkable to her. Selma said she was originally from Riverside; she had been with the Moritas for more than five years. Every day, she came at about 7:30 a.m. and left by 2:00 p.m. after lunch. She prepared breakfast and then lunch and dinner for the household; she managed the kitchen during most of the day.

Her first task was to make tea and breakfast for Mrs. Morita; she was also responsible for taking her lunch to her room. She and Emma typically ate lunch together around 1:00 p.m. The evening meal setup was done by Emma, who lived in the mansion with the Moritas. In the evening, Selma worked at a restaurant in Riverside; on Scott's request, she gave him the phone number and the address of that restaurant. She said that the owner was her cousin. Like others, she was also asked to write down her cell phone number and home address in Jeff's notebook.

They asked Selma to send Emma to Nick's study in fifteen minutes and left the kitchen. The conversation with Emma followed a similar pattern except that she lived in the mansion; her room was right next to Mrs. Morita's. She said she was originally from Bogota, Colombia, but she had lived in the US for nearly twenty years since her husband passed away. Once every three or four years, she went to Bogota to see her few remaining relatives; she considered the Moritas her real family. She said both she and Selma were very attached to Emily. Emma said she was in disbelief when Nick told her about the break-in. Emma could not understand; the involvement of an insider was unfathomable to her.

Scott asked her if she suspected anyone, and Emma said she had no clue. When Jeff asked about hearing or seeing anything unusual in the recent past, Emma said she could not recall any incident that stood out. She said that the house was a quiet place. Emma had a clear recollection of the electric utility repair Mrs. Morita had mentioned. She said a man in Southern California Edison uniform and hard hat came over with Jim, the security guard. It was around 10:30 a.m. Emma opened the door and after seeing them standing there, she went and fetched Emily. Emily spoke with the person from

SoCal Edison, and he explained everything. He said that they had to replace a cable segment.

The man said they would have to shut down the power for three hours to replace the faulty section. He also said once the faults were repaired, they would turn the power on, and he would come by again around 1:30 p.m. and check if everything was working all right in the house. Emily told him that was fine, and the man left. He came back a few minutes before 1:30 p.m. and told them that the power was back on. He waited till Emma went inside, flipped a few light switches, and confirmed that the power was indeed back. Emma also remembered that Mr. Morita was traveling that day, and a black car came in through the gate as Emily was talking to the man. Mr. Morita left in that car for the airport. After Emma was done, Jeff told Emma to request Emily to come over. Emma said that Emily was on a call, but she would let her know.

Before leaving, she asked if the men needed tea or coffee. All three of them said "yes," and she left with a nod. Emma came back with coffee and tea after some time. After she left, Kip told Jeff and Scott that he had already called SoCal Edison and checked on the power line repair, and it was all legitimate. It was in their record, and they had informed Nick three weeks in advance in his personal email account. Nick sent them an acknowledgement like other homeowners on the street did. They even gave Nick the name of their supervisor who conducted the repair and spoke with Emily Morita.

Jeff said, "I had not checked, but I thought it would be totally legitimate because the utility companies have to be careful. It is now clear that something happened that day; we just do not know what." Kip also told Jeff and Scott that he had spent a few hours with Jeff's IT person reviewing camera footage for the front entrance and on the boundary walls. Luckily, Nick had mounted the camera pods in such a way that there were no dead spots.

Kip had looked at the footage of the mansion for several weeks. There was no evidence of anything coming in or going out other than the front gate. He had also carefully reviewed Jack's arrival and departure; he was always empty handed. The footage had shown Martha coming downstairs with two bags on the day of Nick's travel and the limousine driver putting the bags in the trunk. The footage showed Nick coming downstairs after several minutes of that and boarding the limo for Los Angeles Airport. The SoCal Edison person and Emily were talking near the front door as Nick left. Emma stood next to Emily watching.

Emily Morita walked into the study a few minutes after Kip finished. Luckily, Scott, Jeff, and Kip had not started talking again. Jeff requested her to sit down and asked her the similar set of questions. Emily said she was trained as an artist and painter, and from that background, she decided to go into art restoration. Most of what she did was in restoration of very old paintings. She said it was painstaking work that required a lot of patience and attention to detail in each case.

Emily got most of her commissions through references from three well-known art galleries and half a dozen museums in the country. Once in a while, she got exclusive repair requests from private collectors. But those were not often. She also told them that she and Nick had met in college and married four years later. Her parents originally came to the United States from Naha, Okinawa. They were settled in Sacramento now. Emily and her sister were born and raised in Folsom, near Sacramento because her father worked in a semiconductor company in Folsom. She confirmed that her elder sister lived in the Los Angeles area who stayed with her when Nick traveled as he did recently. Her sister was a registered nurse. Emily made that request to her sister these days because of Mrs. Morita's fragile health, just in case she needed medical help.

Emily did not remember seeing or hearing anything unusual; she corroborated Emma's story entirely about the electric utility repair work. Emily said they treated all their staff like extended family. Even though she personally interacted more with Emma and Selma, she knew that Nick was as sensitive to the staff, maybe more. Once hired, they trusted the staff completely. She felt quite let down when she was told by Nick that someone from inside the mansion could be involved in the break-in. Jeff nodded and said he understood her disappointment. Emily also corroborated the process described by Jim about delivering her FedEx and UPS shipments. Her art restoration-related shipments were always couriered. The description matched.

According to Emily, Jim was very prompt with those things. Emily seemed upset about the breach of trust and continued. "Ours is a reasonably organized household with people we trust so we know who comes in or goes out. Each person has a well-defined role," she said finally before getting up. This was unfortunate. She clearly felt that her home was violated. Both Jeff and Scott nodded because they had noticed the warm relationship the Moritas had with the staff - they clearly cared.

All three of them agreed with her that this was no chance occurrence; this was a deliberate breach of trust, and the perpetrators should be held accountable. After they spoke with Emily, Nick joined them in the study. He said, "Emily is very upset about this whole affair."

Scott commented, "I cannot blame her; she should be upset. We'll do our best, Nick." Jeff briefed Nick and said that they had to pursue multiple new avenues for the investigation now to determine who from the inside could have the motive and the means to assist Jack, assuming Jack was man who had extracted the objects from the safe.

Nick nodded. Like Emily, he looked disappointed, but even with that feeling, he stated that getting objects back was the priority. Before Nick left, Jeff asked him, "Nick, could you email the contact details of the limousine company you used that took you to the airport? I would also need a copy of the invoice you received for Jack's physiotherapy services. One other important thing. For a few weeks, please use the laptop my IT guy gave you and use only your personal email account. We have secured your personal account; we would know if any breach is attempted. We are not anticipating any new intrusion; just be careful. In many of these cases, vigilance is the best policy for safety."

Nick said he understood, and he would email the requested documents. After Nick left, they continued their review of the case in Nick's study for some more time. Jeff reminded Kip that his gut feeling that Jack was part of the execution team might be correct, but that did not mean that they could prosecute. They were not there yet.

Scott was quiet for some time, and he suddenly said, "How did Jack even know that the objects were in that room in a safe? That knowledge was in limited circulation in this household."

Jeff looked at Scott and said, "I agree. That is one of the first things we have to establish. I have another gut feeling: the day the SoCal Edison repair work happened had to be an important day. I do not know the why, though. I am also sensing that the objects might not be sold as of yet - something didn't quite work out. There are no large deposits in the bank accounts of the key people; there are absolutely no confirmations from the antique seller and buyer networks that we activated. In fact, most are confirming that the objects never even came up for discussion."

After Jeff finished, Kip added, "Tim has established contacts with the Shans in exile group in Washington, DC. They have been alerted; they have promised to put us in touch with one Shan family that might have a direct connection to these objects. I will try to talk to this family over this coming weekend. If they know these objects could come up for sale, they would be alert. If we are able to locate the objects, this particular family could potentially help us authenticate the provenance and actual ownership in Burma. I am really hoping that we would be able to connect some dots."

Jeff and Scott both agreed. Scott also informed them that the Tracie Wilson background check had been started, and the progress was rather slow; so far, nothing incriminating had come out. They parted ways from the Morita mansion, fully realizing that they needed a real breakthrough. They had a plausible and good theory but not much else. At this point, there was no direct evidence linking anyone to the theft.

Now, they were effectively at a dead end. Kip drove back to his hotel, hoping that they would get a breakthrough soon. He had told Nick that he might visit the mansion on Sunday morning just to look around a bit. Nick said that was fine. Kip drove back to his hotel rather dejected. He took a shower, had a coffee, and then called Tim. Tim said his Shan contact had called and informed him that one particular Shan family in the US should know a lot about those objects based on the timelines. The caller gave Tim the phone number of a law firm in Washington, DC, and Austin, Texas, and said that the law firm would help; the managing partner of the firm was from a Shan Chaofa family.

Kip made a note of the name and the phone number. Tim also said that he had engaged his local boys to stay in touch with Jack and Martha for a week starting Thursday. So, Kip could get a call from the team-leader Rodrigo as soon as they have anything significant. Tim had also done some background checking on the Inglewood company Jack worked for. While there was nothing incriminating, the record was not spotless, and there were a few stains. There were several complaints against them for not following through on reference checking.

Kip forwarded Tim's email and his observations to Jeff and Scott for further follow-up. While on his email, he noticed that Nick had already emailed the invoice with the contact details of the limousine company that transported him to the airport. Kip sent that to Tim with a request for some research on the company and if possible, the specific driver that had dropped off Nick. There were a dozen emails from various antique dealers and insurance agents who confirmed that none of them had heard about those objects in a few months and that they would call him if anything like those objects came up. All the callers were keen to assist the private collector from Palm Springs that Kip was representing. That consistent feedback got Kip thinking very hard.

Not just that - no one even talked about those objects being in the market for sale in the recent past. One agent Kip had contacted reported that he researched and found that no sale of those two objects had been reported in Europe or Asia during the past few months. *That would cover a pretty large swath of the global market,* Kip thought. Kip was trying to label those two objects "stolen" in the visible and in the invisible marketplace for these types of ancient artifacts.

Those messages established that the objects were not yet available in the known marketplace, and that could still leave private collectors. But even private collectors were careful these days; once an artifact was labeled "stolen," its market would shrink dramatically. Private collectors also wanted to show off, albeit to their private audiences. The "stolen" label made that kind of private showing off risky because the owner could become a target for blackmailing quite easily. That was a reassuring thought for Kip because that might mean he had a bit more time than he had originally thought. Kip closed his laptop, switched off his phone for the evening, and went to bed, hoping to get sleep. Until he actually slept, he kept thinking about all those messages - what was the implicit message?

By then, he and Tim had received the same feedback from many different sources. The implication suddenly hit him. Those messages could potentially mean that the objects had not left the mansion! They might not be available for sale yet - there could be only one reason for that. Those were still hidden in the Morita mansion, somewhere out of the ordinary, but those were still there. Something had happened, and the objects could not be taken out as per the original plan. That was it!

He decided to call Tim first thing in the morning and run the hypothesis by him. He recalled that Tim had asked him to keep an open mind about the objects still being in the property during their dinner in Sausalito. Maybe the time had come to consider that option very seriously and do due diligence. Once that scenario started playing in his mind, Kip felt less dejected and drifted off to a very restful sleep.

Shan connection

After Win's 2011 trip to Burma, he had a series of conversations with his father. The more they talked about Burma, the more depressed Aung felt; sometimes, he would just get up and go away. There was nothing Win could do about it. Modern day Burma was actually a bottomless pit of despair for Aung's beloved Shan and Kachins. He could not insult his father by sugar-coating it. He remembered the numerous sacrifices his parents had made during his childhood; the Shan cause was their family's passion. Often, he and his mother were critical of Aung's obsession, but Aung never wavered. Now, Win understood that Aung lived with the pain of their disapproval, even though he never showed that pain or complained about it. It did hurt him inside.

It was not easy for him, but he did it anyway for his beloved Shans and Kachins - a small price for him. Win had a number of conversations on KBC and his visit to the church in Myitkyina with Aung. Aung was really pleased to learn that the church and its congregation were both doing so well. Aung told Win that he liked the church and KBC for their humanity toward the Shan, Kachin, and Lisu. Their approach was one of inclusion. They did not judge the hill tribes of Northern Burma with their Western values; instead, they joined the community.

He was even more thrilled to learn that one of his scouts became a minister; he was not entirely surprised, though. That scout's uncle and aunt had already converted to Christianity when he was with Aung. So that family knew the message of the gospel. Also, in multiple conversations with Aung, that scout had told him that he would consider joining the Kachin Baptist Church after the war if he survived. The war meant uncertainty; nobody could make any long-term plans.

Aung also told Win that Reverend Geis preached to the Kachin and Shan with the mindset of an anthropologist, which is what he was by training. He studied their societies, their customs, and their festivals and tried to relate to those - he did not judge. His preaching made sense to the hill tribes; that was why they were drawn to the church. The Reverend had a calling, he went after that calling with all his passion. He was discouraged by others all the time, but he never hesitated.

That was why the KBC had a lot of credibility as an independent voice among the hill tribes; they may not have had the guns, but the Tatmadaw was afraid of them. Win thought to himself later, that was what Aung was all about as well. He had a calling, and he responded to it in his youth with everything he had, leaving very little for himself and his family. He did not chase material success or possessions; what he built and earned were all because of his hard work and circumstances. Not just his father, and his mother's brother - even Uncle Jim shed blood in Northern Burma for the poor but proud people of the hills. That one cause unified all of them. Win could not let all that suffering go waste.

Outwardly, it seemed like a wasteful effort that had no impact on the lives of the tribes. The idea that all those selfless acts would come to naught did not sit well with Win. At one level, he was very sad to see that his father's lifelong pursuit of the Shan cause was futile. At another level, he was a lot more determined to do something about it. He knew; was, after all, one individual with limited resources, but he reminded himself that it took a small spark to ignite a whole forest. Who knows? There could be other like-minded people who wanted to make a difference. Win had a long conversation with Laura and made a commitment to explore a couple of different ways. Win remained engaged with the Shan exile group as a legal advisor in DC all along.

To the extent he could, he helped them with legal counsel. Sometimes, he would also educate the leadership on how to pitch its cause to the US government. Win knew that for many ethnic groups in Burma, the situation on the ground was getting worse. The coordinator for the US Campaign for Burma (USCB) said so herself. She spoke after a petition signed by about 5,000 Burmese refugees was handed to the US Special Envoy, urging him to influence the Burmese government to stop committing human rights violations by the Burmese Army in particular. That influencing should not be very hard.

The refugees said they were particularly concerned that insufficient attention was being paid to developments in ethnic states. They argued that widespread human rights abuses were still occurring in those states, often committed by the Burmese troops. The special envoy assured the group that he would broach the issues raised by the refugees with Burmese authorities during his next trip to Burma. Organizations like Human Rights Watch reported that renewed fighting in Burma's northern Kachin State had increased in intensity and that some 75,000 ethnic Kachins had been displaced. It also reported that the army burned villages, tortured civilians, and pillaged properties without any due process whenever they felt like it, at will.

Many of the ethnic armed groups fighting Burma's military were also committing atrocities, though their abuses had not been as well-documented as those of the Burmese Army. Through the many meetings Win had with UNHCR, Human Rights Watch, International Red Cross, Doctors without Borders, etc., he realized the complexity of the Burmese problem. He remembered what he had told Aung about the meeting in DC. There was no unifying theme. Today's independent Burma had become a quagmire. That realization of not being able to make an impact and the resulting desperation rang true even now.

The Shan cause was one among many problems in the morass that was modern day Burma. In any case, he told the Shan and Burmese leadership team in DC, "If you all think I can help in any way, please do not hesitate to reach out to me; you have my contact information in both DC and Austin. You are closer to the ground, so you can lead this." The leadership readily agreed to lead the process on the ground.

"I do not think it is practical for my father to get involved because of his age and his current health condition, but I would try my best to help. On my own, I am also going to explore if I can build a coalition of like-minded Burmese people that could help."

The leader of the group had said to Win, "Mr. Lung, you are a second-generation Shan, so you could have looked the other way. Many other asylum-seeking families have done so after arriving. You are a Lung, so you could not have done that. The poor tribes of Northern Burma will always remember that about the Lung bloodline." It was just a statement, but it meant a lot to Win. When he mentioned it to Aung in Austin, he wept, but those were tears of hope. He thought Win would be able to actually help the Shan; perhaps Win would finish what his father Aung Lung could not.

With his age, Aung was getting more and more emotional about the fact that he could not do much about the problems faced by the Shan in today's Burma. When Win considered the problem dispassionately, even he was at a loss. The tribes of Northern Burma seemed to have no political will to fight for their cause. They seemed to be in a vegetative state politically - no engagement at a national level and no interest whatsoever. Win decided to leave the State Department in 2018. He had stayed much longer than he and Laura had originally planned, but the decision to leave in 2018 was because of Aung's health. Aung was almost 95, and his doctors had just detected an early onset of Alzheimer's disease. Win needed to be close to look after him; he could not spend time in Washington, DC, anymore. With Andy and Becky both at UT Austin, Laura could not manage home and work all by herself. The growth of their law firm and Win's involvement in Jim's company in addition to the State Department was taking its toll on the Lung family.

Win had already arranged for a home healthcare professional to assist Aung during the day, but even then, routine things were becoming tough for Aung. By the end of 2018, Win was operating from Austin entirely. Aung loved seeing more of Win in Austin. In addition to Win, he also had Becky because she attended UT from home. Andy was spending more time in Dallas with multiple assignments in Jim's company. Win's plan was to train Andy in multiple business units so that when he actually joined that company, he could hit the ground running. Andy loved the work, and people loved him.

Win still maintained a small presence in Washington, DC, for long-time clients who were connected to the federal government. Lung and Matsumoto had grown as a law firm way beyond Win's wildest imagination; with that growth and the strategic directions of Uncle Jim's company, Win was really busy. Despite his busy schedule, Win always made time for Aung and his family. Andy was in UT studying mechanical engineering with an emphasis in robotics, and Becky was a music major with an emphasis in opera. Both of them were pretty independent, but when they had a choice, both opted to be day scholars at UT, Austin. That gave them the flexibility to operate from home.

Their home was less than half hour's drive from the UT campus anyway, so logistically, it was not difficult. That decision gave them more time to spend with Aung. Aung was thrilled to see more of his grandchildren than he had ever hoped. Andy had to drive down to Dallas often. As his disease progressed, Aung was forgetting many things; his mobility was compromised quite a bit, but his eyes lit up whenever he saw Andy or Becky. Sometimes on weekends, Becky would sing and play her violin for the family. Those were Aung's happiest moments; Win could see that on his face. On some days, Aung would ask Win about the latest from Burma, and Win would update him at a high level, skipping the gory details. Unfortunately, most news items from Burma were not good, and Win did not want Aung to agonize over those. Win could not tell Aung that the Burmese Army was still committing atrocities and human rights violation at will; no one was willing to hold them accountable. The intent was lacking.

He did not have the heart to tell Aung how the jade and rubies that belonged to the tribes were being sold - mostly in the black market, enriching the army generals and the joint venture companies they had formed with the Chinese across the border. In one of the English newspapers, he had read that one Burmese general and his family were planning to purchase a football club in the UK. That club in the English Premier League would have been purchased through a shell company. If the news had not leaked in the Western newspapers, the deal would have gone through for sure. Win was shocked by the audacity of the corrupt generals; the corruption continued with impunity. Clearly, the corrupt generals of Tatmadaw were pocketing most of the money that belonged to the Burmese people. Win knew that none of them were particularly apologetic about it. Their ostentatious lifestyle was Burma's open secret in print and digital media. Everybody knew, but nobody could do anything about it. Those who attempted were promptly put away using the security forces.

In the meanwhile, the restaurants owned by the Lungs were doing very well. Win had brought them under a holding company run by him and Laura so that down the line, the management could consider franchisee operations. Mauricio and the other members of the local teams Aung and Myint had hired were still running the operations; they had had become the best in the business. Shan

Austin in particular was regularly featured as one of the best ethnic restaurants in the state of Texas. Some of the best culinary schools in Texas sent their trainees to Shan Austin for advanced training. Win wished that his mother was alive to see the success of her two restaurants; she built each one with such care. Each time he read a new review of Shan Austin, he would remember how Myint had painstakingly put the whole restaurant together, including the ethnic Shan decorations imported from Chiang Mai in Thailand. He remembered those events.

A lot of credit for the success of the two restaurants went to Mauricio, his brother, and the other staff they hired. They had near zero attrition among employees. He vividly remembered the day when Myint salvaged the inauguration day plans by getting ethnic decorations from the Indian store in Austin. The two other people who knew that story were Uncle Jim and Aung; Aung's memory was fading, and Uncle Jim was no more. Win missed Uncle Jim a lot. Win tried to remain cheerful, but sometimes these thoughts became overwhelming. Luckily, he had Laura and the kids around him. Thanks to the success enjoyed by the two restaurants and the law firm's booming international law practice, the Lungs were financially very well off.

The shares Win had in Jim's company had quadrupled in value; as a permanent member of that company's board, Win was also entitled for other forms of compensation. Win remembered Jim's words to Tom, his attorney. Jim had said that the company and Jim's wealth would do better in Win's hands. Win ran the company with that commitment to its shareholders and its employees as if Uncle Jim were watching him from above and as if he would tell him, "You are doing a great job, Kiddo. I am proud of my favorite Kiddo." Uncle Jim's approval was all he wanted; he was grooming Andy to carry Uncle Jim's vision forward.

Under Win's direction, Jim's company had expanded its services to the renewable energy sector in addition to its traditional focus on oil. Their business from wind, solar, and wave energy did so well that the company had to open satellite offices in Corpus Christi and Galveston. Since Andy was studying mechanical engineering, Win had him do multiple summer internships in different divisions at Jim's company to understand its core value proposition. Andy was doing really well.

Andy was very excited about the potential of wind and wave energy, the two *Ws*, as he put it. Both of those renewable sources had good future in the geography of south Texas. The company had already secured permission for its new wind farm in the Gulf of Mexico. Andy was leading a team that was exploring whether the substructure being built for the wind turbines could be used for mounting wave energy collectors. If that could be done in a commercially viable manner, it would be ground-breaking. Win was excited too. At the current rate of growth, Win expected the company's valuation to at least double during the next year. Andy was already contributing a lot. He was young, but he had already earned the respect of the team; they liked his dedication and work ethic.

The US energy market had transformed itself in the last few years; from a net importer, the US became a global exporter of energy. Jim's company was benefiting a lot from that market shift. The strategic direction Win had set for the company would make it independent of oil-related engineering services in less than five years. With a more diversified energy engineering services portfolio, the company should be all set for growth for many decades. If things went as Win had planned, Andy could be a part of the leadership team in that company in a few short years. On Win's watch, things were going really well. If Jim could see it, he would be pleased with the progress that was visible in many areas.

On the whole, the financial situation of the Lung family had undergone a complete transformation within Aung's lifetime. They came as penniless asylum seekers, and now they were among the wealthy in their neighborhood. None of it touched Win at his core; he had not forgotten how they started and their journey from the refugee camps of Chiang Mai to the relative luxury of Austin. With the financial resources he had at his disposal, he was constantly thinking about a few projects for the Northern Shan State. There was no shortage of the areas. During the initial discussions, Win realized that he would be expected to go through the Shan State government and its bureaucracy for most of his Shan projects; he did not like that at all.

Once that became clear, Win decided that he could get that liaison done by the Shan leadership in exile team in Washington, DC, as long as he supervised it at a high level. Win was also in touch with the Kachin Baptist Convention (KBC) and the Father he met in Geis Memorial Church in Myitkyina. Through those connections, he was aware of the new chapters of the KBC opening up in various cities in the US. To Win's surprise, the KBC was becoming an important voice for tracking religious freedom in Burma. Its moral leadership was feared.

He liked the fact that there was a credible non-government organization he could lean on. Aung loved the KBC, and the KBC had a lot of respect and tremendous affection for Aung; Win thought he would leverage that mutual goodwill for some of his Shan projects. In addition, the KBC was at least trying to hold the Burmese Army accountable for its other atrocities. Win was proud of the two pastors who testified at the State Department's inquiry in 2019. It was reported that the pastors could be arrested on their return; ultimately, that did not happen because of the international pressure and the direct involvement of the United Nations. One of the pastors spoke to reporters in the US, describing harsh treatment during his sixteen-month stay in a Burmese prison. The Burmese government attempted to silence him but could not.

His main offense was he had been helping journalists document military attacks on civilian targets, including the bombing of a functioning church. The other pastor, KBC President Rev. Dr. H. Samson, met the US President at the White House in 2019. His visit was part of a larger delegation that met with the president. He told the US president that ethnic groups in Burma were being oppressed and tortured by the Burmese military government at will. Rev. Samson thanked the president for imposing sanctions on four Burmese Army generals. That news spread in Burma like wildfire.

One Burmese Army officer heard about the meeting and went to court. His lawsuit sought to have Rev. Samson prosecuted for his comments about the military during that conversation with the president of the United States of America in Washington. Rev. Samson returned to the city of Myitkyina after his White House visit; he was waiting for the verdict of the Burmese court. The KBC had strong international connections; as a result, the UN and other international organizations applied a lot of pressure on Burma for the safety of the pastors. Without those timely interventions and the international outcry, the Tatmadaw would have detained those two men of peace.

To Win, these were small but significant signs of progress. If the KBC was becoming the voice of dissent in Burma above all else, that was okay. As Win's great grandfather's ancient Shan saying went, "the flame must not be extinguished." Win knew that recently, a United Nations-mandated fact-finding mission found that the Burmese military abuses committed in Kachin, Rakhine, and Shan States were thought to be serious crimes under international law. Because of his extensive experience, Win was consulted by the government from time to time. Win thought it about time the corruption in Burma was exposed. That UN mission called for senior military officials, including Commander-in-Chief Sr. Gen. Min Aung Hlaing, to face investigation and prosecution for genocide, crimes against humanity, and war crimes. Win had no doubt that the Tatmadaw would face its reckoning at some point very soon. He knew that the United Nations and the International Court were both watching and building up evidence files.

The ruling National League for Democracy (NLD) under its leader Aung San Suu Kyi was accused of stifling dissent using a slew of repressive laws. Aung San Suu Kyi came under a lot of criticism from many governments and NGOs, even the UNHCR because of her alignment with military dictatorship of Burma. When she was under house arrest in Rangoon, the world saw her as a victim. When she and her party the NLD won elections and became the majority party, her international sympathizers had high hopes. In addition to the Nobel Peace Prize, she received numerous awards and recognition from dozens of countries and organizations. A lot of people, including Win, thought that her inclusion in the government could be a turning point. The repressive regime in Burma would start changing for the better. That viewpoint changed completely within a very short timeframe. It was she who changed rather quickly - way beyond people's imagination.

With the NLD doing almost nothing to address the country's lawlessness, the common people had very little hope. The hill tribes were among the worst sufferers because of their self-inflicted isolation mindset. From the outside, it seemed like the NLD would do what the Tatmadaw wanted done. To the surprise of most observers, the 2008 constitution of Burma placed the Ministries of Defense, Home Affairs, and Border Affairs under the control of the military. Win thought that was like boldly announcing their intent to rule by force, not by law. Win was personally aware of the fact that the international community was trying very hard to hold the

Burmese Army accountable on the issue of Rohingya. Those efforts had not made a difference locally yet.

Because of the involvement of Bangladesh and the UN, the Rohingya issue had the most international visibility. More than fourteen thousand Rohingya fled to Bangladesh between January and November 2018 to escape ongoing persecution and violence. Within the territory of Bangladesh, the voices of the refugees could not be stifled; the Burmese government would have liked to, but they had no control. Bangladesh made sure that the Rohingya issue and the plight of the refugees remained front and center, but the situation on the ground remained bad. Win was reading a lot of stories about the atrocities the Rohingya faced even in the US media; that subject was covered widely.

The new refugees joined one million other refugees from 2017 and previous years in precarious, overcrowded camps in Cox's Bazar area of Chittagong in southern Bangladesh. The estimated half a million Rohingya still in Rakhine State remained in extreme danger. The Burmese government always blamed the violence on the armed insurgencies that mushroomed among the Rohingya population. It was their fault - the Burmese Army only responded to potential threats. On its own, it never participated in aggression against the Rohingya. That official version was not acceptable to any serious observer of Burma.

Refugees who arrived in Bangladesh in 2018 reported continuing abuses by the Burmese Army. Sexual violence and abductions of women and girls in villages and at checkpoints along the route to Bangladesh continued unabated. Those refugees who returned faced arrest and torture on arrival by authorities. Many refugees did not make it alive; it was state sponsored terror. Many of the Shan folks now formed part of the internally displaced peoples in their own state since being removed from their own lands by the Tatmadaw in 2000. There were over half a million of these internally displaced peoples of many ethnicities living in Burma. Most of these people had food insecurity to start with; now, the situation was getting worse. Many were trying to escape forced labor in the Tatmadaw; some were trying to escape the many government supported drug cartels. That type of displacement had increased both human rights violations as well as the exploitation of minority ethnic groups at the hands of the dominant majority. That was expected.

With these power structures within the country at regional levels, lasting peace and development was hard. In many cases, crossing the Thai border and going to Thailand was the only sensible option for many poor families. The primary actors in these ethnic struggles included the corrupt Tatmadaw, the Karen National Union, and the Mong Tai Army. The military did give up some of its power in 2011, leading to the creation of a new system, even though significant influence of the military remained under the 2008 constitution. None of the elections could be considered open or fair, so no one knew the will of the people. The poor people had learned to suffer in silence.

Given that backdrop, Win knew he would not get any support or help from the establishment in Burma for any of his projects for the Shan. For the establishment in Burma, the Shan problem did not exist, so there was no case for someone like Win Lung to make noise about it. Win started exploring the possibilities of working with organizations that were on the ground but not entirely controlled by the government. With his other professional commitments, he could only spare a finite amount of time for Burma, so the progress was slow. In time, the idea gained traction, and Win started getting more support.

Where are the treasures?

Kip called Tim first thing in the morning and told him that there was a real chance that the objects were still in the Morita mansion. Tim listened to Kip's analysis carefully and asked him to read out every single message from the agents and dealers.

In the end, he commented, "I agree with you, the objects could still be at the mansion. I think 'something' happened. That 'something' or 'some event' that was not anticipated could have prevented the perpetrators from transporting the objects from the mansion. I am beginning to think that they could not anticipate that last-minute hiccup because they did not know. What if the original method of transportation they had planned could not be used anymore?"

Kip had to admire Tim's reasoning and said, "I did not think of it that way exactly, but now that you put it that way, it makes sense. I think I'll run it by Jeff and Scott and see if I can get their help in organizing a thorough search of the mansion. We have to find those objects."

Tim agreed with the plan and went as far as, "Who knows? This could be the first break we needed in this case."

After Tim hung up, Kip sent out a detailed email to Jeff and Scott and explained the analysis to them. He requested from Jeff that he have two people with him when he visited the Morita mansion on Sunday morning. Three of them should be able to conduct a thorough search of the entire property. Jeff called back within ten minutes and said that he liked this scenario. He said he would arrange for two of the younger detectives from their pool to join Kip outside the Morita mansion on Sunday at 10:00 a.m.; both were very good. Kip requested Jeff to call Nick and give him a heads-up so that Nick could think through and suggest some potential hiding places; after all, he knew the mansion.

Some hiding places were better, and since it was his mansion, he ought to know. Kip was back at the Morita mansion on Sunday. Two detectives, Kevin and Dan, were waiting for him just outside the main gate and chatting with Jim, the security guard. They went in together at 10:00 a.m. Nick was waiting for them and handed Kip a small piece of paper. Kip unfolded it and looked at it. Nick had listed the three locations that could be potential hiding places. Of those, Kip assigned the multi-car garage to Dan and the storeroom behind kitchen to Kevin. Kip himself took on the attic and the grounds; he also told Nick that he would like to take a second look at Mrs. Morita's room and the patio. Nick said he would inform his mom right away and text Kip to confirm right away.

Nick also told Kip to come over to his study for a few minutes to see the insurance company docket he had talked about earlier, and Kip said he would do that before he started with his search. As he sat down with it, Kip realized that he docket was very comprehensive with a whole lot of supporting documentation and valuation certificates. The documents sought to legitimize the increase in the insurance premium by providing information on the sale of similar objects recently. Opinions from a number of experts that valued Burmese jade were also included. Kip felt it was a great collection of supporting documentation. If Martha studied the docket, she would have clearly known an awful lot.

Dan and Kevin had large flashlights and long handled pickers that municipal workers use on beaches to pick up cigarette butts. With their tools, they started immediately. Nick told them that they were free to roam around the property as they liked. He had informed the residents that they were looking around. Since it was a Sunday, only Emma and Emily were inside other than Mrs. Morita. Selma had her day off. Kip thought it was good that they were doing this on a Sunday; he liked the quiet time. It was always good to have fewer people around on this type of search operation. Kip, Kevin, and Dan looked at the specific locations Nick mentioned. Dan was carrying a small handheld metal detector.

They also looked at other places like Emily's studio. They searched every square foot of the house and the adjoining grounds. As agreed, they regrouped in Nick's study after three hours. None of them had found what they were looking for, not even a clue. They gave a list of the places they had searched to Nick and asked if they had missed anything. Nick thought for a few seconds and said that he did not think so. Kip himself could not think of any other place to search either.

Dan suggested that they could come back another day with ground scanners and actually scan the ground to a certain depth like the way armies locate mines in a minefield. Kip nodded and said, "I would call Jeff and brief him on what we did here today. After that, he can decide if we want to explore the option of scanners. He would reach out to you gentlemen and let you know; I think for today, our work is done here."

Dan and Kevin said "bye" and left. Kip did not know what else he could say. Kip went back to the house after seeing them off and met Nick's mother Mrs. Morita. Just like Wednesday, she was ready and sitting on the recliner in her room with a Japanese book. She smiled at Kip and said, "Koniichiwa, look anywhere you want, Kimura San."

Kip looked around, opened the safe again, and studied the drilled holes; he looked everywhere in the room. There was nothing to be found. Then, he went to the patio and then stepped over to the Japanese garden with the koi pond with dark water. He looked at Mrs. Morita's bonsai. Some of those were really great; she clearly had green hands. He could not find what he was looking for. He sat on the patio stool often used by Jack for his massages and tried to think what he would do, but after several minutes, he stood up. None of the options were very appealing to Kip. Finally, he said

"Sayonara" to Mrs. Morita and met up with Nick in his study. Nick was disappointed, but he did not show it outside; Kip briefed him, had a cup of coffee with him, and left.

He wished he had better news or an update for Nick. Sunday traffic was light, but it still took him an hour to get back to West Pico Boulevard because of a construction-related rerouting of traffic. Kip knew he had reached another dead end. He had called Tim and Jeff from the car and updated them. After Kip reached his hotel, he parked his car and decided to visit the supermarket next to his hotel for some bottled water and a few other items. He needed some batteries for his listening gear; he was thinking he might have to opt for his backup plans. Trackers on cars and listening devices were not his most preferred options, but this case was stalling. He might have to consider those finally.

He took the items to his room, washed his hands, and powered on his laptop. Almost immediately, his cell phone rang; it was not a known caller. Knowing the many agents, dealers, and the other stay-in-touch folks who might try to reach him, Kip decided to answer the call. It was a local number; he desperately needed a break in this case. It was Rodrigo, Tim's local stay-in-touch man.

Kip's heart skipped a beat, and he said, "Yes, Rodrigo, Tim told me that you are working. Anything new?"

Rodrigo said, "I think so. We saw the lady meeting the massage man at a Starbucks between Inglewood and Culver City. Initially, we thought it was by chance because the lady said loudly "hello" and that she thought she had seen him in the West Hollywood mansion. Then, when they kept talking for half hour, our young man went inside and got himself a tall café latte. He overheard a heated conversation. The man was blaming the lady for something and saying "she should have known" over and over again. Kip encouraged him to keep talking. She was on the defensive; she kept saying she had no way to know."

Kip thanked Rodrigo and told him to continue to stay in touch and call him if he had anything new. Kip was blown away by Rodrigo's discovery. He called Tim immediately and updated him on the news. Then, he called Jeff and Scott and briefed them together on Skype.

After the call, Jeff called again and said, "This might be the break we needed, Kip. We have the first step toward validating your theory. We can conclude two things from Rodrigo's update. One, we can conclude that Martha and Jack knew each other, and could have planned the break-in. And two, for some reason, things did not pan out the way they had planned. Clearly, Martha was the chief planner. That was why she was on the defensive; Jack was probably venting his agony. That can explain why Jack was upset. Martha doing the explaining leads me to think that she was the one who roped Jack in."

Kip said, "That is quite logical, Jeff. Martha would have known about the objects and their high value. That is why she was my pick as the lead and planner for this break-in right from the start. The prolonged negotiations Nick did with the insurance agents and the agents' claim of the increase in fair market value could have given her all the motivation she needed for execution. In a few days' time, she was armed with all the information.

"When Nick asked her to file the insurance company's docket justifying the higher premium, she could have completed her education on the two objects. She probably thought long and hard about how to extract those from the safe until she had a safe plan with great alibis for her and Jack. We still have many unanswered questions, though."

Jeff and Kip talked for a few more minutes before Jeff hung up. He promised Kip that he would update Nick immediately and tell him to keep it under wraps for now. There was no reason to alert anyone at this point. After Jeff hung up, Kip sent an email to him and Scott and requested a visit by them to Jack's Inglewood company and to the limousine rental company. A visit by two uniformed deputies would loosen the tongue and get the truth out in the open quickly.

Scott acknowledged the email and said he would get on with it first thing in the morning and send a couple of deputies. Kip also requested Jeff to let Nick know that he might visit the mansion again on Tuesday late in the afternoon; this time, he would be alone and take a closer look at only Mrs. Morita's suite. The next morning, Kip woke up a bit late, had his breakfast, and called the law office number Tim's Shan contacts had provided. He was hoping to connect up with the person the Shan gentleman had talked about; he was hitting a wall, and he could use some help on this case right now. Nick's main goal was to find the rightful Shan owners, so that was a priority for Kip.

After a couple of rings, a female voice said, "Law offices of Lung and Matsumoto LLC; how can I help?" Kip said he was "Mr. Kimura," a good friend of Tim's Shan contact in Washington, DC, and it was he who provided this phone number. Kip also mentioned that he was investigating a break-in that involved two Shan artifacts that originally came from Shan State in Northern Burma.

The lady listened carefully and then finally said, "You need to talk to our managing partner, Mr. Win Lung. He is away in Dallas for a board meeting today, but he will be back in this office tomorrow morning. It will be great if you could call anytime during our first half; we are two hours ahead of you. I will let Mr. Lung know that you had called and brief him on what you told me, Mr. Kimura." Kip told her that would be great and hung up. After he hung up, Kip went to the website of the law firm and checked out Win Lung's profile and the kind of legal advisory work he did in detail. What Kip saw was very impressive.

It said he had graduated from UT Austin and then went to Texas Law for law school. He worked for the State Department in multiple conflict zones and also assisted with the planning of the US president's 2012 visit to Burma. Mr. Lung seemed to be quite an accomplished attorney based on his clientele and the broad description of the work he had done. But what drew Kip's attention the most was the last sentence in the website profile of Mr. Win Lung. It said, "Mr. Lung was raised and educated in the United States and Thailand. His ancestors came from a long line of Chaofas (Shan rulers) in Northern Burma." Kip read that sentence twice, and he had goosebumps on his hands. Kip contemplated that this was exactly what he was looking for - a perfect match.

Kip called the other number Tim had given him in Washington, DC, so that he could do an informal reference check. The person was not available, so he left a detailed voicemail and requested a call back. That Shan contact of Tim's called back after two hours even though it was a bit late on the East Coast. Kip picked up the phone and confirmed he was Kip Kimura and thanked the caller for returning his call even though it was late.

Then, the person at the other end said, "Mr. Kimura, I am sorry I missed your call; I was on the road. Am I correct in assuming that you wanted to do a reference check on Mr. Win Lung, the managing partner of Lung and Matsumoto LLC in Austin, Texas? I know him and his father well. Before I got political asylum in the US, our family knew the Lung family of Shan rulers in Burma. I have known about their family through my parents and family in Burma."

Kip responded, "I would not call it a formal reference check; my goal was to understand his family background a bit more. I am investigating a break-in in West Hollywood. We have reasons to believe that two ancient Burmese Shan objects were stolen in that break-in. I was wondering if Mr. Lung's family was from that part of Burma and if they might have heard about those objects from their family members. We have not been able to locate the objects yet. At this point, we are trying to spread the word so that the thieves cannot sell those objects very easily. Once the objects are located, after proper authentication of ownership, the owner might decide to return those to their original Shan owners as his grandfather wished all along."

After Kip paused, the caller remained silent for a moment and said, "It is quite possible, even likely, that Mr. Lung or his father would know about those objects. Let me give you the complete background so that you can understand. The Lungs were a long line of Shan rulers from Northern Burma (now called Myanmar). We call them Chaofa. Mr. Win Lung is the only son of Aung Lung. For us, the people of the Hills of Burma, Aung Lung is a legend not because of his wealth or ostentatious lifestyle, but because he gave up everything he had and went to the hills to fight the Japanese. Aung Lung organized a band of untrained Shan and Kachin scouts and turned them into a formidable fighting force against the Japanese. Working with the US, British, and Chinese, they had a major role in driving the Japanese out of Burma.

"The time frame you are talking about should be the time of Aung's father. Aung Lung's scouts worked with the Chindits, the Galahad, and the Chinese X Forces. They went deep inside enemy lines in the hills of Burma, fought cerebral malaria, scrub typhus, blood dysentery, and the Japanese Army, and eventually won. The Lungs are a highly respected name in our community, Mr. Kimura. If you get to talk to the Lungs, they will do their best to help you in any way they can. I have no way to know for sure, but I think they'll know those objects."

The implication of that narrative was not lost on Kip. He called Tim immediately and updated him, and Tim said, "That means we should have no problems in authenticating ownership. Not just that, but we should now be able to spread the news of the break-in far and wide. That would effectively seal the possibility of the objects getting sold, even in the private collector's market."

Kip said, "This is the best news I have heard today. I hope we can locate the objects quickly; then, we can put this whole fiasco to rest, and Nick can proceed with the handing over. But I do think that many of the moving parts are coming together. Thanks to your contact - this Lung connection was particularly significant."

Kip also told Tim that he was hoping to hear from Scott on the visit to the Inglewood company of Jack and the limousine company that Nick had used to get dropped off at the Los Angeles Airport. After Kip finished with Tim, he saw he had a missed call from Scott. He called Scott on his cell number immediately. Scott had some news; his deputies went to the physiotherapy company in search of Jack, but he was not there. Jack had managed to disappear without a trace.

The company said that Jack had resigned and left the company that morning a few hours before the deputies showed up. They tried his cell phone; the number was disconnected, and the account was closed. When the deputies wanted to look at Jack's apartment upstairs, the company told them that Jack had never lived there. In fact, the company manager took them upstairs and it was empty, never lived in. He confirmed that residential use was not planned or done for that space.

The company manager also said that Jack should not have given that address as his residence, because that space was never used as a residence. Scott's news meant that Jack was feeling a bit insecure, and he was probably on the run. When his latest action was seen in conjunction with the heated conversation overheard at Starbucks, it seemed that he was not optimistic about his financial gain from the break-in anymore. Scott concluded by saying that they had issued a Be-on-the-lookout (BOLO) alert on Jack. Those measures were usually pretty effective because of the large law enforcement network, he said.

He said two of his other deputies had now gone to the limousine rental company to check it out, and he promised to call Kip once he heard from them. Scott did caution Kip that even if they found Jack, it might not mean a whole lot; he might not be ready or willing to confess anything. They did not have any DNA or fingerprint evidence that tied him to the break-in, nor did they have a single credible witness. In the most likely scenario, Jack would refuse to confess and insist on his attorney, which would eventually lead to a long-drawn process involving a court of law. From Kip's standpoint, he was working for Nick, whose main focus was to locate the objects and make sure that they did not fall in the wrong hands. What sort of punishment Jack or Martha got was not a priority for Nick or for Kip. He decided to stay focused on his task.

He had to unravel how the break-in had happened, locate the objects, and call out the perpetrators; after that, the process would be in Jeff's capable hands. Kip was deeply troubled by the fact that they had not made any progress in locating the objects. Kip sent out a long email to Jeff and Scott and explained in detail how he reached out to the Shan contacts in Washington, DC. He also explained how and said that he had established a connection with the Lungs. He informed them that he had scheduled a call with Win Lung the next day. He requested Jeff to keep Nick informed of this important development along with the relevant details. Jeff said this could be a very important development toward Nick's goal. Kip also requested Jeff's opinion on whether Nick should terminate Martha now or wait for some more confirmation.

Jeff responded almost immediately and said that he would call Nick right away, and Martha should continue to work for Nick till they had gathered more direct evidence of her involvement. Jeff also stated that he was not in favor of Nick terminating Martha right now because if Martha came to work, it was easier to "keep an eye" on her and also on her movements everywhere. If she disappeared like Jack did, that would mean more work for his team who was stretched out, and much of that work would be unproductive. Kip agreed with Jeff on the last point.

Scott's deputies got back from the limousine company pretty late, but Scott made sure that they wrote a detailed report before they left for the day. The limousine company was located in Little Armenia; its owner Mr. Ohanian confirmed that they had a call from a lady from the Morita mansion directly to one of their drivers, Johnny. Johnny was a Lyft driver who did moonlighting with them. He had been working with them for about three years, and they had never had any problems with Johnny.

Johnny logged the call in their system, took one of their limousines on that day, and dropped the passenger off at Los Angeles Airport. Johnny had said he had another stop over, but that was not required ultimately, so he came back directly. The company got paid the very next week, and the transaction was closed. The deputies inquired about Johnny's contact information, and they were given a Glendale address and landline phone number. The home address was legitimate.

Mr. Ohanian's company did not have a cell phone number for Johnny. The company car rental used that land line number and the voicemail attached to that number to communicate with Johnny. After he read Scott's report, Kip saw the same pattern that he had seen in Jack's case. He made a note of the Glendale address and sent an email to Scott stating that he would personally check it out the next day first thing. Kip knew Glendale reasonably well - he recognized the locality as well.

Call with Win

Kip knew his next day would be rather busy. He woke up at his usual 5:00 a.m., finished his run around West Pico Boulevard, and did his daily exercises thereafter. The breakfast bar at the hotel opened at 7:00 a.m.; he was among the first guests in the hotel to finish breakfast. After that, he showered and got ready; he knew he had to go to Glendale and then on to the Morita mansion to take yet another look at Mrs. Morita's suite. For his Glendale trip, he also packed some of his specialized electronics, particularly the miniature camera assembly. Kip's detective intuition told him that he would want a closer look at Johnny's Glendale house. He planned to leave the hotel right after he finished his conversation with Win Lung. Kip was hoping for a good lead. The team desperately needed a break, and he tried to remain positive.

Kip called Win Lung's number at 8:00 a.m. sharp, which was 10:00 a.m. for Win in Austin. *It is a law firm, so this should be a good time for them*, Kip reasoned. The same lady with the pleasant voice answered, "Lung and Matsumoto LLC, how can I help?" When she heard Kip's voice, she said, "Mr. Kimura, right? Please wait a second; Mr. Lung is expecting your call. I will transfer the call to his extension, and he will talk to you."

Kip held on, and after a couple of seconds and a click, he heard, "Mr. Kimura, this is Win Lung speaking. Nancy told me you had called yesterday. How can I be of assistance?" Kip was expecting a much older voice. *Some voices do not age, and Win could be one of those.*

Kip continued, "Mr. Lung, at the outset, I want to thank you for making time for my call. I know how busy you are. I am actually investigating a break-in in West Hollywood. We believe two ancient Shan objects were stolen in that break-in. Those two Shan objects came from Northern Burma. The current owner's grandfather obtained those when he was posted in Burma during WW II from a Shan family.

"These objects were gifted by a Shan ruler or Chaofa during the Japanese occupation of Burma. I was wondering if you or your father would know anything about those objects and if you could guide us a bit as to who could be interested in acquiring those. Our goal is to spread the word around the world so that any potential buyer knows that those objects were stolen. We want to make it harder for the thieves to sell those in the open market and also to unethical private buyers. Even private collectors will be reluctant to buy stolen artifacts.

"If the objects are found, the current owner in West Hollywood would like to consider returning those objects to their rightful Shan owners. That was his late grandfather's wish."

When Kip finished, Win said, "Do you have pictures of those objects, Mr. Kimura? It would be great if you could email the pictures to me. I will print the pictures locally and show those pictures to my father when I go home in the evening. My father is almost 97; his health and memory are both fragile because of his Alzheimer's, but he might remember those objects if they are indeed Northern Shan treasures. On Shan matters, his memory is photographic. Often, he remembers details that even I have forgotten.

"We are a Chaofa family from Northern Burma, Mr. Kimura. The Shan cause has been a lifelong commitment for my father; he spent his youth fighting the Japanese with a bunch of scouts and much of his later life helping the Shan in other ways. When my mother was alive, she used to say that my father was with us only in body - his soul was always with the Shan. So, you have probably come to the right place based on the data, but I do not know for sure. Please do call me around the same time tomorrow, and we can go over the details. I will pass on what I learn from my father to you during our call. He had an excellent memory before the disease, so I would be hopeful. I have a court hearing tomorrow, so post lunch I am booked till late in the evening."

Kip said he would email high-resolution pictures of the two objects to Win and wrote down his email address. He also confirmed that he would call the next day. Before hanging up, he thanked Win and his father profusely. After he finished the call and emailed the pictures, he sent an email to Jeff and Scott. Kip informed both them of the call with Win Lung the next day and requested one of them to join the call.

Kip thought, once he had a confirmation from one of them, he would send an email to Win and let him know that a representative from the local police department in LA would join the call. He thought this was the right time to engage Jeff or Scott. Jeff responded immediately and said he would be happy to make himself available. Kip saw an acknowledgement from Win that said he had received the pictures; Kip thanked him and took the opportunity to let him know that Jeff would be on the call the next day. Kip's detective intuition told him that they were onto something here - there was too much coincidence.

Kip left his hotel and drove down to Glendale after his call with Win Lung. The address on Boyce Avenue was actually not far from John's house, could be even less than a mile. He knew that already from his past visits to John. From the outside, it looked like a single-family home with a one-car garage; the house clearly had seen better days. Many of the houses in the mediate neighborhood we very well maintained, but Johnny's house was not. From the outside, the house seemed empty. There was no car in the driveway, but there was an RV parked right in front of the house. That gave Kip an idea. He needed to confirm something that could change the course of this investigation.

He drove down two blocks to the south, found a good street side parking on the other side of the street, and parked his car. Kip waited inside the car for a good ten minutes to observe the surroundings and then came out to see if he could prove his suspicion. He walked down to Johnny's house and crossed it twice to make sure - no one was watching. On his third pass, he used the RV as a cover and quietly entered the property. Once inside, he quickly slipped his miniature camera out of his pocket and inserted it inside the garage through an opening on the side of the garage door; the miniature camera fed a small handheld display on that screen - he saw a reddish Acura Integra parked inside. The make and model were the same as that of John's car! A quick glance or a photo by a traffic camera would not notice any difference.

The place for the number plate was blank. Kip walked around the house and took a peek inside from a couple of vantage points using his miniature camera and the extension. Then suddenly, he thought he heard a noise on the street. He quickly packed his gear and left quietly. Kip left Johnny's Glendale neighborhood quickly and drove toward West Hollywood because he had told Nick he would pay another visit to Mr. Morita's suite. He was still early, so he stopped over at a Pete's Coffee nearby and ordered a tall black coffee, sat, and started thinking.

Kip started playing the scenario of the break-in inside his mind like a movie over and over. He was nearly there; he could now see most of the movie played out in his mind. There were only a few obscure frames or unanswered questions in his mind; most were clarified already. After he finished his coffee, instead of proceeding to West Hollywood immediately, Kip took a detour and visited Mr. Ohanian in the limousine company in Little Armenia. Kip introduced himself with Jeff's card and said he was part of Jeff's team. He asked Mr. Ohanian to explain one part of the statement he had given to Scott's deputies.

"You told the deputies yesterday that Johnny came earlier than expected after the airport drop off because a planned detour did not happen. Could you explain that part to me, Mr. Ohanian? I do not believe our deputies understood the perspective of an experienced owner completely."

Mr. Ohanian's facial expression changed, and he melted immediately. He looked at Kip and responded with utmost sincerity, "In our business, we have to keep track of the number of miles each driver needs the limos for and the duration. That way, we can squeeze in more rides. Johnny was fifteen miles short, and he came back about half an hour early. The customer probably told Johnny that the detour after the drop off was not necessary; it happens all the time. I specifically remember that. How could I forget the fact that because of Johnny arriving early, I could schedule another drop off on that particular limousine for Burbank Airport?"

Mr. Ohanian was quite animated by then, and Kip's body language showed that he was very impressed. "The deputies were not as attentive as you, so I shared the information with them at a high level. You know what I am talking about." Mr. Ohanian's monologue finally stopped. He had conclusively established that he was an astute businessman and the best time manager on the planet. Kip smiled because he got everything he wanted. Much more of the break-in movie became clearer in his head; several obscure frames suddenly became crystal clear in Kip's mind.

When Kip reached the Morita mansion, Emma greeted him outside and took him to Mr. Morita's suite. She was sitting on her chair and drinking tea. As Kip sat down, Mr. Morita asked if Kip would like some green tea as well. Kip said he would, so Emma went to get his tea. After Emma delivered his tea and went back, Kip asked Mrs. Morita typically on her massage days what Jack would do when she was doing her exercises.

Mrs. Morita said, "I cannot say for sure; most of the time, he would be toward my head. The way my recliners are oriented, I cannot see on that side at all. These are heavy pieces of furniture; I cannot shift these on my own. But I have seen him going into the garden to stretch while I was rotating my ankle or wrist. Sometimes, he would look at my bonsai; sometimes, he would kneel down and touch the leaves."

Kip made a mental note of those actions. "How frequently do or your gardener Carlos clean the Japanese garden and the koi pond? I know Carlos works on the lawns two to three times a week, but this part of the garden seems to be taken care of by you."

Mrs. Morita said, "That is correct; this garden and the bonsai are delicate. This part of the garden is tended by hand. I do not allow him to bring his big blunt instruments in this garden."

Kip took out a handheld scanner from his collection of electronic tools and ran it through every square inch of the room, including underneath the bed and the tatami mattress. It did not pick up anything. He checked the walls and floor for any hollow sound. Then, he went inside the attached bathroom and searched that space well. Kip drew a blank again.

As he was finishing up, Mrs. Morita said, "Kimura San, those two objects had spiritual connections; no one can steal those just like that. You and Nick are worrying unnecessarily. I have told Nick that they will be found. They will always be with the rightful owners or with those who got it from the rightful owners in a legitimate way. Those objects cannot be stolen like ordinary valuables."

"Nick's grandfather used to say that the Buddha statue was worshipped by the Chaofa family, and the marriage bowl was used in that family for three generations. It was used for my marriage with Nick's father as well as Nick's own marriage. I know, Jack has broken the safe. But even then, he cannot possess those objects. He cannot violate those and be their keeper. I want to tell you an old story from Japan.

"You probably know from your parents that many homes are made of wood in Japan; those homes withstand earthquakes better than concrete homes. Before Nick was born, there was a big fire in our home near Kyoto. Both Nick's grandfather and his father sustained minor burns in that fire. The room where these two objects were kept got completely gutted and flattened by the fire. After the fire when the salvage team came, Nick's grandfather told them not to use heavy machinery and digging equipment. I asked him, 'Why are you saying that? The bulldozers can finish the job quicker. We have to rebuild the destroyed rear wing after that, right?' Without blinking an eyelid, he had said to me, 'Keiko, those two objects have to be picked up by hand. We are their keepers; we cannot risk damaging those in any way.'

"He was sure that those objects had survived, and he did not want those to be damaged by the bulldozers! He was proved right after two days when Nick's father found those hidden in the rubble. I asked him later how he was so confident. He said he felt it inside his gut; he could not explain anything more than that. I feel the same way now; so, don't worry."

Kip was stunned, but he nodded. He understood that Mrs. Morita spoke from her conviction. Having seen him several times now, she was becoming comfortable with him to offer motherly advice. He did not mind that at all; Mrs. Morita reminded Kip of his mom. He decided to check the garden, the bonsai, and the fishpond once again. Kip walked around in small paces with his scanner. Other than a few hummingbirds and California towhees making noise, it was all quiet. The birds were flying all over, sitting on the plants, on the edge of the pond, and on the bonsai. Mrs. Morita was right - it was a very peaceful place. One felt at peace in this garden and the surrounding pond and bonsai.

He went near the bonsai and kneeled and saw some small holes in the ground. The holes were too small for the two large objects; he ran the scanner near the bonsai to be sure. Nothing came up. He sat on Jack's stool one more time and tried to put himself in Jack's shoes. If he were hard pressed to find a hiding place all of a sudden, what would he do? Would he go into the house? In the garden? The house was not likely because Emma and Selma would be nearby; it had to be this garden.

He sat and thought and thought for a long time but could not come up with anything that made sense. Finally, he said "sayonara" to Mrs. Morita and told her that he might come back again in a day or two. Mrs. Morita told him he should feel free to come and go any time he wanted. She also said he should not worry too much. She knew that the objects would be found. On his way back, he met up with Nick and briefed him on the conversation with Win Lung. Nick was thrilled to hear that Kip had adequately covered the Shan angle; he agreed that the thieves would find it very hard to sell those two objects.

Nick said, "Kimura San, this is why Jeff was so excited to get you to accept this case. Thanks a lot - half the problem is already resolved by your work. We knew there would be an Asian connection, and multiple angles have to be thought through. I am so happy you are on our side; I think there is a chance that you have found the Shan family from Northern Burma that gifted those objects to Grandpa."

Kip responded, "I appreciate that, Nick. Personally, I would have felt happier if I could tell you that I have found those objects. My detective instinct is telling me that those objects are still on your property. Just now, your mom told me something profound that stayed in my mind. She said that Jack cannot possess those; he cannot be their keeper. She said those objects had spiritual connection; they could never be stolen like ordinary valuables.

Somehow, I am feeling that in my bones too. But I have nothing to show for it at this point in time."

Nick looked at him kindly and said, "Mom said that to me several times yesterday. I do not know where her conviction is coming from, but it is infectious."

Kip also told him that they had contacted the limousine company and that they were in the process of checking out the driver. Kip asked Nick if he had asked the limousine driver to drop off a movie tape of something else in another location nearby on his way back. Nick said an emphatic "no." He said if such a need came up, typically, the studio or the postproduction house would send its own courier, and Jim would meet them up at the gate.

Kip had expected that answer; another part of the break-in movie just got clarified in his head. He chose not to say anything at that very moment to Nick. He had another question, "How was your morning the day you left for New York, Nick? Was it a particularly busy day?"

Nick said, "How did you know? It was a very busy morning. There were schedules to be changed, invoices to be paid. I could not complete everything before I left for the airport. So, I had to leave detailed instructions for Martha on several open items. Of course, I explained everything to her first, and then she was to follow my instructions."

As Kip was about to leave, Nick came around his desk and said there was another thing he wanted to talk to him about. "In my office, there is a large drawer in which I keep my video camera accessories like spare camera batteries, folded tripods, lenses, etc. I opened that drawer today and found this bag."

Kip saw a dark tan Tumi duffle bag with a roll of bubble wrap inside. Nick commented, "I had a very similar duffle bag some years ago. I do not use that duffle anymore."

Kip looked at the whole contraption and asked, "Let me guess, your regular travel bags are Tumi? For example, the ones you used for your New York trip, am I right? They are tan in color as well?"

Nick said, "Yes, to both questions; how did you know? Today, you have been guessing everything right. You have got some special powers today, Kimura San."

Kip said, "I wish." But he continued, "Nick, since you are a movie guy, let me try a movie analogy. I think I am able to see this whole break-in movie in my head; only a few frames were missing, and those are now falling in place. This was one of those remaining missing frames that I was hoping to find desperately. For my movie scheme to work, I needed a few pieces of physical evidence; this could be one of those that would support my working hypothesis. I should be able to explain everything to you real soon." With those words, Kip left Nick's study and went to his car. As soon as Kip started his car, his cell phone beeped.

He recognized the number immediately. The call was from Scott, so Kip answered it through the handsfree hook-up. Scott was very excited, and as soon as Kip picked up the call, Scott started talking, "Major development, Kip. Our deputies were able to speak with your Johnny of Glendale. He is John Wilson, by the way, nephew of the deceased Tracie Wilson of Culver City. We have not yet established it completely, but we think his first cousin is a lady called Martha Wilson, also of Culver City; we both know her. Tracie Wilson had no children and lived in a multi-tenant apartment in Culver City before her passing.

"Based on the information we have; we think Martha and Johnny's fathers were two brothers of Tracie Wilson. The siblings were quite close when all three of them were alive. When she passed away two years ago, the owner rented out the apartment promptly. The new occupants had no clue about Tracie, so they declined to receive her mail. There were no relatives on record, so social security checks were returned, and then those stopped coming. Johnny knew that Tracie had her car parked on the street, a bit out of sight from her apartment.

"Once he came to know his aunt was no more, so he simply brought the car over to his home in Glendale. He claims that the car was parked on the street one night when the number plate was stolen. He also claims that he has not driven the car since then; our deputies did not tell him that we know otherwise. We cannot prove much as yet so, so we decided not to confront him. Johnny said that he drives a Nissan Altima for Lyft and Uber, so he has no reason to use Tracie's old car. We saw his Nissan parked in the driveway; subsequently, we checked with the DMV, and we do know that he owns that car."

Scott paused for a bit and then continued, "We asked him about the detour he was supposed to take after dropping off Nick that day at the airport. He simply said that he had no details; he was told there would be a detour, so in anticipation, he gave an estimate for fifteen additional miles and thirty additional minutes - it was a guess. He was surprised to note that we were interested to know how he came up with those time-miles estimates.

"In reality, his distance and time calculations were very precise because they were based on a specific address. I strongly believe he had received instructions about a location he had to go to and drop off something after his passenger was dropped off at LAX. According to our Johnny, that was just an estimate on his part because he really had no idea when he would return the car. We decided not to push him today without checking with you first. Johnny explained to us that Mr. Ohanian was very particular about return time. You could return much earlier but not even a little bit late; Mr. Ohanian was always fine tuning the return times. The accurate estimate of return time allowed him to squeeze in yet another ride and make some additional dollars.

"His regular drivers knew of this practice; they were used to it. When Johnny started moonlighting a few years ago, they had mentioned it to Johnny so that he is prepared. In retrospect, that was not necessary because Mr. Ohanian did it so emphatically when Johnny started. Other than this one idiosyncrasy, there was no issue with Mr. Ohanian. He always paid them on time; all the cars had clean registrations; they were all very good cars and very well maintained."

After Scott finished, Kip said, "You made my day, Scott. I am now able to see this break-in movie play in my mind almost entirely; almost everything fits in nicely. I am able to see the plan A and the contingency plan as well. Can I have you and Jeff on a conference call this evening? I would also have to request my business partner Tim to join in from Bay Area. As you know, Tim has been working on this case in the background even though he is physically in Bay Area."

Scott said, "Let me check with Jeff and text you."

Kip said, "Sounds like a plan, Scott."

Within minutes, Kip had a text from Scott that said the three of them and Tim would talk on a Zoom call at 8:00 that evening. That worked for Kip because he needed to squeeze in a call to Tim before that. Kip called Tim from the car and briefed him in detail; he had to cover a lot of ground, and Tim had several relevant questions and comments, so the call took a lot longer than Kip anticipated. In the end Kip, was happy that they were moving in the right direction finally.

Tim said that he had researched Mr. Ohanian's company as Kip had requested. It was a legitimate business with a decent track record. There were a couple of traffic tickets and registration violations like expired DMV decals in twenty years. Those were non-issues for this case or any other case. Mr. Ohanian seemed to be the most articulate micro-manager in the world who thought very highly of himself. He was otherwise a pretty decent businessman; he was not a lawbreaker.

How did it happen?

Kip got back to his hotel, had a shower, and finished his dinner at the restaurant downstairs. After those were out of the way, he set up his laptop for the long-awaited Zoom call. When Kip dialed in five minutes early, Jeff was already waiting. Since he had Jeff's attention, Kip followed up on the background check he had requested on Martha Wilson. Jeff said that a lot of new things had been found, and she was indeed Johnny's cousin as Kip suspected. But there were many more new things to follow up on, and Jeff would have all the details in another day.

While Jeff and Kip were talking, Tim had already dialed in, and Jeff said he had a text from Scott that he was running five minutes late because he got stuck on traffic. After Kip saw Scott on the screen, he started, "Can all of you hear me?"

Tim, Scott, and Jeff said, "Yes."

Kip had a sip of his green tea and spoke, "Let me walk you through how I think this break-in happened. I have been looking forward to this moment for a while. This has been playing like a movie inside my head for several days now; let me show the movie to the three of you, my expert audience, before its theatrical release. Please feel free to critique my story as you deem appropriate. I think it all started with Nick's conversation with the insurance company and his subsequent quest of reaching out to other companies for lower priced quotes. You would recall Nick was fighting hard to avoid any increase in his premium. He himself said he would often raise his voice and tell the insurance agent that the notion of 'fair market value' had no relevance in this case. In reality though, fair market value has a lot of relevance; insurers use that data point as a reference to compute premiums. When we solve this case, we will probably find that this particular break-in happened because of the increase in market value.

"

"The sudden increase in fair market value of those two objects alarmed the insurance company; they responded by requesting Nick for an increase in premium. Nick had nothing to do with the increase; he resisted the sudden increase like most of us would have done. His reaction to the increase in premium drew Martha's attention. Martha saw the pictures of those objects and the paperwork sent by the insurance company. She knew those could fetch millions. This was a great opportunity, and after reviewing supporting documents, she decided to execute her plan. She was meticulous about the process.

"As we saw, Nick's office is completely open, so Martha could hear most of those conversations that took place. She probably got intrigued and started researching the subject. The way Nick operates based on complete trust, it should have been pretty easy for her to access the high-resolution pictures and know that the objects were in a safe in Mrs. Morita's room. Those details were never hidden. Nick talked about cleaning the objects; for all we know, that cleaning process might have been done in Nick's office, so Martha might have seen the objects closely. For Martha, this was an easy operation to execute; she was not willing to let the opportunity go astray.

"Again, I cannot prove it, but that is within the realm of possibility. Things became a lot easier and much more tempting for Martha when the insurance company couriered a docket with its research on the two objects. Nick had asked Martha to file all that paperwork. That was like asking the fox to guard the henhouse. That was probably when she decided to recruit her crack team and set the ball rolling. For her, the two objects represented an easy way to get her hands on a couple of million dollars based on the insurance company's research. I have seen that paperwork in Nick's office; it is rock solid and probably right on the money. If any of you read the docket, you would agree with me.

"It has references of four reputed antique dealers. If the objects were auctioned properly, they would have fetched a lot more money. On Nick's behalf, Martha might have called other insurance companies for quotes as well, so she was quite knowledgeable on this topic by that time. She probably sought their opinion on the objects and got valuable validation on the value and provenance. She might have even entertained the thought of selling to those folks. I think Martha thought about it for several days and worked out a detailed plan.

"She knew that Nick would travel to the East Coast because she did the hotel booking and air tickets. As Emily remarked during our conversation with her, the Morita household has very well-defined roles for its residents and staff. Anything out of the ordinary is noticed immediately by the people and the cameras. Being intimately aware of that process, she had to devise a method of extraction and subsequent transportation of the objects that would look like a routine matter. Nothing would look out of the ordinary - even if people saw the event.

"The opportunity presented itself when Nick decided to participate in the Motion Pictures Trade Show in New York City. Martha correctly decided that that day would be an excellent window of opportunity when they could transport the two objects out of the Morita mansion practically unseen. The word 'unseen' is the key here. So, she had her crew prepare accordingly. Before transportation, she had to find a suitable person who could extract the two objects out of the safe. That was where Jack was brought in; he might have been an ex-boyfriend who could do with a bit of extra earning or could be another useful acquaintance. An expert locksmith and a good physiotherapist - both in one human body. I think Scott's background checks will reveal more.

"Based on Nick's calls to Dr. Marshall's office in UCLA for Mrs. Morita's arthritis appointments, medications, etc., Martha already had all the details she needed. She could easily use that opening to plant her own person here. Physiotherapy was a very convenient excuse. She knew that Nick was looking for a physiotherapist for Mrs. Morita, and he had asked Dr. Marshall for references - she heard Nick's calls. In a tightly controlled environment like the Morita household, that was a golden opportunity to insert her man. Even more so because her man would work in the room where the safe is. She could not let that opportunity slip by. I do not know for sure, but my guess would be Jack was actually a pretty good physiotherapist who became a thief.

"She easily found out from Dr. Marshall's office that they outsourced physiotherapy services a lot. UCLA probably did not do a thorough vetting of its physiotherapy contractors. Chances are, they passed on a phone number, and the customer and the vendor worked directly. That made Martha's insertion planning much simpler. Dr. Marshall recommended physiotherapy; he did not say anything about the provider. She probably got it all done in one or two phone calls.

"For Martha, it was easier because she was calling them from the Morita mansion; if UCLA Hospital folks checked, the phone number would match. It might have taken her a couple of phone calls and half a day's follow-up to get her favorite company in Inglewood listed as one of the service providers for Dr. Marshall's patients. It was a walk in the park for our resourceful Martha. That office is also a very trusting setup like the Morita household. When I pretended to be Nick Morita on the phone, they never checked. They are in the business of saving lives; they are not in the business of catching people who are lying.

"If they do not care about petty mendacity, it is understandable; I have to say that they have their priorities right. Once that company got listed, it was smooth sailing for Martha because her contact in Inglewood and Jack were both ready. Her contact in that company easily planted Jack for the contracting at the Morita mansion. When we checked, nobody knew Jack for long in that company, and apparently, Jack did not know that the upper floor is not used as a residence. None of it mattered from Martha's perspective; Martha got the job done.

"Jack was probably a temporary plant in the company; his ultimate goal was to come to the Morita mansion. I cannot prove it, but my guess is Jack started working on the safe right from his first or second day. He used powerful precision drilling to break open the safe; those are less noisy and less bulky. His long medical coat could easily conceal those devices as he came in and went out. Mrs. Morita is old but very intelligent; Jack knew she might become suspicious. That was why he insisted on an elaborate routine of music and exercises by herself for thirty to forty minutes right from the start. He could not risk starting the process with a certain pattern and then change it in a few weeks. Mrs. Morita would have asked what prompted the change.

"Mrs. Morita would have noticed if he attempted that, so he did not even go there. He reoriented the heavy recliners in the room and the patio in such a way that Mrs. Morita had no clear view to the safe while exercising. I do not know if you guys ever watched physiotherapy sessions of seniors; very rarely do they involve unsupervised joint exercises for thirty to forty minutes. I have, and I know that is not the norm; it is never done that way because seniors can hurt themselves by stretching or bending their joints the wrong way, and they won't know.

In this case, it was necessary because Jack needed multiple half hour sessions with the safe; Mrs. Morita's safety was not the highest priority for him. He was there to focus on the safe, and that was what he did. He would have transported his small high-power drill, drill bits, and other tools from the first visit and got to work straightaway. He and Martha were both happy with the progress he was making with the safe. That is why it was business as usual. Martha was happily ordering duffle bag and bubble wraps for the next phase of the operation.

"Her duffle bag and a roll of bubble wrap got FedExed in the name of her previous postproduction company to the Morita mansion. Jim received the cardboard box and took it to her as is the protocol at the Morita household; she hid the bag in Nick's drawer for camera spares. She needed to keep the bag close by, far from the prying eyes of Emily, Emma, and Selma. Usually, those ladies do not go to Nick's office often, but there was a risk of exposure. Even if they went in for cleaning, they would not have opened the heavy drawers for camera accessories.

"She would have brought the duffle to downstairs on the day Jack was supposed to complete the drilling. The idea was to transport the objects in that bag safely in bubble wraps once the objects were out of the safe. This was not the work of a novice; the detailed planning was admirable. For example, the brand and color of the duffle bag was the same as that of the carry-on Nick used for his New York travel. Because she knew of it sufficiently in advance, she could advise Jack to set his pace of drilling and extraction. Getting the objects out of the mansion on that day was indeed a very good tactical plan. It was easy to execute; it would not have been noticed, and most importantly, it would have been completely safe for both Martha and Jack with airtight alibis. If it was executed, most likely, nobody could ever blame Martha or Jack.

"Thinking about the plan and flipping it many times over inside my head, I have to say I thought it was a very good plan. As a matter of fact, it almost worked. She did not make any mistake; it was pure luck that saved us if I may say so. Unfortunately, luck was not on her side that day. For a casual observer like Jim or Emma, it would look as if Nick were traveling with a carry on and a duffle. You would not question why Nick would need two big pieces of luggage for such a short trip unless you were trained to see the unusual. Martha was counting on typical human behavior of 'seeing' but not 'noticing.' She almost nailed it.

"Luckily for Nick and us, Martha's plan was upended by SoCal Edison. They had decided to do a routine maintenance on Nick's street on the day of his travel and shut down the power for a crucial three-hour period. I spoke with SoCal Edison and its supervisor in charge; they planned it over a long time and took formal permission from all the impacted house owners. Nick got lucky with this one. Because of that power shutdown, Jack could not finish his drilling work on the safe and extract the objects out of the safe on time for transportation.

"The planned transportation came and went back, but the objects could not go. The limousine that came to pick up Nick was Martha's planned transportation for the duffle bag with the two objects. That was why her cousin, Johnny Wilson, was the hand-picked driver. Our Johnny was told he would have a detour. I cannot prove it yet, but my guess is the detour would have been to a certain address we know in Culver City. Johnny knew it, hence, his estimates of an additional fifteen miles and thirty minutes - exact calculation. He had to satisfy his obsessive time manger Mr. Ohanian; my guess is it was not a guess.

"Martha could not have anticipated the SoCal Edison repair work because that notice came to Nick's personal email account directly. She had no way of knowing that Nick had even acknowledged it and confirmed the date and time. Not just Nick. All owners in the neighborhood agreed on the date and time for the SoCal Edison repair work. Martha was probably angry inside; she could not do anything about it. She hid her frustration very well; that was all she could do.

"SoCal Edison shared the information with me in the interest of customer transparency. That was why on the day of Nick's travel,

Martha had to be downstairs. To a casual observer, she came down with Nick's bags and loaded those into the limousine trunk. The real reason was quite different. You see, she had to talk to Johnny and tell him that the detour would not be necessary; the duffle could not be loaded because Jack could not complete his drilling and extract the objects. Nick was in the office, and it was a very busy morning for both of them. Because of Nick's travel, there were many things to do. Nick had given her a lot of instructions on a variety of things, so she could not call Johnny on his cell phone and discuss a duffle bag or a detour. Nick would have asked questions - would have suspected something.

"To her horror, her plan A for transporting the objects was unraveling in front of her own eyes. There was no power in the house. That was why the drilling had to stop; Jack got upset and left early. Mrs. Morita asked him to stay back and complete the massage, but Jack did not stay. Jack was probably seething inside as well because he thought Martha should have been aware of the SoCal Edison repair work. Once Martha's plan A failed, Martha had to work on a plan B. Most probably, Jack had already broken into the safe during his next visit to Mrs. Morita's room. He could have taken the objects out or left those inside the safe intentionally because he was still not sure of a hiding place.

"He did look around in Mrs. Morita's garden multiple times. Mrs. Morita noticed it. It was in Jack's interest to get the objects out to start the process of selling. He did not gain anything if the objects sat inside the safe, but he had to be careful. Martha knew that the process of selling was going to be long; that is why she needed time on their side. Inadvertently, SoCal Edison made their mission very complicated; they were on the verge of losing it. Each day of delay was increasing the size of the problem; after all the trouble, they had nothing to sell.

"You can call it divine intervention if you like; I am calling it Nick's luck. Once again, we do not know for sure, but it is likely that this was when Jack started losing faith in Martha's impeccable planning that was so inspiring to him at the beginning. Martha had two problems brewing by then. One, she was unable to pay all these willing participants in her scheme from the proceeds of the sale. And two, keeping the objects on the property had its own risk; somebody like me could get lucky and locate those. That is where our fearless Johnny Wilson played an important role for the second time. I don't know if he knew that he was he was involved in the illicit transportation of Shan cultural treasures for his cousin. Martha could have compartmentalized the tasks well, particularly if Johnny is not bright.

"Martha probably told him that she or Jack would get the objects out of the property in a duffle bag. Johnny would then pick up the bag from the vicinity of the mansion - the exact location of the bag to be communicated later via text or call. The method could have been something like Jim came inside the mansion, and at that time, Jack walked out with the bag. Jim used to leave his post at the gate and come inside the mansion during his lunch break or visits to the restroom. Exactly at that time, Jack could have walked out with the duffle on his back. Or Martha herself could have taken it out and left it on a nearby landmark street side and texted Johnny. Time was running out; she needed to transport those off of the property quite urgently.

"Once those were out, she needed to prepare for the sale. Johnny was instructed to be in the vicinity so that he could rush to that location and pick up the bag. Johnny had to be close by so that the bag with the objects did not remain unattended for long. That was when our Johnny decided to take out Tracie's old car because there was no limousine for Nick's travel, and he could not involve his Nissan in a major crime. Johnny decided to drive around the neighborhood in Tracie's car because he did not want to be connected to the crime. Johnny also knew that Tracie's car and its number plate would be a dead end for the police, and it would buy him a lot of time. He had to do the rounds several times because he could not find the duffle bag; it wasn't there. The bag was not there because nobody could take the bag out.

"Neither Martha nor Jack could find a way to take the duffle bag out of the mansion without drawing attention. Based on Nick's directive, Jim was not leaving his post even for lunch. If Jack or Martha had walked out with the bag, the cameras would have captured their movement and recorded it with a time stamp. With the changed protocol, Jim would have noticed it too, might have stopped them, who knows? Martha could not risk that because that would destroy the carefully crafted alibi. Martha and Jack would have tried many different scenarios, but Nick was watching; Jim was alert; nothing worked out, and they were stuck. Nick's directive to Jim to be at his post had a role.

"In the meanwhile, Scott decided to issue an alert on the number plate of Tracie's car. Johnny was worried. Bad luck - by now, Martha's plan B was also in serious jeopardy. Nick had noticed the theft, and he had taken action. The decision by Scott to issue an alert on Tracie Wilson's number plate suddenly made our brave Johnny panic; he was not hidden any more. Loss of anonymity threatened his livelihood: both Lyft and Mr. Ohanian would have fired him if they knew he was involved in a theft. Knowing Mr. Ohanian, he would have done it first.

"In his panicked state, Johnny promptly found a similar parked car less than a mile from his home and swapped the number plates to distance himself from Martha's scheme. He felt if he did that, he would be safe. At this stage, even Johnny was losing faith in his cousin's formidable planning. By this time, Martha's plan B had almost entirely unraveled. The sale did not happen, the promised fortune did not show up in anyone's bank account, and the anxiety of exposure was increasing each day. Given this backdrop, Martha's confrontation with Jack at Starbucks was quite understandable. She should have been on the defensive and she was; Jack should have been upset and he was.

"It is possible that Jack decided to go underground right after that conversation. It had less to do with our actions and more to do with Martha's ability or the lack of it at that point to come up with a viable plan. I think Jack lost faith in Martha's planning, and he wanted to cut his losses. Martha's attempt to deceive anyone within earshot with 'Hello, I think I have seen you before' routine was in vain; it only proved she had something to hide. It did not even deceive Rodrigo's men, those men stayed in touch despite that. We might not be able to prove or explain some parts of this story yet, but I think the story has come together. The duffle bag with bubble wrap in Nick's office was probably the most direct piece of evidence I have seen so far to support my hypothesis. I understand that we are not going to get these crooks to confess. For that, we will need to spend more time and energy.

"I myself would like to be able to explain some parts of the story better. For example, I would like to know who helped Martha in the Inglewood company and why. I would like to more about how she planned to sell the objects. Yesterday, I spent a lot of time in Mr. Morita's suite. Mrs. Morita told me something profound: she said those objects have spiritual connections - they cannot be stolen just like that. They will be found. She said Jack might have drilled a few holes and broken a safe; he could try very hard, but he could not possess those two objects. Those objects do not belong to Jack. Don't get me wrong. I am not proposing that we go and tell Nick that the objects will be found eventually and wash our hands off. What I am saying is Mrs. Morita got me thinking. We have already seen something close to divine interventions in this investigation.

How else could I explain my borrowing John's car or SoCal Edison doing maintenance work on Nick's lane on that particular day? We got lucky on that one; SoCal Edison's maintenance crew might have saved all of us from big trouble.

"Both of those events impacted Martha's timelines adversely. If I had not borrowed John's car, our Johnny would have gotten away with his number plate swapping for another few weeks. If SoCal Edison was not there that day, the objects would have left the property for sure. If those were off of the property, they could have been sold quickly. Who knows? It depended on Martha's ability to leverage her network.

"I am keeping an open mind, but I have started believing in Mr. Morita's conviction. I think the objects are still there in the Morita mansion, not easy to find, but those are still there on that property. We have to think like Jack and restart the search. There could be another wrinkle; Jack might have kept the hiding place a secret from Martha as an insurance. He would disclose the location only when he sees a viable plan for transportation. I thought of this wrinkle while driving back to my hotel today. Jack does not gain anything by disclosing everything to Martha upfront. Jack would have had another legitimate concern if Martha knew she could have recruited others for help!

"This way, Martha is under pressure to come up with a plan sooner than later. From our perspective, this last wrinkle is not very material; we have to find those objects anyway. If we can locate those, what Jack or Martha thought is not an issue. Mrs. Morita said to me that those cannot be stolen like ordinary valuables. She also said they have to be treated with respect or given wilfully as an act of goodwill, not by force. These objects cannot be violated. That Buddha statue was worshipped for centuries; it will not fall prey to man's greed. Greedy men can try hard, but they will not succeed - they cannot be their keepers. She told Nick not to worry repeatedly; she expressed that same sentiment to me when we met."

Kip finished his long monologue, gulped multiple sips of his green tea, and then asked, "What do you gentlemen think?"

Scott was the first to react. He said, "Wow, good work, Kip."

Tim said, "Makes a lot of sense to me."

Jeff spoke at the end, "Good theory, great hypothesis, but are you trying to say there are no gaps in this story right now?"

Kip responded, "Not at all, Jeff. There are several big holes. Remember, we have not found the objects yet. Dan, Kevin, and I searched every square inch of the property and the grounds, we did not find anything. In order for this story to work, we have to find the two objects in the Morita mansion, and we have not done that yet. Until we do that, much of my hypothesis is just pure speculation. The facts that the objects are not in the market for sale and there are no windfall deposits in any of the suspected bank accounts keep me going. But still, I do not have anything direct that would stick on the suspects. If we can locate the objects, I will say my story is the real story - until then, it is a theory."

Jeff commented, "I like your honesty, Kip. But I do think this is the most plausible story; nothing else comes even close. Let us redouble our efforts toward the search of those two objects within the compound. There might be places we have overlooked. Luckily, Jack did not roam around the entire property; he was confined in the rear wing mostly. Dan had some ideas. I will talk to him and send you an email first thing tomorrow."

Before he hung up, Kip asked Jeff if Nick should terminate Martha. Jeff said he thought so and that he would speak to Nick right now and advise termination with immediate effect. Kip was not expecting that answer so quickly, so he was a bit taken aback by the response.

Kip had to ask, "What changed your mind so much?"

Jeff responded immediately, "The duffle bag with bubble wrap - that cannot be brushed aside as a mere coincidence. Nick does not owe her an explanation; he could simply say that because of the COVID-19 lockdown, he needs to reduce staffing - that's all. I do not want to alarm her too much. It is she who violated his trust. We do not have a case that we can take to the DA right now, but I am hoping that we will. I would like to see Martha and Jack behind bars soon."

Scott added, "We will also redouble our efforts toward due diligence on her finances and see if we can find a motive. That exercise should not take us very long at all. Also, we could get lucky and locate Jack somewhere nearby. These are seasoned hands; it is unlikely that we would get a confession, but we have to keep an open mind and try. In this case, Jack worked on the safe for a while - pretended to be a physiotherapist for a while but got nothing in return. That would make him frustrated and desperate, fertile ground for his next set of mistakes. Typically, these types of people get caught in problems of their own making, and that is when they open up. They have an unhealthy disrespect for law enforcement, they think all of us are stupid, and as a result, they make one mistake or sometimes two mistakes - that is what helps us in nabbing them. Kip mentioned that Rodrigo and the team are still staying in touch, so there could be a 'Jack sighting' soon enough." There was a pause after Scott finished.

Before concluding the call, Kip said, "As we discussed in the past, prosecution and pressing charges based on what we have is going to be up to Jeff and Scott. You both know that subject better than Tim and me."

Scott responded for both of them, "It is our jurisdiction; that is how it should be. We'll take care of that at the earliest. The process is long and arduous, so we will start building up our paperwork from today. It is going to be a hard slog, not easy."

He also added that he would talk to the district attorney's office and seek their advice pro-actively. Jeff also said that Martha and Jack were both pretty experienced in their tradecraft, so he did not have high hopes with them, but Johnny Wilson could be a weak link. Jeff also thought Johnny could be more malleable because of his employment with Lyft and Mr. Ohanian. Both would fire him if they knew he willingly participated in a major heist in West Hollywood - even a small leak could hurt Johnny. Johnny could be persuaded to cooperate with law enforcement with relative ease.

Kip reminded Jeff to call him at 10:00 a.m. Pacific time the next day so that he could patch him in on the call with Win Lung. Jeff said he would, and all of them hung up. Kip was really looking forward to their call with Win. He was hoping that Aung Lung would remember something of value about those ancient Shan artifacts. That was Kip's only hope to conclude this investigation. Otherwise, Martha and Jack's stonewalling could take months of negotiations and approval process from the DA.

As things stood now, Martha, Jack, and Johnny all could deny everything and say there was no direct evidence. Coincidences do not work in courts. Kip went to bed immediately after the call, but he could not sleep for a long time. Various possible hiding places in the Morita mansion were creeping up in his mind, and after a few seconds of thought, he was discarding each place. This process kept repeating in his head for the three-car garage, then the living quarters, then Nick's office and study, then the kitchen and storage area, then the grounds.

Every single time, the mental scanning would stop at Mrs. Morita's suite and garden. In his subconscious mind, he was going back to Mrs. Morita's suite again and again. There was something he saw there or heard from her that kept bothering him. He could not pinpoint what that was. Finally, after a long time, he drifted off to a fitful sleep. In his dream, he kept seeing Mrs. Morita's garden, her bonsai plants, and the fishpond over and over again. The moment he attempted to focus more - tried harder to see the different birds - the dream would break up.

Authentication of ownership

Kip woke up earlier than his normal 5:00 a.m. and went for a longer run in the morning. He always liked to observe big cities in the wee hours of the morning. The locals said that Los Angeles never slept; that might actually be true, but Kip always managed to find subtle differences. A fresh new day meant new possibilities, uncertainties, and also opportunities. He thought that was why people and places were a bit different in the early hours of the morning. There was anticipation in the air; he could almost smell it in every city. Most of his friends and his family members mostly laughed at him when he shared his feelings about early mornings with them. But for Kip, that did not matter; he loved early mornings, even in crowded and smoggy Los Angeles.

He got back from his run, showered, and started eating his breakfast while glancing at the *LA Times*. There was a lot of news coverage on the upcoming elections in November. There were many news items about the increase in COVID-19 hospitalizations in the LA area as well. Kip had a busy day, so he finished breakfast and settled down with his laptop to clear email; he saw a few emails from Scott and Jeff. Scott's team had found that someone from the Morita mansion had made multiple calls to UCLA a few weeks before Nick's travel to New York. There were three calls made on one particular afternoon; all the calls were made between 12:00 noon and 1:15 p.m. Kip smiled and thought that some more pieces of the difficult puzzle were falling into place neatly.

He also had a voice mail from one of Rodrigo's men that said that a person who looked like Jack was seen in a chiropractic clinic in Pasadena. Kip immediately relayed the name and address of the clinic to Jeff and Scott via email. He informed Tim in Sausalito as well. The physical description of the man matched that of Jack except the hair color and glasses. Rodrigo's man thought those were easily alterable attributes; that was why he brought up the surprise sighting. Scott said he would get two of his deputies to follow up right away.

The detailed report Jeff had promised on Martha's background check was not yet in; Kip thought the deputies were probably still checking a few things. Tim had sent an email stating that Kip should call the Shan contact in Washington, DC, when he had a moment. Apparently, he had some new information. Kip was quite encouraged; he had started to like that person. It was already 11:00 a.m. in Washington, DC, so Kip decided to make the call to Tim's Shan contact right away.

Unlike the first occasion, he picked up the phone on the second ring and said, "Is this Mr. Kimura? Thanks a lot for calling back. Based on our conversation last time, I made some inquiries on your behalf. I basically called our local contacts in the Shan State in Burma. Not many people in the Shan State capital Taunggyi remember the Japanese occupation anymore. It has been a long time. Those few who do are in their mid-nineties or older with mostly fading memories. But we did find people who remembered hearing from their parents that a few Shan Chaofas were trying to endear themselves to the Japanese.

"By this time, the Shan Chaofas were rulers all right, but they had very little disposable liquid cash. Their cash resources were just about adequate to maintain their big families. Their houses and heirlooms were the only real assets these Chaofas had at that point. Some of those heirlooms were really valuable, one-of-a-kind major works of Shan and Kachin artifacts. Two of the Chaofas were known to have given their family heirlooms to the Japanese Minami Kikan people. Those Chaofas hoped for a better future for their tribes in post British Burma. They had recorded those by hand with their Chaofa seals. The current Shan State Hluttaw or the state legislature is trying to document those, but their challenge is that it is mostly oral history.

"They have some written documents that confirm the events indirectly. I was told one Chaofa's handwritten note to the Japanese officer receiving the heirlooms as gifts had been located. That could be an indirect proof of the transaction. This is still work in progress, but I thought given the context of your investigation, I should let you know. It might help your investigation, particularly with respect to the authentication issue you had mentioned to me."

Kip quickly summarized the conversation in an email to Jeff, Scott, and Tim. Then, he grabbed his mug of coffee and dialed Win Lung's number in Austin. This time, the lady did not go through the whole ritual of telling the name of the law firm and her name; she probably recognized Kip's area code.

She simply said, "Please hold, I will transfer you to Mr. Lung."

After a short click, Kip heard Win Lung. He told Win to hold so that he could patch Jeff in. Win said he had seen Kip's email, and he had no issues if Jeff joined the call. In a few seconds, Kip, Jeff, and Win were all in.

Kip started the conversation, "Mr. Lung, once again, thank you for making time for this call. As I mentioned in my email to you, we have Jeff Bloder, the detective in charge for the West Hollywood break-in, with us today. In a sense, Jeff is the one who got me involved in this investigation."

Jeff said, "Good afternoon, Mr. Lung. Really appreciate your sparing some time for us today. I know you are a very busy man."

Win responded, "No worries, Mr. Bloder. I had the context from Mr. Kimura's email."

Then, with a pause, Kip made his request, "I hope you were able to talk to your father. If you don't mind, Mr. Lung, why don't you please tell us what you learned after he saw those pictures?"

"Win cleared his throat audibly and started, "I talked to my father for many hours, and I learned a lot. When my father saw those two pictures, his first question to me was, 'Where did you find these?' Then, all of a sudden, he broke down before I uttered a single word. With his age and the onset of Alzheimer's, he has become very emotional about anything Shan. He somehow thinks he has not been able to do much for them and that he has let them down personally. He thinks he should have worked a lot harder. He has an overwhelming feeling of guilt for no apparent reason. Such agonizing emotion is not good for his health, so on his doctor's advice, I consciously try to avoid such exposure for him. I was totally unprepared for what happened with your pictures, Mr. Kimura. It was like a release of bottled-up grief of many decades.

"Something akin to a collection of lifelong regrets all gushing out at once. I waited for several minutes for him to regain composure; nothing happened for a while. My daughter is very close to him, so I called her in after some time. Then, my father recounted the story for both of us. I had heard the story partly in Bangkok when I was eleven. My daughter had not, but in her family scrapbook, she had one of my father's napkin drawings from that time. So, she was able to connect the dots pretty quickly. We sat with him for over three hours! My father said those objects were actually our family heirlooms, treasured by our Chaofa family for many generations. That marriage bowl was used in the marriage of my grandfather, great grandfather, and his father. That Buddha statue was worshipped by our Buddhist family.

"My grandmother, great grandmother, and other ladies of our family would perform ceremonial offerings to that statue on auspicious occasions. The marriage bowl had similar stature; it was used in many generations of marriages in our family. Those two objects were gifted by my grandfather to one Major Yoshikuni Morita of the Japanese Army in 1942 as a token of goodwill for the work he did to unify the Shan and other tribes of Northern Burma. Major Morita worked for the Japanese Army's intelligence unit at that time. Along with the two objects, my grandfather had issued a handwritten decree or letter that said these objects were gifted as a token of goodwill; he signed it in his name as 'M. Lung' with his Chaofa seal. Major Morita was working for Colonel Suzuki of Minami Kikan at that time as part of the Japanese efforts to build an anti-British coalition. Major Morita was trying to unify the hill tribes; it was a necessity for an independent Burma."

Win continued after a pause. "My father does not remember the exact date. He thought Major Morita was recalled to Japan, along with Colonel Suzuki in mid or late 1942; he probably took these objects to Japan with him when he left Burma. My father was dead against the Japanese occupation because of the atrocities committed by the Japanese Army in Manchuria, Malay, and other places. My father was convinced that Burma and its people had no reason to fare any better than the other nations that had endured Japanese occupation. My father had a disagreement with my grandfather and the Shan leadership over their proximity to the Japanese occupiers. One night, after a heated outburst, my father accused my grandfather and other Chaofas of bowing to the Japanese; he called them totally uneducated.

"He also stated these two specific objects should not have been given to the Japanese at all. He said that the Japanese were in Burma to further their cause. Being young and angry, my father branded all of them 'naïve.' Those objects were symbols of Shan culture. Giving away symbols of culture was as bad as giving away the culture itself - that was how my father saw it and said so. My grandfather thought my father was obstinate and ungrateful; he could not tolerate it anymore, and he ordered my father banished from his home. My father never returned.

"That was the last time my father saw my grandfather or any member of his direct family. Most of them perished during the war. After the war ended, my father went and searched for them in their village many times. Our village and our ancestral home were flattened by Allied bombing. There was nothing left. With his legendary Kachin scouts, my father went to the Thai border looking for his father and family members, but all his efforts were in vain. That heated outburst over these objects was the last time he spoke with my grandfather.

"As I said earlier, our ancestral home in Shan State used to see a lot of air raids by the Allied forces; it was reduced to rubble. He still feels guilty about leaving his family in that manner and not having seen any of them since. When my father was a little boy, his grandmother used to tell him many stories about those two objects. She believed those objects had spiritual qualities. My father's grandparents were already deceased when the objects were gifted. Every one of those heart-wrenching memories came flooding back to my father last night when he saw those two pictures after many decades, and he broke down. My daughter and I were taken aback; we had no idea about the intensity of grief associated with those objects. For my father, those two objects were symbols of Shan culture and unforgettable personal grief."

Jeff and Kip were in stunned silence! Kip regained his composure faster, and he managed to say, "Please continue, Mr. Lung. Please do not stop. We are both captivated by your story; please tell us what else came up."

Win started again, "After the war, we crossed the border and went over to Thailand before we got political asylum in the United States. We were in Bangkok for a few years. My parents had a restaurant in the Bangkok waterfront. When I was young, my father and I would go on long walks along the waterfront. My father used to talk about his days in Northern Burma and how he and his Kachin scouts had helped a small number of US and British forces fight the vastly superior Japanese Army and win. When all customers were gone and the kitchen was closed, my father used to educate me on the Shan culture and the Shan cause. He tried very hard to locate his family members after the war; on weekends, he would go to the NGOs that were active in the Burma border for updates. He would talk to his Thai friends in Bangkok and ask if they could help. His efforts did not yield the result he was expecting.

"One day, our conversation drifted to his disagreement with my grandfather, and he mentioned these two objects. I had never seen these objects, and as refugees, we could not bring much across the border to Chiang Mai in Thailand. We had no photos of our life in Burma; it was all very obscure for me as a kid. As a curious eleven-year-old, I asked my father to draw these objects for me. My father took a napkin from our restaurant and drew these two objects by hand for me. As a kid, I had no real idea about the place I came from or my cultural heritage. My father's words gave me a glimpse of that world for me. Yesterday, after you emailed those pictures to me, Mr. Kimura, I compared those with what my father had drawn on a napkin many decades ago in Bangkok. The pictures are strikingly similar, including all the minute details of the rubies and all the etched inscriptions.

"Someday, I would like to show those napkins to you. My daughter Becky maintains a family scrapbook with all my old stuff now; that is why we still have those napkin drawings. Otherwise, we would have probably thrown those away. The Shan cause was a lifelong obsession for my father; in the early 1940s, he was already upset with the Shan attitude toward the Japanese. He called it 'servile.' But he said to me yesterday that the frustration had been building up inside him for a while.

"The symbolism of these two objects being 'gifted' ended the relationship for him. I never met my grandfather; he was probably a pragmatist Shan leader. He probably saw a good reason to endear himself to the Japanese. He did not have much cash to give. Even though they were rulers, Chaofas did not have liquid assets; family heirlooms were the next best thing. Being in his twenties and a bit hot-headed, my father thought that act was disrespectful to the Shan. To my father, those symbols of Shan cultural heritage were sacred - inviolable. My grandfather's act of giving those away showed that he wanted to please the Japanese at any cost, and my father rebelled. His was in the minority view in Burma of 1942. Most tribal leaders, even my father's relatives, liked the Japanese because they were Buddhists."

When Win finished, Jeff said, "Mr. Lung, words cannot express our gratitude to you and your father. The current owner of these objects is the grandson of Major Morita. Your grandparents met under very different circumstances, one as the victor and the other as the vanquished. Mistakes happen on both sides in the fog of war. You should tell your father that the cultural significance of these objects was never lost on Major Morita. Before he passed away, he had instructed his son to find the rightful owner and return the objects.

"His son, the current owner's father, tried hard through the Burmese Embassy in the United States but could not locate your family. The Embassy was not interested. Major Morita's grandson visited their ancestral home near Kyoto many times when he was a boy. He spent a lot of time with his aging grandfather. Every time the objects came up for discussion, Major Morita reminded him that the Moritas were merely keepers, despite some of their own difficulties. Those treasures had to be returned to the Shan family who owned those as soon as they were found after the war. Perhaps your father would find comfort in the fact that those objects were treated with the deserved respect in the Morita household in Japan and in the United States."

Win responded, "Not just comfort, Mr. Bloder. My father will be thrilled when he gets to know this part of the story. It is the disrespect that hurt him. If the Moritas saw and treated those the way you just narrated, they respected Shan culture as if it were their own. That act will not be lost on my father - he will consider that an honor. I have a court hearing in about an hour. After that, I will go and talk to my father and share this news with him. He is unwell and not very mobile, so he cannot travel outside. You both should know that my wife's family is originally from Japan; we harbor no negative feelings toward the people of Japan. In fact, ordinary Japanese people suffered the most in WWII. My father used to say in Bangkok that of all nations and peoples, Japanese suffered the most, remembering the nuclear explosions in Hiroshima and Nagasaki. My wife's family came from Hiroshima originally; we know what many of them had to go through.

"Our frustration is with the Japanese government and the misguided Japanese War Ministry of that time. They were the reasons for so much distress and despair in Southeast Asia. I assure you: my father will understand Major Morita and his family's views on this subject. What the Japanese Army did during the war was not a reflection of the will of the Japanese people. In large measure, it was probably Hideki Tojo's megalomania for which he was punished after the war. My father believes that there were other parts of the Japanese government that were not held accountable. Be that as it may, almost all observers, like my father, believe that ordinary Japanese people were not the real perpetrators. They were probably the victims who remained silent."

After Win finished, Kip added, "Mr. Lung, we will take the information you provided to us to Mr. Morita and talk to him. After that, we might need to regroup to discuss the next steps. I will reach out to your office in a day or two and set up a suitable time. I have to let you know that despite our best efforts, we have not been able to locate the stolen objects yet. We think we have figured out how the break-in happened, but that has not led us to the objects yet. That effort will go on in parallel. Be that as it may, it will be necessary for us to talk after we discuss your inputs with Mr. Morita. I hope to be in touch.

"We are confident that we will be able to find the objects. When we do, we would like to do our best to right a wrong that happened in Northern Burma in 1942. It is poignant that the two grandsons will probably iron out a wrinkle that was created by their remarkable grandfathers in the fog of war way back in 1942. I am sure Jeff and I would love to witness that historic moment when that happens." Win said that was totally understandable, and he was quite comfortable with the idea. After that, he hung up since he had court duty.

Jeff called Kip back almost immediately. "What a story, Kip. This is why I knew we needed someone like you to investigate this case. This was not just about getting the objects back; we also had to right the wrong that was committed, maybe inadvertently, during WWII. I think Nick will be mighty pleased with this part of the development. Now, let us hope we can locate the objects quickly. I still owe you that report on Martha; I will email that today. I will call Nick and update him; I am meeting Scott in a bit for another case, so I will keep him informed as well."

Kip said he might visit the Morita mansion again, so if Jeff could have Dan call Kip about his new ideas for searching the property, that would be great. Kip sent an email to Nick requesting him to check with Mrs. Morita if he could come by around 4:00 p.m.

In a few minutes, Nick responded, "Mom said you can come and go any time you want. She has asked you to have green tea and special tempura with her."

Kip responded, "Much obliged, Nick. Please do tell her I'll be there."

He then had a short conversation with Dan from Jeff's team. As the day progressed, Kip remembered his dream from the previous night multiple times. Was there a message? Was there something he was missing? He played that tape in his mind over and over again but could not quite resolve it. He decided to go to the Morita mansion about an hour early and take a look at the surrounding houses and roads. For nearly an hour, he drove around the property.

He considered the possibility of someone tossing a bag with the two objects over the boundary wall and having the bag picked up on the other side. Jade was pretty high on the Mohs scale of hardness, so that fall would not damage the objects, but would someone like Jack really risk that? That would mean Martha would have to involve someone like Carlos who could put it inside a dry leaves bag and then toss it; it would also mean that they would need access to the property where the whole contraption would land. Kip had not seen any such attempts in the camera footage. He considered several other possibilities like getting those out using the trash collection service or the courier folks. That did not work out because Selma put all trash in a plastic bag, and she would notice if the trash bag was four times heavier on a certain day. Courier service would not work either because those came and went through Jim. After a while, he discarded those ideas and went inside.

He was told Nick was on a call with one of his directors, so Emma took him to Mrs. Morita's suite directly. Selma was already doing the set up for Japanese green tea and special tempura on the tatami in Mrs. Morita's room.

She said, "Koniichiwa, Kimura San" cheerfully.

Kip returned the greeting in Japanese and sat down. As he sat down, he could see a glimpse of her garden and the birds flying back and forth. Suddenly, something clicked in Kip's brain: it was like a sudden flash of lightning. He jumped up from the tatami, almost toppling his green tea saucer and startling Mrs. Morita. He looked at Mrs. Morita, bowed, and apologized in Japanese.

"Gomen nasai, Morita San. Chhotto matte kudasai." He had just figured out the last missing piece of this puzzle!

Kip suddenly understood what was bothering him and where the stolen objects could be. He called out Emma loudly, and when she arrived, he asked for a pair of household rubber gloves that people use for cleaning. Emma and Selma both came running with a pair of yellow gloves, and Kip asked for a large bucket as well. His intuition was on fire; he knew he had to have it. Kip wore the gloves, took the bucket, and went to the koi pond. He rolled up his pants and went in - the pond was about a foot in depth in places. He took a few steps on the edges and went to the center. In the middle of the pond, there was a mound-like formation - covered in slime, there was a small heap. Kip bent on his knees and pushed his hands into that mound of slime. He groped for a minute or two. His fingers were touching surfaces, and then he got a grip.

And then, another minute later, he pulled out the Buddha statue and the marriage bowl in two hands and straightened up! As he stood up, he saw Nick and Emily standing on Mrs. Morita's patio; both were looking at him and his two hands, completely bewildered and speechless! They probably came down when they heard the commotion.

Kip looked up said, "Sorry to disturb your fish, Nick; somebody kept these two objects in your koi pond - well hidden in plain sight from my prying eyes. I had to go into the pond to get these out." Nick asked Selma and Emma to get a tub of warm water to wash the slime off. They did so immediately, and in less than half an hour of cleaning, the two jade objects were gleaming in their ancient glory.

Jade is hard, so the slime and dust had done no harm. They were placed in the middle of the pond gently to form a mound so there were no scratches. Nick wiped the two objects and inspected those carefully with a magnifying glass he had brought from his study.

After that, he announced, "No problems."

There was a bit of celebration all round after Kip washed up in the attached bathroom. Nick and Emily also sat down for green tea and tempura. After they all settled down, Kip apologized to Mrs. Morita one more time for jumping up from the tatami and scaring her, but she had a very pleasant indulgent smile on her face. It looked like "I told you that you will find the objects, didn't I?"

Then, he started his explanation, "As you know by now, I visited this room many times over the past three or four days. Every time I came here, I tried putting myself in Jack's shoes and thought what he would do. He had to hide those two objects at a short notice. He could not go looking for a place. During my last visit here, Morita San said something profound to me. She said those objects will be found. Most definitely, she was absolutely certain, no doubts. She said those objects would not fall prey to man's greed; Jack might have drilled a few holes and broken the safe, but he would not possess those objects. No way. Her statements increased my conviction that the objects had to be hidden somewhere nearby. Also, there was no evidence to the contrary; no one reported a sale; no one had a big deposit in a bank account yet.

"If the perpetrators actually had the objects, what were they waiting for? Then, I reasoned, probably, they did not have the large deposits because they had not sold the objects. They had not sold the objects because they could not. If the objects were not with them yet for sale, then those objects had to be hidden within this property. During my last visit here, I asked Morita San to explain Jack's behavior in great detail. She told me how he would often spend time in the garden - look at her bonsai, kneel down near those plants. He would ask her to exercise her joints, rotate those for twenty to thirty minutes in each session, and then invest that time in exploring the garden. He was clearly looking for a suitable place in the garden for many days.

"I did the same set of things last time, retraced his steps, looked at every hole and every corner in the garden, but nothing clicked. You have to understand, my mind is trained to see the unusual; my mind observes and captures what others might not. I was hoping desperately that something unusual in the garden would act as a trigger, even subconsciously. Something unusual happened. I must have seen it, but nothing triggered in my mind while I was at the garden or near the pond. When I was kneeling down near Morita San's bonsai, I noticed some hummingbirds and California towhees flying around the garden. Sounds quite normal, right? One particular bird, a towhee, seemed to sit in the middle of the water in the koi pond. When I saw it, nothing clicked, but that peculiar image remained in my subconscious mind.

"That image of the bird in the middle of the pond was not quite normal at all. I went back to the hotel. I felt a discomfort but could not pinpoint what it was. The water in the koi pond is pretty dark mainly because of the moss. The moss and slime are both good for the fish. Because of the recent California fires, it also has a layer of fine ash on top. As a result, you could not see the bottom. During my last visit, I walked around the pond multiple times in circles. I noticed nothing unusual. My discomfort kept increasing, but I had no answer that I could lean on. I saw something unusual; my subconscious mind registered it as an anomaly, but my conscious mind could not resolve it.

"I went to bed early yesterday, but that scene kept coming back in my dream all night. All day today, that dream was playing in my head, but despite trying hard, my conscious mind could not resolve what I was supposed to see. I saw something that wasn't normal. My subconscious mind saw something unusual, a disconnect, anomaly, or abnormality. I tried hard to remember, but my conscious mind could not figure it out. So, I went about my day-to-day work with that tremendous discomfort.

"Just when I sat down for tempura and green tea this afternoon, it clicked. The towhee was sitting on something solid; otherwise, it would sink! Hummingbirds can hover, but towhees have to sit -

they cannot hover for long. That was the abnormality! Given the koi pond's depth, that something could be the objects we have been looking for. The dimensions of the marriage bowl and the Buddha statue would work perfectly for the depth of the fishpond if those are placed to form a mound. So, I called Emma and asked for the rubber gloves. You saw the rest of story unravel in front of your eyes with bewildered expression. Call it divine will; call it luck - it is up to you. Morita San, domo arigato gozaimashita." Kip again bowed deeply to Mrs. Morita.

Kip ended his explanation and finally started munching the lovely tempuras. They were so delicious; Selma was trained well.

Mrs. Morita was the first to speak, and she said, "Do itashimashte, Kimura San. Arigato Gozaimasu."

Emily went next, saying, "Don't know how to thank you. Mr. Kimura; this is like a movie unravelling."

Nick was still in a dazed state, but he finally spoke, "You are just amazing, Kimura San. I am blown away; I am talking, but I want to say I am totally speechless. I will call Jeff and ask him and Scott to come over for a conversation."

Kip said, "I think that is a great idea, Nick."

Jeff and Scott both dropped everything they were doing and came over to the Morita mansion separately but within the hour. Scott came first and shook Kip's hand; Jeff came a few minutes after that and rushed to Kip and hugged him.

Jeff said, "Wow, Kip. This was an awesome display of detective's intuition and dogged persistence. My mentor in LAPD always said, 'Every good detective must learn to trust his intuition in challenging times.'"

Emma brought some coffee, tea, and more tempura and left the room after serving all of them. Both Jeff and Scott said that they had never had such tasty tempuras before. Nick said it was Mrs. Morita's recipe that Selma practiced and perfected with great care.

Apparently, the tempura batter was made differently in Mrs. Morita's ancestral place in Western Japan, and that was what made so much difference in the taste. Kip thought part of the reason could be that everyone was relieved that the two objects were finally located within the property. Nick certainly looked very happy and relaxed.

After they all settled down, Jeff started, "First things first. Nick has already terminated Martha. Our background research ties her more strongly with the break-in, so we would complete the research and then decide on how we go about pressing charges. Same applies to Jack and Johnny. Both are in trouble. Of the two, I would like to focus on Jack a bit more because he did the most actual damage, including the drilling.

"Scott and I will review what we have, fill in the gaps in our story, and then decide what is next. We still have some distance to cover. Nick has indicated that he does not care about the exact nature of their punishment as long as they are held accountable. Scott and I will sit down and look at all the aspects and evidence in hand and then make those calls. We will talk to the District Attorney's office in Los Angeles as soon as we are able to get an appointment from them."

He paused for a few seconds and continued, "Now, coming to the more important part of the discussion. What do we do with the Lungs? Based on what I told you on the phone about our conversation with Win Lung, what would you suggest, Nick? I think we have to get back to Win Lung and his father - the sooner the better, given his deteriorating health condition and age."

Nick thought for a few seconds and said, "I would like to return the objects to the Lungs and fulfil my grandfather's wish. I think the best way to do that would be to do a face-to-face meeting in Austin or a place of their choice at the earliest.

"I do not believe we should keep these objects in our home; this break-in has taught us a good lesson in safety. Maybe one of you can join me for that meeting with the Lungs, and after that, we can decide the process of the handover. I do not believe the paperwork will be complicated. If there is any specific permission needed, we will have to go through all that process."

Kip commented, "Win Lung might be able and willing to help us with that as well. His law firm had done this kind of assignments in the past and has had extensive experience."

Jeff agreed; he felt Win would be in a position to help with respect to the handover process. Scott nodded his head.

Kip continued, "Do you think I should reach out to Win for a date and time? I hinted that to him during our call, so he will not be entirely surprised."

Jeff and Nick both said, "Absolutely, please go ahead, and please ask for the earliest date he can accommodate. Since his father is in Austin and he has a travel restriction, we can travel to Austin and meet up with him."

Scott was quiet for a while, and then he commented, "I think you should accompany Nick to Austin, Kip. As public employees, Jeff and I have to go through a lengthy process to get that kind of travel approved. Also, in this case, you are Win's primary contact, so it is entirely appropriate."

Jeff said, "I agree, I was about to suggest that myself. You are the best person to travel with Nick; you resolved the background of this case. Also, the Shan folks and the Lungs are all your contacts; we had no connections. I think you should travel as soon as Mr. Lung is available."

Meeting the Lungs

Kip sent an email to Win from his car and also left a voice mail requesting a face-to-face meeting in Austin. Kip also informed him that Nick Morita would be traveling with him. Win called back while he was on the road a good ten minutes away from his hotel. Win said he could not meet the next day but could do the day after, so Kip confirmed that day with him. It was agreed that he and Nick would take an early morning flight from Los Angeles, arrive in Austin mid-morning, and take a flight back in the evening. After finishing the call with Win, Kip called Nick and updated him on the travel plan. Nick said the plan was good and that he would have his travel agent book the air tickets right away.

On the way, Kip also called Tim from the car and updated him on the day's events, Tim was thrilled. He said such a loud "yay" that Kip almost thought something exploded in the background but then realized it was Tim's scream. Kip thanked Tim for contributing so much toward the resolution, particularly the Shan connection. After he got back to the hotel, he saw an email from Nick. The email said that Mrs. Morita had suggested that they do another round of authentication of ownership on the features of the objects. Kip thought about the request for a moment; he felt Mrs. Morita's request made sense. So far, what they had learned about the Lungs was solid, but if somebody spent a lot of resources, much of it could be fabricated - at least, theoretically, that was possible. What Mrs. Morita was suggesting was a complete proof.

In Kip's mind, the Lungs had already come through. For example, no one told them the full name of Nick's grandfather Yoshikuni Morita or his boss Colonel Suzuki. He was not sure how the Lungs would react to the request, but he had to make the request. Nick suggested that he would email one specific question on each object; these would be very easy questions for someone who had seen those objects. If the objects were in their possession and they had seen those objects closely, they would know the answers. The questions could not be answered from the high-resolution pictures. Nick also saw an email from Jeff that stated he agreed with the idea. Kip drafted an email accordingly and sent it to Win Lung. After an hour or so, he received a response that said Kip should send the questions, and he would have to ask his father.

Nick's first question was on the statue. It asked, "How many rubies were there on the statue?" The question on the bowl had two parts: "What was etched inside the bowl and how many?" Kip relayed the questions to Win. By that time, it was time for his dinner, and it was pretty late in Austin. He finished his dinner at the adjacent restaurant and came back to his room. To his surprise, he found that Win had responded already; he was probably home and was able to talk to his father as soon as he saw Kip's email. The answer to the first question was "seven dark red original Burmese rubies." The answer to the second question was "Four dragons were etched inside representing four seasons or four stages of life as per Hindu and Buddhist belief."

It was not too late on the West Coast, so Kip took a chance and forwarded the email to Nick. Within a minute or two, Nick responded. He said, "Amazing, Kip. Both correct answers. My mother says these objects belong to them without a shade of doubt."

Jeff also emailed, "That settles it, then."

Kip was blown away. He immediately called and briefed Tim on this development, and Tim was very happy too. Kip was happy that the Lungs came through this last-minute test of authentication with flying colors. He knew it, but he had to go through this last step for others. It was good that it ended this way. He was thrilled that the Lungs did not object one bit and went through the process as if it were a routine matter, to be expected from anyone. Kip was quite impressed.

His respect for Aung Lung went up several notches; he could see why the Shan tribe called him a legend. Kip and Nick had an early start on the day of their trip to Austin. Because of the COVID-19 lockdowns, the airports were not crowded. Kip arrived at the airport a bit earlier than Nick. After parking his car in the long-term car park, Nick came by a few minutes later. Win had sent an email to Kip stating that he would send his admin Nancy to pick them up at the Austin Bergstrom International Airport arrivals hall with a placard with their names on it.

Given their schedule, they would have less time with the Lungs if they tried to navigate Austin by themselves. It was not a big deal for Win, so after checking with Nick, Kip had agreed. Win said Nancy would bring them to the offices of Lung and Matsumoto, and from there, they would go to the Lung residence and meet with Win's father. After that, they would do lunch with the Lungs and depart. Kip thought that schedule made sense. Given Aung's health, Kip hoped that they would get a chance to talk to him. It was Nick who noticed Nancy and her placard first; she was a tall lady. She said hello to both of them and directed them to a parked Lexus outside. To the driver, she simply said "office." Traffic was light; it took the about forty minutes to get to the law offices of Lung and Matsumoto because of construction on I35.

The car dropped them off at the door, and Nancy took them straight to the conference room. She asked if they would like to drink anything, and both promptly opted for coffee. Nancy went out, and another younger lady came in a few minutes later with their coffee, creamers, and sweeteners. Win Lung came into the conference room with a coffee mug as the other lady was exiting, and he held the door ajar for her. She was carrying a wide tray with mugs, so it helped. After she left, he closed the door and turned toward them. Win was about five feet nine, looked thin and fit, and had sharp Asian features. He was dressed formally; he had a court appointment late afternoon for one of his Austin-based clients. Austin was the seat of the state government.

Kip thought he was sixty based on his profile, but he looked and sounded a lot younger. Win said, "You must be Mr. Kimura, and that would make you Mr. Morita." Win was looking at Nick.

"Correct on both counts, Mr. Lung," said Nick, extending his hand.

Win thanked them both for making the trip to Austin and said that they should leave in about ten minutes to meet up with his father. After the introductions, Win talked about his work with the State Department a little bit and asked about Nick's work. It turned out that Win's wife Laura was a fan of several of the movies made by Nick's team. Nick promised Win that he would send them some first screening invitations. After a few minutes of getting to know one another, Win got up and led them outside. The same car and driver were waiting; Win nodded at the driver.

Win asked the driver to go home. The drive to the Lung residence was quite short, probably just a couple of traffic lights from the office. As soon as the car stopped at the portico, a young lady came down the stairs. Win introduced her as his daughter Becky, and he said she was a music major at UT Austin.

He said to her, "Beck, these gentlemen are here to meet Grandpa. I told you about their visit last night. Could you please get him on his wheelchair and bring him to the living room?"

She said, "I will get him ready and bring him over right away" and left.

The Lung residence was a spacious place very tastefully decorated with different kinds of artifacts. Kip recognized some Japanese origami and other paper art, but there were several he did not recognize. Win led him and Nick to a large living room toward the left of the entrance.

The room had a classic grand piano that looked used on a regular basis. Soon after Nick and Kip settled down, Becky came in pushing a wheelchair. Kip immediately noticed the striking facial similarity between Aung Lung and Win Lung. Aung was frail because of his age, but he could feel that he would have been quite feisty in his youth. Win introduced Nick as Major Morita's grandson and Kip as Nick's friend Kimura San. Aung nodded to them both. Aung waved Nick to come a bit closer so that he could talk to him without raising his voice; perhaps his eyesight was weak as well. Nick came closer to Aung and bent on his knees to talk to Aung so that both of them could hear each other clearly.

Aung said, "I met your grandfather many times. He used to come to meet my father whenever he visited Northern Burma from Rangoon. Your grandfather had a knack for learning languages. In barely a couple of months, he picked up the Shan, Kachin, and Lisu dialects. Whenever he came to our house, he spoke with my father in Shan and ate our ethnic Shan food. I had never seen any British or American officer do that. That was quite remarkable, I thought. I want you to understand that while I respected your grandfather as a person and his ability as an officer, I did not like the Japanese government and the Japanese Army. They committed atrocities in Burma and other places.

"I did not like what they did in Malay, Manchuria, and Burma. Japan's own citizens suffered the most in the war. My conflict was not with your grandfather; my conflict was with the organization he worked for. I thought the Japanese were in Burma for its natural resources and its strategic location. They had no real interest in Burma or its indigenous people." Nick nodded his head in understanding. He actually agreed with Aung's assessment entirely, and he said so to Aung in as many words. Aung said, "I am not surprised to see that you agree."

After Aung finished, Nick spoke, "My grandfather became a well-known university professor of linguistics after the war. His abilities with languages were legendary; I benefited a little bit from that because when I was a boy, I learned Japanese, Mandarin, and Hindi from him. As a person, my grandfather did not like the ways of the Japanese Army; he suffered from chronic depression after Hiroshima and Nagasaki. He always said that Japan and its people were used as pawns by a few in the war ministry and the Japanese people suffered unnecessarily in the war. As a nation, Japan paid a very high price for those awful mistakes.

"On my grandfather's behalf, I want you to know that the cultural significance of the two objects your father gifted to him was known to him. He made sure my father, mother, and I knew that always. Our family treated those objects with the utmost respect and affection. Grandpa instructed my father to try to return those objects to you. Despite a lot of efforts, my father could not locate you or your family. The Burmese Embassy in Washington, DC, was not very helpful. When my father passed away, he gave that task to me, and I did try from time to time but did not succeed because that part of Burma is a bit obscure for outsiders, and we did not want those objects to fall in the wrong hands. It is only after the recent break-in occurred that I contacted Kimura San, and it is because of him we are sitting here and talking to you."

Aung looked at Kip and said, "Thank you for your help, young man." Kip nodded and bowed to Aung. Aung was not a big man, but he had a presence.

They talked for a few more minutes, and then Becky peeped through the door and said, "Grandpa, lunch and medicine time."

Aung looked at her, smiled, and said, "Yes, Beck dear, let us go." Aung said goodbye to Nick and Kip, shook Nick's hand, and left."

Then, Becky waved, said "bye" to everyone, and pushed Aung's wheelchair away. As she was getting out of the room, Win called her and said, "Beck, could you please tell Mom to meet us at the restaurant for lunch in fifteen minutes?"

She said, "Will do."

After their meeting with Aung, Kip informed Win that the objects had been found a few days ago. And Nick inquired if he and his father had any thoughts about how the handover of the two objects to the Lungs should take place. Nick was sure there would be a bit of paperwork at both ends, but he said that he would like to do what Aung wanted regardless of how much time it took. Win said that he had briefly talked to Aung about it, and Aung suggested that they donate the objects to a suitable museum.

There were two reasons for that suggestion. The first reason was it is not easy to keep such valuable ancient artifacts safe in a private home setup. The recent break-in at the Morita mansion was a good example of that kind of risk. Aung's second reason was more profound: he thought more people would get to see those if they were kept in a museum. That would mean more people would get to know of the Shan and their struggles, and Burma would get visibility as well. Kip could understand that the second reason meant a great deal to the eternal Shan warrior that Aung Lung was. That was why he was a legend for the Shan. After the meeting with Aung, Win took them to Shan Austin for lunch.

It was a lovely ethnic restaurant very well appointed; the manager himself came by and greeted them and took them to a table at the back. A Japanese looking lady was already sitting at that table, and she rose as they approached.

When they were near, Win introduced her, "Morita San, Kimura San, this is my wife Laura. She is also a partner in our law firm. We were classmates at UT, Austin."

Laura asked, "Have they met Dad already?"

Win said, "Yes, just met him at home and came."

Kip thanked both Win and Laura for their time and their exemplary hospitality. Since Kip and Nick were not familiar with ethnic Shan cuisine, Laura did the ordering for them. After the food came, she explained what each dish was made of and a bit about the preparation technique. Win said the restaurant belonged to them and that his mother had designed the interior and the menu. The chefs, all the waiters, and management were all hired by his parents when the place opened.

They were all like extended family to the Lungs. Kip and Nick saw how Aung ran his businesses. Midway through the lunch, Laura asked Win, "Have you told Morita San what Dad wanted to do with the objects?"

Win said, "Yes, I did mention it as we were driving here. I also told them why Dad thought donation to a museum was the best option."

Nick picked up on that and commented, "Personally, I like your father's idea. But how do we go about doing it? Logically speaking, I think I will have to transfer ownership of those objects to you or your father, and then you will have to transfer ownership to the museum that is selected. What will be the process from the other side? In other words, what steps would be required of the museum? You both are practicing attorneys - what would be your professional advice?"

Win thought for a moment and said, "Perhaps I can talk to one my friends in the State Department and find out."

Laura added, "You might need to talk to a couple of museums in the DC area as well. At state level, things could be done differently, but the museums in DC will come under federal jurisdiction. We have to do a bit of due diligence before we know the entire process."

Win said, "In that case, Laura, why don't you take the action item of due diligence on the state and federal government?"

She said, "Sure."

Win added, "I would take the action of talking to the State Department and the museums in DC and make a shortlist of candidates. One of my friends might know a curator. Not every museum might be interested in those type of ancient artifacts."

Nick agreed, he said "Quite true. We do not want to give it to a museum that had no interest in displaying it. That would not work."

They agreed on a broad action plan and who would do what before it was time for them to leave for the airport. As they got up, Nick shook Win's hands and said, "Mr. Lung, it was an honor meeting your father, you, and your wife. What our two grandfathers did in the fog of war in distant Burma is getting sorted out in America by us, their grandchildren; that idea itself is so thrilling." He said to Laura, "Mrs. Lung, it was indeed a pleasure meeting you too, and thanks a ton for your due diligence on the procedure for donating the objects. Thank you both for your great hospitality. If you happen to be in Los Angeles, I would consider it an honor if you could please let me know."

Win said, "We reciprocate the feeling, Morita San. We will be in touch via email and phone." He looked at Kip and said, "Kimura San, thanks a lot for bringing us together; this meeting could not have happened without you."

Laura said, "Morita San, domo arigato gozaimasu. Daijobu desu."

Nick said, "Matsumoto San, do itashimashte."

After those goodbyes, Kip and Nick left for Austin Airport in a hurry. Nick dozed off as soon as the flight took off, so Kip did not get to talk to him much during the flight. After they landed, as they were exiting the plane, Nick said he was very impressed with the Lungs and he thought he was doing the right thing by handing over the Shan treasures to the original Shan owners. Kip felt the same; he was really moved by Aung Lung and his commitment to the Shan. Kip told Nick that he agreed, more so after hearing the rationale from Aung.

Kip also told Nick that he would need to wrap the investigation up and get back home to Bay Area. Nick said he understood but asked him to be around for two more days so that both of them could plan a joint meeting with Jeff and Scott in Los Angeles before Kip departed for Bay Area. Kip agreed; that was reasonable because Jeff might ask him to tie up a few loose ends. Jeff and Scott were busy with jury duty the next day, so they decided to meet the day after at 10:00 a.m. at the Morita mansion. As was the protocol, Emma greeted them and took them to Nick's study; she said Nick would be with them in a few minutes and that he was finishing an East Coast call. Nick came by before Emma returned with coffee for them.

Nick sat down and said, "Sorry, I got quite delayed."

Jeff started the conversation, "Great work in the last few days, gentlemen. I think we are ready to wrap up the case in relatively short order. I did not get a chance to update you: we did finally locate Jack. When we confronted him, he said he had no knowledge of the safe or the two objects. He even had the audacity to ask if those were valuable. He also claimed that he left the Inglewood company on his own accord. He showed us his resignation letter and also said that he switched cell phone companies with a new phone number because he got a cheaper calling plan with unlimited data from T-Mobile. Apparently, Jack was planning to move to Pasadena for a long time; it was just a coincidence that it all happened now. He also said that he did not know Martha but remembered meeting her in a Starbucks when she helped him with rental property information on Pasadena. He said she knew a lot of real estate folks in Pasadena because she had lived there in the past."

"What about the background check on Martha?" Kip had to ask.

Jeff responded, "Money was the clear motive; her husband lost his job just after the COVID-19 lockdown in a movie production company. All movie production in Hollywood has stopped, so the job loss was understandable. Martha's Culver City property had mortgage due for four months already. Cash was in short supply. When confronted with the presence of the duffle bag and bubble wrap, she denied any knowledge; we checked, and there is no DNA evidence on either. She said she had never seen such a bag leave aside buying or owning one, and she suggested we check with the bag company. When we asked her why the duffle was couriered from her previous company, she said Nick used to know the CEO of her previous company. We should ask Nick. She simply received the package from Jim and stored it in the only large drawer she could find. She was so ready with answers for every question we had; it was almost practiced and premeditated.

"Also, according to the Tumi company record, the bag was purchased by a man named Tom Jones in Miami, so that did not help our case against her. When we asked about Johnny, she admitted he was her cousin and she got him some business, but that was not a crime in California. Martha also said that she had used Johnny's limousine service in her previous post-production company for people requiring drop off at LAX or Burbank. Nobody had any objection to it. If Nick had issues with Johnny's reputable limousine company in Little Armenia, he should have told her not to use them. She completely denied any knowledge of a person called Jack who did physiotherapy.

"She said she had no clue. She even asked us if Jack had claimed he knew her, seemingly confident that Jack would not betray her trust. She was totally ready and knew how to handle our questions. Her demeanor told me and my deputies that she would have rehearsed those answers many times in front of a mirror prior to the interview. Breaking her is not going to be easy, but that does not mean that we are not going to try. For the record, we are going to put in more efforts.

"When we showed the video footage from Starbucks, she said she remembered meeting the 'physiotherapist' at Starbucks. The physiotherapist from the Morita mansion was looking for a rental home in Pasadena. Somehow, his face was familiar to her, and she said 'hello,' to which he responded. He then asked for help on apartments in Pasadena. He had a lot of questions about rental properties in Pasadena because he was moving there, and she was helping him with that information. She had lived in the Pasadena area before, so she knew.

"Apparently, she always tried to help others in need. The only area where we thought we had cornered her a bit was with respect to Johnny's role, but even there, it was just a transition; she recovered quickly and put up a wall around her that we could not penetrate. That sort of an attitude could come from experience or ignorance. The experience part could mean that she did this type of thing in the past and managed to evade justice; the ignorance part could mean that she is unable to comprehend that we know a lot more than what we are announcing. We subtly informed her that we found Tracie's Wilson's Acura Integra being driven in this neighborhood by a hooded figure. We also let her know that Tracie Wilson's red Acura Integra was found in a Glendale. We said that somebody swapped Tracie's number plates with another car. She was totally stoic, did not show any emotion.

"One thing we did manage to communicate unequivocally was that we were not letting this go away. As of now, the case and evidence we have might be a bit thin, but that would not be the case always. These people are being watched by multiple agencies; they do not know that. They think that they have pushed us away by blocking us and denying everything. We will get them in the end; I shall see to it personally."

"So, what does it all mean? They go scot-free after what they did and took us through?" asked Nick in a sarcastic voice. "They tried to steal valuable ancient artifacts, violated our home - there has to be accountability. I cannot believe what you are saying, Jeff. Seriously!"

Jeff answered, "Nick, it simply means these are seasoned crooks; this is not the first time they are doing this kind of stuff. We need to do more work using taxpayer money and resources to nail them. Frustrating indeed, but what can you do? That is life in today's law enforcement!

"If we do not follow through and do appropriate due diligence, Scott and I will face questions. In the worst-case scenario, departmental inquiries. We will nail them, Nick. I promise you that; what I cannot promise you is the timeline. It could be tomorrow; it could be next year. But they will not go scot-free. Trust me. Look at the way Martha is talking to us; it is pure audacity. These types of crooks think they are very smart, and the law enforcement folks are all stupid. The first part of the statement might be true, but the second part is almost always false, and that is how they usually get caught and get put behind bars."

Nick started shaking his head. So did Kip in disgust, but he know their case would not have a good chance in a court of law as yet. They had no option but to be patient; it is always better to wait a bit and build a better case. There are numerous reports of District Attorneys deciding not to prosecute cases when the trail of evidence was thin.

Treasures to the world

It took couple of weeks of non-stop work from Win, Laura, and Nick to finalize all the necessary paperwork. It was decided that the ownership of the two objects would get transferred to the Lungs in Aung's name. Thereafter, Aung would formally donate those to the selected museum. After a great deal of searching, Win was able to convince a major museum in DC to host those two objects as part of its upcoming Southeast Asian Cultures Gallery. It was pure coincidence and luck that they had already planned the expansion and one of Win's ex-colleagues from the State Department knew the curator. Win called the curator and helped her establish the provenance through his channels in the Shan State in Northern Burma.

Once she heard the story of the two grandfathers and how the two grandsons had united to make it happen, she was all for it. Nick loved the idea too. Win also got the Shan exile group in DC to connect up with its contacts in the Shan State in Burma to develop a detailed historical background of the Chaofa family ownership. When all the documentation was almost finalized and ready to ship, Aung called Win and Laura to his room. He told them to make the paperwork in the name of Aung Lung and Yoshikuni Morita; he felt that was the right thing. Win was not surprised, knowing his father and how his mind worked. Win had overheard Aung explaining the rationale to Becky at home when she asked, "Why are you doing this, Grandpa?"

Aung responded, "Beck dear, even though the two objects belong to our family, we should not forget that the Moritas took care of those for many decades. That contribution should not be forgotten. Our ancestral home was reduced to rubble by Allied bombing; if these objects were in our home, they could have been destroyed. I went there after the war - nothing survived. You could argue that by donating those, my father actually saved those two objects; my grandmother would have called it Lord Buddha's wish. The other thing to remember is, if Yoshikuni Morita wanted, he could have sold those objects for money three times over to a private and invisible collector in Hunan. He and his family went through difficult times in post war Japan, but he chose not to do that."

Win had not thought about that angle. It was true; the donation had become possible because of Nick's grandfather. He actually saved the objects from the ravages of war twice, once in Burma and then subsequently in Japan. *We should be grateful for that*, Win thought.

Nick was pleasantly surprised when Win called and explained the change, and Nick had to sign in a couple of places for the Morita family on behalf of his deceased grandfather. The paperwork had to change a bit because now the objects had to co-owned by Aung Lung and Yoshikuni Morita; that was how they could become co-donors. Mrs. Morita was quite pleased to hear that news.

She told Nick, "Your grandfather definitely deserves that recognition. Those two objects would not be here today without his foresight. I am sure Mr. Lung realizes that contribution and decided to act on it. From what I have heard about him, I am not surprised. In fact, part of me was anticipating this move. The Lungs are good people, and they are doing the right thing. Your grandfather would not have expected this, but he would have been pleased."

The museum management wanted to wait for confirmation from the Shan State folks so that there would be no counter claims by anyone later. Luckily, the contacts of the Shan leadership in exile came through, and Win was able to submit all the supporting paperwork authenticating the origin band ownership to the museum for their carefully planned inaugural day display. In the end, the museum management made a formal announcement on the two ancient artifacts getting displayed during the inauguration of its brand new Southeast Asian Art Gallery. Win was totally thrilled. He called Nick and informed him as soon as he knew and requested him to attend.

It was decided that both of them would be present for the inauguration to draw attention to the Shan cause. The museum curator liked that idea a lot. Along with them, representatives from the Shan leadership in exile and Kachin Baptist Convention agreed to join in as well. After all, the Kachins and the Shan mined that exquisite jade in Hpakant. The artists who carved those objects were probably local tribes, so the Kachins and the Shan most definitely deserved a place at the table. The museum management loved the idea of the donors and the tribes participating in the inaugural; it was their culture, after all.

Win told Nick that the Hpakant jade mines were in the news recently in 2020 for a massive landslide that killed a hundred plus freelance miners. The locals freelanced in dangerous jade mines because there were no other jobs. Win educated Nick on how Burma became the largest supplier of jade worldwide. Today, the Chinese, the Burmese Army, and the local tribal militias control roughly $30 billion in jade revenues; most of the benefits go to the corrupt generals. He said that only a very small percentage of that huge revenue directly or indirectly benefits the local Kachin and Shan population. Win said that much of the proceeds is pocketed by the Burmese Army officers through their joint venture companies with the Chinese. Nick was not aware of so much of suffering in today's Northern Burma; it was a scary picture all over.

Nick and Win arrived in Washington, DC, separately. Nick flew directly to Dulles from Los Angeles. Win had a few other action items for Jim's company, so he came to DC from Raleigh. Since they were both flying out of Dulles two days later, they decided to stay in the Reston area; the airport was an easy half hour drive away. The day before the formal inauguration was reserved, so Nick and Win got a great ringside view of the whole process. That was the exclusive view for the designers, staff, donors, and patrons. That was their opportunity to view and appreciate the gallery without outsiders crowding the place.

By then, they were on first name terms and gradually becoming friends; both of them were staying back for the next day for the formal inauguration, so Nick proposed that they do dinner at his favorite Japanese restaurant. Win gladly accepted. During the dinner, Nick got to know a lot more about the life the Lungs had since they left Burma in the mid-sixties. Nick was particularly moved by the story of Aung and Jim's friendship and Win's relationship with Jim. The more Nick spoke with Win, the more he was reminded of his late grandfather. He decided to share one specific story with Win. Nick used to love stories from his grandpa as a boy; he had a huge collection of great stories.

One time, he was visiting the famous Rokuon-ji Zen Buddhist temple in Kyoto, Japan, with his grandfather. It was Nick's reward for doing well in the Hindi lessons with Professor Morita. After the visit, they were both standing near the adjacent lake and admiring the beautiful world-renowned golden pavilion glittering in sunlight. It was a crisp and sunny Kyoto day; the lakeside was completely tranquil with one or two visitors.

Nick asked, "Grandpa, why do people fight wars?"

Professor Morita thought for a few seconds and said to Nick, "It is all about people and their leaders, my son. All wars are inflicted upon societies by a few narrow-minded and insecure people who got elected to or chosen for positions of leadership. Such people should not have been leaders in normal circumstances. In most cases, there were signs that should have alarmed their supporters, but those signs were ignored by the enchanted masses. Such people usually ascend into leadership by simple chance or by manipulation or by using even greater insecurity among the masses at that specific point in time."

Professor Morita continued, "In order to start a war or to attack another nation, you have to convince yourself and your nation that what you have is not enough or not good enough. Sometimes, they say that war was necessary to 'right a wrong,' like Hitler kept saying about Germany's treatment and surrender in World War I, and he used that to justify World War II. Mussolini had a similar strategy in Italy. That is how the insecurity played out. And then having started the war, if those leaders won, they convinced themselves that they were somehow superior to those they attacked and fought. Then, more atrocities happened, and people forgot to treat other people like humans. That is how the narrow-mindedness played out. By that time, those leaders were synonymous with their countries. Like Germany was Adolf Hitler, Japan was Hideki Tojo, and Italy inadvertently became Benito Mussolini. By then, those dictators were gods - they were worshiped.

"Very often, other important details like how they won the war, who they exploited, how many unarmed and innocents were butchered or tortured were forgotten. You have been studying Hindi today, so let me start with the example of India. The British came and occupied India for several centuries; they plundered India's wealth, destroyed much of India's multiethnic rich ancient culture. It all started because of the greed of a trading company called the East India Company. Its leadership was insecure and short-sighted. It should have done trading; instead, it shifted focus on empire building. It was unhappy with what it had and its role as a British trading company.

"So, it seduced the monarchy with promises of untold riches from the colonies. Unfortunately for the world, the British monarchy agreed with that viewpoint and endorsed the idea of creation of colonies. The Mughal Empire in India at that time was declining, and the multiethnic Indian principalities were not ready for organized foreign invasion; India was relatively peaceful when the British came. If the British, French, and Dutch trading companies did not have an expansionist agenda and did not create colonies, the world would have been more peaceful. Smaller number of people would have been impacted adversely; exploitation, human rights violations, famine, hunger, ethnic cleansing, and atrocities would have been significantly less.

"But that was not to be. The British won the key battles in different parts of India with relative ease. And then having won the wars, the British told the Indians that they were somehow superior because they were British, and they were white. The Indians were told that they were inherently inferior to the British. They created elaborate systems and procedures in Indian society to perpetuate that myth. That system continued for many years after the British left. To make it look legitimate, the British had it more or less mimic the caste system in India. Many educated Indians actually believed the British. They forgot that the caste system was based on profession and not on skin color.

"After the war, most British voters did not like the idea of colonies in faraway places anymore. People were unwilling to feed those inflammable insecurities and narrow-mindedness, so many erstwhile colonies became independent countries quickly. The French and the Dutch had similar stories. Very similar things happened in the case of Japan. Hideki Tojo and his friends influenced the Japanese emperor during WWII, and the emperor endorsed their warmongering. When those leaders came to power, their countries were already in trouble.

"For Germany and Italy, it was World War I and the subsequent extreme economic hardship that followed. For us in Japan, it was the aftermath of the wars with Russia and the misplaced national pride. They used that window of opportunity or national insecurity to grab power, often making many fake promises. Once in power, they unleashed their evil aspirations. War, atrocities, annexation of neighbors, and other horrible things followed in quick succession.

"In the case of Japan, Hideki Tojo and his war ministry became the face of Japan. No one asked why, not even the emperor. In almost all those cases, the nations that chose the path of war like Japan or Germany suffered the worst outcome. You know about Hiroshima and Nagasaki. I have discussed that with you, my son. Nobody asked, 'Did the common people in Hiroshima deserve that? A generation suffered from radiation sickness, cancer, and other diseases - was that deserved by the common folks in Hiroshima and Nagasaki?'

"Nobody asked me in Kyoto if I wanted to invade China, Malay, and Burma! Similarly, nobody asked Wolfgang Schmidt, the clockmaker in Bavaria, if he wanted to invade Austria or Poland. I was happy researching and teaching the world's languages; probably, Herr Schmidt was happy making clocks in the Bavarian Black Forest. People made wrong assumptions about others - never questioned their leaders' motives and went along. We, the common people, are guilty of our deafening silence. We did not realize that by remaining silent, we became victims.

"That was the price our nations paid. If there was ever a real national dialogue in those countries, WWII might not have happened. There was no national dialogue; people had such deep faith in their leaders or gods that they had no time for dialogue. It was apparently a waste of time, and nobody wanted to waste time. Instead, they attacked a neighbor and started a war!" Nick knew his grandpa was no fan of the Japanese Imperial Army and its exploits in the war.

After he finished, Win said, "Your grandfather was a great man and even greater intellectual. I have never heard such simple but powerful explanation on what causes wars. I wish I could tape that analysis and publish his views like a book to educate others. It would do an awful lot of good!"

On the inauguration day, Nick and Win thought they were arriving early, but when they entered the hallway, the representatives from the Shan leadership in exile and the people from the Kachin Baptist Convention were already there and chatting; both greeted Win and said hello to Nick. Win introduced Nick to them as Major Morita's grandson. The inaugural function started on time with representatives of various Southeast Asian cultures making a short speech and presentation about their specific exhibits. There was a strong representation from South Asia. When their turn came, the gentleman from the Shan leadership in exile went to the podium and spoke. He recounted the story of Yoshikuni Morita and Aung Lung in great detail. He also said that their grandchildren are in the audience today for the inaugural. Nick and Win stood up for a few seconds and waved at the entire audience in the midst of a loud applause. They loved the energy.

He also articulated Aung's desire to have the objects in this gallery so that the Shan culture and cause are known globally and to the future generations. He thanked the Morita family profusely in his speech for taking care of the two objects for close to a century in two different continents. He said that the Moritas saved the objects from WWII; otherwise, this day would not happen. He concluded by saying that the Lungs and the Moritas were really giving the Shan treasures to the world today. On the whole, it was a well-planned, well attended event.

Clearly, the museum and the curator knew what they were doing. They probably hosted such events quite frequently; all the historical and cultural contexts were very well presented. After the function, Win and Nick were walking toward their cars in the multi-storied parking lot. Win was leaving the next day, and Nick was taking an evening flight back to Los Angeles. They were about to say "bye" to each other when there was a vibrating sound from Win's phone.

He said, "I put my phone on vibration mode - must be my DC office trying to reach me. They always want attention for one last thing that could not wait." Both of them smiled and laughed about it. Then, Win's phone made a different sound and vibrated again.

This time he said, "Somebody is texting me and calling me; let me check." He pulled his phone from his pocket and saw the number and the text message. Win's face turned pale suddenly.

Nick got alarmed, and he asked, "What happened, Win?"

"Dad is very unwell; he is in the ICU in Austin. That was Laura - Becky is with Dad. I have to leave immediately. Nick, when you get back to the hotel, could you please let them know that I had an emergency and I had to fly back urgently? They can box my stuff in the room; I'll have someone from our DC office pay the bill and pick it up tomorrow."

Nick said, "Of course, Win. Please do let me know if you think I can help in any other way. I hope your father recovers quickly."

Win said, "Will do" and ran to his car. In a few minutes, Nick heard tires screeching and Win's rental car getting out of the parking lot and merging into airport bound traffic in a hurry. Nick prayed for him.

Win was lucky he found the last seat at the very rear of an Austin bound Delta flight within twenty minutes. He had already called Laura and Becky; he had advised Andy to come over. He had also informed his offices in Austin and DC that he would not be available for a few days. Win's mind was racing at the speed of light. He hoped and prayed that was, *all was not lost.* By the time he got to Austin, it would be late evening. He was worried. Luckily for him, the flight was on time. Fortunately, because of a strong tailwind, it landed in Austin early. As soon as Win got out of the terminal, he saw Nancy waving at him in the arrivals hall.

Laura would have asked her to come to the airport knowing Win's state of mind. Nancy drove straight to the Seton Medical

Center where Aung was. On the way, she said that Aung had complained of chest pain two days ago right after Win left for the East Coast. Initially, it was mild, and then it increased. Within an hour, Becky called Laura, and with the help of Aung's nurse, they admitted him at Seton. The doctors put him on oxygen, conducted several tests, and said he was stable; he seemed to be improving. The doctors were getting ready with a treatment plan.

The next morning, when Laura went to see him on the way to work, he seemed fine. Around midday when Becky went, she found him very weak and requested the doctors to check. He had been in the intensive care unit since that request; he was under observation, but his doctors had not issued any update. Because of Aung's advanced age, a team of doctors were involved in his care from multiple specialities.

Loss of a legend

When Win arrived at the hospital, Andy had already come in from Dallas. He and Becky were just outside the ICU; they said Laura had just gone home a few minutes ago. Win knew that because he had texted her as Nancy was driving him to Seton. Win asked the doctor if he could see his father; the doctor said yes but only for a few minutes. Win went inside and saw tubes all over Aung's face. He looked very tired - just that quick glance reminded Win of Uncle Jim in Dallas.

There were monitors all around him; the face that was so familiar to him all his life was barely visible. His eyes were closed, and the doctor said he was heavily sedated. The doctor asked him to wait outside with other members of the family; he said he would come out and call them in when Aung could see them. Win came out and flopped on a seat next to Andy, and he turned and gave him a hug. Win was wiping tears from his eyes when Becky came to him. She hugged him and broke down. Win tried to console her as much as he could; it was very hard.

Win knew she was very close to Aung, so he had to be strong for her. He wiped his own tears, patted her back, and consoled her. He said, "You are a big girl now, Beck; please calm down. What will Grandpa think?"

That seemed to work for a bit, but she kept sniffling. Andy was not crying but was very quiet, which was not normal for Andy. Win got Becky to sit next to him. With Andy and Becky sitting on his right and left, his own eyes were tearing up. He had no idea whether he would get to talk to Aung again. He longed for just one more chance. He did not know how long he sat there thinking about their days in Myitkyina and Bangkok. He could not count how many days and nights he and Aung had spent just talking about the Shan cause. He missed those days so much.

In his teens, he had started detesting Aung's Shan obsession. Win had wanted him to be like others. Later in life, he realized that it was that obsession that had brought the two of them together. Aung did not have a lot of people in the outside who were interested in that topic, so Win was his sounding board for decades. As he grew older, Win realized that he respected his father a lot more because of his Shan obsession, because of the purity of his commitment. He was obsessed when he had no material wealth; he was still obsessed when he had a lot of material wealth. He never got anything out of it except suffering, but he never wavered. Aung Lung did not change even one bit; his integrity, sincerity, and commitment soared above all else around him.

Win had not realized when Laura had come in - he suddenly felt a hand on his shoulder and looked up. Laura was standing there in casual clothes with a bag on her shoulder; both her eyes were tearful. She had probably gone home, changed, and came prepared for a night in the ICU waiting room. Win got up and hugged Laura. Seeing her mom, Becky got up, embraced her, and started weeping on her shoulders. Win had no idea what he could do or how he could help.

The duty doctor came out after several hours and called Win aside, "Mr. Lung, we need to talk. Could you please come inside with us for a moment now?"

When he went in, the doctor told him that they were about to put Aung on a ventilator to ease his breathing difficulty. Before they started that process, Aung might be able to talk to him. It was a short window because breathing was becoming difficult for Aung. Win requested the doctor to allow his family to come in as well and rushed in. He went in and took Aung's right hand in his palm.

There was a slight twitch, and Aung said, "Kiddo?"

Win responded, "Yes Pho, this is Win. Why are you lying down in bed with so many tubes all around your face? You need to get well right away and get up. I need to take you home as soon as possible, Pho. You do not like hospitals, remember? You never wanted to get admitted to the hospital after your stroke; you stayed at home, remember? Please listen to me, Pho. Please get well now, and we'll go home."

Aung seemed to smile. By then, Laura, Andy, and Becky were all inside the small room. He smiled at them and said to Win in Shan, "Look after Laura, Becky, and Andy, Kiddo."

Then, his grip on Win's hand became loose suddenly! Win was startled, first by Aung's use of the Shan language - he had not spoken with Win in Shan in years because the kids did not understand - and then by the grip becoming loose. He looked up to the monitor; the line in the middle was flat. Something beeped loudly, and the duty doctor came running, bent over Aung, and tried to resuscitate him, the doctor kept trying, but nothing worked.

After several minutes and many attempts, the doctor straightened up and said, "Your father just left us, Mr. Lung; we will not need the ventilators anymore. I am so sorry for your loss."

It was Becky's voice that startled Win. She screamed, "Oh no!" Andy took Becky outside, but Win remained on the chair. Speechless. Frozen.

He was holding Aung's hand; he released it after several minutes, then closed Aung's eyelids and went out of the room. The world seemed so empty to Win. He realized that a big chapter in his life had just ended, leaving a gaping hole. The world would not be the same for him, ever. Outside the room, Becky and Laura were crying, completely out of control, and Andy was trying to console them. Win came and hugged them. They remained in that state for several minutes before Win spoke. He told Andy to take the car and drive Mom and Becky home. He also told Andy that he would be required to stay longer because of hospital paperwork pertaining to Aung's passing. Andy nodded and took Laura and Becky with him towards the car park.

When Win was alone, he sat on a nearby seat and wept for a long time; he poured his heart out in grief. Win kept thinking, *Could I have done anything differently?* He went through the list in his head over and over. Maybe, he should have avoided going to Washington, DC, for the inauguration? Maybe he could have returned earlier. But Aung had told him to go and stay. Should he have admitted Aung to the hospital proactively? But Aung had always hated hospitals. He said so incessantly. Two years ago, when Aung had a mild stroke, there was a talk of going to the hospital for an extended period of time, and Aung himself had shot it down.

After a while, an elderly nurse came along and called Win for some paperwork. She also offered him some coffee from the hospital machine; she said that was all they had. Win took it and swallowed the lousy, cold coffee in one gulp. It did not help reduce the grief one bit.

He did not feel any better; nothing seemed good or comforting any more. After a couple of hours, the nurse said he was free to go. The nurse had told Win that he could email them the location of Aung's funeral the next day so the hospital could take the necessary steps. She gave Aung's belongings in a plastic bag for Win to take home; Win wept some more when he saw those. The realization that nothing would bring his Pho back hit him like a ton of bricks. Eventually, what seemed like a lifetime to Win, the nurse called a taxi for Win, and he went home. He felt uniquely alone in this world - nobody shared that loneliness with him. A part of him had gone away forever, and it would never come back, no matter what he did. Even though he knew he had Laura and the kids, he had never felt so lonely ever before.

Win remembered that next part of the process well from his mother's time. He had decided a few years ago to have his parents rest next to each other; he had arranged that with the funeral home already. Win went through the next few days in a dazed state; he could not even remember how he went through the motions of talking to the funeral home, selecting the date and time, and arranging a celebration of life lunch at Shan Austin just like they had done for Mom and Uncle Jim. There was much to do; Win felt he had no energy left in him. Andy took a leave of absence from UT and Jim's company; his presence helped a lot. He needed very little instruction - he just took charge.

Among the special guests, he decided to send invitations to the Shan in exile leadership, the Kachin Baptist Convention, Nick Morita, and also to Kip Kimura. In addition, he had a large list of guests from Austin that included his and Laura's friends from UT, Laura's family in Arizona, Mauricio's family, and many others. Aung was a father figure for the staff of their two restaurants and also to many in the Travis County Restaurant Association. Win had to invite all of them too; they looked up to Aung like a role model. They had all suffered a major loss.

Several people from the offices of Travis County informed Win that they would attend too. One of them said Aung's life and his story were an inspiration to all of them. The news of Aung's passing reached Nick when he was in the Canadian Rockies in connection with a movie project. He and his team were deciding on a site where most of the on-location shooting for the film would take place. He sent an email to Win expressing condolences from him and his mother, Mrs. Keiko Morita, and informed Win that he would certainly be in Austin. Kip also responded immediately, saying how sorry he was, and that he would try to attend, but since he was out of the country in Cambodia, he was unsure if he would be able to get tickets. Kip said in one short fifteen-minute meeting, Aung had inspired him enough for three full lifetimes. Amazing!

Win thought given the short time; he might not make it. The service was pretty elaborate with both Christian and Theravada Buddhist traditions. Aung was born a Buddhist, but he liked the Kachin Baptist Convention and its teachings from his youth in Burma till his later years in the United States. When Win informed the church in Myitkyina that Aung had passed away, the Father and the Kachin Baptist Convention rose to the occasion and coordinated everything. The Christian part of the service was coordinated by the one of the US chapters of the Kachin Baptist Convention. Win was very impressed.

They were all over the place all day making preparations. The Father wrote a note to Win that said, "The proud Kachins of these Hills considered your father one of their own sons. They embraced him when he came to them in his youth, and he reciprocated the same his entire life. Please accept our heartfelt condolences and allow us to celebrate his life with you and grieve with you." After the regular proceedings, the Shan exiles leadership performed the unique Shan ritual of the passing of a leader into his next life. If Aung had not left home in his youth, he would have become a Shan Chaofa; the Lungs were a long line of Chaofas by birth.

That was what the Shan rituals reflected - essentially welcoming a lost son back to his eternal Shan home and then letting him continue his journey to his next life. The Shan rituals were a bit different; it involved a lot of chanting by the monks and a process that had a lot of similarities with the pujas in Hindu temples.

When the time for the eulogy came, several people spoke. Mauricio stood up to speak, but his voice choked up; he somehow finished a few sentences and came down. He remembered how Aung and Myint had visited him and his brother in their small apartment many years ago. In that meeting in Round Rock, Myint had asked one of them to join The Shan. He also recounted how Aung and Myint had guided them like their own parents, through all the ups and downs of life, even after their own parents came to the US. Even though their own parents had migrated from Mexico sometime back, when they needed important advice, they would ask Suu Myint. Since Myint's passing away, it was exclusively Aung. Aung and Myint never let them down over these many years.

He concluded by saying, "Like Win, we lost a father."

The Kachin Baptist Convention also delivered its eulogy, recounting how Aung had helped Geis Memorial Church in Myitkyina, Burma, after the war. Win did not know that Aung had also taught a Sunday School with the Father for Kachin kids; somehow, Aung had never mentioned it, but the KBC representatives had a record. One of Aung's Kachin scouts became a well-known KBC minister in later years; he probably kept the records. The Kachins said that they lost one of their own beloved sons.

The Shan exile leadership spoke toward the end; theirs was the most memorable eulogy. The same elderly gentleman who spoke at the museum in DC rose. In his raspy voice, he started speaking slowly.

"Today, some of you have lost a father, father-in-law, mentor, grandfather, and a good friend. That is a very big loss. Such losses are not easy to live with because the void remains forever. With time, you learn to live with it. Our loss is not like yours; it is of a different kind. We think it is unique to us. We, the Shan, have lost a legend. Aung Lung was the last legend who walked among us. Aung Lung was a legend not because he was born a privileged Chaofa; he was a legend because he chose to be a commoner. For his tribe, he left a life of relative security and luxury, willingly accepted a life of struggle and starvation, fought one of the most powerful standing armies of the time. Most days, he did not know if he would live to see the sunrise the next day. Not many human beings do such things as a conscious choice.

"You might erroneously think he got huge rewards for those choices. He did not. He did not get anything in return except unearned suffering. No one, not even us, his tribe, acknowledged his efforts. Our legend was a modest man, as legends are. He once counseled me for praising him in public. He told me that he had nothing to show for his efforts, so no praise was due. He thought so because his beloved Shan people were still suffering in Burma, and he couldn't stop that suffering. That self-appraisal was not fair.

"Today, the day we are celebrating his passage to next life, we should correct that. I rose today to ask, should outcome be the only measure of contribution? Should we not consider the personal sacrifice, the commitment? I think you would agree with me when I say that for our Aung Lung, we should. We think the commitment - the purity of purpose - should count. Outcomes are often not knowable; despite that, great people do selfless acts. When our great saints and preachers left their homes and started preaching, they did not know how many lives would be impacted. They had no way to know how many millions would benefit from it and when and where those unknown benefits would accrue. They had a calling, and they responded with a purity of purpose without expectations. That's what legends do.

"It is hard to explain such acts rationally. That is what our legend did too. He responded to his calling to the best of his ability, without expecting anything. He did not forget his tribe and shared his bread with them in the Kachin Hills of Burma. He was poor then; he did not have food for the next day, but he did the same when he was a well-recognized business owner in Texas, when he could feed hundreds. He never forgot his tribe or its cause; our Aung Lung never changed.

"His parents did not approve of it, his own family did not like it sometimes, but he did not waver. Never, ever. Not many people can traverse the path of our legend Aung Lung, for that journey is difficult and dangerous - but most importantly, thankless. He was always very alone in his quest, as legends often are. We hope all of you here can understand the depth and intensity of our loss. Our last legend has passed on to his new life." The Shan speaker wiped tears from his eyes when he finished and got down. Win noticed many others sitting in the audience were also wiping their eyes with tissues. It was very moving.

At the very the end, a speaker named Morita rose to speak. Win saw Nick from a distance. He was surprised because Nick's name was not there in the list of speakers he had seen. Nick probably made a request to Laura after he arrived in Austin and she added him later, Win thought. Win was not sure why Nick had decided to speak.

Nick had started speaking, "Most of you do not know me; my name is Nick Morita. Unlike you, Mr. Lung was not known to me for a long time. I met Mr. Lung only once, for less than one hour. My connection with him was tenuous. I was told our ancestors were enemies. His father gifted two objects of great value to my grandfather, a Japanese Army officer posted in Burma, in 1942. Those two jade objects were exquisitely crafted examples of Shan cultural heritage. I was told Mr. Lung's father gave those to my grandfather as a token of goodwill for his attempts to unify the hill tribes of Northern Burma. Mr. Lung did not like the idea of giving those away. He disagreed with his father's decision, and that led to a big, heated argument between Mr. Lung and his father. So, under most normal circumstances, I should belong to the enemy camp. Am I right?

"In today's market value, those gifted Jade objects would be worth millions of dollars. My grandfather and father wanted to return those objects to the Lungs, but we could not locate them. To honor my late grandfather's wish, my father contacted the Burmese Embassy in DC multiple times and requested them to help us locate the Lungs, but the Embassy did not help. The two objects remained with our family for nearly a century, initially in Kyoto, Japan, and then in our home in Los Angeles, California. Win and I are the grandsons of the two remarkable grandfathers who started this saga in 1942. This story started in the hills of Northern Burma; with Mr. Lung's passing to his next life, we are ending that story this morning, here in Austin, Texas.

"Win and I were able to connect up here in Austin only a few weeks ago. Thanks to Mr. Lung's photographic memory, we were able to authenticate the ownership and return those objects, as my late grandfather wanted. Immediately after getting those objects back, Mr. Lung decided to donate those to a museum in Washington, DC, so that the world can learn about the rich Shan heritage and culture. The act of donating those highly valued artifacts, worth millions of dollars, could be a story by itself. After all, how many people would do that?

"But that story is for another day. As you might imagine, the donation of cultural artifacts of that vintage requires a lot of paperwork. The process is comprehensive for a good reason. The museums do not want to expose themselves to claims and counterclaims later. Win and Laura worked on those processes for many weeks. When Win and Laura had almost finalized the paperwork for the formal donation process, Mr. Lung called them aside and instructed them to include my grandfather Yoshikuni Morita's name as one of the co-donors.

"That was the name of an enemy soldier! Can you imagine anyone doing that? There was no reason for him to do that. Remember, the Japanese Army was occupying Burma at that time; the Japanese Army committed many atrocities including the infamous Kalagong Massacre. For us here, it was a distant event; we might not be able to relate to those events. That was not true for Mr. Lung. He lived through all that horror - saw much of it with his own eyes; he was at the receiving end of the Japanese Army's atrocities for no fault of his. His decision to include my grandfather's name should be understood with that background.

"A few days ago, when I mentioned to my ninety-year-old mother that I was planning to come here, she insisted that I speak to all of you today. She asked me to rise and remind all of you of that background. Many of you might not know otherwise and think this was a routine matter. It was anything but a routine matter. My mother, Keiko Morita, insisted that it would be my duty to rise and speak today, so here I am.

"I speak today on behalf of the Moritas to tell you that it was an extraordinary act by an extraordinary man. When future generations go to that museum and look at those two exquisite jade artifacts, they will see two donor names: Aung Lung and Yoshikuni Morita. Along with his own name, Mr. Lung had my grandfather's name, the name of an officer of the Japanese Burma Command, etched on the plaque. That plaque is now mounted in front of the two objects.

"We learned earlier from his tribe that he was a Shan legend. You all can see why. He did what legends do; it came to him naturally! Today, as we celebrate Mr. Lung's passing to his next life, that is my story for you. His tribe, Win, and his family were lucky to have him in their midst. He was one of a kind. Irreplaceable. A true legend."

Nick sat down in the midst of thunderous applause; it continued for a long time well after he took his seat. Win wept uncontrollably.

© Ashish Basu 2020